THE WAR LOVER

Books by John Hersey

THE WAR LOVER   *1959*
A SINGLE PEBBLE   *1956*
THE MARMOT DRIVE   *1953*
THE WALL   *1950*
HIROSHIMA   *1946*
A BELL FOR ADANO   *1944*
INTO THE VALLEY   *1943*

These are BORZOI BOOKS,

published in New York by Alfred A. Knopf

THE
WAR LOVER

BY

JOHN HERSEY

ALFRED A. KNOPF

New York 1959

15133

Fic
Her

L. C. catalog card number: 59–13177
© John Hersey, 1959

THIS IS A BORZOI BOOK,
PUBLISHED BY ALFRED A. KNOPF, INC.

Copyright 1959 by JOHN HERSEY
All rights reserved. No part of this book may be reproduced in
any form without permission in writing from the publisher, except
by a reviewer who may quote brief passages in a review to be
printed in a magazine or newspaper. Manufactured in the United
States of America. Published simultaneously in Canada by Mc-
Clelland & Stewart Ltd.

TO

BARBARA

CONTENTS

CONTENTS

THE WAR LOVER

CHAPTER ONE

THE RAID

0200–1119 hours

1 /
    I woke up hearing a word break like a wave on the shells of my ears: *Mission*.

    I sat up on the edge of my sack and fumbled with my feet for my flying boots, for even in August I liked to nest my toes in the lambskin lining first thing in the morning. I hunched there and scratched my back.

    As usual I had forestalled Sully. In those days I had a clock in my head which would rouse me, on the mornings of missions, just before Sullivan, the waker, came in and flicked on the sun, in the form of a flashlight, right over one's face, and said, "Come on. Roll out. Breakfast at two thirty. Briefing at three." The rising hours varied, but my headclock almost always anticipated Sully by a few seconds.

    Today's was to be my next-to-last raid. I felt as if tiny taps were opening in me and ice water were going into general circulation. I counted the credits I had, trying to make sure of their number, because I never could seem to make sure enough:

    Lorient, Bremen the day I met Daphne, St. Nazaire, Antwerp, Meaulte when my feet were cold, Helgoland, Lorient when Braddock blew up, Kiel when *The Body* caught fire, St. Nazaire and flak, Wilhelmshaven when we were hot, Bremen, Le Mans, Hüls, Hamburg when we went around the second time on the bombing run, Le Mans, Nantes, Heroya at the beginning of the July Blitz, Hamburg, Hamburg again when Lynch got it, Kassel recalled, Warnemünde with leaflets, Kassel after my separate peace, and finally Poix, a milk run.

That made twenty-three; the twenty-fourth today; twenty-five and home. . . . I leaned back and touched my knuckles to the wooden wall.

Where was Sully? Why didn't Sully come this morning?

By the dim wash of a light that some poor gink down the hall had left lit over his bed because otherwise he would have split open a nightmare, I saw across the way in our room the bulk of my pilot, Buzz Marrow, lying on his side with his legs pulled up in the deep, warm sleep of the not yet born. I could see the white lump of sheet over him and the rectangles above him on the wall of pictures of dames, sprawling for him, giving him the old eye. He could reach up, as he said, and pat Danielle right on her Darrieux. He was cranking off sleep the way the hill used to sleep outside my window at Donkentown.

Then I remembered the dream, or parts of it. There was a passage with Daphne; we were walking in a dry place, rocks, haste. That was not the part. Yes, this was it:

We broke out of the undercast and saw the dawn, a great sheet of mother-of-pearl, wrinkled with altocumulus and cirrus, over the continent ahead. Under us, like mud, lay the flat, damp wad of weather that always seemed to cover England and her Channel in those months. Each time we ventured out and back, we cut through it, our wings like spades, sometimes in the dark before sunrise and sometimes, returning, in the dark after dusk. The dawns and sunsets provided my keenest pleasures, in those days, I guess, except for those that Daphne gave me. In the dream the dawn was bags of gold, heaps of oranges, fires in hedges, snow on mountains, piles of smoking autumn leaves, cotton gods and cotton cherubs, sheets of flesh, films of oil on water, flying seas of wine. I dreamed the colors. Mostly and finally it was mother-of-pearl, dark, blue-gray-green, a fundamental range that would have been depressing but for its infinite variety and its shimmering changeableness, like that of the watershot silk in one of Daphne's dresses when she walked.

Daphne was in the pilots' compartment with us, standing behind my seat where stolid Handown, the engineer gunner, usually stood on take-offs.

I could see vividly in the dream our cockpit: the two columns and wheels, Marrow's and mine, and the dials and switches and lamps and gauges and throttles milling around like a New Year's Eve crowd in Times Square.

We broke out, as I say, into the huge oystershell of heaven, and I looked across at Marrow, to see how he was taking the sight.

Marrow was being Marrow; a hunk of machinery, concerned only with his work, which was to drive twenty-seven tons of metal up a road of thin air. F—— dawns; they were for co-pilots. The big man sat, as always when he had the controls, leaning forward toward the pilot's column. He bulged in his leather coat, and its huge collar, lined with yellow-tan fur, was folded down over his shoulders, and the throat was not zipped up all the way. He looked like a motorcycle cop, arrogant and sure of his victims. We couldn't have been high enough for oxygen, because his helmet was loose, and the hard leather chin cup and pointed strap hung down on my side, and the fur-lined visor was turned up, and the bulge of the earphone and the chin cup and the goggles were the only precise shapes in that whole pile of shapes; the goggles were up on his forehead, their elastic strap bunching the crown of the soft head-gear. A hank of oily blond hair stuck down on the right side of Marrow's forehead, under the goggle strap.

I saw Marrow in the dream as I had seen him early in our tour, not as I saw him toward the end.

Buzz did not wrestle with the ship, as some men seemed to do, and as I think I did, for I am a shorty and also was much impressed with the law of gravity. He handled all that airplane with his finger tips, and his movements were gradual, and the ship's were smooth. He was a powerful figure, an impressive organization of flesh and cloth and leather and fur and rubber, yet he handled the plane not with power but rather with tender, sad care. His fingers adjusting the trim through a button on the automatic pilot were as sensitive, as plastic, and as modest in relation to the whole man as the knob itself in relation to the tremendous strength of the cables and stress of the wings of the plane. He held the wheel the way he'd hold a martini glass and a butt when he thought he was snowing a dame.

I watched him, and his face was no more and no less expres-

sive than the altimeter or one of the r.p.m. indicators. His eyes
moved without haste from dial to dial, and at times he looked out
at the shoals of atmosphere beneath us, or at the gaps of toplessness
in the clouds above—but in a calculating and not a sensuous way,
and now and then he checked his wingman and the element ahead
of us, higher than we. He was calm and automatic.

All of a sudden I, Charles Boman in the dream, could stand
the sight of Marrow's complacent ease no longer, and I grasped the
wheel on my side in my tight, muscle-bound way, and I stamped
my feet onto the rudder pedals. I fought to push the column forward and turn the wheel to the right, and I tried to kick right rudder. But the controls would not move under all the strength I
could bring to bear.

I looked over at Marrow, and he was still flying with his finger
tips and with his legs relaxed. His fingers and his unforcing feet
were holding the plane smoothly on course against the currents of
air and against all my strength.

I fought frenziedly to take the plane off course, but the turn-
and-bank indicator was level, and the rate-of-climb indicator was
as steady as a stopped clock, and nothing I could do would change
anything.

Again I turned toward Marrow. Buzz was staring across at
me. His face was white and broad and too big, and it wore an appalling look of disapproval.

After that, Buzz and I were playing acey-deucy in the officers'
club, and Daphne was whispering, and everything became pleasant
in the dream.

2 /

I looked at my watch and saw that it was two minutes
past two in the morning. They had told us, up at two. I wondered
again where Sully was. He usually started at our hut.

Then I was wide awake and I remembered the other thing. I
hated Marrow. For three days I had hated him.

When I had first seen Daphne's face, that previous Saturday,

I had realized there had been some change. It was not in anything she said or consciously did, but rather in some kind of conviction that came out through her skin from inside her, for she was such a feminine one that essences, odors, and colors seemed to be expressed out of her at the slightest stirrings of her innermost feelings. I ran up the creaking stairs of the house in Bartleck where I had taken a room for her, and my heart was beating as it did on take-offs. I opened the door and stood in the doorway. Daphne was sitting in a straight wooden chair against the wall by a dormer window on the opposite side of the room, reading and waiting, and at the sound and sight of me she started up, dropping the book and apparently not caring whether she broke its back, and she ran across the room, and as she came toward me her eyes restored my beat-up leather jacket and brushed my hair, and she said, "How beautiful you are!"

That was guff, and I knew it, but I ate it.

She did not run all the way into my arms—she never had—but stopped in front of me and waited there for me to move or speak.

"Darling," I said.

"That word," she said, and she moved under its influence, just a swinging shift in her stance.

But I was uneasy. Had I forgotten something? There was a shapeless doubt at the edge of my mind. Some change. Yes.

"Work?" she asked.

"Stand-down for the day," I said.

"Oh, darling, I'm so glad."

But it was done. In those few moments I had stood as if before a judge, hearing—yet not clearly hearing because of the murmuring in the courtroom—a sentence pronounced. It was not much. Just a hint of a change. In the afternoon we went to an exhibition cricket match at Lishton and sat on the grass in the shade at the edge of the grounds seeing the white flannels of the players flickering in the sunlight, and the bowler, like a primitive cartman, rolling the big wheel of his stiff-armed pitches endlessly, endlessly, and the restless Yank uniforms around us, and a loudspeaker explaining the ins and outs of the interminable performance. And later we walked in the village, along the narrow sidewalks, and she held my arm. The black of the thatch, the damp stone of the walls, the windows squintingly small as if the light of English days could not be trusted to have the free run of a man's castle; the elegant Caledonian lettering of PONGREN & KNEE, APOTHECARIES, and the honey-varnished buns in the baker's window, and the strong smell of dung at the end of the High Street, where inside a courtyard could be heard a plainsong of cattle—these familiar things in the village were unchanged, yet everything was changed in my eyes and in my heart, which lay in my chest like a bag of gravel, because of the slightest shift in the balance of Daphne's and my feelings. Not a hard word had been spoken and it could not be said, by any means, that we had run into disaster, but there had been a change, there surely had been a change. I kept juggling the pieces of the puzzle in my mind, and finally, remembering my having had the duty in Ops on Thursday night, and remembering, too, the way my pilot and best friend in the group, Buzz Marrow, whom I myself had told that Daphne had been due back to Bartleck from Cambridge that afternoon, had jounced along the corridor of our Nissen hut with his comical tippy-toes walk, hoisting his huge form at every step on his incongruously delicate feet, saying he was just going to have one lousy limey beer at the officers' club, and it would probably be warm as p——, as usual—but he hadn't come in until two in the morning; remembering all that, I put together the most improbable notion I could devise: that Marrow had had my Daphne.

And when I got back to our room I woke him up, to find him grinning at the very moment of his return from pit-bottom sleep, where he was such a familiar, and I asked him to his face whether he had been with Daphne.

He rolled over on his back, hugging the pillow he had brought from the States with him, his eight-dollar pillow which he called "Down Girl," and he leered, and he denied it. "Wished I had been," he said. "You lucky son of a bitch; I bet she's a lay and a half."

It seemed to me that he was lying. We had had a late alert. I slept little.

3 /

I found out, to my cost, from Daphne, that he had been lying, in a way; or partly. But this was not why I hated him. Daphne had told me everything he had said and done, and it was much worse than I had thought. I hated him because his magic and strength had been illusions. I hated the taint in him. I hated the insight that he, through Daphne, had given me about certain men and war, and the despair for the future this episode had given me; the sense of degradation, the glimpse, as in a nightmare, of clawing, bestiality, filth, worms, blackness of tombs.

But I also felt a new strength of my own. I had at least a clearer eye.

I looked across at Marrow again, for he had sighed deliciously, and I think that part of my hatred at that moment must have stemmed from the way he slept—just like a hill in a peaceful landscape. He was a specialist of sleep. He went to bed each night in fresh underclothes, so that in the morning, at the next-to-last moment, he could pull on shirt and pants and socks and, walking into a pair of shoes, keep right on walking, without shaving or brushing his teeth or even really waking up, to the Nissen hut that served as a lounge attached by a corridor to the Number Two Officers' Mess, and there he would lie down, curled up like a cutworm, on one of the fake-leather sofas with steel-pipe arms, "catching five," as he put it, while the rest of us shuffled in and took our places to eat. Yet he was never quite the last to sit down at table, and he was every bit awake when he did.

Here he was, conked out, with an arm crooked around his private pillow. Tacked above the head of his bed was a sign he had had Chan Charles, the squadron painter, letter for him, and that he'd covered with transparent talc as he had all his pictures of dames. "This pillow," the sign said, "is NOT Government issue. It belongs to W. S. Marrow. It cost eight dollars. Do not borrow. This means you."

"I bought that pillow in Woolman's furniture store in Dayton," I had heard him tell other fliers a dozen times. "It's a hundred per cent pure goose down. Eight lousy bucks. Jesus, that thing has been everywhere I been. It went all around the phases with me:

Spanner, Lowry, all around. Why s——, that pillow's paid off eight *hundred* bucks in sleep dividends alone. And that ain't all, son. That's my 'Down, Girl' pillow. I used to tell a girl, 'Feel that,' and she'd put her hand on it, and I'd say, 'No, no, put your cheek on it, just feel that with your cheek, you never felt anything that soft.' Well, the minute she put her cheek on it, s——, she was a pushover. Down, girl! Any son of a bitch steals that pillow, I'll cut his b——s off."

My dream came fleetingly into my mind again, and I thought of the changing sky in the dream, and for some reason I remembered the sky the morning of our mission to the Heinkel plant at Warnemünde, the day we carried the leaflets and when Buzz about blew a gasket because, as he shouted, we weren't going to clobber the squareheads but only drop a lot of bull s—— on paper. The ship was going along fine, its vibration as soothing as the sound of a coffee pot perking, and the sky, as we moved in it, up and out, was giving us its fantastic gift of variety. A tree slowly changes its lights and stirs in the morning breeze—the great oak in the corner lot by Aunt Caroline's house, I remember it!—but the sky is like a human mind, with uncountable shifting pictures and caverns and heights, and misty places, and lakes of blue, and big sheets of forgetting, and rainbows, illusions, thunderheads, mysteries—and in it, all around us, as we went on our work of those awful days, death and the dealing of death. That day, however, I felt happy, because we weren't going to drop any death, only leaflets, "bumwad," as Max Brindt, our bombardier, who was just as angry as Buzz, called them. And I remember the clarity when we got all the way above the cloud cover. The sky above us, where the fighters were dogging, was just solid with contrails, long, feathery paths of condensation; from a distance it seemed as if there were a hundred giants, skating and cutting up the ice of the sky. It was brilliant on top.

I began to dress. I threw my pajamas on the floor of my metal locker. I had taken a shower before turning in, and now I powdered myself and put on some long G.I.'s, and a pair of silk socks and woolen ones over them, and light coveralls, and a pair of ancient, cracked, stretched patent-leather dancing pumps that I'd bought in a moment of insanity in Denver, when we'd been at Lowry, which now were as light on my feet as old slippers; I'd worn them ever since that gruesome Meaulte mission, back in May, when my feet nearly froze and Buzz ate me out because of my putrid formation flying. He said I flew according to poop—no imagination. Actually I flew according to having a couple of blocks of ice for extremities, but I wouldn't tell *him* that. Oh, no. Proud Charley Boman. Not your typical sassy shorty. Not me. Grin and bear. Band music by Sousa.

Where the deuce was Sully? Two-oh-nine in the morning. And if he wasn't coming, what was I doing getting up? Must be a postponement. I went right on tying up my shoelaces, with a prickling sensation in my buttocks that I'd understood from tenth-grade Hygiene to be the preparation of the body by the adrenals for an act of self-preservation but that I'd learned in my post-graduate course at Obscenity University was really something called chicken s——. I began to speculate as to *what* was being postponed. Where did they plan to send us today? For a week, since the tenth, we'd been expecting the bad one they'd briefed us for that morning; they sent us out to the dispersals to our planes, and then scrubbed the mission because of a foul sky. Schweinfurt. That city was too far away. We knew we'd get it sooner or later; they always gave us the ones they set up and briefed and scrubbed. We'd tried to get Kassel started three or four times before we finally got there and wished we hadn't. I began to flub my shoelaces. My heart was taking off and my palms were beginning to spout like Old Faithful. I began to think about not thinking about the mission they would give us.

4 /

I heaved myself over to my locker and got my shaving gear and went down the corridor to the latrine. The guy I saw coming around the corner into the mirror was myself but I hardly recognized him, because he looked like some gazabo in a Halloween mask, one of those clammy rubber face-masks, of a guy about twenty years older than I, and I was supposed to be twenty-two; forty-two counting the mask; a middle-aged mask of some tired businessman whose business was . . . well, let's say, unsavory. Both to him and to his customers. This unshaven middle-aged businessman in the mirror was a shorty, but you could tell from one look at him that he was not your typical cocky shorty. No would-be Napoleon he. No Little Corporal. No, sir. Maybe he was a ruin, but he was tall in all but stature.

And skinny. I had lost fifteen pounds since March. March, April, May, June, July, August. I talked funny; I'd noticed lately that I talked funny, even to myself. Slow, and like an obstacle race.

At the end of the row of basins a shoulder-high window was open, and I shuffled over to it in my dancing shoes and looked out and saw a fog with which you could have packed chinaware in a barrel.

Straight ahead as I peered out would be the Admin block, and I thought of the lights burning in Ops and Intelligence over there behind blackout curtains, beyond the fog, and I decided: I'll mosey over there after I shave and ask them what gives, where are we going to bomb, what's the dope about the postponement?

I'd ask Stormy Peters, the Group Meteorologist; he was a good joe, he might give.

So I turned on the hot-water faucet and let about a mile of water run, but it never got warm enough for a proper shave, considering that an oxygen mask was so tight that the least bit of beard would itch and chafe under it till you thought you were going to jump.

I cut myself. I had no styptic pencil. I made several little blotters of toilet paper and stuck them one by one on the bleeding spot. I looked in the mirror and saw: blue eyes, intense and direct, the whites not very white; dark brown eyebrows that went straight across the whole face without a break over the nose; a high forehead with a soft vein running indirectly down the middle like an aimless trickle of water on a windowpane; a pair of thick lips, which before the mirror I twisted and tensed in an effort to persuade myself that I had the mouth of a lieutenant general, which I was, all except for the last part; a fair chin, with its little scarlet-hearted blossom of toilet paper; brown hair in a military, or frigid-ears, haircut; and, at the center of everything, a shame of a nose, narrow-ridged and bulging at the end like a swiftly oncoming auto-hood flanked by two dented fenders for nostrils. It was not a face to make shaving a pleasure the first thing every morning, even in peacetime.

For pleasure I tried to think of Daphne's face. I couldn't. The sore spot was too raw.

So I thought of my other girl, my so-called former fiancée, for Christ's sake, back home, Janet. I thought of the little dark thing that she was, on a bicycle, that summer between junior and senior years, when we got a little tight one night and were riding bikes up over the beach road among the pines, with the house lights on the Vineyard and Naushon winking at us across the way, and she steered into a ditch and fell sprawling on a sandy place and accused me between giggles of having pushed her over, though I'd been squarely on the white line, up on the middle of the crown, seeing if I could ride the line, a sobriety test, and I dropped my bike on the macadam and ran to her, and she lay with her brown legs all showing on a spread-out fan of light linen, laughing, and brother, I thought she was the cat's pajamas. I was working as assistant head-waiter—big title, much skidding of thumbs in hollandaise on used plates—at the Sea Breeze that summer, and Janet had a job in Tuckers' in Falmouth, and life was so promising, so easy, so in our hands. And then—oof, the drop! like a hole in a cold front—I thought of what a teaser she was. That girl could really douse a fire.

It was two twenty-seven when I stashed my shaving things and put on my flying boots and scuffed out into the fog. Talk about flying blind. It took me about ten minutes to do a one-minute walk over to the Admin block, feeling my way along the asphalt path with those heavy sloggers. I'd get off in the mud once in a while—though actually it was less soupy than usual, as we had had five days of good weather—and then feel my way back onto the hardtop; and poking along that way I got there.

The burst of light nearly blinded me when I first pushed my way into the concrete building, inherited from the R.A.F., that served as our center of command. I went down the hall to the door marked METEOROLOGIST, and pushed in, and there was Stormy on the phone to Wing H.Q., giving the higher-ups some stuff about altitudes of undercast tops that he'd picked up from our weather ship above the mess. You could see he was exhausted, but he was unruffled and polite, even to Wing.

Stormy Peters struck me as the healthiest guy in the Group, for he had the look you see on the faces of those who cope with elements, that you see on the faces of most men who work in the soil,

even when times are hard, and sailors, fishermen have it; a look of
unhurry, of deep respect for Nature even where there's hatred, too,
a look perhaps of resignation. Anyway, on Stormy it was indistin-
guishable from one of calm, peace. He was simply a nut about
weather, and knowing that I'd always watched the sky, and
dreamed about it, and read stories about it, ever since I'd been a
kid, he gave me more time than he gave most throttle-jockeys.

He hung up. "Aren't you a little early for the ball, Cinder-
ella?" he said.

"Cut the crap." I was testy, and he respected the mood, as if
it were some kind of a disturbance of the upper air. "What's the
story?"

Stormy stood up and walked over to his map. He raised a hand
toward it, with fingers spread, and it was like a Michelangelo hand,
as if he were giving weather to the land outspread on the map, and
he said, "Up here, over the —th Wing Bases, there's advective
North Sea stratus, and it's going to stay that way. But here, over
the —th Wing, our clouds are dissipating, and the cold front is
weaker than expected, so we'll get some fog . . ."

"*Will* get some. Christ's sake, Stormy, don't you ever look out
the window?"

". . . well beyond the take-off time in the field order . . ."

"So there'll be a slight postponement."

". . . so there'll be a slight postponement."

"How much?"

"Three and a half hours. Briefing at six."

I shuddered at that. "Then they scare the s— out of us, then
they scrub. Huh?"

"No scrubbing today."

Stormy was uncanny, he was more dependable than the whole
U.S. Weather Bureau put together; if he said we'd go, we'd go.

"How come you're up?" he asked me.

"Because of a dweadful old big nasty dweam. Come on,
Stormy, be a pal, where are they sending us?"

"Briefing at six," he said. Then he must have seen the look on
my face. "I can't, Bo," he said. "They got me under lock and key.
You ought to know that."

"Big friend," I said.

"Why don't you go get some sleep?"

"J–o–k–e," I said. I spelled it out for him to save the trouble of laughing.

So I went back to my hutment, skiing along on the asphalt the way I'd come, and when I got inside I looked at my watch and saw that I had two hours and a quarter before they even wakened the others, one hundred and thirty-five minutes hanging around my neck like a mariner's curse.

5 /

I sat down in the can—the only place with decent light at that hour—with *The Good Soldier*, one of Kid Lynch's books that I'd copped from his room after he was killed, and I must say the book had me completely flummoxed; I couldn't concentrate, I couldn't have told you who was who. My eye lit on a sentence: "As I see it, at least with regard to man," the narrator said, "a love affair, a love for any definite woman, is something in the nature of a widening of the experience. With each new woman that a man is attracted to there appears to come a broadening of the outlook, or, if you like, an acquiring of new territory. A turn of the eyebrow, a tone of the voice, a queer characteristic gesture—all these things, and it is these things that cause to arise the passion of love— all these things are like so many objects on the horizon of the landscape that tempt a man to walk beyond the horizon, to explore. . . ." Explore! New territory! Jesus Christ! I thought that I had *lost* a continent, a land of fable named Daphne. I threw the book across the latrine, and it hit the tin paper-towel receptacle and made a hell of a noise. I was in bad shape and I knew it. And just at that moment, as if through an aural hallucination, there was a roar of an airplane engine in my ears.

I stood up and hurried to the window, and then with a rush of relief I realized that the sound really was there: some contraption-loving crew chief giving a final roll to an engine that had been running rough on a recent mission—for he wanted his million-dollar baby to come home again when next she went out, because she had so many hours of his life's work, like gallons of his seminal fluid, in her parts.

I thought, as I stood at the window looking out at the drifting mist, which was given substance, like that of new steam, by the bathroom light, that one way I *was* lucky was in our having a ship that was sound. Our plane, which Marrow had nicknamed *The Body*, was one of those aircraft that announce, on the first day's flight, that they are all right, in every response and utterance they are like a Lincoln Continental or a perfect pussy cat. Some ships were lemons, quite unrelated things going wrong one after another, cowl flaps one day, a turbo the next, interphone the next; and little things all haywire, such as juice for heated suits fizzling out—all in the same plane, day after day. Those dud-planes shook, as if scared of their function, or guilty, perhaps, over their defecations. Bad planes. I guess they came back as often as the good ones did, but it took a lot more sweat to get them back, and we were glad to have a peachereeno. We'd missed only one mission—Kiel it was, back in May, and that was when Marrow and our crew chief, Red Black, began feuding—on account of pure engine trouble; the other times, including Abbeville-Drucat just the day before, there'd been a nick of flak or a tiny shell fragment somewhere in the works, and *The Body* couldn't help *that*. And she'd had little enough of that sort of trouble, practically nil. One of our mecks, who had an unspellable name, it sounded like Perzanski but it had about a dozen extra c's and z's and y's in it, so Marrow called him Alphabet Soup, and we all called him Soupie—Soupie actually put in to be shifted to another ground crew because he said it was a f——ing bore to take care of *The Body*, it was like being a f——ing gas-pump winder at a service station; but the powers-that-be wouldn't transfer him. "What a way to fight a God-damn war," Soupie said one day. "In my opinion I avoid all pigs that there's no risk of the clap if you put it to 'em. Life's short. S——! You got to gamble." And he would spit on *The Body*, she was so perfect, so clean. No clap in *her*. But the rest of us were satisfied. Oh yes, we were.

Then, with a sudden jolt of the old feeling in my chest, I was able to think about Daphne. I went back and sat on the john, with my pants pulled up, and I saw *The Good Soldier*, poor Kid's book, lying butter-side-down on the concrete under the leftmost washbasin, and I put my chin on my fists, and I thought about Daphne at the bar in the officers' club, the first moment I ever laid eyes on her, hadn't spoken a single word to her. She was looking down her

arm in that self-loving way of hers, and across her bosom, checking
everything, just making sure she was as nice as ever. And afterwards
I remembered her sitting down at her mirror, the first time she'd
locked the door of her room in Cambridge, with me in it, and looking at herself as if to say, "Aren't I the clever one?"

I went in our room, thinking I'd savor some images like these,
and better ones, too, and I lay down on my bed, flying shoes and
all. It was a mistake. The minute I stepped in the room I was aware
of Marrow—of the Marrow whom Daphne had helped me to see;
who was such a fake, such a shallow fake. I knew. I knew about
Buzz.

But I knew, too, how magnificent he had been, and could be.

I saw in my mind Braddock's ship blowing up, and Kid Lynch
in the radio room of his plane with the unspeakable smear that a
piece of twenty millimeter had made of that beautiful brain of his,
and Senator Tamalty, slobbering his cheap patriotism on us out
there by the control tower. Let me put it mildly: I had a despair-
ing view of the world and of what men were making of it. War
equaled s——, and peace equaled s——. There would never be peace
so long as there were men with Marrow's taint.

Gradually all that became blurred, and I saw a meadow, and a
river with couples in punts, and a blue sky, and the fresh green of
early spring, and I was flat on my back, and my head was in Daphne's lap, and her soft hand rubbed and rubbed my temple.

6 /

There was an explosion! A brilliant flash of flame.

Then I realized it was Sully. My headclock had screwed up.

Then I understood: no, it hadn't. I'd fallen asleep again in my
clothes. I'd be damned.

"Roll, boy," Sully was growling, with the light in my face. You
never could see flabby Sully in the shadows beyond. "Well, look at
old Bo," he added, "beating the f——ing system." He must have
thought I'd put my flying clothes on the night before. "Briefing at
six."

I batted at the flashlight and said, "Up yours."

But Sully, who I guess caught more abuse from us glory-boys in any given morning than the Luftwaffe caught in a whole month, was quick, and he'd pulled the torch away before I could have the satisfaction of banging it against the wall to smithereens.

Then Sully went over toward Marrow, and as he walked across the room, Buzz said, clear-tongued as Satchmo's horn, "O.K., Sully-boy, I'm awake." Of course it was a lie. He was about as awake as Stonehenge. But his subconscious had managed to keep that third-degree light out of his face.

Being all dressed and ready, literally, to take off, I was able to lie there, as Buzz always did, awhile longer, I listened to the clamor in the hut of the men getting up and shuffling to the latrine, metal lockers slamming, johns flushing. I heard Wilson's off-key voice strike up, "Oh, what a beautiful morning," missing that haunting, unexpected interval on "morn-" by plenty; he must have peered out of the latrine window and seen the fog. Schuman, a new man with probably only three missions under his belt, but loud, the way Marrow had been at the beginning of our tour, was bitching about the tepid water, and Maltitz, the boy with the mouth full of sugar cane, who was awake in his room in spite of the fact he couldn't go on this mission because his ship had been beat up on the Abbeville-Drucat raid and was having to get some grafts from the Hangar Queen, bellowed to us all, "Have a nahss trip, chillun', y'all sen' me a postcard, heah? And come back real soon, heah?" And then the chorus of abuse: "Aah, go flog y'self." "Kiss my ass." "Jag off, Titty." Maltitz laughed, high-pitched and screeching, as a loon laughs in the dark.

In time the men began to leave the Nissen hut. The door at the center of the arch at the end away from the runway, pulled shut by its strong spring, slammed again and again and seemed to shake the whole building.

I thought once more of my session with Daphne the day before, and of what I now knew of Marrow, and how this waking was different from every one that had gone before it, and I had a bitter sense of regret and loss—loss of that other Marrow I had admired so much; or loss, perhaps, of the other Charles Boman, the other me, who had done the admiring, who had been so naïve.

Finally Marrow heaved himself out of bed and into his clothes, as if all in one motion, and sleep-walked out of the room.

He didn't notice me, his eyes probably weren't even open, but then, he never noticed anyone, except once in a while, for effect.

I followed him.

On the days of missions we ate in the senior officers' mess, the Number One Mess. It was exactly like the Number Two Mess, only it was ordinarily for field officers and visiting muck-a-mucks. I guess they thought they could make us captains and looeys feel important the mornings we were to risk our iddy-biddy lives, except that all it did, most times, was to burn us up to see all the top-heavy brass among the ground-grippers eating there, who, if breakfast was at two thirty, say, were all on hand, to a man, because they'd stayed up, they'd had a duplicate-bridge party, or a tatting and needle-work evening, or some God-damn old maid's affair, and usually some of them were squiffed and much too breezy. Jokes from the bicycle squad. Awful.

On account of the postponement this morning breakfast was so late that the joint was a mausoleum, and the only desk-fliers present were some of the working boys from Ops and S-2. Stormy was there, looking like an occluded front with occasional drizzle.

Perkins thumped down onto the bench beside me; his eyes were puffy. "I see," he said, sourly, "as how the rank is all gassing in the sack."

"Couldn't stay up *this* late," I said. "Simply teddible for the bally old team spiddit, you know."

"The sons of bitches," Perkins said.

Toward the very end of the influx I saw Marrow drift in. I guess he'd washed his face in the senior officers' latrine off their lounge, because he looked as fresh as the day he was born. He was making some crack, and I saw Stedman wince and glower as Buzz thumped him on the back.

They brought in heaping pans of bacon which looked like oily rags, and of yellow mush, with water oozing around it: scrambled powdered eggs. And pancakes and toast and chipped beef and also beans (just the thing for high altitudes; ask Prien, our tail gun-ner!). I held my nose when they put those water-logged eggs down.

"Cock-a-doodle-doo," Perkins said.

I poured a cup of coffee, and another, and another. I knew I was supposed to eat, but I just couldn't, no matter what Doc Randall had told me.

Some days of missions I didn't eat anything at all. Coffee for breakfast, then four, six, eight hours in the air, and of course I was too busy in the plane (let's put it that way) to eat the delicious K-rations supplied by Uncle Sam for his fighting boys, and then by the time we got through interrogation and other post-raid chores it was too late for evening chow, anything but cold leftovers, and I figured I'd sleep better on an empty stomach anyway.

I'd seen Doc just a week before. He had sat in his bare office, at his desk beside some olive-green metal files, his indomitable eyes wandering from the touched-up studio portrait of his field-mouse wife; to my sallow face; to his fingernails, each of which was chewed halfway to the moon, and you couldn't blame him, because Doc carried about fifty pooped aviators around on his back day and night; and now and again to a pile of case histories of aviators' deterioration stacked on the desk before him, like so many reproaches against psychiatry and patriotism; to his pipe; to the wall; to the sky outside which carried all his many troubled men to the enemy and sometimes back again—and he had told me to eat in the mornings. All about calories. Sitting under tension in a plane without nourishment. Reserves. All that.

I had told him I just couldn't eat breakfast, ever.

He had said I'd simply have to force it down, the mornings there were missions.

"Doesn't this world ever make you want to throw up, Doc?"

At that question of mine he'd looked at me, and his purple-rimmed eyes had said, "Constantly." But the flesh around his mouth had moved in convulsive waves, and soon a sunny smile sat on his lips, and he told me a fable which I think he made up as he went along.

"Once upon a time," he said, "there was a crow with the appetite of a condor, or perhaps a goat. It didn't care how things tasted, but only how they looked. It liked bright objects, silver and shining blue things, and one day it ate a lady's ring, a nickel a child had lost by the roadside, a priest's collar button, a sequin, a violinist's mute, a juke-box slug, and a lot of other junk like that. In the afternoon the crow began to feel nauseated, and he said to himself, 'Must be something I ate.' His crop got more and more uncomfortable, and finally he oopsed everything. The morsels he had thrown up looked so pretty that he wanted to eat them all over again, but believing that one of them had made him sick he decided not to eat any of them at all, and he flew away with a sense of forfeited pleasure. Do you know what the moral of this fable is?"

"Don't eat breakfast before going on a mission," I said.

"Wrong," Doc said. "The moral is: People don't know what's bad for them until after the fun's gone out of it."

"Doc," I said, "you're the God-damnedest man I ever met."

"Sometimes I think I'm plumb crazy," he said, grinning.

And maybe he was. What the hell did that crow have to do with me? Nothing. Only I came out of there feeling great. Doc's eyes just kind of poured willingness into you.

7 /

I was among the first to reach the briefing room—an outsize Nissen hut with enough folding chairs for about two hundred fifty men arranged in rows on a concrete floor facing a low platform. A blackboard rested on one easel on this stage, and a big map with a black cloth draped over it was on another. Clamped to an overhead steel beam, about a third of the way back, were several theatrical spotlights, which made the platform end of the room dazzlingly bright. The crews, both officers and sergeants, were beginning to wander in, and they were a raunchy bunch, in coveralls or leather jackets, the officers wearing hard caps or leather flying helmets with the earflaps turned up, and the gunners wearing fatigue caps or flying hats or black woolen skullcaps—each to his own taste, a ragtag mob altogether, sleepy, bad-tempered, curious but not zestful-curious, mumbling, elbowing, with no sense of drama at all, just a dull ache of wishing the whole f——ing world-wide mess was over.

Even on this clammy August Cambridgeshire morning the room was stiflingly hot before all the men had arrived, like a railroad car in which the thermostat has gone blooey, and soon the passengers' tongues will become dry, and their collars will swim, and the children will draw cross-eyed faces in the steam on the windows. Those bright lights had something to do with it. We called

the place the sweatbox; of course the actual heat wasn't to blame
for all the perspiration.

I jostled my way up to the front of the room. Before they'd
covered the map they had stretched a length of red twine out on
pins over the course to the target and back, and the spare twine at
the end was rolled on a bobbin, which hung down and kept the
line on the map under tension, and we'd figured out that if there
was a lot of twine left on the bobbin there couldn't be much on
the map, and we'd have a milk run to one of the sub bases or maybe
Holland or at most a shallow penetration of France; but if the
bobbin was almost empty . . .

Some bastard had got wise to us and had tucked the bobbin
around back, and I couldn't see it, even with one foot up on the
platform and craning my neck. I heard a croaking voice say, "Tut-
tut, teacher spank." I whirled and saw that of course it was Merchant, our flak officer, who was batty about sunbathing, and though
he'd come to the wrong country for it, was deeply tanned; every
time the sun peeped out you'd see Merch flat on his back out on
the grass in his drawers. He often had the sniffles because of sunbathing under clouds. He'd caw, "You really get a burn through
this stuff; 's like a billion little magnifying glasses." Then he'd have
to run like stink because there'd be a cloudburst. Still, he was pretty
black, maybe from a secret sunlamp. Out from his larynx that
sounded full of BB shot came a rattle: "Curiosity killed the cat."

"Don't say that!" I snarled. Merchant represented flak, and I
didn't want death at his hands, or at curiosity's either. Since the
end of July, since Kid Lynch had his beautiful brains eviscerated,
and Daphne had opened my eyes, and I'd made my separate peace
with the enemy, I'd wanted as much of life as I could grasp in my
hands. No mention even of the end of life. Merchant's bronze lips
twisted in a friendly grin which I didn't trust.

I drifted five or six rows back, and there Marrow grabbed the
cloth of my coverall on my right shoulder and hauled me into a
row of seats and sat me down beside him.

"Morning," I said. "Hope you were able to sleep last night."

Buzz, ignoring my sarcasm, began prattling about some Red
Cross doughnut girl he wanted to get his hooks into, and suddenly
I had to go to the latrine.

The can of the briefing room was hair-raising; the buckets

hadn't been emptied or limed since the battle of Hastings, and of course there wasn't any paper except some formation blanks from the Abbeville-Drucat mission.

When I went back the arched room was filled. Marrow had saved my seat, and pretty soon Old Man Bins came out and said, "All right," and the place was like church.

The Old Man was twenty-nine, a tall, wasted figure, and he stood there grinding his teeth, and we thought him a passable C.O. Had guts, was firm. This morning, after what Daphne had made me see yesterday about Marrow's "courage," I looked at our famous Colonel Bins with new and more skeptical eyes. I remembered Marrow's reaction when we came back from the rest home in mid-July and Bins had just been promoted over Marrow's head (Marrow thought), and in his absence, and the two men were just like a pair of roosters, on tiptoe trying to look down each other's gullet. And now I wondered if Bins, too, was like Marrow. I squirmed in my seat. I wanted my tour to be over.

Colonel Bins didn't stand on his prerogatives, the way most Group C.O.'s did, outlining missions themselves at briefings. Bins knew that he read out loud like a first-grader, haltingly and stupidly, and he said a few rapid words and turned things over to Steve Murika, our S-2, who was an articulate man. This practice didn't diminish Bins' grip on the fliers; they admired him, called him the Great Granite Jaw.

Murika stepped up with his black loose-leaf notebook in one hand and his pointer stuck under his arm like a swagger stick. He stood straight and pressed his lips primly together, and his hair, what little he had, was greased, and his forehead glistened in a startling way, as if coated with aluminum foil. We examined his face for a sign, like boys in an examination room searching the teacher's face as he comes in with the test in his hands, trying to make out from his expression whether the paper is going to be stiff or a gut; but Murika never showed anything. Mystery man. All day and most of the night he sat in what seemed to be a locked wire cage in Intelligence, with a teletype machine clacking in a corner, and he was always writing. He was bald, and there were liver spots on his bare dome. He was well built and worked with his collar open and his sleeves rolled up, and Marrow, who claimed he could spot a fairy from a city block away, said that Murika wasn't one in spite of be-

ing "an intelleckshul," and Buzz considered Murika's information
reliable on the sole ground that it was delivered in what Buzz
deemed a manly wise.

Murika didn't keep us in suspense. He poked his pointer up
under the black cloth and lifted it off the map.

8 /

In a flash I remembered the briefing on Schweinfurt the
week before—the portentous way in which Murika had responded
to the wave of horror that went over his audience when the men
saw that stretch of twine across Belgium, past the Ruhr, deep, deep,
across Germany into Bavaria, to a place they'd never heard of and
didn't want to see. "Yes," Steve had said, as the gasps and whistles
died out, "you will have the honor today to make the deepest penetration of enemy territory in the history of American aerial warfare." Steve Murika was the only person on the base who used
words like "honor" and "courage" and "loyalty" and "morale" out
loud. He had flown as an observer on two missions and knew miles
of Conrad by heart.

And I remember how Buzz, beside me then as he was now,
had shouted, "Hot diggety! This one'll separate the men from the
boys." Buzz was forever talking about men and boys. He called us
on his crew, "son," "sonny," "junior."

Murika, with his superb sense of showmanship, and with his
expression that seemed to say that he had more stored away under
that shiny forehead of his than any of us would ever learn and forget, had worked up a fair amount of enthusiasm among us, telling
us why Schweinfurt had been selected as a target: ball bearings, a
potential bottleneck, stocking impractical, Schweinfurt complex
one half total Axis production, pervasive effect, all high-speed
equipment. . . .

We saw what he was driving at: If we did a good job on the
Schweinfurt ball-bearing plants, soon there'd be less Focke-Wulfs
and Messerschmidts and Dorniers and Heinkels, less of all the bees
that swarmed to torment us. And some of us exclaimed with sounds

oddly like those of pleasure, and I could see men rubbing their hands, eager to go—for a moment. . . .

Marrow stirred; I think he sighed.

I thought of him in the corridor, on his way to Daphne, the previous Thursday night, and I tried to recall the exact shade of slyness on his face as he lied about going over for a beer; the subtle print on his face of his enjoyment of deceiving his co-pilot and closest friend. But I drew a blank, I saw in my memory only the open, honest face of a thirsty Nebraska youth.

"This time there will be two great forces," Murika was saying, standing very straight, his metallic forehead and bald crown and greased hair effulgent under the floodlights. A better plan than the previous week's. A huge force of the —th Wing would go in first, its target Regensburg, not far from Schweinfurt; it would fly on over the Mediterranean to North African bases. (Exclamations; a swaying of shoulders in leather jackets.) We of the —th Wing would penetrate enemy territory ten minutes after the first force, go to Schweinfurt, and come back on a reciprocal course. The Regensburg task force would get most of the fighter support because it was thought it would get the preponderance of enemy opposition. (Profanity expressing satisfaction.) Murika raised his pointer with the assurance of a symphony conductor, and he half-turned toward the chart. "Our Schweinfurt force, consisting of two boxes of two combat wings each, will cross the Dutch coast here at zero plus nine and zero plus twenty-one. The gaps in timing are necessary because the Regensburg force will be carrying Tokyo tanks and so will have a slower i.a.s. than we, and also to avoid jamming in the target area. . . ."

For me the incentive for this mission—to reduce, in due course, the enemy's fighter strength—had a slight catch. I would fly only one more mission after this one, knock wood, and any effect we might have on the Schweinfurt ball-bearing works couldn't possibly be felt soon enough to help me.

Could anything help me?

Why had I even asked Daphne about her hours with Marrow? I had sat on the edge of her bed and asked the irrevocable question—on her bed in the drab room where she had so often, heartbeat by heartbeat with mine, pushed the sense of finality, of maybe-the-last-time, back out of mind, and no matter how tired I might

have been, no matter how danger's foul breath had been blowing, she had made everything perfect, for she was responsive, so it
seemed that what I wanted, she also deeply wanted, and I had only
to search my needs in order to serve hers, and we became a single
personality in our passion. I sat on the edge of the iron-framed bed
and asked her the question, and she looked at me as if we were
about to be parted, and she nodded and in the act of nodding said,
"But wait!" At that a word was shaken out of me, like a cough or a
sob, because I only saw the nod and could not listen to the warning that there was much to say, and all I wanted to know was *why*.
She said simply that I was the one she adored. But it was no use. I
was deaf. Much later, when she had made me some coffee and I
was calm, she told me all about my pilot, too much about him,
really. Marrow, the Lover-Boy! About what he really loved.

Murika was telling us about the diversions they'd set up to
help us: Mitchells and Bomphoons and Typhoons were going to
hit around Amsterdam, Woensdrecht, and Lille. As to fighters, the
Regensburg strike was to get P-47s, Murika said, but there would
only be four squadrons of limey Spit-9s with the first box of our
force; all this time I was taking automatic notes, but my hand was
trembling so that I could scarcely read my own writing. Marrow
was sitting on the edge of his seat, like a kid at the circus, responding to the surprises and delights, as he apparently regarded them,
of Murika's show with grunts, sighs, flexes, and little yips like those
of a happy fornicator, and my loathing of him was almost beyond
bounds. I mean I wanted to do something about it. I had a terrible
moment and missed altogether some sentences Murika spoke that
might have been keys to survival during the day. Then a thought of
Daphne, of the old Daphne, a thought of her such as had calmed
me many times in the air, came to me, and I felt better, for Daphne
had an influential serenity like that of a pond in the Maine woods,
in the evening, its face reflecting the wind-spent sky, when the wa-
ter-birds are still and the beavers haven't yet begun to slap and
gnaw.

"But the second box of the Schweinfurt attack"—Murika was
suddenly like a stern teacher—"and I remind you that our Group
is to lead that box—will have no fighters at all on penetration."

Marrow shifted his bulk, whopped out a handkerchief, and
swabbed his streaming face. He was known as a great sweater; at

meals he showered his food with salt. Now he was driving out fluid by the pint. "Christ!" he exclaimed, in a loud voice that turned faces his way for several rows. "Too God-damn much body heat in here." Then, with a crazy, cackling cheerfulness, he added, as Murika paused to see what the disturbance was, "Next briefing the place'll be like a f——ing refrigerator. S——!" And the men around us who had heard both utterances laughed. Good old Buzz! How healthy his jokes about death!

There had been a few seconds, back there, when my hatred of Marrow had almost flown out of control in the slow, heavy, side-slipping way of a Fort with a broken cable. I had lost all track of what Murika was saying, and I had clamped my left hand across my forehead and over my eyes, but then I saw the sweat of my terror and anger gleaming like a morning cobweb in the wrinkles of my palm, and I thought: I'm in lousy shape. Maybe I'd better go to Doc Randall after the briefing and tell him I was going to have to chicken out on this mission. I'd be a danger to my crewmates.

But then Stormy Peters was on his feet, who'd been up all night, and he was talking about the sky, and I guess I must have thought of Doc Randall, building his jaws on a pipe stem and worrying, deep in those unconquerable eyes of his, about all *his* troubles, which were aviators, and I guess I was so sorry for Doc that I got some courage back; what we call courage.

". . . six- to eight-tenths stratocumulus at twenty-five hundred to three thousand, tops five thousand, decreasing to nil just off the English coast; three- to five-tenths altocumulus at twelve to thirteen . . ."

I almost enjoyed this part, for I could see in my mind pictures of the fantastic skies Stormy dryly told us about—until something about Stormy reminded me of Kid Lynch, my other best friend, who was dead; dead as the body on the beach at Pamonassett that I never could forget. This was all I needed: to have to think of the Kid. Now there was a marvelous half-trained mind. The Kid had squandered his assets—all that corny clowning on the Tannoy system—and maybe he'd have been that way all his life, throwing half of himself away. But what use was that maybe? The world, this f——ed-up ball of s—— we lived on, had blown the top off his skull and thrown all of him away.

After that we had our sunburned friend Merchant, whose nickname was Feather (What else? Were ever Rhodes not Dusty?) on the flak prospects, and he was ridiculous, as usual—". . . expect meager-to-moderate at Bingen, Hasselt, Maastricht, moderate at Antwerp, meager at Diest . . ."—for he had to get off the stale line that had once been regarded as a joke, about the flak being mainly a deterrent, men.

The sergeant gunners left for the armament shop, and the navigators and bombardiers and radiomen got into clumps and received their special briefings, and Flying Control, in the obnoxious person of Major Fane, with his air of just having taken a morning dip in a dry-cleaner's vat, gave us the order of taxiing and we found out where *The Body* was to be in the formation: she was to lead the second element of the lead squadron of the lead group of the second box of the Schweinfurt strike. No fighter support. Translated into English, that meant: sucking the hind tit. Lousy.

And we ended up, forty-one minutes after Old Man Bins had opened the briefing with that rumbling, "All right!," with a time tick, synchronizing our watches.

For a couple of seconds, as we stood up and stretched, exactly, for me, as if it were the end of a movie at the ancient Fox Poli in Donkentown, I caught Marrow's gaze. It seemed to me that as he looked at me his eyes were surprised, puzzled. I wondered if he knew that for the first time in all our months together I saw right through him.

9 /

Nine of us rode in a weapons carrier out around the five-mile perimeter track to a dispersal point where, surrounded at a distance by vague, lumpish trees and shrubs, our ship huddled in the mist like a great dark sea lion among some wave-worn rocks.

When the carrier stopped, our sergeants lifted out their guns and parked them for the moment on the engine tarps which the line crew had stacked on the grass beside the hardstand.

I stood in a daze on the paved area; I was puzzling out a queer sensation I had had a few minutes before. In the equipment room,

as I had pulled on my bright-blue electrified flying suit, and once
again, as I had stood in the co-pilots' line for kits, I had felt waves
of funk. Like gusts of cold wind they had hit me and had passed.
Marrow had stayed behind in the briefing room with the squadron leaders to talk formation, so I didn't, at the time, associate the
flashes of fear and despair with him. I had been fortunate; I had
not had too much of that sort of trouble, especially since I had
made my separate peace with the enemy and had devoted myself
to survival. I had had plenty of fear all along but very little panic.
And now, as I walked with my crewmates across the hardstand toward *The Body*, I had all my usual symptoms of pre-strike anxiety,
but I was free of anything like those thrusts of agony I'd felt in the
equipment room and kit line. I think that when those had hit me I
must have been struck by deep urges to avenge myself on my once-
friend Marrow—though at the time I'd have sworn on a stack of
Air Force regulations that nothing could have been further from
my thoughts.

We walked toward the ship through nacreous pools of oily water on the asphalt parking area. Visibility was less than a hundred
yards. We couldn't begin to see *Erector Set* and *Finah Than Dinah*, the Forts that were parked on hardstands on either side of
ours on the perimeter. Marrow hadn't been driven out yet.

I heard Jughead Farr, our right waist gunner, sniff the fog and
say: "Great day for an abort, hey Brag?"

And Bragnani, left waist and Jughead's stooge: "Aw, kiss my
ass."

This was Bragnani's way of expressing enthusiastic agreement.
Long since, we had come to understand that Bragnani, who was no
good (whereas Farr was dangerous), put a reverse twist on everything he said. Thus, "Go f— yourself!" meant "Sure, pal," and
"What a horse's ass!" meant "He's a prince." Black was white; lies
were truths in Bragnani's mouth. Farr, who had Bragnani under his
thumb, could parse and scan this imbecilic double talk for the rest
of us.

I heard some of the others, in whose minds our Gelsenkirchen
abort, Farr's single-handed fault, was all too fresh, jump him now.
He talked back. Even little Junior Sailen snarled at Farr. Our crewmates began snapping at each other like vicious hungry dogs. It was
Handown's peremptory, "Cut the chicken s—, Jug," that brought

the flurry to an end, and we stood silent, breathing hard as if
burned out by a sudden violent run, in the thick morning beside
the silver ship as Handown fumbled at the underside hatch handle
to let us in.

When *The Body* was open the sergeants went for their guns,
and I scrambled up through to the pilot's compartment for the preflight check.

I sat in Marrow's seat. I was in charge. For a moment I took
Marrow's wheel in my hands, holding it lightly, in his manner, between thumbs and forefingers—but of course the controls were
locked, and I snapped out of it. I reached to the central control
panel, forward of the throttles, and threw on the big ignition
switch; then, to my left, on Buzz's side wall panel, I checked each
battery switch with either inverter on, and turned on the master
battery switch. I threw the hydraulic pump switch to automatic.
The list and order were clear and immutable in my memory like
lettering engraved on a headstone: landing-gear control switch in
neutral, flap control switch in neutral, set parking brake. . . .

I was conscious that Marrow was standing in the aisle looking
down over my shoulder. As I glanced up at him he began heckling
me. What was I doing in his seat? Had I remembered to do this?
That? The other thing?

For weeks, during the middle stretches of our tour, Buzz had
entrusted the preflight to me. Indeed, in all that time when he
had played the bloody hero, especially after he got his D.F.C., he
couldn't be bothered with the boring routine of life in *The Body*;
that was all left to underlings. His time was sky time. Ho-hum. But
lately he'd become irritable about routine checks, erratic, incon-
sistent, and I didn't know any more whether the responsibility was
mine or not.

This particular morning I knew that I'd had it, where Marrow
was concerned, and I startled him, no less than myself, by saying,
"If you don't like the way I do the preflight, you can do it yourself," and I started to get up out of his precious throne.

"That's O.K.," he said, like someone turning off a hot-water
faucet, and he was suddenly on his hands and knees crawling down
the passageway to see Brindt and Haverstraw.

So I hollered to Handown to take the blocks out of the controls and still sitting in Marrow's seat I moved the wheel and the

column and the rudder pedals to the extremities of their operating ranges. And across the way my own co-pilot's wheel, unmanned, my column, and my pedals moved in perfect automatic harmony with the movement of the pilot's controls.

10 /

I crawled down to the greenhouse, where Marrow was going over the mission in a cursory way with Brindt and Haverstraw. The three of them hunched like conspirators there—Brindt sitting backwards-to in his bombing seat, Haverstraw at the navigator's desk, Marrow in a crouch by the desk, all washed by queer gray-green light that came through the plexiglass of the astrodome and the nose. They had already covered the target and most of the flight plan out and back, and I must say I resented Marrow's going into all that with Max and Clint without my being present—as if they didn't really need me. I had to horn in, as it was.

Haverstraw began to give the Gee information: the Eastern Wyoming and Southern California chains on Grade A would operate during the entire mission. I loved those codes; I wanted to cling to the fantasy that it was all a huge game of Cops and Robbers. The bombers' call sign for the day was Windbag. The fighters' call sign was Croquet. (Bins or somebody had spelled it Crokay on the blackboard.) The target was a German city that *we* called Alabama . . . and at the word "Alabama" I had a glimpse for a moment of the stately curve of the high-rankers' homes at Maxwell Field on the way out to the officers' club, the grass new-mown by the sidewalk and vividly fragrant after a sudden shower, and a splash of bougainvillea, too brilliant to be true, and some officers' wives getting out of highly polished cars, going to a quiet luncheon in the club, probably an afternoon of bridge; and I yearned, with a nostalgia that was like a lover's pain in the chest, for those days that I had thought so dull at the time, those days in that other world before the killing began.

For it had turned out not to be Cops and Robbers.

Marrow was leaning forward now, his eyes bugging out at Max

Brindt, who was so mild on the ground and so ferocious on the bombing run, and they were almost drooling as they talked about our loading, and its distribution, and the fusings: we were carrying ten five-hundred-pound general-purpose bombs. Both of those men would have preferred to carry thousand-pounders. The bigger, the louder. Voom! Voom! Marrow was full of sound-effects, like those of a ten-year-old boy. Skidding tires. Crunching fenders. Colliding aircraft. Above all, explosions, the trembling of foundations, falling masonry, the collapse of cities, the rumble of the end of civilization. He could do it all so hauntingly in his throat, with a grin.

As we piled out through the lower hatch we saw that most of the sergeant gunners had finished their work and were standing in a clump in the grass having a smoke. Red Black, the unpredictable crew chief, sweet as taffy this morning, moved in after us to polish the glass of the nose. Our radio gunner, Lamb, was still aboard, moving around checking the interphones. We four officers walked out across the hardstand toward the others. Marrow was raving again about the doughnut girl—saying that taking a uniform off a girl was better than taking an ordinary dress off her, it was more like a gift wrapping, and this Red Cross girl, he'd studied her uniform. . . .

But I thought I detected a new strain in Marrow's voice, an undercurrent of some kind of uneasiness. Perhaps he suspected that Daphne had told me a few things about him. Or perhaps it was only in my mind, that he was a man who ought to be uneasy.

The pickup truck came around with K-rations and candy, and we had a rhubarb about the sweets. The driver tried to pawn off peanut brittle on us. Marrow stood on tiptoes and began flailing his arms.

"Hey! We want O. Henrys," he shouted.

"Tough titty," the driver said.

"I got to have my chocolate," Buzz said.

"Better tell General Arnold about that," the driver said. "Hap Arnold *wants* his boys to have chocolate."

"You God-damn sergeants," Marrow said. "Always wising off."

I thought Buzz was going to reach in and poke the guy.

"What's more," the driver said, as saucy as ever, "stations time's postponed forty-five minutes. Till eight fifteen."

"—on account the inclement weather," Handown said, mimicking the driver's prissy voice.

"Big news, for Christ's sake!" Marrow said.

"And that ain't all," the driver said, and then he ground the gears and fussed with the gear shift. He knew how to twist the stiletto in a man's guts, especially in those of a man like Marrow, who just couldn't stand waiting for anything, least of all news. Finally he gave. "I got word they've scrubbed the diversions." And with a pert little glance at Handown he added, "On account of the inclement weather." And he gunned the pickup and zoomed in a sharp curve out of our hardstand, practically on two wheels.

Marrow took off with a torrent of obscenity against Wing Headquarters, which was the only institution he hated more than the sergeancy. The idea that Wing could send us on a deep penetration without any fighters, and without diversionary raids to decoy the squareheads—well, Buzz's tirade was a dusey.

11 /

The men, in a knot, groused and joshed back and forth, using their bizarre nicknames for each other—Dopey, Negrocus, Butcher, Slop-jar, Jughead, Rum-Boogie—and soon they had broken it up and were passing the sluggish time as well as they could. Butcher Lamb, Prien, and Sailen went in and messed with their guns, and I could see Max Brindt fumbling around looking for something in the greenhouse, with a flashlight, like a prowler on a country estate, and Buzz kicked the huge tires; I suppose that was a check. I heard Bragnani, Farr, and Marrow strike up a razz about dames, and then: San Francisco, Brag was saying, was the meat-heaven of the world. "Why, s——," he said, "those babes out there *like* it. You can't fight 'em off. We'd no sooner get in there to the hotel, you know, on an overnight, when, Jesus Christ, the dames would be lined up with beds on their backs." Later Buzz walked along the perimeter track part way to the next dispersal point, and I heard him holler down to Stebbins, who was to be his left wingman on this one: "Hey, Steb!" and when an answering hail came,

Buzz shouted, "Listen, you son of a bitch, you owe me four hundred and seventeen cokes." That would be from acey-deucy. Stebbins' answer swirled off in the mist, too hollow for me to hear. I did hear Negrocus Handown's thick Southern wail, as he stood with his head and shoulders between the open bomb-bay doors, probing the shadows with a light beam to see whether the eggs were securely racked:

"My mammy calls me sugar-lump
My pappy calls me apple-dump,
Oh Mammy, Mammy, ain't it a shame,
That Snowball ain't my name?"

I had turned an engine tarpaulin inside-out to find a dry part, and I had stretched out on it on the grass, and I was burned up at Marrow—this surely was balmy of me—because he wasn't the guy he'd seemed long ago. I guess what really made me furious was that I'd been taken in by him—by his look of being a happy animal in those early days. The very first time I met him I was struck by his vitality, by a fine tension he had between pouring out and holding in, which made him look pneumatic, blown up with energy. I saw him that day for the first time in the assembly hall at Spanner Field when our group was being formed. I was in a cluster of men around Major Bairn when Buzz came up, walking expressively, like a man doing a tango, lightly but with a dance-floor self-consciousness, a being-watched look, with a rhythmic heave up onto his toes at each step. He was pretty old, twenty-four or -five, and I, being short and slight and envious of big men, could estimate his height fairly exactly at six feet and one half inch, and his weight at one ninety-five; I could have made a lot of money at country fairs guessing the sizes of big men. Buzz had a centaur's chest and a head like a great statesman's and hands big enough for a steeplejack or a sea-going rope handler; but his feet were tiny, in dainty brown saddled brogans. His face was a muscle playground, ugly, square, and active—rippling with little spasms that might have been taken for thoughts. Major Bairn introduced him around our circle, to perhaps seven of us, and I remember his looking down at me, in my turn, as if I were some kind of freshman initiate, and when the Major had gone all the way around Buzz said with great animation, "Glad to meetcha, gentlemen. Or *are* you gentlemen?" His face exploded, and out came a booming laugh, and his shoulders heaved so energetically that soon we too were convinced that he had said something funny, and we laughed. Then Major Bairn told us that Lieutenant (then) Marrow had used to be a test pilot for Mildress Aircraft and that he'd been famous for his reckless power dives, and Buzz said, "S——, sir, they were afraid those cowlings would crack because of the temperature change, but I never could crack one of the God-damn things. I tried. By Christ, I tried!"

On a small table at the end of the Number Two Officers' Mess here at Pike Rilling there was a ledger, with a title printed by hand on a piece of adhesive tape across the front: *Beef Record*, and underneath the title: "Register here all suggestions, recommendations, reports of good or bad work or service, and all personal insults to Mess Officer." On the pages within the fliers had written according to their kind. "Let's have some fruit turnovers." "A meringue on the butterscotch custard pie would be 100% improvement." "Suggest that brief passage of reminders as to conduct becoming an officer be posted in mess hall or passed around." In very small letters: "Let's go home." Only one entry in the whole book had initials after it, and that had appeared late in March, when Marrow was brand new and hadn't flown a single mission, and of course the initials were W. S. M., for William Siddlecoff Marrow, and before these initials Buzz had written, in sprawling capital letters, "I WANT MORE STEAKS."

One day every time you went into our hutment you could see Marrow throwing darts into our room, with the board propped up on the head of his bed diagonally across from the door, and Buzz toeing the sill of the door, his sleeves rolled up and his shirt wet with sweat, alone, playing without an opponent in order to master a game he had just discovered, shouting when he made a good hit and laughing at himself when he missed the board altogether. Whenever a new game came along, in those early days, Buzz took it up with violent enthusiasm and did not drop it until he got bored with winning: gin rummy, backgammon, acey-deucy, canasta, darts—he collared men to teach him and then made victims of them and won their money at the game they had taught him. Buzz threw darts ten hours that first day, and the next morning he went up and down the whole base groaning about his stiff

arm, and he made a medic give him a rubdown. No one ever beat
Marrow at darts after that, except when he was very drunk.

Then I was on my feet, really mad, thinking of things that
Daphne had helped me to see. I had a five-pound note in my wallet that Buzz had loaned me a week before, because I wanted to
get Daphne a better electric hot plate for her room in Bartleck, and
I don't know just why, I'd been short on cash. That note of Buzz's
began to feel bad in my wallet. I didn't want his God-damn money.

I opened my electric suit and pulled my wallet out of a pocket
in my coverall, and I took the huge thin crackling white English
bill out and opened it up, and I asked Bragnani, who was nearest
me of the men then talking on the edge of the grass, if he had a
match, and he, thinking I wanted to light a cigarette, produced a
Zippo and with a flourish snapped up a flame, and I put a corner
of the bill on the lighter's tongue, and the white paper caught fire.

Bragnani popped his lighter shut and drew his hand back as if
he had lit a firecracker. "Jug, you see what the man *did?*" he asked
Farr nearby.

"That ain't money, idiot," Farr said. "That's just this lousy
limey bumwad. Leave him be. He maybe had a chill."

Bragnani laughed loudly. "Chill, my ass," he said. "Firebugs
we got."

"Douse that!" Handown sharply shouted from near the ship,
and I came to my senses and dropped the flaming paper and
stamped on it.

I hated Marrow through and through. Finding out what he
was really like had been a shock; I had been stupid and blind. And
it came over me, thinking of the two Marrows, one that I'd imagined and one that was real, that there were two kinds of courage:
the courage that comes from turning fear outward on behalf of others, that wants company and life; and the courage that wants to be
alone, that really wants death for all. The two kinds often looked
alike but were opposites; they often dwelt side by side in the same
man, but one was bound to predominate. And now, thanks to
Daphne, I knew that in Marrow the upper courage was that of the
annihilator.

12 /

It was nearly eight fifteen, the new stations time. For something to occupy my mind, I was checking my personal gear— my escape kit in the knee pocket of my flying suit, my sheath knife (as if I expected to meet cougars or savages in the jungles of the clouds) strapped inside my left flying boot. A jeep drove up, its two amber foglights, close together, swerving off the perimeter track at the mouth of our hardstand, and a voice called out, "Ninety-minute postponement. Do you hear me, pilot?"

And Buzz: "Again? What in Christ's name goes on around here?"

And the crackling voice in the jeep of some leather-larynxed old sergeant who had seen many a Marrow come and go: "You got complaints, sir, lodge 'em at Operations."

And Buzz: "You can tell Ops to go f—— itself."

And the voice of disenchantment: "Thank you, sir. Operations don't like to f—— itself so early in the morning."

So we had an hour and half more to kill. The fog was beginning to thin out now, but visibility was still borderline, five hundred yards at most. Buzz was sore at Wing, and he said they'd keep us waiting all morning and then scrub the f——ing mission. I said I didn't think that would happen. Marrow turned on me as if *I* were Wing Headquarters. What the hell did I know about anything? I only knew, and I certainly had no intention of repeating, what Stormy Peters had said. I stood silent, staring at Buzz.

Then Marrow came close up to me, over me, his big face squashed down toward mine, and he said between his teeth, very softly, making sure that no ears but mine would hear him, "You little son of a bitch, you think you're so f——ing smart."

Well, it seemed to be a meaningless flash of impatience, as much at the world as at me, so like Buzz lately, cranky before missions, but suddenly I turned away, for I was suffering as I'd suffered in the briefing; I felt a pang like those I'd experienced in the equipment room and on the kit line. I had to face it: I wanted Buzz Marrow to be dead, dead, dead.

As dead as the body on the beach at Pamonassett. The curve of the bay at Pamonassett was gentle, a big easy bite of a sated sea,

and we would run along the clean yellow beach and across the
sandbar out to Tiger Rock at low tide when the bar broke water,
and we'd dash through the sand pools in the lee of the Tiger, with
water clear as the magnifying glass on Father's desk in the summer
house which smelled of damp wicker and damp straw matting, and
we would chase the schools of minnows, throwing crystal splashes
into the sunlight as we sped through the safe shallows, and we
caught puffers off the head of the rock, fish that always made us
laugh at their audacity if they thought they could frighten us by
blowing out their bellies like ridiculous little pigeons of the sea, yet
when it came time to get them off the hooks it was strange how we
lost interest in fishing. Then we'd dive in the hole there off the
head, a deep, ominous, dark, round place with a couple of light
shadows, undersea ghosts of round rocks which we could feel with
our outstretched hands when we dived down, the roundness hairy
and slimy with weed. We thrilled at the danger of the hole every
time we saw it, and diving into it took a lot of vaunting and dou-
ble-daring, and we did it seldom enough. That lowering cloudy
morning, oppressive, hot, and damp, a day so still that it must have
been readying some horrible thunderclaps for its evening sky, Rod
and Vinny and I went out on the rock just because there wasn't
anything else to do, and there was the body, bobbing in the hole,
held from the foamy reaching of the sea by the paws of the Tiger.
We ran to the village, our scalps crawling as if with ants, and they
came and got it out and stretched it, flecked with dirty spindrift,
on the beach, the end of a man in working clothes, a stranger; the
feet were bare. One man said he'd seen the fellow drunk along the
Old Post Road. The face was purple and puffed out so that I never
could bear to go fishing again, and the eyes of the first death I'd
ever seen stared into a distance such as I could not imagine then. I
wondered what they saw so far away.

13 /

Marrow had lost interest in me. With scarcely time for a
transition in mood—and how like him *this* was; he was mercurial
—he got into an argument the men were having about the differ-

ence between a lady and a woman. They had spread out a couple
of engine tarps and were sprawled on them. Farr and Bragnani sat
hugging their knees. Prien was curled up pretending to be asleep.
Negrocus Handown, in a black knitted skullcap, drops of moisture
on his prominent blond eyebrows, sat working with a rag and a can
of metal polish on a crank handle he had removed from his beloved
top turret. "A lady," he said in his calm Southern voice, shaking
the can of polish and pouring some out on the rag, "is when you
don't want to fool around, like your own mother."

"Aaah, Neg," Farr growled, "you God-damn mother lover."

Little Junior Sailen, standing by the tarps, lit a butt and blew
a deep inhale onto his match, and spoke up. "It's a question of
money," he said.

"Ladies are frigid, and women aren't," Marrow suddenly
barked. He threw himself down on the oily canvas. The men were
respectfully silent. "I knew a real lady once," Buzz said, and he was
off on one of his tales of his swordsmanship. . . .

Just as Buzz finished his story, a recon car rolled in alongside
The Body. The mist was definitely burning off now, and a thin
sun could be seen swimming through it toward the west, moving
fast through the wreathing, luminous material. A voice called Buzz
from the car, and I recognized it as that of Curly Jonas, the Operations Officer of the Group, an ally of Buzz against Old Man
Bins. "Come over here a sec," the voice said when Marrow answered. Marrow stood up, surveyed his audience with satisfaction,
like a glutton looking at an empty plate after a meal, and then
bounced over the hardstand, going up at each pace onto the balls
of his feet. Jonas had opened the door of the car, and we could see
Marrow standing with one foot up on the steel step. For a while
we couldn't hear their murmuring, then suddenly we heard a shrill
protest from our pilot: "What're they trying to do, kill us all?"

To me it was a bloodcurdling cry, because it seemed to me to
have in it the sound of delight ill-concealed. Again, though, I realized that this might have been all in my mind—what I thought I
should be hearing in the voice of the Marrow whom Daphne had
exposed to me, the voice of a lonely courage, of a war lover.

Soon enough Jonas had left and Marrow came back to us. The
men stirred, stiffened, at his approach, because they knew Marrow
wouldn't hold out on them.

It was Clint Haverstraw, the navigator, Marrow's pet pup, who dared to say, "What have they dreamed up now?"

They were always inventing something to torture us with. They knew what They could do with Their war.

Marrow stood with his feet wide apart looking down at us. He was a fine figure. He *was* courageous, but he stood apart, his courage was selfish, pale, deathly.

"They've sent the Regensburg strike on ahead," he said. "They sent it out at eight o'clock."

14 /

It was stations time, a quarter to ten, and we went into *The Body*. The pearly ground fog had lifted; low clouds were running down to the eastward like suds in a rocky river bed. From my seat in the cockpit I could see the cubical control tower in the far distance, and I could even make out some tiny figures—members of the operational staff—on the iron-railed balcony of the tower. Eight or ten Forts were visible, scattered at their hardstands along the perimeter track, dark and squat, imponderable, rooted to the ground by their tail wheels. A big camouflaged R.A.F. gasoline lorry and trailer moved slowly along the main road toward the hangars. Jeeps busy-bodied up and down the perimeter track.

A two-pronged red flare arched over the center of the field. Start engines!

Our ritual began. While Buzz supervised the turning over of the props by hand, I ordered Negrocus Handown, who as aerial engineer and top-turret gunner manned the area right behind Marrow and me, to go back in the bomb bay and open the manual shut-off valve of the hydraulic system and set the selective check valve to servicing position, so I could check the hydraulic pressures; seven hundred pounds, more or less, in both accumulators, O.K., so I got Negrocus to reset the valves. Then Marrow and I each had both hands flying. I opened the cowl flaps and locked their valves; made sure the fuel-transfer valves and pump switch were off; set the fire-extinguisher selector valve to the number-one engine, which

I'd start first; moved the intercooler controls to cold; opened the carburetor air filters after Buzz cracked the throttles. . . . In his temper Marrow was slamming things around and spoiling this passage, our partnership in bringing to life the power of the ship, a process which had used to thrill me even when I was in extremities of fear at the beginning of the early missions; had thrilled me partly because it was I, in the end, who actually started the engines, and partly because I had always been staggered by the beautiful complexity of these great fortresses of the sky—by the myriad dials, switches, knobs, handles, and warning lamps; nerve-ends leading to the great vitals and muscles of the plane. Marrow and I were the twin-lobed brain of the ship, and the starting was the awakening of the huge creature before its miraculous act of flight.

Had been. This time I had to force myself through the steps.

Marrow was carrying on a furious subversive monologue against Wing. He saw better than the rest of us what the decision to let the Regensburg strike go ahead meant to us. He had gathered from Curly Jonas that the decision had been based on the idea that the Regensburg force could not be delayed, lest its planes should reach the unfamiliar North African airdromes to which they were destined after nightfall. But the whole point of the two-pronged attack had been that the heavily escorted Regensburg strike would attract and exhaust the German fighter defenses so that our strike, following in train, would be spared. Jonas had said that our take-off had been delayed three hours in order that the friendly fighters with the Regensburg force could return, refuel, and go out again with us. But so could the Germans land and refresh themselves.

Buzz got all this out, and much more, in incoherent sputters seasoned with profanity. He was so mad I was afraid he'd goof off on something important, fuel valves or prop controls or some such.

But finally he gave me the nod, and I pressed the starter button for number one, and I could hear the whine of the inertia starter in the wing. I unlocked the primer and set it to number one and pumped up a solid charge of fuel. Buzz was counting off the seconds, and he nodded again—still yammering about those murderers in Wing—and I flipped the switch to mesh and craned and saw the momentary burst of blue smoke sweep out into the prop wash as number one caught and we heard the roar and felt the shaking of all that energy. We went to work on number two.

I had a strange lonely feeling. Then I remembered the day I was left behind—a milk run to St. Nazaire on the twenty-eighth of June, when Marrow took Maltitz along as co-pilot to check him out on combat before they let Titty fly first pilot, and I stood gripping the rail at the control tower and I heard, out across the vast spread of the dispersal areas, the first ragged fusillade of the starting engines, and then gradually a powerful roar built up, and I felt as lonely as a solitary climber freezing to death on the slopes of a mountain to the sound of a distant avalanche.

Soon all four engines were going all right, and I had my eyes on the oil temperature and pressure gauges, two meaningful circles for each, on the panel straight ahead of me, and the engines were warming up, when in the one ear that I'd covered with an earphone I heard Marrow rasp out, "Lamb, did you remember your IFF?"

By no means for the first time Butcher Lamb, our radio operator, who could find a thousand ways of pretending there wasn't a war going on, had forgotten to test the homing device before taxiing time. "Oh-oh," he said into the interphone.

Then Marrow shouted on the interphone—all ten of us were plugged in, of course—one of his elated, abusive cries which we had all loved so much over the hard months, and which, so far as I knew, the others still loved that morning, but I hated with a taste of rust in my mouth: "I don't know how any you bastards would ever come home, only for me thinking of these things."

That had been Buzz's hold over us. It couldn't happen to our ship, not with Marrow in there; so he had often said. "See that?" he had shouted the morning Braddock's ship blew up almost literally in our faces. "That won't happen to us. Not while I fly this bucket." And then a burst of indignation: "What's the matter with that son of a bitch Braddock? Don't he know evasive tactics? . . . I got to speak to these bastards"—meaning the other pilots. "They're all going to get 'emselves killed!" Ours was the one inviolate vessel, and Buzz was our magic charm. "It can't happen to this bucket, son." The crew believed it, particularly the enlisted men. Marrow's ship was famous in the enlisted men's barracks as the one that didn't know how to fall down. We'd had our share of troubles—our eighth, May 19, the Kiel strike, those friendly incendiaries!—but it was a fact that ours was a lucky ship. There *was* such a thing as luck up there. It was one of the things I hated about flying in war. I wanted a world in which a man could be in control of every step on his way.

But I, and only I, on the plane as we trembled on the hard-stand, was the custodian of a horrible piece of knowledge. Marrow's personal magic was not there. It was all bluster. His strength, as we had imagined it, outgoing and luck-coated, wasn't there at all. I had had the word straight from Daphne.

How vulnerable we were!

Yet even now, I found, I still had a hangover of admiration, envy, some feeling of having to hand it to him.

He called Sailen on the interphone and asked if his turret was secure. Junior Sailen—*all* of us called *him* Junior, why, he was half *my* size—was stationed in the ball turret, slung down under the fuselage, where he sat huddled up like an embryo, and if the turret weren't locked with its guns pointing rearward, when you taxied out, there was liable to be a loud scraping noise, and you'd have a couple of bent barrels on those underbelly guns. Buzz really was a commander; he knew what every crewman was supposed to be thinking at every moment. Junior Sailen hadn't forgotten. You didn't have to worry about him; he was a scrapper. Yet Marrow—even though he was probably way below par—made sure.

But it was when he put his hand to the power controls that you really had to give it to Buzz. Maybe this wasn't good, maybe it was neither good nor bad; anyway, he looked as if the power flowed from him into the ship. With the mixture controls in automatic rich, he tuned the throttles at around fifteen to sixteen hundred, then he checked the propeller governors, moving them to high-pitch position, and then—and this was when it seemed as if some kind of juice flowed through his hands into the fierce motors: he cocked his head and listened, his back was straight, his chest could have been a generator—he ran up each engine at full throttle and twenty-five hundred r.p.m.'s, and with marvelous dexterity and precision and speed, he adjusted the supercharger control stops for forty-six inches of manifold pressure.

The thing he'd said so often, that he was part of it and it was part of him, seemed true.

Marrow gave a signal out of his window, and Red Black

yanked the chocks out from under the wheels. Buzz and I closed our windows. I checked the tail-wheel warning lamp to make sure the wheel was unlocked. We were ready to roll.

15 /

At a corner of the perimeter track, down the line from us, we saw *Angel Tread*, Colonel Bins' ship, lumber slowly out from his hardstand and swing to lead the procession of taxiing ships. As she passed their dispersal points, *Gruesome Twosome* and *Erector Set* heaved out behind her. We waited. We were to be fourth in line.

Two big English meat wagons stood waiting at the end of the runway; I hated to look at ambulances.

The sun came out from behind a low cloud, and three or four of the ships in the distance turned from gray to silver, and the great meadow inside the triangle of runways was drenched with yellow-green light. Despite its patches of camouflage the control tower stood starkly rectangular against the dark of the forest where we lived, and the distant alleys of lime trees and great elms and the woods of oak and ash near Pike Rilling Hall were still under cloud.

Starting and stopping, her brakes screeching above the roar of her engines and ours, *Angel Tread* went by us, and the other two followed, and then Marrow, with the throttles of the inboard engines locked, swinging his big right paw on the throttles of one and four in subtle, sinuous moves, gunning our tail around first and then easing our huge weight forward, pulled us out into line. Now our own brakes joined in the outcry, as we started and stopped while each plane stepped out and tacked on.

Taxi time was hard for me. We knew from experience that from the time *Angel Tread* made her first move to the time when all the ships of our group—twenty-four this morning, including stand-bys—would be stacked up at the head of the runway, taking into account the five long miles of the track and the usual hitches, but not allowing time, as we often had to do, for some idiot to run a wheel off the edge of the paved way and get stuck hubdeep in mud, so a cleat track would have to clank out and haul him free, more than an hour would have passed. There was nothing for me to do but move my eyes from gauge to gauge: be sure that fuel pressure didn't go above sixteen pounds per square inch, cylinder-head temperature didn't go above two hundred and five degrees Centigrade . . . oil pressure . . . oil temperature . . .

We went slowly along, and I, being on the outside of the great perimeter, saw each ship on her hardstand, her props whirling—one caught the sunlight in all of hers and stood holding up four beautiful golden dishes of light for me to see—and to some I waved an ambiguous wave that might be a nonchalant top-o'-the-mornin' or might be, might prove to have been before nightfall, a farewell, for good and all.

The ships, waiting to fall in line, were like old friends. *Finah Than Dinah, Hoor's Dream, Chug Bug, Howzat Again, Round Trip Ticket, Baggy Maggie, Expendable VI, She Can't Help It, Flak Sack, Eager Virgin, Big Bum Bird, Miss Take, Friggon Falcon, Ten Naughty Boys, Heavenly Hooker, Rats Wouldn't Stay, Torch Carrier, Betty Grable, Alabama Whammer, Lady Be Good* —one by one they joined us, and we knew how many lives *Chug Bug* had taken, and the extraordinary escapes of *Heavenly Hooker*; each one was a personality. Some were ancient crocks, camouflaged a dun green above and sky blue on the underside, patched and oil-stained, and some were slick new ships that had been left unpainted except for the huge identification letters they all carried on the upright tail surfaces.

When we had picked up the whole parade *Angel Tread* turned in at the head of the east-west concrete runway, which some of the early pilots had named Crunch Alley because of a series of accidents on it; we would take off into the west wind. We began to close up tight. Marrow spotted *The Body* no more than twenty feet behind *Erector Set*, and I locked the tail wheel for the take-off.

We had another long wait, while the twenty ships behind us closed in and spotted themselves, and then we had to burn up some time Wing Ops had left as leeway.

This was almost the worst wait of all—strapped in with nothing to do.

There was practically no ground haze; the clouds a thousand feet up were scattering, though there was still about six-tenths cover.

Negrocus Handown was standing behind me, and having him there, solid as the Alleghenies, was a big help on this of all mornings. After all, Neg was a grown man, thirty-six years old. He had his problems, all right—that business of supervising the education of the young in London was very odd—but of one thing I was sure: Handown was not one of those I knew I must hate to the end of my life, he was no war lover.

Just as I thought again of that streak in Marrow, Buzz turned slowly toward me, and his face was weirdly close to the face I had seen in my dream the night before—broad, swollen, pallid, and distorted by a ferocious look of disapproval.

"You God-damn smart aleck," he shouted over the roar of the engines.

He must have known Handown could hear him.

"What the hell did I do?" I screamed back.

"Never mind," he said, waving me away with a slab of a hand.

I shrugged, I guess for Handown's benefit. I had no idea what had brought on this curious temper flaw, but I had begun to understand, this morning for the first time, the underlying fury that had long been there—fury at the whole f——ing world, and even at himself, and especially at me. Daphne had given me a great deal to ponder, and now, after Buzz's outburst, I felt an urgency about thinking him through, or perhaps it was thinking myself through, because I was sure that this mission on which we were about to launch ourselves was going to test him, and test me, to the very heart of our hearts, and that while my life might be at stake against the Germans, something more important than my life might be at stake against my own pilot and best friend: I mean my self-respect, my honor, my faith in human beings.

A flare popped up from the center of the airdrome meadow. Marrow hung his left hand at the top of his wheel and began to follow the second hand of his wrist watch. We heard the thunder of *Angel Tread* under full power. *Gruesome Twosome*. *Erector Set*. Forty-five-second intervals. We could see the great curl of condensation off *Erector Set's* props as she rolled away from us, like streams of fluid from the lips of four great pitchers.

Marrow flipped the generator switch. On interphone: "Clear, Max?"

Brindt must have looked around from the greenhouse. "Roger," he said. "Skiddoo."

Then the tower came in. "Go ahead, six one four."

Marrow on liaison: "Roger." And he began to ease the throttles forward.

The plane moved, and I felt the great push of acceleration on my shoulder blades and spine and buttocks. We gathered speed; the tail lifted. . . . Again I remembered the day I was left behind —the sudden cracking open of thunder when the props of *The Body* were right in front of me on the tower, my trying to lift the plane bodily off the ground by rising up on my tiptoes.

Now *The Body* was on her own tiptoes. We were well above air speed. And I said in my mind, "Bye, Daph. Goodbye, Daphne. Goodbye, goodbye, my darling."

We were airborne. Buzz gave me a mechanical nod, and I reached out to the central panel for the landing-gear control switch, to pull up our wheels. I saw the black tire marks at the end of the concrete runway, twenty feet down.

CHAPTER TWO

THE TOUR

March 1 to April 17

1 /

As we eased down out of some low clouds the color of soft-coal smoke and saw England, after the strain, boredom, and cold of those many hours over the ocean, it was not haycocks and hedgerows and heydownderry that attracted my eyes, but rather the black streaks at the end of a long concrete runway where rubber had burned from the wheels of other men's ships as they touched back to earth.

Tired as he was, Marrow put us down among those beautiful stripes so gently that we could not have left much mark. We taxied, to the music of the thumping of our tail wheel on solid ground, behind a jeep with FOLLO ME painted in big yellow letters on a high backboard. We parked at a dispersal point and opened a hatch and went out to stand on English soil under the wing. It had begun to rain.

"Filthy place," Haverstraw said.

"S——!" Marrow said. "This is nothing."

The rain slanted under the wing on a raw northeast wind. Of Cambridgeshire we had only an impression screened through the deluge—somber flatness, and mud; mud oozing up over the edge of the asphalt circle where we were parked; mud in the tread of the jeep, which rolled away on twin tracks of ocher, leaving us ma-

rooned; a vast plain, or lake, of mud stretching off toward a cluster
of barely visible buildings.

A recon car drove up, and we officers ran to it through the
downpour, and to our surprise we found the Group C.O. at the
wheel, himself. We wrestled our valpacs aboard, and the Colonel
said, "Boy, are we ever glad to see you guys!"

"Who you mean, 'boy'?" Marrow asked, craning around. "No
boys around here I know of."

Colonel Whelan did not react; he had no ear for bumptious-
ness. "And look at that!" he said.

The plane. It wasn't any great shakes, a B-17E with war camouflage on her that had been used awhile for training. But badly
needed, it appeared.

Marrow started right in giving his first-person pronoun its daily
constitutional. "I didn't have any trouble," he said. "Haverstraw
here tried to miss Iceland; he can carry figures in his noggin but he
can't *use* 'em. . . . I didn't hardly stop at all at Goose Bay, just a
cup of coffee. . . . I . . . I . . ."

The Colonel looked shot, a man of perhaps twenty-eight or
-nine with an overlay of false age—deep lines in a stubbled face.
He was sloppy, and to my eyes, unschooled in pain, his sloppiness
was as glamorous as grease paint. He was the sort of man I had
trained all these months to become.

A weapons carrier came up, and our sergeants piled in.

Marrow said, "Somebody be out to give my ship a rubdown?"

A bleat of sound that might have been laughter burst from the
Colonel's lips. "Your ship? That Fort's going in the hangar for
modifications, and as soon as she's ready, she'll fly missions, and
who's going to drive her is me. *Your* ship? Ha!"

Marrow shrugged. "I don't give a s——, I'll fly a f——ing trundle bed if I have to."

A trundle bed sounded good to me; I was pooped. I remembered a part of the trip that I'd spent lying curled up in the bombardier's greenhouse on a pile of valpacs and duffel bags, under a
brown blanket, shivering, trying to read an old copy of *Night
Flight* that I'd borrowed years before from the Donkentown Free
Library and never returned, which I'd picked up at home on my
last leave, and I plugged away at it until the shaking of those four
Wright Cyclones got into my eyes, and my retinas became like

oscillatory sanders wearing away the images of the words into a
finely finished blur. Bleak, it had been bleak up there over the ho-
rizonless sea actually going to a war that had, during training,
seemed remote and imaginary, like a legend.

But Marrow was so full of bounce that you'd have thought we
had just taken a routine training flight in the sky as blue and light
as a jay's wing over Lowry Field. His vitality and his boasts were
invigorating and restorative. He made you want to forget you were
dogged; laugh and sit up straight.

Colonel Whelan started off on the two-mile drive to the Ad-
ministration block, and suddenly, as we went along the mud-
decked concrete track, the rain stopped, and the clouds broke up
like a crowd at the end of a game, and in no time we saw snatches
of blue overhead, and the wide panorama of Pike Rilling Aerodrome opened up.

How moved I was by that sight!

Within the great irregular five-mile loop of the single-laned
perimeter track there lay a triangle of concrete landing strips, each
one a mile long, and except for the outer ring of mud on which we
traveled the whole area was a great meadow, and even at the beginning of March a vivid, hopeful green carpeted the ground. To
our north, near where our ship had been spotted, we could see a
forest of bare-limbed trees, and what seemed to be a cultivated
park, and a visible shoulder of a country house, where Wing was
set up "like a bunch of God-damn noblemen," the Colonel told
us, communicating to us in a flash the hatred of the combat unit
for the next higher echelon. Ahead of us, south of the runways, was
our objective, a camouflaged box-like building with a glass-win-
dowed penthouse on it and, atop that, a dark cubic water tank, on
which an enormous number, 79, was painted in figures that must
have been eight feet high. Several Nissen huts lay like old discarded beer cans around the control tower, and beyond the tower
crouched a row of factory-like buildings which housed, the Colonel
said, repair facilities and armament shops and the service organization.

The view from a distance of all these ominous low-lying buildings, which, like the Colonel, looked tired and experienced, filled
me with a kind of tension—an eagerness to know what combat
would be like, and a desire to acquit myself decently, yet also an

apprehension, a wondering about unknown dangers, altogether a vague sadness of which I could not have named the cause.

To our left, as we drove down the line, we passed an area of roofless walls draped with camouflage nets and a series of mounds which evidently covered underground vaults—the bomb dump, the Colonel said, a treasury of explosives, incendiaries, flares, ammunition, protected by pillboxes, and by a brier patch of barbed wire, and by sentries hugging themselves to keep warm. I felt a slight chill of a different sort from theirs.

Across the field to the west, abutting the concrete emplacements and striped sentry boxes of the entrance to the base, we could see the village of Bartleck, a couple of rows of gray stone houses with thatched roofs and chimneys capped with pots—the first proof I had seen that we really were in England.

Through Bartleck, the Colonel told us, ran the main road to Motford Sage, six miles away, and to Cambridge, fourteen miles distant. London was an hour off by train, he said.

I heard some shooting. Rather sharply I said, "What's that?" and then wondered if I'd sounded jumpy.

"Some gunners shaking out their guns," the Colonel said. "We got a clay bank over there as big as an Alp that they can just barely hit. . . . We got a skeet shoot, too. Pike Rilling Huntin' and Shootin' Club for Gents—you know?"

Buzz wasn't going to let me off that lightly. "Boman thought it was the f——ing Krauts sneaking up on us."

Everyone laughed but the Colonel.

At the Admin block Colonel Whelan turned us over to the Ground Exec, a captain named Blair, who smelled of Vaseline hair tonic, and after checking our orders he drove us south of the flying line, where the land sloped upward into wooded groves in which, widely dispersed and well hidden, were the living quarters of the men. The enlisted men lived in prefab Nissen huts, officers in slightly more elaborate hutments with single and double rooms. Here, too, were sick quarters, the motor pool, the officers' club, the Red Cross Aero Club for the men, two officers' messes, a shed for movies, and the big enlisted men's mess.

It began to rain again as we drove.

Marrow said, "Chawming climate out heah in the tropics, old chap."

Captain Blair said, "You don't like it, just wait fifteen minutes."

"What's that mean? It get better or worse?"

"It gets different, only the same."

"S——, that doesn't make sense."

"You'll see."

After fifteen minutes it was teeming harder than ever.

Blair took Marrow and me to a room about halfway along the
north side of a hut in a grove of oaks and scrubby hawthorns. The
Captain pointed to one of the beds and said it was jinxed—eight
pilots had slept in it in twelve weeks, all eight missing in action.

Marrow said, "I'll sleep in that sack, you can't flak me up with
that kind of crap."

"The other sack, the guy finished his tour. Ready to go home
—Happy Warrior," Blair said. "Hope you sleep good," he said to
Marrow.

"Go s—— in your hat and call it curls," Marrow said, and he
flopped on the bed and was sound asleep before I could get my
shoes off.

We got up in time for supper and afterwards ran in the rain
to the king-sized Nissen hut they called the officers' club. Club? It
was a slophouse. Once, later on, when I was low on things to do, I
counted forty-seven stuffed armchairs, covered with cracked brown
leather, which looked as if they'd been scavenged from a bankrupt
old folks' home. A plywood bar stood at one end, and some low
round oaken tables were scattered among the heavy chairs.

A big iron stove in the middle of the room had a sign over it
saying not to spit on it, but that notice worked like a fresh-paint
sign; newcomers couldn't resist doing it once to see their spittle
bounce, and then they understood the reason for the sign when
they took a whiff of their own personal steam. Oof!

Brindt and Haverstraw and I sat back and watched Marrow go
to work. Ordinarily he talked loud; he was afraid of nothing. That
evening he seemed to hold back, pulling on a cigar, waiting for his
opening. Fliers were sitting around rolling horses for drinks and
flipping half-heartedly through limp magazines, and gradually a
group formed, and one of the aviators, a mechanical nut, was telling how he'd converted a silent movie projector into a sound machine, making a photo-electric cell somehow out of a tube socket

and using a dime-store pocket telescope to focus the exciter light on the photo-electric cell; I couldn't follow it. But Marrow followed it like a bird dog, and when the guy was finished and there was a momentary lull, Buzz cleared his throat and spoke up with a ringing voice.

"I knew a dame once that was wired for sound from her c—— to her throat."

Marrow paused for the idea to soak in. "Thing was," he went on, "I was catching this commercial plane from Newark on to Denver, see, and by the ticket counter . . . ."

I had heard the story several times before. It was impressive, quite funny. The story happened, in passing, to reflect handsomely on Marrow's prowess. The old hands enjoyed it. Marrow was shrewd. He shut up after that.

From out of doors there suddenly came—I nearly jumped out of my seat—a huge, crackling, deep, doom-heavy voice, sounding like our common Pilots' Fate calling to us out of a cloud. It announced that the base was on alert: mission in the morning. Not for us in Marrow's crew, of course. I watched closely the faces of the men who would have to go, but all I could see was a slight deepening of the weariness they all shared. The bar closed. We broke it up. On the way out one of the guys told me that the spooky voice was called the Tannoy, some kind of English public-address hooter that was hung in trees and on poles all over the base.

I couldn't go to sleep for a long time, thinking of that booming voice, and of the men who'd been in the club with us who were going to die the next day.

2 /

I could have spared myself that anxious charity. Marrow slept hard and late, but I got up early and heard the briefing and eventually climbed the tower to watch the mission take off. The planes began to taxi at nine forty-five, and just before the last of the Forts had positioned itself at the end of the runway, Wing scrubbed the strike. Gave no reason. It was a frightful letdown for the pilots, and I felt the first stab of an anger that was to be my frequent companion in the coming months, at the capricious authority of Wing Headquarters.

It didn't take them long to deflate our egos; they sent us to school. Our self-esteem got quite a knock that morning, when some desk pilot told us that our training in the States might have made good kiddy-car drivers out of us but that we weren't combat aviators by a long shot—for we had a month of rugged training ahead of us before we could be trusted on a mission.

Marrow was wild. As I've told you, he was quite old, twenty-six and a few months, and he had racked up a lot of hours as a pilot, even if they weren't in the heavies, and he had figured he was going to win the war and get home by Christmas.

So he went over to squawk to Colonel Whelan, the minute they had sprung us from a class on British code. The C.O. had been up since four thirty, and had run a briefing, and had gone out to his ship, and had sat in her for nearly two hours, right up to the verge of take-off, and then Wing had canceled, and he must have been fit to be tied; and here Buzz stumps in and announces he's not going to sit on his ass and listen to schoolmarms for a month, he's come over here to *fight*, he wants to bomb squareheads.

Buzz never told us what the Colonel said, but I can imagine; it was six weeks before we took off on a mission.

By nightfall Marrow had that impulsive visit to Whelan all rationalized. On account of it he, Marrow, was going to be known, among the higher-ups, as a scrapper, and he'd be marked for command. That was what he figured.

Marrow hacked all the way through ground school; lipped the instructors, doodled big goggle-eyed beetles and spiders in his notebooks with bold heavy strokes of his pencil, and stared out the window presumably revisiting triumphs between the sheets. I, on the other hand, ahem, a sincere and capable young man, if somewhat on the short side, was conscientious to a fault. I memorized and stuck my hand up in class and manifested a clean-cut willingness to learn. *Stars and Stripes Forever.* I was shocked at Marrow's indifference to the classes, and once told him so; said he might be jeopardizing the lives of his crew some day.

"Boman," he said, for he always called me by my last name,

never "Bo" or "sonny," or anything else, whereas he often used nicknames for the others in our ship, and this used to puzzle and sometimes enrage me; "Boman," he said. "You study your books, I'll fly."

When we were finished with ground school he knew ten times more about everything we'd studied—or that I'd studied and he hadn't—than I did.

There was a simple reason: Marrow was a genius. At least, he was a genius in one narrow sphere—that of handling an airplane. I later had spurts of wanting to be a command pilot and to have my own plane. Kid Lynch told me before he was killed that when he took the controls on missions, he changed seats with his pilot, he took command in every way. Marrow let me spell him, but only in the co-pilot's seat, and this made me sore after what the Kid had told me; I hated being an assistant, a tourist, it made me boil—until I thought of having to land my own ship as a command pilot and then thought of Marrow's landings in *The Body*. Genius in flying, as in the performance of music, lies not in precision, not in being exactly on pitch and in time, but rather in the ability to perform with absolute accuracy and then to break the rules by inspiration for the sake of a higher perfection. Genius rearranges old materials in a new way never seen on earth before, and Buzz handled the plane with constant shimmering variations of standard techniques; especially in his landings. Each time Marrow let me land the plane, what one saw was simply an effort to get down alive. Each of Buzz's landings was an experiment, a delicate search for a new and better way to find that breathtaking split moment when all those tons of metal ceased being carried by the wind and were accepted back by the mother ground. He held the wheel of the column in his finger tips and seemed to be feeling, with the sensitivity of a blind man reading Braille, for the very very very end of flight.

3 /

In the late afternoon of our fourth day at the base, which was also the fourth day of March, Marrow and I stood with others out on the oil-blackened apron in front of the control tower to watch the ships of our Group come in from a mission to railroad yards at Hamm, in Germany. The meat wagons were drawn up at the far end of the runway. The day was clear and mild; our shadows were long. There was a shout from the tower, and we heard a rumble, like the one I had often heard out my bedroom window at Donkentown, of a distant freight train on a foggy summer night when the air seemed to carry most easily the deepest sounds. As the formation came around and began to form a traffic pattern, men of experience near us began to count. They could not believe their tally, and they checked again and again. Five planes missing out of the nineteen that had gone! Gloom settled on the base with the planes. We hung wide-eyed around the edges of the interrogation. Pilots talked excitedly, gesturing with their two hands, palms down, to demonstrate the maneuvers of ships. ". . . came in from twelve o'clock . . . down from three o'clock high . . . a four-o'clock attack . . ." I thought: That clock in the sky must whirl at a terrifying clip, in combat, because those men are the same age as I, more or less, yet their faces show that they've grown far older than I; time hasn't run at the same speed for them and for me. The fliers spoke of the fearless enemy fighters, who used coordinated attacks of half a dozen planes at a time, with pairs attacking simultaneously from both sides and from above; but mostly they came from the nose. I tried to picture it all. We went to supper. There were many empty seats. For an instant I saw myself as an empty seat, and I shakily wondered: What would be lost, if I were lost? But at once I rejected that possibility. I was too young. I hadn't lived my life. I *couldn't* be lost. I had many agonizing thoughts alone in my room after supper, for Marrow had disappeared.

He came in late, looking sheepish.

The next morning he and I passed the bulletin board outside our mess together, and there was a notice signed by Colonel Whelan, saying, "It has become necessary for me to call attention again to paragraph 4, VIII AF memorandum 50–8a, dated 18 September 1942, which prohibits fraternization between officers of the VIII Air Force and other ranks or enlisted members of the WAAF and the ATS."

Marrow began to whistle *This Can't Be Love*, off key.

"They catch you?" I asked him.

He nodded and looked eager beaver.

"Where?"

"In the village."

"Didn't take you long," I said.

And he said with glittering eyes, "Try and stop me, either. Your enlisted English servicewoman really throws herself into the war effort. Who am I to discourage her? Know what I mean?"

4 /

We flew our first practice mission over England just a week after our arrival. Over the patchwork we made our way down to Land's End, then around to starboard on the second leg, at two thousand feet. I looked out to sea across the Bay of St. Ives and out over the Atlantic. It was three thirty; in Donkentown it would be ten thirty, mid-morning. Janet would be at her office, at her typewriter, but not writing me a letter, if I knew her. We flew over the tin mines of Cornwall, with their white hills of tailings and pools of vivid copperas-colored water, and then we were over fields being turned for planting, and I saw many cyclists on aimless roads, and some pigeons flying, and in open meadows flocks of sheep with their heads down, and everywhere crooked lanes and trees at random—no ruled lines at all. We soared over a moated castle, and suddenly I thought of my schoolroom England and my bedtime England—the Fish Footman, Hotspur, and Long John Silver, and knights' tents, and a sword plunged in stone. For a moment I felt intense longing for the pleasures of my childhood days; I remembered a shield cut from plywood, with crate-strap handles, on which my father had painted for me a lion rampant, gules, on field azure. We went up Salisbury Plain and the Downs.

We saw some flights of the R.A.F., Stirlings, Halifaxes, and Bos-
tons, and in the midst of nostalgic daydreams I suddenly imagined
an enemy attack, which I built on the basis of an orientation lecture we'd had from Colonel Whelan: "To attack, the FWs fly out
about two thousand yards ahead and get all lined up and figure
their deflection and so forth and come in to about eight hundred
yards, roll over on their backs and start firing. They can hold the
ship right in there. The FW is a well balanced airplane and can fly
like a brick s—— house. After it rolls in at eight hundred yards it
keeps firing and does a split ass at a hundred yards. I'd say about a
third of them are good pilots and that presents quite a problem to
us, because it's pretty hard to bring a gun to bear on 'em. . . ."
Marrow asked me on interphone if I'd take a look around the ship,
so I got up and went toward the rear, and when I opened the aft
door of the ball-turret compartment and, with head down, pushed
through into the forepart of the waist, I got the shock of my life.
There were Farr and Bragnani, our waist gunners, having stowed
their machine guns on their brackets, inside the ship, crouching
on their respective firing platforms, aiming pistols—at me. Both of
them. They were snarling and shouting to each other, and I could
see Farr's mouth fall open and his Adam's apple bounce as he
made in his throat the rattling sound of shots. The pupils of their
eyes were ringed with white. The illusion, for a moment, of their
sincerity was overpowering. The weapons they threatened me with
were flare pistols. I suppose that Farr and Bragnani, too, were trying to recover childhood raptures of some kind, just playing a game
of guns, but they were so convincing! I long retained the idea that
those two were linked in hostility against all of us.

5 /
          On March the ninth, the Special Events Officer staged a
screwy athletic meet for our amusement, and the big event was an
obstacle race in full field equipment. Amusement? That one was
straight out of the manuals on basic training. Marrow, out to prove
that he was as much of a man as anyone, entered the thing, and

he didn't do very well, but at least he finished, and he was walking
back from the finish line with me, panting like a dog and saying
he'd be screwed if he'd ever do anything like *that* again just to
entertain a lot of lazy flat-footed sergeants—and he darted a furious look at the crowd of spectators standing along the edge of the
course.

A crippled German fighter, caught on a solo sneak raid,
smoked in a slant across the sky, and we heard a terrible ground-
shaking clatter as it plowed into a beet field about a mile down the
line.

The R.A.F. boy who'd got him came down and made a pass
and gave us goose pimples with a victorious slow roll over the
remains of his fallen adversary.

That broke up the field day. We all got on bikes and rode out
to see the junk heap. It happened we'd had an orientation lecture
on German equipment a couple of days earlier, and they'd dis-
played several German uniforms, and for the first time I'd had a
sense of the enemy as a human being. It had bothered me, because up to that time I'd thought of the enemy as a pickle barrel.
Viewed from extreme altitude. And soon I stood on the lip of the
crater that an ME-109 had exploded in a field of beets, and I saw
what was left of a young man. Fire had obviously killed him before the impact. I stepped back, for I was engulfed by a wave of
deep pity for our race, which for all its progress and civilization was
so barbarous. It seemed to me that like some of the lower creatures,
moths or salmon or lemmings, we were launched on a process of
purposeful self-destruction—for all of us.

"Come on," I said to Marrow, for I was unable to stare at the
dead German.

As we stepped away Marrow started talking cheerfully about
his father. A sergeant in the First World War—a man's man. Took
great care of his mother. But away from home a lot.

6 /

The weather that awful first month! We were treated to an endless succession of weak cold fronts, and as Blair had told us the day we arrived, there was plenty of variety, but all the changes seemed to be for the worse. We used to watch the take-offs of missions, and one day the Group taxied out in passable weather, and the planes began to roll, and ten ships got off the ground, when bang!—the sun disappeared as fast as if a light switch had been thrown. A ground fog had materialized, so sudden and so thick that a plane that had started its take-off in plenty of visibility was on instruments before it was airborne at the other end of the runway. Our feet were always wet. I had long thought the muck in the bog between my house and the Shaushohobogen was as sticky a mixture as earth and water could make, but the ooze at Pike Rilling was worse. Low shoes were a joke, because the prehensory mud would pull them right off. We were wet and bored and dreary, and we played shove ha'penny in a desultory way in the officers' club, and read and re-read the months-old magazines on the oaken tables, and dreamed of sunshine.

Marrow, who was irrepressibly ebullient, took the weather, the wetness, the constant chill, as challenges. It was quite a trick to get a decent fire going in the odd contraptions in our rooms that the British called stoves, and the coke supply was inadequate, so Marrow, having scrounged a bucksaw and a hatchet from somewhere, dragged me out into the woods, and we chopped down small trees and cut them up, but the wood was green and burned poorly. Marrow discovered that shoe polish made fine kindling. He used to smuggle his electrically heated flying suit to the room, in the face of strictest regulations, and he'd sleep in it, while I obeyed the rules and shivered across the room. We bought a hot plate for cooking, and he'd have that going all night. He and a big ox with whom he spent a lot of time, a pilot named Braddock, discovered that the ash piles out back of the enlisted men's kitchens contained many "big pieces" of unburnt coke, and there were mornings when you could treat yourself to the sight of those two enormous heroes, both of them captains in their country's defense, poking around like a pair of desperate beggars in the heaps, their bristling chins and broad shoulders frosted with ashes, and they'd fill fire-prevention buckets with this undignified loot and run to their rooms and holler back and forth all day about their marvelous conflagrations.

In mid-March the entire complement of sergeants attached to our crew came down with bad colds. Marrow attributed this at first to the inborn weakness of the current generation of sergeants, but Negrocus Handown informed him one day that the men had caught cold in their concrete shower rooms. Their latrines, Neg said, weren't fit for cattle. Paper and dirt were littered everywhere; the toilets were sickening; worst of all, there was no hot water for showers. There was, it seemed, no coal or coke for the hot-water heaters. Marrow became furious in an almost comically exaggerated way; at the time, it seemed that he was moved by a touching loyalty to his crew, but now I see that he may simply have sniffed a fight. At any rate, he went to Group Headquarters to protest on behalf of his sick sergeants. He told me later how he had gone over to the Admin block, down a neat white hallway with signs—S-2, S-3, ADJUTANT, AIR EXEC, GROUND EXEC, and, finally, C.O.—and he'd knocked. By this time we had, under the influence of the blooded pilots, come to a somewhat less romantic view of our Group Commander than we had taken on the day of our arrival, and we called him, with everyone else, Grandmaw. At Marrow's knock, Grandmaw cleared his throat and called to Buzz to enter. Inside, Marrow found the Colonel sitting in an easy chair, in woolen slippers, reading an Agatha Christie paperback, and Buzz could see through the old man's bedroom into a spic-and-span bathroom, where there was a shower curtain with mermaids on it, and, worst of all, he saw in the living room, toasting Grandmaw's tootsies, a sparkling grate ablaze with cannel coal. Marrow reported the shocking condition of the enlisted combat crews' ablution sites. Whelan stood up, nervously rubbing his bristly little mustache, and gave Marrow what-for. The enlisted men, he said, deserved pneumonia. They were lazy, undisciplined, ill-trained babies. I can imagine that Marrow, himself accustomed to speak of the sergeant gunners in that way, must have blinked to hear such words. They took the fight out of him. If the men had no hot showers, Whelan said, it was because they had stolen for their hut stoves eight tons of coke that had been deposited near the ablution-site boilers. Well! Marrow came back to the room and let out a stream of obscenity, not at Grandmaw, but at the sergeants of the world.

A week later a new large consignment of coke was dumped at the enlisted men's ablution site. Marrow was among the first to steal from it a very large supply of coke, which he stored under my bed, the space under his own bed being reserved for his pajamas and damp towels.

7 /

Marrow treated our tiny ball-turret gunner, Junior Sailen, as if he were a child. On the afternoon of the seventeenth of March there was a terrible accident at the field, one of those horrors of lethal carelessness that a war seems to bring, displaying to the world not heroic killing but gratuitous homicide. A mission bound for Rouen had been recalled by Wing after the planes had got out over the Channel, and the fliers were furious, because they'd reached altitude in fair weather, but the fighters had missed the rendezvous. In a disgusted frame of mind, back at the base, a ball-turret gunner, removing his guns, accidentally whacked the trigger bar of one of them, which he thought he had locked on safety, and it began to fire and perversely jammed and ran away, spraying the village of Bartleck with fifty-caliber bullets and killing five ground-crew men in a matter of seconds. Marrow and I were in our room and saw none of it, thank God, though we heard the distant firing.

Marrow's reaction to news of the tragedy was to go to Sailen and say, "Listen, Junior, if you ever do anything like that I'm going to stop your allowance."

8 /

We had climbed in an easy spiral, and as the houses below became toys and fields became a quilt, we sailed for a while among islands of cotton. At ten thousand Marrow called us on in-

terphone and told us to put on oxygen masks, because we were
ascending for our first high-level practice flight over England, and
he ordered Prien, our tail gunner, to run oxygen checks of the
crew every ten minutes. We had flown at high altitudes over Lowry
Field, but somehow this was different, for our being in foreign
air-seas and very close to war made us seem interdependent as we
hadn't been before. All ten of us were linked to the ship and to
each other by those life-keeping hose lines, and we were like an
unborn litter of young in the belly of our common mother. Never
before had I—or since have I—had such a feeling of being part of
a brood in a plane.

"Check in," Prien said. "One."

"O.K.," Max Brindt responded.

"Two."

"Yup," said Haverstraw.

Prien numbered us off. We climbed higher and higher, and
now the earth through the clefts was a mottled, hazy blue. The
clouds close around us were gray and soft-edged, but as we climbed
away from them their outlines appeared hard and sharp; other
clouds above were a dazzling white against the Sahara-dry sky
overhead. I watched the tiny ball of my oxygen gauge, jumping
up and down, as if it were alive with my life, and I was aware of my
oxygen bladder, and of Marrow's, swelling and waning, alive with
our lives. Prien checked us again. I switched my earphones to liaison, and Kowalski, our radioman, was tuned in to B.B.C., and
for a while I listened to a contralto voice singing opera; maybe it
was Verdi. We were at twenty thousand. The music became passionate, and I began making a childhood world of the sky, when
suddenly Marrow cut in on CALL, which interrupted everything
else, and said, "Prien! Off your ass. Give us a check."

I heard some gurgling and a moan.

Marrow jerked his thumb to indicate that I should get back
there, so I got all unhooked and went onto a walk-around oxygen
bottle and squeezed back through the bomb bay and radio room
and ball-turret compartment and scurried along the waist and
found Prien slumped forward on the tail gunner's seat, doubled up
tight and wrestling with himself, and although the temperature inside the plane was probably twenty below zero, he was pouring off
summer sweat, and his skin was yellow, and when he turned his

head toward me I saw his eyes rolling behind his goggles like the little metal balls that you're supposed to roll into the holes in those glass-covered puzzles.

I hooked myself in to Prien's interphone jack and told Marrow that Prien was sick—looked like the bends or some sort of reaction to altitude.

Right away Marrow began laughing and diving the plane. I shall never forget that macabre descent, the immense Fortress screaming down the sky and my ears full of Marrow's crazy cackling and pealing. Marrow had understood at once what the trouble was: that in rarefied upper airs a man may be unable to belch or break wind. Prien's stomach was already famous among us, for he stored immense amounts of gas in it, and sometimes he emitted *flatus per rectum* for what seemed like minutes on end. And indeed, that was all there was to it. At twelve thousand Prien took his oxygen mask off and got relief, via both exits. In a big way. I mean, it was remarkable. Right away he was himself again—a mousey, blond man, rather cold, inflexible, and remote, except that on the surface he could turn on a mechanical enthusiasm, always said everything was just great; he was in the best crew in the E.T.O.; Marrow was a better flier than Jimmy Doolittle. You wondered whether he meant what he said or just the opposite.

As soon as we landed, Prien began stiffly saying that Captain Marrow had saved his life.

9 /

A notice went up on our officers'-mess bulletin board that the American Red Cross Aeroclub, properly the enlisted men's social center on the base, was offering lessons in ballroom dancing to both enlisted men and officers who had never happened to enter into this pastime. Marrow, who regarded himself as an accomplished dancer, announced that he was going to take the lessons, as a gag, for he thought there might be a number of Red Cross nifties on hand as teachers, possibly Arthur Murray girls gift-wrapped in Red Cross uniforms just for him, and he did in fact attend the first session. His joke fell disastrously flat. He was the only officer who turned up. Some thirty enlisted men, who were bashful and really wanted to learn to dance, were his companions. The sole teacher was Miss Lobos, the manageress of the Aeroclub, a remarkable woman of about fifty-five with a profile that might have belonged to a pioneer woman a hundred years ago—a face of iron determination, yet one dominated by sweetness and a full-blooded but controlled feminity. I heard afterwards that she had put Marrow in his place. Quickly discovering his bluff, she had made him demonstrate steps to the enlisted men. He came back to our quarters afterwards and vented his evident shame and anger in a blistering attack on sergeants that came from the blue. This was not the first time he had done such a thing. Indeed, one of the themes of Marrow's war was that enlisted men, and especially sergeants, were "weak." They were a bunch of gold-brickers, lazy, ingenious only in avoiding peril and work. But this time the tirade was out of all proportion to the occasion—a sickening outburst, a kind of nausea of obscene, violent verbalizations of hatred, a torrent of vague generalities about weakness, inadequacy, shirking, cowardice.

10 /

The Tannoy pulled me up from a sound sleep, blaring out a deep Georgia drawl: "'tintion to 'nouncemint . . . 'tintion to 'nouncemint . . . Evabody proceed to shelters at once. . . . Air-raid wawnin', red . . . Repeat . . ." I had a bruiser of a time waking Marrow, but when he heard what it was he jumped out of his sack, and we were outdoors by the time the sirens in Bartleck began to moan with their triple-throated Cerberus howl. Searchlights, like huge staves, began to belabor the scattered clouds, and we could hear a throb of planes somewhere far away. Buzz had picked up some lore. "When you hear those motors say, 'It's for you, it's for you, it's for you,' that means it's Jerries. They're lousy engineers, don't know how to synch their motors." I was in favor of the shelters, but Buzz said, "We've got to see this," and we climbed up a ladder on the big water tank on top of the control tower, and when we got there all we could see was the play of the sticks of light.

Buzz said that the sound of the planes reminded him of a day when he was six years old, seeing and hearing a tri-motored Ford fly over his house in Nebraska. He thought he'd decided to be a flier that day. He said in a booming voice that he loved the *roar* of that big Ford ship.

I thought he was talking about the sky, and I told him that I vividly remembered having had powerful feelings about the sky from childhood days, myself. I recalled standing on the porch at home all one afternoon, when I was about seven, having over-heard Father mention that a new Philadelphia-to-Pittsburgh mail plane was due to fly over Donkentown at about two o'clock, and I watched the clouds and the interstices of blue, and I had the im-pression that the clouds were moving with an incredible swiftness, as if they were big potatoes rolling down the sky; I never saw the plane; later in the afternoon several direct stares at the sun gave me my first experience of multiple black suns burning in the retinas of my eyes.

From then on I studied the weather, and what I loved best was to daydream as I gazed at clouds, about what they looked like, and what they meant.

I told Buzz this: On the first flight I ever took, on a commer-cial plane, flying eastward into the dawn, I looked back at the cap of night slanting toward the Mississippi Valley astern, and then down at a gray layer of haze and smog so thick as to appear to be the earth itself. Deep in that seeming earth, ahead, I saw a huge flattened vessel of a reddish sun, coming up, it seemed, out of the middle of the world, out of the ooze of time.

But Marrow was impatient, for he wanted to talk about power, and about speed, and he got me going, up there on the water tower after the all-clear, and I told him what he wanted to hear: about the old Grand Prix, and Blériot, Curtiss, Rougier, Calderara; about speed merchants, about frightful crashes; about all the devil-may-care boys I could name. It was more than an hour before we climbed down and walked home in the weird glow of a flashlight masked with blue paper.

11 /

Late in the afternoon of April Fools' Day, when we'd been on the base exactly a month, training, we were taken out to have a look at the ship we had been assigned to fly, eventually, in combat. After a morning of rain it had cleared; the sky to the west was soft and opalescent, and the field was bathed in slanting light. Being taken out to the dispersals, Marrow was sulky, suspicious—thought someone was trying to make an April fool of him. Or, if we really were to be shown our plane, he thought it might be *Chug Bug,* which was the hexed ship of the Group; she had killed seventeen officers. The driver stopped our recon car, and there, about two hundred yards away, we saw our Fort. A jeep flying a yellow warning flag was inching along the perimeter road, and behind it came a cleat track towing a brand new B-17F that was one of the first, under a new policy, not to be camouflaged; her long tapering fuselage and enormous vertical stabilizer glistened in the fading sun. She was a sight! Max Brindt said, "Holy cats," and we got out of the jeep on the edge of a hardstand covered with puddles of grease and black oil and watched as she was stacked on her dispersal point.

In a marvelously honest gesture, to show how the sight made him feel, Buzz raised his arms and flexed his muscles and posed, like Mr. America, and Max said, "What the hell do you think you are, one of those fairy strong men?"

Marrow pointed to the ship and said, with unaffected sincerity, "It's part of me, kid."

A few minutes later, though, as we walked around the plane he seemed to think of the ship as a *her,* and he came close to giving her the name she eventually carried. "Some torso, huh?" he said. "Just seeing that thing makes me feel horny. I can't wait to get my hands on her."

12 /

He got his hands on her the very next day, when we took her up in a formation practice flight of the squadron to which we then belonged, under a man named Gurvine, who was later killed. Horncastle, Worcester, and home, three hours in calm air. What a stickler Marrow was then for inspections and checks in his brand-new plane! I think the ship was an object of erotic love for him. At that stage, because he had already fallen for her, his relationships with the ground crew, who also loved her, and particularly with the irascible crew chief, Red Black, were smooth; they were lechers together. After each flight Marrow and Black whispered about *The Body* like two wide-eyed adolescents talking about a hard dame with elegant gams. Anyway, on that flight I remember the close turn of our six ships at the Worcester apex of our course as, following Gurvine's lead, we veered to port, and I saw the long, graceful, painted Forts on our left tilt their wings and show their undersides of pale sky blue. The sun was high above us. We flew over Oxford. Spires and courtyards like those of Cambridge, but a bigger city . . .

Marrow reached across the aisle and tapped me on the shoulder. He pointed downward beside his window, and then at his own chest. I had seen him peering down. We were over open country. I looked out but couldn't make out what he meant. He told me to take over, and he crawled down into the nose. On interphone, in a few seconds, he excitedly called the men, two or three at a time, to come forward and see something.

Finally he said, "Boman, you got to come see this."

"And let the gremlins fly us?"

He came up and relieved me, and I crawled down, and my first impression was of the ample space in the greenhouse of the B-17F, and of how open it seemed without the metal ribs that divided the plexiglass in the earlier E's that we had been flying. Then, far below, I saw what had excited Buzz so much. On the surface of the silvery ground haze six swift shadows of Forts moved in formation. Around only one of them, on the rear right side, the shadow of our ship, there was a shining nimbus, a halo, like a ring around the moon. Haverstraw later explained to us the physics of this phenomenon, which we often saw, but the way the sun singled us out from the six shadows, that first time, seemed so eerie that I couldn't put away a feeling of uneasiness as I remembered Buzz's pointing at his own chest when he had first seen this apparently magical sign of our distinction.

13 /

Marrow's last flight before he was cleared as a combat pilot was an afternoon's joy ride he took with three Army nurses. He had left me on the ground. "S——," he'd said to Haverstraw, "Boman's engaged, he wouldn't want to go." But I didn't feel engaged any more, not having had a letter from Janet for three weeks, and I *had* wanted to go. Marrow took Handown to keep an eye on the engines and Haverstraw to navigate and Max Brindt, who was crazy to be a pilot, to keep the plane level while he, Marrow, entertained the ladies.

That evening Marrow hopped around like a kid on a pogo stick, mysterious and all charged up. Finally he took me into his confidence. "That's the first time—the first *three* times—I ever had it in the air."

"Was it good?" I asked, but I didn't really have my heart in the question, because I was still miffed, now more than ever miffed, at having been left on the ground.

"Listen!" Marrow said. "Flying's as good as getting it, and when you do it, too, bang *bang!* You're as big as a Fortress up there. I mean, the whole thing is just twice as good as real."

"Six times as good, you mean," I bitterly said, multiplying for him.

But now I believe it was all imaginary. I asked Haverstraw and Handown about it, and Haverstraw said he'd been too busy trying not to get lost to notice anything, and Handown was wild with excitement at the idea that he'd been sitting in the co-pilot's seat when right back there in the radio room . . . It was later that we came to realize that Handown considered sex a spectator sport.

But I don't think they missed a thing. I think Marrow made it all up in his head.

14 /

The following day was the sixth of April, the twenty-sixth
anniversary of the entry of the United States into the war that
made the world safe for democracy, and the weather was cold and
windy, and they stuck a little notice up on the Ops bulletin board,
saying we were cleared to go on the next mission, and I read it over
the shoulders of some of the old hands, and they began discussing Marrow.

"He's green," one of them said. "A real country rookie."

"He's got diapers on," another said. "I had him on my wing
that last practice mission."

It was obvious what was eating those joes: they knew they
could fly a hundred years and never touch Marrow. I didn't even
bother to tell them what they were full of, I just raced over to see
Stormy Peters, to see how the weather looked. It looked stinking,
for days to come. And that was just our luck: there was no mission
for nine days.

15 /

Marrow said that if we were going to fly missions we'd
have to have the name painted on our ship, which we had had for
about a week, and of course a suitable picture to go with it, so one
afternoon when the day's showers had cleared Marrow and I rode
out to the dispersal point with Chan Charles, the squadron
painter, to explain the project to him, and we stood throwing three
long splinters of shadows across the hardstand while Marrow gave
orders, and Charles, a bald-headed man with heavy tortoise-shell
glasses who had a way of wrinkling his nose as if subject to twinges
of pain, was sour on life and on our idea, said he couldn't promise
to get it done before the next alert, but we knew he would, and he
did. Chan was in his fifties and was dyspeptic and negative—complained about having far too much work and cursed the childish-

ness of pilots. He would never engage to do anything on time, yet he always quickly finished exactly what was wanted, and his little paintings on the noses of the ships had great wit and warmth. His deep bitterness, declared to the world, was that he wanted to be a creative artist but had somehow been forced to do his bit in the war as a glorified sign painter for a lot of cheap-minded men with banal ideas who only wanted replicas of Petty and Varga girls on their ships, anyhow. It never occurred to him, as it did to us, that he was exactly fitted for what he was doing. He seemed to get no pleasure whatsoever from the delight the men took in his work.

Two days later he painted us the name: *The* BODY, and he did it in such a way that the emphasis seemed to be on the first of the two words; and he put a nude above the name that justified the emphasis. We had sergeants hanging around for days gaping at her. Marrow stood around with them by the hour, too, drooling.

When we congratulated Chan Charles, he said the painting was a piece of s—.

16 /

That evening, in the officers' club, we heard on B.B.C. that the Belgian ambassador to Washington had protested against the inaccurate bombing done by the United States Army Air Force on Antwerp three days before, which had caused heavy civilian casualties. Max Brindt, our bombardier, usually so mild, took off in a rage about that; without ever having flown a mission he was hipped on pickle-barrel bombing. Once before, we'd heard in a broadcast that the French had complained about a bombing on rail yards at Rennes which had left three hundred French civilian casualties; the French had thought this a high price to pay for "*un si court délai et ralentissement du trafic*." Brindt was sore at the French because they *liked* the R.A.F.: "*une arme de précision remarquable*," compared with the Yanks.

Marrow laughed at Brindt's excitement and began calling him "G.E.," for Gross Error. "Why don't those Frogs go jump in the lake?" Buzz asked. To Marrow, war was a simple matter. It concerned his potency, his destructiveness. That there might be human beings with him or against him scarcely entered his head.

17 /

By the eleventh, five days after we'd been cleared, Marrow was nearly off his rocker with impatience, and he took us up in the rain on a practice flight. In talking us into going up, he'd said, "It's too tough here on the ground. I got to take that thing up and beat it around and then I'll be all right."

They announced a stand-down that night, and we decided, as a crew, to take our first trip to London.

18 /

That whole visit to London was a search. We were looking for something, only we didn't know what. A moment of tender love? A fight? A world's record hangover? It wasn't anything so exact. We were looking for something fugitive, a receding oasis, a something perfect that was beyond our reach.

We raced through the city looking for it, taking a drink here and there along the way. We must have been looking for *something*, else how account for my standing with Marrow, of all people, both of us bareheaded, in the Poets' Corner? The great white words in Picadilly Circus jumped at us, and whirled: *guinness is good for you gives you strength votrix vermouth the merchant navy comfort service comes to town odeon bile beans we've got to keep on saving.* We saw the white tower and the bloody tower and Marrow pinged the knights in armor with his fingernail and said, "What those guys needed was a good five-cent can opener." Marrow decided to collect squares. He started with Trafalgar, and we collected Berkeley, St. James, Russell, Grosvenor, Belgrave, Chester, Gordon, Brunswick, Mecklenburgh; until we realized we were blitzed—I mean overcome, each in his way, by the accumulation of gaps, fallen walls, boarded-up windows, memories, regrets, endings. I see now that I was overcome with sadness and fear, Marrow with excitement. I thought we were together, but we were at poles.

Next thing, we were standing side by side, Marrow was guffawing, we were staring at Henry the Eighth and his wives in Mme. Tussaud's. The monarch appeared surprised, the women wore calm expressions.

"Quite a guy," Marrow said. "Those dames look satisfied."

"He wasn't married to them all at once," I said.

Then we had an eerie feeling, maybe we felt as if we were coming close to what we were looking for, because we were witnessing the death of Nelson. Nelson was lying on his back. There was a basin at his side. Four men, with anxious thoughts for England, were leaning over him, tensely peering. One held a lantern. Its light picked out the sturdy beams of the ship.

I said, "Let's get out of here," for I could no more abide the idea of death in a waxen Nelson than in a charred young German flier.

After that we walked a long time in silence. We were at a gate of St. James's. Two enormous Coldstream Guards—only we didn't know they were any such thing till later when we asked a geezer in a pub, because they were wearing ordinary British battle dress—seemed to jump out at us from ambush, and they began the damnedest ceremony. They slapped their rifles and stamped their hobnailed boots on the flagstone path and shifted and banged—went through a unison drill that seemed to last a whole minute and ended with a present arms as rigid as bronze. Well, I looked at Marrow, and Marrow looked at me. Then Buzz ripped off his hat, pitched it in the air, yipped, and did a breakdown stomp. It was a good American answer, but the Guards stood there like statues until we left them, shrugging our shoulders.

We joined up with the others at the Dorchester, and Marrow said he thought he'd leave us for a while; thought he'd make out better as a lone wolf.

"They're a dime a dozen around Piccadilly," he said knowingly, "but you'll find the real class along by Hyde Park, up by Grosvenor House, in there."

I was paired with Max Brindt, and we found ourselves, moder-

ately drunk, eating a meager roast-beef dinner with horse radish
and Yorkshire pudding in the Ford Hotel, a stuffy little Victorian
stage set full of people who looked like drawings by Pont, my favorite artist in *Punch*—which (I didn't know it then) Kid Lynch
used to smuggle into our officers' club at Pike Rilling every week.

After coffee Max said, "I'm horny."

I said, "O.K., Max."

We walked along Bond Street, where we'd heard there were
some French ones, and soon a pair of babes stepped out of the
shadows, and Max had one of those little pencil flashlights, he was
a systematic bastard, maybe he'd brought it from the States just
for this purpose, and he shined it in their faces, and they were
crusty old dreadnoughts, and we sniffed and walked on. But we'd
had a lot of brandy; libido lived where judgment had vacated.
After a few steps, Max said, "Oh well, they prolly need the money."

So we went back, and they were Flo and Rose, about as
French as kidney pie, and we took them to Covent Garden, a big
dance hall that made the whole world smell of cabbage, and Flo
and Rose danced like pushcarts, so we had a change of venue, we
went to the Captain's Cabin, to drink, for Christ's sake, and before
long I decided that whatever it was I was looking for, Flo or Rose
didn't have it, so I went back to the Dorchester.

Marrow was there in our room with Haverstraw and Neg
Handown and some other guys, strangers but fliers and so not
strange, and he was giving an account of his successes as a lone
wolf. Claimed he'd had it four times, twice with a WAVE and
once each with a couple of Piccadilly commandos. For several
days Marrow had been affecting British slang terms but distorting
them to his own ends. "She sure was butt-pranged," he said of one
of his companions of the evening. The three dames had been
"laid on," he said, "by me." He loved to mimic the British accent,
but always kept a Nebraska twang: "Gooseberry tarts. . . . You're
looking simply wizard. . . ."

Haverstraw could do lightning calculations in his head, and
Marrow began showing him off. "Hey, Clint," he shouted, "multiply these." And he'd reel off a couple of big numbers. It was a
trick of the mind, and Haverstraw was quite good, and somehow
this was endlessly fascinating to Marrow. I couldn't see it, myself;
just a trick.

I guess we must have been getting pretty loud. The telephone rang. Marrow answered. He covered the mouthpiece and said, "The manager," and he winked, and then he said into the phone, "The occupants of this room have been staying here four years off and on. They never made a noise yet." He hung up.

In a few minutes there was a knock on the door, and it was the manager, polite, stiff, genteel. Marrow stood up; his jaw was sticking out. "We're not making a noise," he said. "This is just a conversation. Maybe you want to make some noise? If you want to make some noise, why don't you kick the door down?" And he slammed the door in the manager's face.

Later two Aussie infantrymen came in, one belligerent and one not. They began telling *us* that night bombing made better sense than our kind, and you'd have thought Marrow had been on twenty missions. It got hot, and after a while Marrow said to Handown, real sore, "Neg, pour me a drink."

One of the Aussies, who seemed to want trouble, said, "I always understood, when you called a Southern gentleman a nigger, he would fight."

We didn't call Handown nigger, his nickname was Negrocus. Where that came from I'll never know, and maybe it amounted to the same thing. We regarded the Aussie's crack as especially offensive because Handown wasn't an officer. He was, however, thirty-six years old, solid as an anvil, and able to take care of himself.

He shuffled over to the Aussie. "Foot sojer," he said, "I fight m'own fights." Then he jerked his thumb at Marrow and said, "Fight his, too."

The Aussie said, "If you like to be called that, it's all right with me."

So Handown said, "All *right*. Mind y'r business."

There was some more shouting, and the manager returned and asked who was responsible for all the noise, and Marrow said, "This Austreyelian," pointing to the belligerent one, and the manager politely asked the Aussies to leave, and they did.

We were glad to be rid of them, for we were full of the feeling of separateness, of the unity of those who flew against those who did not. We had the illusion that between aviators there was a mysterious bond, that we were sharers of a secret, that only in the sky could that secret manifest itself, for only in the sky could we men of this special and separate stamp fulfill ourselves. It was much later, with Daphne's help, that I realized that all that was shared between Marrow and me was a certain free play of the mind in the sky; but his dream in the sky and mine were far apart in kind. I did not know that then.

Toward sunup, when all the others had left, Marrow sat on the edge of the hotel bed and began to cry and to beat a big fist into a big hand. "I'd like to kill 'em all," he sobbed. I thought he meant Them. Wing and all authority. I thought I understood, that I was tied to him by a close bond. But now, after Daphne's insight, I supposed he meant people, humanity, really all of us. I should have been horror-struck. He blubbered like a baby.

19 /

If a famous hangover had been what we'd been looking for, we'd have been satisfied travelers, because we really caught one that next morning. We went back to the base on the train; it was like riding inside a dentist's drill. Handown and Prien sat in the compartment with us four officers, and it developed that Negrocus had taken Prien out to educate him the night before, but after Neg had picked up a dame for Prien and had taken a room for all three of them in a fleabag, Prien, said Handown, got hoity-toity.

"Thinks hoors are naughty," Handown said. "In fact," he went on, "he thinks *women* are nasty. Take advantage of a fella. Want money, clothes, a good time. Don't want to cook. Fake a man out all the time."

Prien sat there like a dummy, and finally he got out a sentence. Thought he'd change the subject. "For Englishmen," he said, "those people in London speak the brokest English I ever did hear."

"Always bellyachin'," Marrow said to Prien, and then Marrow rocked with laughter, because mere mention of Prien's stomach made Buzz roar.

20 /

Back at Pike Rilling the sky was a soft linen blue, and by mid-afternoon, after a nap in my own sack, I was feeling human again, and Stormy Peters came by and asked me if I wanted to take a bike ride.

"We could pedal up to Ely," he said, "and see the Cathedral."

"How far is it?"

"Not too far with this following wind."

"How about coming back?"

"Oh-oh," he said. "Didn't think of that. This wind is going to hold. Might be rugged coming back."

So we just rode out through some turnip fields along a lane that farmers must have used, and we came to a field where infant barley was up, glistening in the sunlight, and suddenly overcome with spring fever we stopped and lay on our backs on the almost-daffodil-covered new growth and looked up at the empty sky, and naturally we began talking about the sky and fliers in it. I wanted to know what a comet looked like close to, and Peters told me, and I'd read, and I told him, about the remarkable navigational powers of the honeybee, and we discussed the false peace, which seems like the peace that nations make, in the eye of a hurricane. I told Stormy that I'd had curiosity about the sky and flying since I'd been a kid—and so, I remembered, as I lay there, had Marrow, and I felt for a moment that this fascination and study, this primitive curiosity, was the simplest common denominator in the community of aviators; I thought then that Stormy was not quite in it with Buzz and me.

Now, my eyes having been opened by Daphne, I can see that Peters was closer to my way of thinking and feeling than Marrow, for Marrow's passion deep down was for engines that pull, power, speed, some wild exhilaration and defiance in the air, while Stormy, drawn to a life force, was satisfied with the clouds, the rain, and the sunshine that fed the growth on which we lay. If Stormy talked of flights he liked to talk of fabulous ones—of Icarus, Cyrano, Rasselas; he was content to imagine the Blanchard balloon, with its curious feather-like oars, drifting slowly over the English Channel. With Buzz it had to be speed, daring, records, accidents, death, self. For Marrow the vault of heaven was only a mirror; while I think that Peters gazed into the sky as into a living forest.

21 /

For the next two days the weather was still ideal, and we were really itching to go. There was a vending machine for cokes against one wall of the officers' club, and on the evening of April fifteenth, after dinner, the men crowded around the machine, and Marrow said to me, "I'm buying you a coke."

"My turn," I said, fumbling in my pants pocket. "I already owe you five."

"Five! Perl owes me forty-three. I won 'em at gin rummy. Five's nothing. What's five? I'm buying you a coke."

I discovered that Marrow had a couple of bucks' worth of nickels in his pocket, which he had got from the PX, done up in paper rolls like Life Savers. He apparently liked having nickels when everyone else was running around saying, "Got the change of a quarter?" and I suspect that he also liked having people indebted to him. Whenever he heard a man asking for change from the bartender, who kept a cigar box full of coins under the bar, Buzz would shout, "Hey, you, I got plenty nickels. Come over here, I'm buying you a coke."

In this way Marrow bought audiences for his stories of his valor in the Battle of the Sheets. The one that night began, "The most beautiful body I ever saw was in the moonlight. I just pulled back the covers and there it was. . . ."

We played bingo later, and Buzz called the numbers. He was on top of the world. "All ready, ladies and gent'men? Now, an honest shake for the little lady with the ceegar in the back row. *And* the draw. Under the N, thirty-*two*. You! Get out of here! Hey, White!" He called to a pilot who was trying to read a book off to one side. "There's a place for aviators over at Flight Control. Out! Here we're all bingo players and con men. *Under* the B, fifteen! Anybody like to sell their cards back to the management? All *right*. Under the O, seventy-five. . . ."

After a while Stebbins shouted, "Bingo!" and laughed at the boos of the others. Stebbins had won twice the previous night.

"Ladies and gent'men," Buzz gravely said, "on behalf of the parish bingo committee, I wish to state that that son of a bitch is lucky."

It was during the second game that the fateful booming voice of the Tannoy thrilled us with the announcement we had waited for so long. We were on alert! We went to our rooms and Buzz and I sat down and wrote letters. I lay on my stomach on my bed and wrote to my mother, and I supposed that Buzz, at our desk, was writing to some dame. When he'd undressed and had gone off to the john, his letter was still unfinished and lay on the desk in the cone of light from the hooded lamp over it. Outside a cold wind rustled the dead leaves caught all winter in the spurs of a low hawthorn near our window. I read part of what Buzz had written. The second page was showing. It was to his sister.

". . . and also in your very subtle manner you might let Mother in on the obvious need of things sweet over here. Anything and everything, but soon. Never ate much candy in the States but right now I could use a hardball or even a lollypop. I mean it. I'm getting so old in the service I'm in my second childhood. No, check that. I figure a flier is entitled to three childhoods. One at the regular time, one when he's on his tour, and one when he gets over eighty the way I'm going to get. Anyway, tell Mother. I'm not brazen enough to throw a hint quite that broad, so please ask Mother, or suggest it, don't send the stuff yourself . . ."

I wished that I had not read it. It upset my stomach to realize that William Siddlecoff Marrow, the mighty hunter, my pilot, was a homesick kid like me.

22 /

We hit it lucky. They gave us Lorient for our first mission. At that time there was a big buildup going on in North Africa for TORCH, and they had been using the heavies in England to try to hit the submarine pens and ship-building yards on the theory that this would help secure the lifelines. It was disheartening work for our pilots, because the pens were insignificant, to put it mildly, from twenty-one thousand feet, and they were made of concrete twelve feet thick, and trying to pockmark them didn't seem like a way to win a war by Christmas. Germany was where the enemy lived. Besides, the TORCH buildup meant that our own strength was not being increased, and we felt like—in fact we were, then— the second team. Nevertheless we of the crew of *The Body* were perfectly satisfied to be going to Lorient on our first day out, be- cause it meant a routine strike, and most of the flying was over the sea rather than over enemy-held land; and in the hours before the mission we were so eager it was funny—looking back on it.

We were in for a shock. The day was just one long fog of con- fusion. To begin with, the field order called for an indicated air speed during the climb of one hundred seventy miles per hour, and for a lot of the crocks our Group was flying that was too much of a strain. There were eight aborts from our Group on the way out, and as luck would have it the lead plane of our element turned back before we'd even formed up our squadron, to say nothing of our Group, so we and the other wingman of the element washed around up there not knowing whom to join up on. In the air one group looked like another. We flopped around and finally tacked onto the wrong squadron of the right group.

It was obvious, besides, that we weren't the only ones who were screwed up. My heart sank. Was *this* the glorious combat in which I was to be asked to lay down my trifling life—trifling, that is, to everyone but me? Looked as if somebody had done a snow job on us. This shambles didn't look like the raw material of a proud communiqué of the kind I'd swallowed whole so often.

Marrow, on the other hand, grew more and more elated. Just before we had boarded the ship at stations time he had gathered us in a knot, and he had said, "You can't be hurt in the plane with me. My mother told me I brought luck in the house." We sincerely believed him. His great square face was working and was wet; he was perspiring with patriotism, it seemed, with hating to wait for the desirable fight ahead.

And in the air, while everything was utterly confused and a hundred things were going wrong, he shouted in his throat mike: "Carry on! Carry on!" (He had learned that this was what we should have said to the Coldstream Guards at St. James's gate to unfreeze them. Were the poor guys still standing there?) He kept checking things like mad, now peering down at a dial as a killy hawk hovers above a field mouse, now shouting a reminder to some member of the crew. But in his euphoria Marrow was also recklessly abusive to the rest of us. Sailen would call up with some timid, conscientious observation from his mantrap of a ball turret, and Marrow would shout, "What's the matter, Junior, you nervous in the service?" At one point I told him that because of our fast climb the cylinder-head temperatures were all pretty high, and he said, "What are you, Boman, chicken s——?"—as if manliness consisted in burning out your power plant. Yet at the time, for some crazy reason, we were buoyed up by his hateful calls. He was having such a good time that it seemed churlish to feel confused, disappointed.

My own greatest strength was that I had always considered myself weak. I was an old chum with anxiety, irritability, restlessness, sleeplessness, headaches. It was nothing new for me to rally my defenses. In the long run I suppose this was why, on that final mission to Schweinfurt, I found I had deeper reserves than Marrow. The one thing a war lover cannot deal with is the imminence of defeat.

But I suppose I had another strength that day which was even greater: ignorance. I simply didn't know what was going on around me, and I had to learn about what happened over the target much later. The mission was to have strong R.A.F. withdrawal support, but over Lorient itself we were unprotected, and I was given to understand later that enemy fighters reacted to the tune of fifty or sixty, and that they came in from all directions, but particularly from ahead, in waves of four to seven aircraft approaching in co-ordinated attacks, and that a couple of FW-190s dropped the new time-fused aerial bombs on us from wing racks, and that there was a continuous-following flak barrage that was vicious and accurate—but of all that I saw only a brief flicker of a rounded wingtip and a few puffs of blackish smoke.

Just before the initial point, where our bombing was to begin, Max Brindt called me on the interphone and said, "Come on down here a second, Bo, help me figure something out."

So during the run I was down in the greenhouse with a walkaround bottle of oxygen peering over Max's shoulder—I don't be-

lieve he ever did find in the ground haze the power house alongside the sub base that was supposed to be our aiming point—and
Marrow, who was not yet subtle in his evasive tactics, was roller-
coastering the nose, up and down, and once, while I was standing
beside Clint Haverstraw leaning over Brindt, we swooped downward so hard that Clint and I left the floor, and for a perceptible
moment we hung suspended in mid-air, like swimmers in the fluid
of eternity, surrounded by weightless objects floating around us: a
cushion, a log book, somebody's parachute. Buzz pulled up, and I
landed on the floor in an immobile crouch with everything dragging down; my face felt like a tired old bloodhound's. Haverstraw,
who felt compelled to reduce all human experience to numbers,
figured later that at the moment of strongest centrifuge, I had
weighed four and a half G's, or six hundred seventy-five pounds,
or, as Haverstraw said, "in British terms, forty-eight stone three."
That remained for me the memorable experience of my first strike
against the Hun—being, for two seconds, as heavy as a circus freak.

When we had broken away and the Spits had picked us up—
I *did* see them because of the nice, cautious habit they had of pulling up their wings out beyond range, so the triggerhappy Yanks
would recognize their brothers in arms and not plug them full of
fifties—and we were gurgling along over the Atlantic in the rag-
gedest formation since Napoleon's retreat from Moscow, I experienced for a few moments my kind of thrill from flying. We were,
for a short first hitch of a dogleg, on a course for Penzance, and
looking out at the ocean of atmosphere I began to daydream
about pirates of the sky. I was free from the stifling confines of
reality on the earth. I was a happy child again.

Buzz interrupted this mood, coming up on interphone to tell
Max Brindt that when Max had shouted, "Bombs away!"—which
Max had done as he toggled the bombs in response to the ships
around us, without the faintest idea of aiming—that he, Marrow,
had had the best feeling he'd ever had in his life outside of inter-
course. That was not exactly the way he put it, however. He gave us
a laugh.

It came time to let down. "Prien!" Buzz shouted. "Shall we
descend to fart?"

At twelve thousand I took off my oxygen mask. It was sopping

with drool and sweat, and I realized that I had been terrified
somewhere along the way.

We landed, and one look at the expressions of Red Black and
his boys in the line crew made me think maybe we'd done something great, after all. I was so pooped I could hardly drag myself
out of the plane.

By the time we reached the interrogation room, Marrow
looked as composed and blasé as if he'd flown most of his tour.
There was a Red Cross girl handing out doughnuts, coffee, and
cigarettes, and she was really a sad case, but Marrow went up to
her, looking as springy as a high-hurdles man, and he said, "So *this*
is why we fly." She really was an exhibit. She was, but for great
bosoms attached to her like a mail carrier's endless burden, surely
a man. She was bound to be a man in disguise. Yet Marrow
flirted with her as if his life depended on her charms.

After a while he came over to me and confidentially said, "You
never can tell about those ugly ones. Sometimes they're hot as a
pancake."

"Down, Fido," I said. "You're barking up the wrong tree."

"Boman," he said, "caution never earned me a single dime."

We didn't have anything to tell the interrogator, except that
we'd probably missed the aiming point by a mile and that the
enemy planes had all zipped past us before we'd had a chance to
fire a single round in anger.

Our whole crew stood around for a long time afterwards talking about our day; we were like men in a decompression chamber.
Someone asked Handown how he could remain so calm all the
time. He said he'd felt tense over the target, but he kept busy and
just wouldn't allow himself to dwell on the possibility of disaster.
"It's like I have a governor in my head—shuts off the juice when
the worrying begins to go too fast." Prien was a bit more carefree
than a man with a tendency to flatulence had a right to be. Said
there'd been some white flak. Looked sort of like popcorn.

23 /
We had no sooner had supper than they hooted another
alert at us. This was not funny. We had had our blooding, our first
mission; we'd been through the rites of initiation. The reaction
was setting in. We had learned that over Lorient *Woody's Wooden
Pecker*, Woodman's ship, had been shot down; no parachutes; ten
men, exactly like us, dead. One drink had made me feel as if the
top half of my head were made of Vermont marble. My legs
hadn't been so tired since New Year's Day two years before, and
that was because I'd stayed up all night, dancing, drunk. I was
mincemeat, ready for the flak house after my first sortie . . . and
then the Tannoy opened up, with its deep but tinny sound of
doom, and said we were going right out again the next morning.
Up at two, briefing at three.

I went straight to bed. It is hard to know what I thought about
when in bed, but not sleeping, in the days before Daphne; or
rather, it is hard to recapture the quality of the thought, for
Daphne opened up my mind, set me free in ways I had never been
free. I cannot return to what I was before. That night, at any rate,
I never did tumble all the way down into deep sleep; I groped
around in a haze of thinking-dreaming.

They sent us next day to bomb the Focke-Wulf aircraft factory
at Bremen, and this was without question the worst engagement
the Wing had ever been through. Of one hundred fifteen Forts
that went out, nine aborted and sixteen were lost. We could thank
our stars that we knew so little about what was going on. A blurred
horror is more blur than horror; perhaps this is why ignorant and
stupid men seem to have no nerves.

We took off at nine thirty at thirty-second intervals and assembled over the base, and our Group flew to Thurleigh and made
a big sweeping turn to the left and fell in behind the Thurleigh
group, a thousand feet higher, and together the two groups
rounded out the full circle and headed for King's Lynn, whence
we were to leave the coast of England; two more groups joined
up on the way. We left King's Lynn exactly at zero hour, at about
ten thousand feet, and we steadily clicked up over the Wash to
twice that high.

Over the North Sea Handown in the top turret spotted a lone Fort way out ahead at two o'clock. We used the clock system for spotting, which meant thinking of the great round pan of the earth's atmosphere as the dial of a clock, face up, in the sky, and that we were at its hub, and that twelve o'clock was dead ahead, six o'clock dead astern, and that the other hours pointed their various directions. The Fortress that Handown saw at two o'clock seemed to be black, and others of us saw it, and we wondered how any ship had got so far from the formation; maybe it was a weather ship. We had theories but none right, because that Fort—we later learned—was one the Germans had reconditioned after a crash landing, and it was a spotter, and it radioed ahead our course and speed and altitude, so Jerry was up and ready for us at the target. We saw the spotter often later on; it was Kid Lynch who called him The Black Knight.

Looking back, I see that those pilots in front of the bulletin board before our first mission had been right: Marrow *was* a green-horn. He actually enjoyed that frightful second mission, to Bremen. I was infected by his off-handedness. The whole show seemed unreal to me. I became fascinated on the bombing run by the puffs of flak—the sudden formation of cute little clouds, as if by trick photography in a movie; you could imagine it done to music, with Paulette Goddard, bare to the waist, appearing in the middle of each burst of fluff. Unreal, unreal. I saw some enemy fighters this time, but it was hard to take them seriously, because all I could get was a feeling that they were *skidding*. They weren't flying, they were sliding sideways. The impression was a product of our speed plus or minus theirs. When they came at us head-on, the rate of closure was six hundred miles per hour, but it was never a bee line; they *skidded*.

"Look out," I yelled once, but I'd forgotten to cut into the interphone.

Somebody on our ship fired a gun, and Handown shouted into my earphones, "It was a Spit."

"Spit, my ass," Farr said. "The God-damn bastard!"

A smell of the Fourth of July drifted forward into the cockpit and eventually came in through my mask, and I saw a dark beach, and dimly my father bending over with a glowing piece of punk in his hand, and then Father running, and the basic whoomp, and a flat crack overhead, and the mops of blue and green light up above, and finally the drifting smell of burnt powder, and my laughing delight—not so much, I think, at the noise and colored sparks among the stars as at the sight of Father running as if all his sternness toward me had suddenly turned on him and was chasing him as fast as he could go in the heavy footing of the sand.

"Oh, holy Christ, there goes *Old Crow!*" Prien screamed in the phones.

"Any chutes?" Handown asked.

Sailen spoke in a quavering voice. "If this God-damn turret sticks, will you come and get me out, Neg?"

"Relax, Junior."

Now I see that, wet behind the ears though Marrow may have been, his mind was fully alert to the one thing that mattered to him: the attack, the huntsman's kill. Buzz prepared everything, including us in the crew, well in advance. "We've come a long way," he said several minutes before the initial point, "so let's not waste it. You all through arming, Max?"

"S——, yes," Brindt said.

When he toggled the bombs, Brindt gave out a yelp: "Banzai!" After the mission Haverstraw told me that as Brindt saw his bombs dropping down he couldn't contain himself and jumped up and down on his seat like a baby celebrating the flinging of a stool into world—Brindt who was so bland and taciturn on the ground.

Our losses were frightful—though you couldn't have proved it by me—on our return flight, when the edge was off our keenness, and, in the middle of the worst of it, Marrow reached for his chartboard and held it up for me to see. Behind his goggles his eyes were like Eddie Cantor's. Clipped to the board was a Varga nude. All I could think was that it was thirty-four below zero in the cockpit, but Marrow pawed the picture with a hand in a flying mitt.

As soon as our escort picked us up and the enemy fighters left us, we had a lot of elated chatter on our interphones. I was supposed to keep phone discipline, but Marrow himself was in on the racket; what could I do?

"Their flak is lousy," Marrow shouted.

"Don't *say* that," Handown cut in, with mock alarm. "If you got to say something you can say, 'I jus' hope their flak ain't any better next time.' Man, you got to be more *careful*."

"Their flak is lousy," Marrow shouted again.

At the interrogation after the mission, Marrow had his chartboard under his arm. We caught Steve Murika for our questioning, and I sensed that Marrow was talking a bit too big. But Murika was dead level with Buzz, till, on being questioned about types of enemy aircraft, Buzz held up the clipboard and said, "Look, I even took my recognition chart along."

Murika didn't seem to think that that was According to the Rules of the Game, and he stiffened.

Marrow saw this, and he said, "No, listen! I search and I fly, too. No one searches better than me. I surprise myself. That's why I get tired, see, I got to rest my eyes once in a while"—and he held up the picture and made his eyes look as if they were resting comfortably.

24 /
On the way out from the interrogation hut Marrow asked me if I planned to go to the officers' dance that night. I said I was pretty tuckered, I didn't know. What really was on my mind—a reflection that would have been the last to enter Marrow's—was that I was a new hand, with only two missions to my credit, and I guess I figured it would be somehow inappropriate for me to mix it up with the experts.

To my surprise, however, I found myself taking the day's second shave and a hot shower back at our hutment, and I got into my good uniform, and I ate a big supper, for me, and around nine thirty, when a fleet of R.A.F. buses and vans, bringing girls from Motford Sage and Cambridge and Ely, began to pull in at the turning circle in front of the Number One Mess, I was already established inside, at a table back against a wall not far from the bar they'd set up, with Marrow and Maltitz and a jerk named Benning whom nobody liked.

There was some thrashing around—I saw legs in skirts, and I

tried to work up a little ache in my chest in honor of Janet, my so-
called fiancée, back in Donkentown, but nothing happened—and
everybody but us went by and shook hands with two old curtain
rods who were the official chaperones, and then the station orches-
tra, with *The Pike Rilling Jive Bombers* printed on the big drum,
began to let go from a wooden platform with a banner over it pro-
claiming the Group motto: *Our Foot on the Hun's Chest.* That
was the Englishy influence of the first Group C.O., Walkerson,
whom the higher-ups had practically certified out on a Section
Eight, as a madman. I couldn't take my eyes off the face of the
alto-sax player, who inserted the reed of his instrument in one
corner of his mouth and looked lopsided and grotesquely earnest.

There seemed to be a great deal of confusion, and friend
Benning, who wouldn't have known the difference between a
wedding and a wake, finally figured out what the trouble was.
There were a lot of extra girls. Among those who had come to the
dance were a scattered few in uniforms of WAAFs, WRENs, ATs,
and FANNYs, but most were starchy young hopefuls from the
homes of merchants and farmers and professional men in the
nearby countryside. Decent girls with potato-and-brussels-sprout
complexions. The extras stood around in awkward clumps awhile,
then began to sit together at tables. Benning said they were dead
men's drags. The Wing had lost a hundred and sixty men—sixty-
four officers—that afternoon, and a good number of the officers
who were missing from our Group must have had dates for the
dance, and their girls had arrived all keyed up for a flurry with the
Yanks, only to learn that their escorts had not come home from
Bremen.

One hundred and sixty! It was beyond my comprehension. I
had been worse shaken by the image of one ship's having gone
down the day before, Woodman's.

"Gret naht fuh scavengers," Maltitz said.

"I'm taking my time," Marrow said.

"You dumb bastard," Benning said, "the good ones'll all be
snapped up." And Benning drilled off to see what he could appropriate.

We sat and drank. It was a slow party. Many of our fliers had
lost their companions, and there was a shadow across the evening.
Maltitz left us to find a dame. Marrow talked about what he be-

lieved, and what I, too, then believed, had kept us alive that afternoon.

"I'm ass deep in luck," he said. "I can't lose, seems I can't lose.
Braddock owes me twenty bucks. Church owes me twenty-seven.
Handown owes me eleven. Benny Chong owes me thirty. I used to
know a guy at Spanner Field, I owed him money all the time, because, the thing was, he had a bad inferiority complex, so I used to
make a point of borrowing a few bucks from him every week to
give him confidence. . . ."

That was when I first saw her. I was facing the bar, and I saw
her over Marrow's shoulder. She had paused for a moment near
the bar, because some unattractive character was trying to get her
to drink with him, and she was squinting, letting her eyes get used
to the half light at our end of the big room. She was blessedly
short; shorter than I. Yet she was slender, fine-boned, and her neck
was a stem, and she held herself as if she were tall, like some delicate weed grown fast in a summertime field. She was wearing a
navy-blue dress trimmed with a narrow standing edge of white
piqué around her fragile neck, and she stood with one arm on the
bar and began to survey herself, looking down at her arm; then her
glance ran up over her shoulder and across her bosom. Her skin
glowed. She was openly happy at what she saw of herself.

Marrow, evidently sensing that my attention was vagrant,
talked louder. "You know Apollo Holdreth collects coins? F——
that! That's something I can't see, collecting old jack—foreign
jack. Money's to spend! The other night over at the club Martin
Foley, you know Foley, he came in there with two old silver coins
and he told Apollo he'd sell 'em to him. Foley said he'd bought
'em in Panama, they just looked like silver dollars with this Spic
writing on 'em you could barely make out, but he said they were
Pieces of Eight. So I said to him, 'Eight what?' and he couldn't
answer me, so I said, 'When I get to be President of the United
States, we're going to mint nothing but twenty-dollar gold pieces,
and that's what I'm going to collect. I'm going to be a coin col-
lector, like F. D. R. collects stamps.' S——, he has his Postmaster
General print 'em up specially for him."

I didn't dare look at her too steadily, for fear Marrow would
turn around and see her, and that, I figured, would be that.

Marrow seemed gloomy. "We lost a lot of dumb jerks out

there today," he said, as if to stress that it was a man's own damn-fool fault if he died. "I don't care when I lose. I guess that's why I win so much. I just don't care. Another thing. I don't believe in the law of probability. I just say to myself, 'Maybe the f——ing law's not working right this minute.' Like I always play the winner in roulette. The hell with statistics. By the law of probability I'm probably going to get killed in this war, but I say the hell with that, maybe the law's on vacation. I don't like these guys that add up how much back pay they got stored up. What they think they are, squirrels? I like to spend my money. I budget my cash very careful, so as I can be sure and spend every cent."

You couldn't tell whether he wanted to live forever or be ready to die any minute.

He was getting kind of sore at me for not saying, "Yup, yup, sure, I agree," every ten seconds, so he looked around and saw her, and he said to me, in a voice that had conceit in it, and ruthless-ness, "Brother Boman, follow me. We got work to do." He started over toward her.

I tagged along as usual. At that time I thought Marrow had hung the moon.

25 /

It happened that as we moved toward the bar the girl got up and started to walk away, maybe to go to the can.

The way she walked took my breath away. There was a straightness about her, not of a small person trying to be big, but of someone serene, and though I wasn't crazy about cats I admired her catlike control, tense-relaxed, in balance like a spring, and she had an odd way of putting her legs forward, setting her feet down pigeon-toed, toe first and then heel, it seemed, like a ballet dancer, but not affected, simply answering the demands of a certain kind of pelvis and faintly suggesting superior fruits in that basin of bone —a provocative walk, believe me, her head turning with hooded eyes that seemed not to look at, but certainly saw, men.

Buzz hurried and blocked her way, standing nearly on tiptoe, blowing like a porpoise, with his overseas cap flipping in his hands in front of him and then beating on his leg, and with a big Don Juan simper all over his massive face; while I posted myself like a docile footman behind him and somewhat to his right. My heart was beating hard, considering that Buzz was leading the charge.

"Par' me, madam," Marrow said. "Can you direct me to the Dorchester Bar?"

"Mademoiselle," the girl corrected him, with dead eyes.

"Apologies."

Buzz's shoulders were stooped forward, as if he had a public grab in mind, and I saw the girl look up at him in perfect calm, neither accepting nor rejecting his winks and lip-licking.

"Will you join my pal and me in a cup of tea?" His reference to me was on a deploring note, hinting that it would be a cinch to ditch me later.

The girl looked around Marrow at me, and my heart nearly cut loose its moorings and came sailing out my ear, because there was a distinct change of expression on her face, for the better, and she said, with a simple directness that I later came to think of as Daphne's trade mark, "Yes. Love it."

So we went back to our table, it being evident that she had not been going to the loo but only unloading a problem man, and all three of us ordered gin, not tea, and Buzz went through his routines, like an acrobat, flexing his jokes, posing proud and poised as if hearing a drumroll of danger at the edge of certain stale compliments and premature suggestions he always plunged into. And I, in the meanwhile, suffered a most extraordinary shyness, hardly daring to look at the girl. My heart was still racing and tripping, and most of the time I kept my eyes on my glass of warm gin and soda, which I kept revolving, like a troublesome thought, on a ring of moisture on the table top. It seemed that each time I raised my glance to the girl's face, her gaze was fastened to mine.

Was her man m.i.a.? Marrow asked the question as off-handedly as if being lost on a mission was like having a hacking cough.

He was.

Who had he been?

Pitt. The girl spoke the name with ease, with what might have seemed too ready acceptance of her loss.

I vaguely remembered Pitt, a navigator in *Houdini's Trunk,* a

mild and undistinguished gent, so far as I knew. But this girl. He
must have had something.

"Sure," Buzz said, who had apparently run a check on every
woman in Cambridgeshire and all East Anglia. "I heard Pitt had a
classy steady, and no one could figure it out." It was thick-skinned
of Marrow to run Pitt down, but the girl didn't seem to mind.
"A navigator!" he exclaimed, as if she'd thrown herself away on a
pickpocket.

"He was a dear man," she said, without emphasis; Pitt might
have been a fellow she'd met for a minute at a party, but her coolness itself was enough to stop Marrow's mouth.

Various men dropped by our table, each for a drink at a time,
because the word seemed to have spread that the Pitt Special was
on the loose, Pitt being regrettably absent. I watched the girl.
Daphne. She had the knack of sizing men up before they opened
their big mouths, and she knew exactly which side of herself to
show a man in order to make him feel like the whole cheese. With
one she'd make herself scarce and small; with another she'd be
taciturn, a deep well; with a third she'd make common-housefly
wings of her eyelashes. As for me, she looked straight at me, into
me. She patted her hair and fluffed it up a lot, and she constantly
worked over the Pitt legacy of lipstick, compact, gold-plated Zippo.
I don't mean to give an impression of her as a winsome flirt. She
was a grown woman. In the mirror of her compact she was great:
dealt with herself as her own best friend. It was obvious that the
admiration of men, of which she was getting a heap, stirred up unaffected joy in her. Wooing by heels was not ruled out, so long as
it was spirited. She was in love—not with poor Pitt any more, but
with everyone, herself, life. She poured out warmth to a lot of men
who were chilled to the bone. I had the illusion, however—and
whether or not I was justified, I clung to it, a lamppost in my reel-
ing world—that the only person to whom she communicated real
feeling was me.

I didn't dare ask her to dance: the risk of losing her was too
great out there where, by now, the band having reached altitude
and having cut in the supercharger, feet were flying and hands
across the sea were in some cases also across the seats. Calais glide,
jitterbug, big apple. But a dozen others did ask Daphne for a turn.
She declined, never saying, but somehow the men got an idea, that

it was in deference to the departed. But I had a different idea, because each time she turned one down she got in a look at me.

There were ten minutes, toward the end, when she and Marrow and I were alone at the table again, and during that time Buzz, under the impression that he was, as usual, sweeping the field to victory, incessantly talked, and I asked one unobtrusive question: Did I have her permission to see her sometime? This she gave so quietly that I think Buzz, going off like a pinwheel, never even noticed the exchange.

The party was getting rough. Some throttle-jockeys from the —th Group had crashed the dance, and during a fist-fight on the floor we had a soulful bass-viol solo, very drunk, by Major Walter M. Silg, commanding officer of the —th Squadron in our Group, who had had four ships torn from his flanks during the day. Then some damn fool blew taps, and everybody stood up and cried. Daphne's eyes were dry, but they had a half-covered look, as of a Moslem woman's face withdrawn behind cloth in unassailable privacy. I couldn't tell anything about what she felt.

That was the end. There was a scramble for buses in the blackout outside, and suddenly, to my amazement, there we were in the darkness, Daphne and I, hand in hand, groping from bus to bus to see which was Cambridge Number Four. We found the right one, and she boarded it, and she touched me lightly on the shoulder to thank me and was gone.

Ten minutes later, undressing, not wanting to face Marrow because in the end he, not I, had been ditched, I came to my senses.

I didn't have her address. Didn't even know her last name. Where she worked. All I knew was: girl named Daphne, lived in Cambridge. Sure, she'd be glad to see me.

CHAPTER THREE

THE RAID

1119–1337 hours

1 /

    We flew in a low, wide circle around the airdrome and formed our element, a slanting vee of three, with *The Body* at the apex, and Stebbins in *Finah Than Dinah* on one wing, and Schuman in *Expendable VI* on the other. Those two had taken off after we had, and they caught up by flying slightly tighter radii than ours. My job on the climb was to watch the temperatures and pressures and keep an eye peeled for maniacs flying collision courses, and I had to close down the cowl flaps little by little to maintain the proper cylinder-head temperatures, as Marrow gradually eased the manifold pressures and reduced the r.p.m.'s. We had more than an hour ahead of us of climbing and forming up. By the time we'd taken a turn around the field, *Finah Than Dinah* was packed in on our left wing, about fifty feet astern and fifty feet lower than we; and *Expendable VI* was in a corresponding slot on my side, but fifty feet higher. We settled down to the work of our long ascent at three hundred feet a minute, riding out on our first long northeastward leg over the mysterious, steamy fens, where soft white pads of the morning fog were still to be seen alternating with flats of grain rippling in the westerly breeze like patches of golden sea. I saw dark fields of sugar beets and strawberries, and some of the broad dikes of the Dutch reclaimers of English swamp, shadowed ridges on the plain, and the Ouse and the Cam, which

I thought of as Daphne's and my river; and then—familiar land-
mark from many raids—the great hundred-foot-high dike, the
straightest line in all England, I think, thirty miles from Erith to
Downham Market. I had come to have vivid, powerful feelings
about all that damp green plate of landscape, seen in many lights.
It had meant, so often, departure toward danger and then arrival
back to safety; parting from Daphne, perhaps for the last time, and
then prospect of reunion, relieved and weary, glad to be alive for
her sake.

Our group was to proceed to splasher beacon number two for
assembly. I was listening on VHF for a call from Croquet Red,
Colonel Bins' call signal in *Angel Tread*, and scanning the sky for
planes of our Group. Marrow was unusually glum and quiet, speaking to us in short, choppy queries.

"Anybody see any flares?"

The sky was full of Forts and shrinking clouds. We watched
for flares from *Angel Tread* and from other group and squadron
leaders, but so far there was only confusion.

"Hear anything, Bowman?"

"Not yet."

The sound of Marrow's voice acted on me as some sort of
warning. I looked quickly at him, and it was on the tip of my
tongue to ask him if he felt all right, but I checked myself, for I
wouldn't have wanted to give a man I hated the satisfaction of
scorning my solicitude—and besides, I was not ready to undermine
Marrow with the crew. But his voice was certainly strange—unsure, absent-minded, edged with strain.

How different these tones were from those in which the Marrow of the early days shouted in the plane! He had been ebullient
then, and I had thought him full to bursting with life. I remembered how he would curl up for a catnap on one of the sofas in the
lounge outside our mess, after lunch, in those days, and how, after
a deep sigh, he would give an attribution to Keats and then bal-
locks up the quote: "The art of living is a joy forever!" But now
Daphne had helped me see that he had always been in love with
something quite different from what I had thought; not with living
at all. I could picture him, just before curling up on that sofa, in
front of the officers'-mess bulletin board, the day after a mission,
gazing at the strike photos of the first bursts, the smoke heads rising,

the chaos of dust and ruin; and at the P.R.V. photos, taken later, of the carcasses of buildings and the pockmarks of our bombs. He would stand there for a very long time with squinting eyes and a set jaw; a grim face. This morning, after what Daphne had told me the day before, I knew that it was not at all an expression of horror and regret, but rather the grimace of a man who has just taken a big slug of strong booze, when the throat burns and the first relaxing ecstasy shoots through the chest—with the difference that he seemed to be able to savor that first stab, prolong it, hold onto it.

Then I remembered the first time he had let out his battle whoop on joining with enemy fighters, a cry which had grown, through successive missions, into his prolonged, hair-raising shriek that I hated, I believe, more than anything else in all our work of these later days. And that first shout, come to think of it, had been early in the tour—on the mission to Meaulte, our fifth, on May thirteenth, and I barely noticed it at the time, because that was the day I wore the shrunken socks and my feet were nearly frozen. Yet I remembered it vividly: It came just after Handown called in an attack from eleven o'clock, and Buzz and I could see the fighters swing over and begin their run on us, and they got within range, and *The Body* trembled as our guns began to fire, and Marrow shouted, a long "Oo-oo-oo-oo!," happy, fierce, and oblivious, a shout like that of a certain kind of kid going down the first dip of a giant roller coaster.

Now we flew through a cloud, and I must say that while there may have been a signal of distress in Marrow's voice, there was absolutely nothing yet in his handling of the ship that was not steady, firm, the touch of the master. Flying through a cloud in formation during assembly was pure nightmare for me; he had always thought it a lark. You had no horizon on which to orient yourself; your wingmen had to tuck in so close that you expected one of them to chew off your tail section any moment; and the sky was full of madmen flying every which way trying to find their formations. But Marrow was on course for splasher two; he had no idea of dodging a piddling cloud, so through it we went. It was small, thank goodness.

Marrow kept riding Haverstraw for our position. Buzz was on the pilot's controls of the radio compass himself half the time picking up the bearings of splashers, yet he expected Clint to have everything in his head as well. Finally Haverstraw did something he never had done before: raised his voice in protest. "If you want me to keep track of these bearings," he said, "then get the hell off the tuning crank."

I remembered the way Marrow had meekly scuttled himself down the passageway to the navigator's compartment when I'd let loose a similar blast during the preflight check, and I wondered whether he'd pull another docile retreat in the face of Haverstraw's surprising anger. Not at all. "Keep your shirt on, junior," he quickly said. And he raised his arm and began tuning again.

"Red-green flare at two o'clock," Handown said from the upper turret.

"I see it," Marrow said. "Keep your eye on that ship, son." Marrow even called Handown, who was thirty-six years old, "son."

We were climbing all the while, and as we rose in the sky I saw, lit by the thin sun which was near its zenith, the many wriggling rivers of that haunch of England: the Nene, the Ouse, the Lark, the Rhee, the Granta, the Pant, the Stour, the Wissey, the Wensum, the Nar, the Yare. It was Kid Lynch who had put me onto all those beautiful names from the warehouse of ancient time. "Lynch," Marrow said once, when the Kid got on the subject of English place names, "you're a God-damn limey lover." Really he was mainly a lover of sounds in his mouth. You'd hear him reel words off with dazzling speed: "Whelk yak joke clink udder under mood purl ousel osprey loam dome dimity stoat notch niggard noodle dump." Good names for watercourses, he said. Some you'd call rivers, some not. Yak Creek. Purl Pond. The Upper Dimity River . . . For a moment I saw Kid Lynch sprawled in the radio compartment of *The House of Usher*, the brain with those filaments of outlandish association quite lost, all smashed, and I felt a thrust of bitter sadness.

2 /

Max Brindt snapped me out of it, calling for me on interphone.

"Yeah, Max."

Max asked me if I'd made a note of the co-ordinates of the
i.p. "I must've wrote 'em down but I can't find the God-damn
thing."

Max was a baffling one. He was two people—so mild, dutiful,
and damply depressed on the ground, worried about Gross Errors
in bombing, convinced at times that we were losing the war; so
cocky, aggressive, and energetic in the air. On the early missions he
had been a simple guy from Milwaukee with an overdrive going
when he was in the ship; he used to joke about possible disasters—
until that mission to Lorient in mid-May, our seventh, when Braddock's ship blew up right in front of us. No more jokes after that.
Lately he'd been heavily sentimental and methodical, more and
more German, it seemed; a beer swamp. Perl whispered in my ear
one night that Brindt was a Nazi. Max had been showing up the
last few times in my bad dream, my bombing-and-being-bombed
dream. Being German-American and the bombardier qualified
him for those nightmares. How he loved to drop his bombs! Just
about a week before, I'd taken a walk with him out to the bomb
dump, and he had sat morosely astride a thousand-pounder under
the camouflage nets and waved an arm out across the heaps of
hogshead shapes and said, "Look at all that s——." On our mission
to Hamburg during the frightful July blitz—the day Lynch was
killed—Max got so excited at the prospect of *dropping* the bombs
that he forgot to fuse them; dropped them safe. Marrow really cut
into him about that, said Max only had three things to do on a
mission: Arm the bombs. Open the doors. Toggle on the lead
bombardier. "Sometimes I think you want us to lose the war,"
Buzz said. That remark really got Max where he lived; he'd never
really recovered his high spirits, even on bombing runs.

"Hold on a sec," I said.

I found the information and gave it to him, for I was the
methodical one, old Scotch-Irish-Presbyterian me. Oh, yes, I was
secretively conscientious, and during briefings I usually wrote
everything down; being just a lowdown co-pilot I felt I had to
cover for every expert, and this call of Max's wasn't the first time a
specialist had come to me to get straightened out. I was Dependable Charley. Ha!

My notes of that morning's briefing were full of holes, and it
was by sheerest chance that I did have what Max wanted. I remem-

bered the swerving of my attention that morning during my fury
at Marrow; that had been uncharacteristic of me, because I had always kept a tight control on divagations at briefing time, the life-
and-death time. Apparently Max's mind had swiveled that morning, too. Then I had a shock of alarm. What if everyone in the
plane—what if everyone in the entire strike had been woolgather-
ing when a certain vital fact of the mission had been thrown out?
This was one of the things that made that day dreamlike: Ideas as
fantastic as this one, of a momentary universal nod during separate
briefings all over the Wing area, came to me with the clarity of
revealed truth. With an effort I shook that one out as absurd.

3 /
Handown was a plane shark. He kept his eye, as directed,
on *Angel Tread*, which he'd spotted firing the red-green flare of a
group leader, and we had no trouble attaching our element to
Colonel Bins', so that our squadron of six planes was formed:
*Angel Tread, Erector Set, Gruesome Twosome, The Body, Finah
Than Dinah, Expendable VI.* Marrow hung our element underneath, slightly behind, and slightly to the right of the Colonel's.
We were all experienced fliers in the lead squadron, and we made
a snug box, no outside dimension of which was more than four
hundred feet, and that wasn't bad, considering that a Fort had a
wing span of one hundred and four feet, and there were six of us
packed in the box.

Over splasher two we wheeled, and there we could see the
other two squadrons of our Group coming up, and as we slowly
swung in the sky they closed with us, to form the larger box of the
Group. The low squadron, led by Buzz's friend, Curly Jonas, in
Baggy Maggie, was behind us and down to our right, and the high
squadron—Apollo Holdreth commanding in *Round Trip Ticket*
—was behind and above and to the left. For tightness the squadrons were slanted in the opposite direction from the elements—
the high wingman to the right, the high squadron to the left.

Two big circles, climbing all the while, and our Group was

formed. We leveled out then to fly along the line of splasher beacons to join up with the other eleven groups of our attack.

4 /

We were at about nine thousand feet, and it was time for me to take a turn around the ship and make a manual check of everyone's oxygen-hose connections—a practice which Marrow had instituted after a navigator on the man-killing ship, *Chug Bug,* had died of anoxia at twenty-four thousand feet. I made the rounds, exchanging shouted greetings with some of the men, working silently at the stations of others.

I left the nose till last. In the navigator's compartment, Clint Haverstraw was bent over the right-hand side of his desk watching the radio-compass indicator, but when I leaned over him he swiveled his chair and looked up at me. Clint had the cleanliness madness, and his compartment was fussily housekept, pencils lashed with bowknots, the driftmeter hood weirdly shined with shoe polish. I remembered that early in our tour we'd had ground-school dinghy drill one day, and Marrow got Clint's goat talking about mud. "If it rains much more we'll need these dinghies," Buzz said, "to ride the mud around here." And, seeing Haverstraw's loathing of our dirty, disordered life welling up, Buzz took off. The clean war of the Air Force. No marching, no foxholes, no mud. Clint wanted a bath right on the spot, by the time Buzz got through. Marrow was merciless. Most of the time, though, Marrow was gentle and protective with Clint, whose trick mind for numbers dazzled Buzz. Haverstraw was really Marrow's toy. The favoritism was clinched when Haverstraw came up with a most unexpected talent—for baseball. This was revealed to us on April Fools' Day, after we had been shown *The Body* for the first time, when, in the late mildness of that spring afternoon, a bunch of us organized a pickup hardball game. Haverstraw said he'd like to play third. Marrow insisted, of course, on pitching, and the opponents began pasting him, and Haverstraw made some stops that took your breath away, and his pegs to first went like telegrams. Marrow

became ecstatic. "See that wing?" he shouted. And after the game
he said to Clint, "You got to go out for the Group ball team, son.
We got to keep those God-damn sergeants off that ball team."

Clint never meant to do any harm but often managed to do
some, and now, at his desk, after we had shouted over the engine
roar a few commonplace complaints against this mission we were
on, he turned the full glare of his insensitivity in my direction and
cried out, "I hear Marrow's f——ing your girl."

I couldn't believe my ears; the vibration of the motors suddenly seemed to get into my knee joints. "*What?*" I shouted.

Clint repeated his happy announcement.

"Who the hell told you that?"

"Three guesses." Clint gave me a grin like the chrome grille
on the radiator of a Buick.

Marrow, then, was already making a story of going to bed
with Daphne, and a lying story, at that, and probably purveying
it, as he did his many accounts of his swordsmanship, in the officers' club, buying anyone he could collar a beer or a coke so he
could have a bonded audience, and letting the others talk until, at
a general pause, he would lean back in his chair and get off a fine
lead sentence. "Did you ever clamp it to your co-pilot's best girl?"
Something like that. And all a lie. In the past, when I had listened
to Buzz's stories of his epic successes in bed, I had always thought
of his girls as figures in a homemade myth, not as flesh and blood
and breathing reputation, but now I saw that the coin he spent so
freely was human, and I was in a rage standing there looking at
Clint's delighted face—but my rage was mixed with a sadness for
Marrow, too. I saw for the first time, after what Daphne had told
me the day before, a pattern in the recitals of these tales of his
prowess. All lies? There was some insatiable repetitive driving
need in him.

I turned my back on Haverstraw's table, and on him, and
made my way in a daze of thinking and anger back up to the cockpit and sat in my seat and looked over at Buzz. He had buckled
his helmet and buttoned the collar of his suit, and he was ready
for whatever the day would offer, and like the cadaver on the beach
at Pamonassett, he seemed to be looking into distant times and
spaces—only of course he was simply scanning the sky for signs of
our other groups; very much alive, damn his alert green eyes.

I shuddered. I think I must have wanted to kill Buzz. Yes, I
wanted to kill. I, who had such a horror of killing. Who had guilt-
fraught nightmares about our work of killing civilians: the faces
looking upward, in the dream, and I among them, watching the
killing coming down from the sky, and Max Brindt standing beside me in a thick crowd of innocents with upturned Picasso faces,
and the horrible feeling of being rooted to the ground and unable
to run away, and yet knowing that it was also I up above who had
dropped the killing that was falling on also me below.

To overcome this fearful anger I, too, looked into the distance.
There were broken clouds below us, but around us the sky was
porcelain. We were flying southeastward over Norfolk. I felt somewhat calmer.

Suddenly I had a new understanding of one of Marrow's
favorite stories about his own flying—about the dive that had
really scared him. While testing at Mildress he had flown as a stunt
pilot in several movies: *Through the Thunderhead*, *Wings Over
the Desert*, *Mail Run*, and some others. "This one movie, when
they were making it," Marrow once had told us, while we were still
in training, and he had repeated the story many times, "they said
to me, 'Go up, stunt as crazy as you can, and then take a long dive.'
So I did what they said, and I didn't ask any questions; they paid
me to fly, not to yap at 'em. When the picture came out, I bought
me a ticket and went in to see it, and I found out it was about this
pilot, he got p——ed off at his wife, so he went up to spite her with
some wild flying that was going to pay her back, he figured. I could
see where I took over with the stunting, I mean, the flying got
good. I looked around the theater at the faces to see how they were
taking it. Boy, was I scaring some of those women! Anyway, I
looked back at the screen, and I was going into this dive, and
diving was my specialty; it was real clean. Then I noticed, God, I
was getting low, and I didn't remember I went that low, and I still
wasn't pulling out. Then they showed the ground coming up—too
fast. It was too late for me to pull out. I shouted right out in the
theater, the people must've thought I was off my trolley. The lousy
plane crashed and the pilot was killed, and I was almost dead myself. They should have told me about what they pasted onto the
end of my dive. . . ." And Marrow laughed at the memory, with
too much laughter.

5 /

"All right," Marrow said, "prepare to go on oxygen."

We were at ten thousand feet, and it was twelve minutes past noon. I unhooked my mask and ran a hand across my jaw; I'd shaved too early—nearly ten hours before—and I could see that I was going to have stubble trouble, as Handown had once called it, under the tightness of an oxygen mask.

Colonel Bins was taking huge easing turns, so that two groups behind us could attach themselves to us.

Now I was in my mask, cut off from the world. I regulated the flow. In a few minutes Prien called for an oxygen check, ticking off the numbers from nose to tail, and each man answered in his way.

I said, "O.K."

Marrow always said, "I'm here, son."

At splasher six, where our task force was to achieve its final assembly, we all made an enormous S of two semi-circles, so that the whole formation could close up, and on the way around to the right I looked out and, seeing group after group tacked closely onto the great loop, I had a sense of our strength, our growing strength. It was always a thrilling sight to see a strike tighten into ranks, and that morning it was breathtaking.

"Four aborts," Farr said. He meant from our Group. "Lucky bastards."

After the huge turns, which took nearly ten minutes, we unwound on a southwesterly course, sailing over the Suffolk downs for Orfordness, where we would break with the friendly coast. We were all put together.

Our great strike was made up of two task forces of about a hundred ships each, which were flying in train twelve minutes apart; each task force consisted of two combat wings, one behind the other, five minutes apart; each combat wing comprised three groups of eighteen ships each. The groups had now joined up into these combat wings, slanting wedges exactly like the basic vee in which our three planes, *The Body, Finah Than Dinah,* and *Expendable* VI, were stacked in our element, and like that in which the three squadrons of six ships each in our Group, Bins', Jonas', and Holdreth's, were formed up in their turn. The combat wing had a lead group of eighteen, a high group of eighteen stacked up behind to the left, and a low group of eighteen astern, below, and to the right. We in *The Body*, in the second element of the lead squadron of the lead group of the second combat wing of the second task force, were about three quarters of the way back from the head of the procession. Actually we felt more exposed than that sounds, for thanks to the gaps between combat wings, we were right out on the nose of the last big fighting box of the strike. All that shielded us from the very nose was Colonel Bins' element, *Angel Tread*, *Erector Set*, and *Gruesome Twosome*.

On the way to Orfordness something happened which was very curious, which struck me at the time as being strange, but whose meaning I did not then even try to fathom, for I was busy thinking of other things.

Junior Sailen came up on interphone. "Ball turret to engineer," he said, though we usually had none of that radioman's-manual kind of formality on our ship, *Roger*, *over*, and *out*, but simply spoke to each other by name and shut up when done. "Roger," which was supposed to mean, "I understand you," was occasionally used by our sergeants with a heavy accent on the second syllable to express mock alacrity, and for a while, during Marrow's phase of enthusiasm for English slang, we had bandied around "Rodney," which Buzz had said was the R.A.F. equivalent for "Roger." On the whole we were sloppy because Marrow thought it was manly to be raunchy. "Cut that kid stuff," Marrow had said on an early mission when our first radioman, Kowalski, had gone formal on us.

Anyway, Sailen said, "Ball turret to engineer."

"What's up, Junior?" Handown said.

"Come down here a minute," Sailen said.

Junior Sailen was a tiny guy; one look at him made me feel burly. He was five feet and one inch tall, weighed a hundred fifteen—and a good thing that he was so tiny, too, because his station in combat was just a small plastic bubble full of machinery down there under the ship, where even he had to sit with his knees drawn up like an embryo. He was strong for his size, and well coordinated, and needed to be, because it took a natural athlete, if a small one, to gyrate those Sperry K-2 power turrets around, traversing through range and deflection at the same time, by means of feather-delicate touches on the hand grips of the guns, to get a bead on a German fighter coming from underneath at a skidding angle. And though he had this litheness and quickness and was twenty-one years old, we all treated him as a baby, and he loved it. He was our mascot. He told me once that his father had died early and that as a kid he'd been brought up by a brother ten years older than he, and that from the time his brother had left home he'd always been restless; he would take a job, and there'd be no one to look out for him, and he'd quit in a few days and mope around the house, and then take another job, and the same thing would happen. In our crew he was in clover—nine older brothers, who fought each other to take care of him. Even Farr: "Did you remember your gloves, Junior?" Junior couldn't take a p—— without getting permission from one of us.

Marrow hated not being in the know, and when Sailen asked Handown to come down to his turret, Buzz cut in right away, saying, "What's itching you down there, Junior?"

"Nothing," Junior said.

"What do you mean, 'nothing'? Wha'd you call the engineer down for if it was nothing?"

Usually at this point Junior Sailen would have been eating out of Marrow's hand, but this time he seemed inspired with gall and he said, "It's just between Handown and me."

I was amazed at this: it made me think there must be something seriously wrong in the turret about which Sailen was too scared to tell Marrow, for fear it might mean turning back. Handown had an amazing knack for getting things straight in the plane. In the heaviest of action he could retain the cool, systematic logic of a case-hardened mechanic on a trouble-shooting quest, eliminating one by one the possible causes of malfunction in the order of their probability. He had saved us all more than once. I think that what made me sure something was wrong in the turret was Sailen's having started the whole thing off in that formal way, using the word "engineer" in calling Handown. Power of suggestion.

Rebuffed by the tiny man, Marrow went wild. He loosed a fantastic torrent of obscenities against sergeants, which reminded me, in its excesses and its vileness, of his tirade the night he had gone for a dancing lesson at the Red Cross Aeroclub.

And what came out now was distorted in sound, because a throat mike couldn't take more than a certain amount of volume.

When it was over, Sailen said with astounding quiet courage, "You must have the wrong number, sir. No one here by that name."

"Listen, you God-damn yellow-bellied mouse . . ."

Handown was apparently back at his post in the upper turret, because he now spoke one word that cut Marrow short. "Sir."

"Handown, what the f—— is this all about?" Marrow shouted.

"I gave Junior a loan of my lucky dice couple days ago," Handown calmly said. "He thought maybe I'd want 'em today. Gave 'em back."

I had no idea whether that was the truth or whether Neg was covering for the Little Brother.

6 /

As we approached the coast of East Anglia the broken and scattered cumulus clouds, far beneath us, lay like scraps of lint on the floor of a careless home. The sky above us was clear. We could see for fifteen miles all around. The sun was already behind us, and ahead, low in the sky, a slender moon was rising, and the Channel beneath had the cold blue-gray cast of finished steel.

We went over Orfordness at twenty-six minutes after one, at fourteen thousand feet. From the coast onward our briefed cruising speed was one hundred sixty miles per hour, indicated air speed, and, as Colonel Bins adjusted to that rate, Marrow followed suit. We were still climbing.

About five minutes out Marrow told me to fly awhile, and I took the controls. There were no problems now; just a matter of keeping hooked snugly underneath the first element. This kind of flying had at long last become second nature to me. About fifty miles out over the Channel I remembered to remind Butcher Lamb to cut off the IFF. *Erector Set* overhead was the first ship I could see test-firing her guns, flinging out momentary puffs of smoke, pale blue against the deeper blue above; then our ship began to shiver, and through my earphones and the engines' roar I could hear the crackle of short bursts as our men shook out their barrels and then left their guns cocked and on fire against the danger we were so soon to face.

Prien barked off an oxygen check, and afterwards Haverstraw sang out, "On flight plan," stretching out the pla–a–a–n, like an echo among hills. That meant that we were on course and on time; the report rang in my ears like the "All's well" of a watchman in the night, a cry of defiance against would-be thieves, murderers, disturbers of the peace.

There came back to me, then, a warning I had indirectly taken, the day before, from something Daphne had said—that men with Marrow's taint might, in an extremity of facing defeat of some kind or other, try to destroy everyone around them, along with themselves. She had not put it so explicitly, of course. She had been talking about an R.A.F. pilot she had once loved—a man much like Marrow, she had said; the warning I had inferred myself. I thought there was some analogy between the tale of the last hours of her R.A.F. boyfriend and the legend of Samson's death, and I was not sure that the fact that Samson was surrounded by enemies when he brought the roof of the temple down deprived the analogy of its force. I felt, at any rate, a sort of chill of bracing myself for whatever my pilot might pull.

My eyes drew me away from these thoughts. For a few minutes, as we climbed through the eighteen-thousand-foot mark over the Channel, all the planes of the great attack began to give off short, non-persistent trails of condensation. Each ship was like a huge brush leaving a stroke of whitewash on the ceiling of the afternoon. Fortunately—for beautiful though the contrails were, they were a menace to planes in formation and a cover for enemy fighters—they faded quickly away, and as we ascended they no longer formed.

Far ahead, over the enemy-held land, higher than we yet were, I could see a thin plate of cirrus clouds, and it briefly crossed my mind that that cover might cause us trouble. Directly under it, like an indistinct shadow, I could just make out the dark line of the enemy coast. What was ahead was like a huge mouth, the upper lip of vapor, the lower lip of earth. In between, on our course that would lead us to be swallowed in that maw, there was only a misty vagueness, a gray uncertainty, an atmosphere almost opaque.

CHAPTER FOUR

THE TOUR

April 17 to May 18

1 /

Sleep is a mystery. That was a night I should have spent going round and round on a barbecue spit, but not at all. I dived asleep before Marrow even came in the room, and I was in a black void from then until nine thirty in the morning, when Sully wakened me, shaking my shoulder, saying, "Breakfast at ten. Briefing at ten thirty. Out, you slug."

No. Not again. Not three days in a row.

It was not a dream. Sully persisted. "I mean it, stupid. Get up. And get your fat-ass pilot up while you're at it."

When Marrow finally came to, he was so furious at Wing he seemed to have forgotten all about the night before and Daphne.

They briefed us, and we went out to the ships, and we taxied, and we had three postponements, and then they scrubbed the strike.

In our weeks at Pike Rilling, before we'd flown a mission ourselves, we had seen many a scrubbing, but this was our first direct knowledge of how pernicious these cancellations were. They had got us believing we really were going on our third in a row. They'd worked us up to the pitch of reluctant willingness known as slight cramps in the bowels, and they'd made us wait two hours, missing lunch, and then, like puppeteers grown tired of the weights on their fingers, they'd let us down.

In the truck, going back in, Marrow was pleasant to me. I was amazed. He seemed to have no hard feelings whatsoever about Daphne. Didn't say a word. It was four thirty when we got to our room.

I washed up and changed into O.D.'s and went to the PX and asked the tech behind the barred window for a box of three condoms.

For once I almost had to agree with Marrow about sergeants: always a razz. "Officers' dance last night, sir?" this tech said, with his enamel hanging out most agreeably, a first-class ad for some miracle ingredient. "Congrats." On the speedy work, he must have meant.

I wasn't a great hand at this particular transaction, and I could feel a blush start at the back of my skull and push out around my hairline, so that my face felt sheathed with blotting paper, but I'd picked up enough of wising to say, "They're a present for those bastards up at Wing, so the Situation won't get pregnant."

"Have a nice ride," the tech said. "Sir."

I drew a pass and caught the liberty run to Cambridge at, as they said, eighteen hundred hours—appropriate that day, because it had seemed at least that many from Sully's fracture of my peace in the morning until now, six o'clock, when with a snarl of poorly maintained gears our grown-toy R.A.F. bus took off into a haze-softened sunset. I had been in a strange fluctuating mood all day, even during Wing's interminable hoax, for I had felt as a firefly must, aglow and luminous at times, cold and dark between. In the periods when the coils were lit I had rehearsed Daphne as a presence: the swift rushes of eagerness to please in her expression as she sat and talked with the big ox, Braddock; her left hand trembling around her compact, as if holding a living bird; her sincerely hospitable face as it met its twin in the small round mirror, almost saying, "Oh, it's you! Delighted to see you, my dear." Above all her straight look into my eyes. Again and again. I had a sense of wonder at her subtle favoring of me, as if I had been given some least-expected honor—been made Mayor of Donkentown just because people trusted my phizz. Then the intervening chill. I wondered how much I had kidded myself about her election of me, for Daphne had, to be honest, made every man look as if he felt chosen. Maybe the reason Marrow wasn't sore today was that he thought *he* was in the driver's seat. My imbecility—not getting her address, her name, even. Had I been drunk? No good could come of my challenging Marrow in the very hearth and parlor of his conceit. What in the world was I doing on this bus?

The men in the bus were meanly silent, like released criminals, men pale from living in the shadow of prison walls, oppressed with a feeling of the immensity of the world, yet eager to be in it again, to prove themselves or get revenge. I heard them murmur, one to another, plans for their rehabilitation: Let's have a beer first, or, Why'n't we wait and see they got a movie house.

As for me, I was just going to walk around the streets looking for a face.

The square bus ran along at about twenty miles an hour with a whine of a hurtling Spitfire. I saw glimpses in the dusk of the East Anglian farmlands, gently breathing contours under a blanket of mist; then, as it darkened, the Gog-Magog Hills off to the right, two-hundred-foot bumps looming in that flat land like noble distant sierras. Then suddenly we were being dumped out on Trumpington Street.

I began with a semblance of system—by looking for bright lights, but there were none. My eyes were so wide open I saw nothing. Past a small church into a market square. Faces blank in the caverns of the night. Under a street lamp some students in idiotic truncated academic gowns, not even as long as their suit coats, with mortar caps under their arms. A sound of military boots against a wall. Bicycles, singly and in packs, dangerous as wild dogs.

Then I stood opposite the great gate of Trinity College, like a huge, upside-down, four-legged butcher's chopping block; what it really was I did not then know. An iron grille was locked. Indeed I had again and again at what must have been college gates an impression of being shut out.

I entered lobbies and restaurants and stared in corners; told headwaiters I was expecting someone. The Lion. The Bull. The Hoop. I had the honor to be thrown out of a gentlemen's club called, I was given to understand, The Pitt. Daphne had been Pitt's girl; I remembered, in a game of hidden treasures in a strange living room, a woman playing the piano very loudly when I got "warm," near the object of the quest but still unable to see it.

I squinted to make out, on plaques on the faces of houses on street corners, the names of streets, as if the deficiency of not having an address could be overcome by close concentration. Maid's Causeway. Petty Cury. Many. I scowled at the doors on Paradise Street, for surely . . .

On King's Parade I saw a middle-aged gentleman, with a face shut tight, jaw shadowy, looking like an F.B.I. man wearing a silk top hat, a cutaway, and striped pants, running headlong down the middle of the street in pursuit of three clearly drunken students in those crazy short gowns like black shoulder-wings, and I felt relief at the sight of their eccentricity. For me it was a consolation. We were all in this world together.

Long since I should have given up, but I see now that my desire to be near Daphne Whatshername was very, very great.

Like a gloomy voyeur I stared in rare un-blacked-out windows for a chance sight of her face. I seemed to hurry faster and faster the more absurd my search became. I saw none of the great sights of the ancient seat of learning, and late, once, in a disturbing open place, I cried out to ask a distant walking man where I was, and he shouted, Jesus College Cricket Ground.

I caught the Pike Rilling liberty bus at the Bull on Trumpington Street at eleven o'clock, twenty-three hundred hours—uncountable hours since I'd seen the girl who had said her name was Daphne. I slept hard in the bus, with my head fallen forward and, I guess, bouncing on the bus window; I had a stiff neck for a week. The station was on alert when I got there, for a mission the next morning, and Marrow was still up, and keyed up.

"I been looking all over for you," he said. "Where the hell you been?"

"Bike ride," I said.

"Where the hell you go, Cincinnati?"

"Just around," I said. "Stopped for a bottle of stout."

"Some bottle," he said. "You look bushed."

Buzz was really revved up. He said he'd been investigating "that dish of yours last night." I was too tired to give a whoop; he'd calmly surrendered her to me. Said to be a great piece. Lucky bastard. Something about some sort of tragedy—lost an R.A.F. fiancé, or some such, no one knew exactly what. Was known to have had several relationships, here and there, Pitt having been the last, but during each one was absolutely monogamous. "Boman,

you really hit it lucky if you can effect a tie-up there." Marrow was
actually glad for me—either that, or he was wiring up a booby trap.

2 /

  The next few days were a bad dream—exhausting activ-
ity and frustration. The morning after I went to Cambridge they
scrubbed a mission for the marshaling yards at Amiens; the morning after that we had wind, rain, and what the English newspapers
call bright intervals, and Colonel Whelan sent us up on a Group
practice mission, to tighten up our formation flying, but all we did
was dodge the intervals that weren't bright; the following day he'd
scheduled another practice mission, but someone slipped a cog,
and Sully didn't wake any of the fliers in time for the take-off, and
Whelan was infuriated and restricted all personnel to the base,
pending an investigation of what he deemed to be sabotage of his
will. The next day after that they sent us on a prolonged low-level
practice mission.

  That was the morning it came to me that maybe Marrow
knew Daphne's last name, or her telephone number, for he collected such things for their own sakes, and he could have found out
that night while I'd gone to the boys' room. Only I couldn't figure
out how to ask him without giving away too much.

  The practice mission had Marrow in a tizzy. He had connected two things: our being sent on a hedge-hopping practice
flight, and an order from Wing, that very morning, that all combat
crews were to be given new lectures on security, and he was convinced that they were planning to send us on sneak strikes against
heavily defended targets at zero altitude. He was furious. He said
Fortresses had been designed in every particular for extreme high-
altitude attacks; they weren't mosquitoes, they hadn't the maneu-
verability or stamina for grasscutting missions. It was true that
weather interfered with our usefulness high in the air, but . . .
how could a man tiptoe in hip boots?

  Marrow fumed away till we got in the air, then suddenly he
was transformed, because he saw what our low-lying thunder did

to the countryside. Flocks of sheep, herds of cattle, the myriad specks of barnyard fowl in their open runs—all were thrown into panic at our approach. Marrow's chest expanded. The calm smile of a powerful man spread on his face. The flight gave me curious new sensations, I must admit. When we went across woodlands, treetops whipped past my ears, it seemed, and looking out my side window I saw the intricate patterns of bare branches, like the ordered barbs, barbules, and barbicels of great feathers, and I saw a wagon in a stone-fenced yard, a car in a road, a clutch of thatched roofs like the backs of huddled badgers—all in instantaneous camera-shutter glimpses. That was what made the mission eerie for me: the flickering sensation, sizes and shapes confused in my bewildered eyes.

But for Marrow the thrill of power grew and grew, and finally he said, "You take her, Boman, I got to see this closer." He unstrapped himself and crawled down in the greenhouse and he plugged in on Brindt's interphone and began giving the crew a running account, as of a radio announcer, of the impact of our roaring threat on all living beings below. He cackled as he talked, the swift laugh of seeing pie thrown into faces. "Listen, you guys . . ." He told of a farm crew, spreading manure from a wagon, cringing, one or two running blindly nowhere, at the sound of our hundred engines. Then he almost killed himself laughing— "you should've *seen* this"—when the driver of a tractor threw a gear to halt his machine and tumbled off and sought shelter under his slender vehicle.

Out of nowhere, as I strained to stay in formation and maintain minimal altitude, I had a thought. I would ask Clint Haverstraw about Daphne's number.

Haverstraw, the math demon, had a trick system for remembering phone numbers, and during the phases, back at home, at first in fun and then for ready reference, Marrow had filed in Haverstraw's head several score, maybe a couple of hundred, telephone numbers of various women he claimed as his all over the United States; now the United Kingdom was also beginning to figure in the catalogue. Sometimes, to show Haverstraw off, Marrow would just give a first name.

"Margie."

"Which one?"

"That's right! S——, I forgot, there are three of 'em. The blonde."

"Denver. Decatur six, four four oh nine."

"You see?" Marrow would say, looking around at the audience. "The son of a bitch has a f——ing *machine* in his head. Too bad he can't put it to some good use. Like, say, navigating a ship."

The only number Haverstraw couldn't remember was that of his own best girl. Marrow had found that out somehow, and always announced it to the audience, and you'd just be thinking that this was a gag when Clint would blush.

I couldn't wait for the mission to be over. We flew north over soft heathery hills and turned back before we reached the Scottish border, lest, as Max said later, we bump into a stuffed cloud, up there where they had real hills. I was very busy flying and began to have cramps in the right cheek of my fanny. We finally got home, and of course Marrow came up and took the controls away from his idiot co-pilot to be in charge of the landing. That was all right with me. I was drenched with sweat.

They had an interrogation which was also a sort of critique, and on the way out I managed to catch Haverstraw for a minute. Clint wouldn't have seen Daphne, because he hadn't been to the dance; he was soldering the connections of a homemade radio receiver in his room that night. I asked him if Marrow had registered with him the number of a dame called Daphne from Cambridge.

Haverstraw said, "The Marrow Meat File is not open to unauthorized personnel."

Sometimes I have a hard time taking a joke, especially when it's on me. I didn't want to sound too eager, but I barked out like a kid who can't take a slash, "Cut the crap. I got to know."

Clint saw that he had me on the ropes. "I can't remember any of that stuff only when Marrow asks me. It's like he's got me hypnotized."

I was afraid that if I pushed any harder Clint would tell Marrow how riled up I was about someone named Daphne, so I dropped it.

3 /

We had eight days of maddening weather after that—not bad enough to keep us on the ground but not good enough to fly missions. The older hands, particularly those who had nearly completed their tours, began to get fidgety at having no mission scheduled and Marrow took us up a couple of times but really didn't drill us on anything; he just wanted to fly.

On the eighth of those mizzling days, the thirtieth of April— I have a good reason for remembering the date—a batch of replacements came in, and although we of *The Body* had only been on two missions, the sight of their faces in the club that evening made me realize how raw, how childish, we must have looked when we had first arrived.

After supper we were sitting around, and Marrow said to big Braddock, jerking his head toward a chilled clump of new officers, "What say we flak 'em up a bit?"

"Why don't we go over and do it to the new sergeant gunners? That's more fun."

"Let's warm up here," Marrow said.

So we drifted across the room, and Marrow began the hazing in the most natural way in the world, because of course the new boys began asking questions. They got onto the subject of friendly fighter escorts, and Marrow said, "Under eighteen thousand the Spit-5 with the clipped wingtips, that's a capable ship. It's given us a lot of support, wouldn't you say, Brad?"

"Sure," Braddock said, "and above twenty-four thousand the Spit-9 is a *very* good airplane—right?"

"Check," Marrow said. "But in between, the Messerschmidt, the 110, seems to be the ideal ship."

"Trouble is," Braddock said, "right in there is where we fly."

A few minutes later the Tannoy announced an alert, for the next day, and even I was strangely relieved at the announcement, but I noticed the new cheeks go pale, as my own must have when I had first heard the fateful, hollow, metallic voice from Out There. After the alert Benny Chong, going off to his sack, left the club door ajar, and right away Marrow called out, "Benny! Hey! Close

that f——ing door. You think you're coming back tomorrow or
something?"

Chong poked his head in, said, "Up yours, Marrow," and
slammed the door.

It got much worse. Braddock and Marrow fed each other horrors to frighten the new men with. The way that gunner (invented) looked with the top of his head blown off by a cannon
shell. What splashed here, and what splashed there. His lower lip
was untouched, he needed a shave, there was some cigarette paper
stuck on the lip; but his upper lip didn't exist, he was like the Invisible Man from there upwards. About the gunner's pal who had
to take the rag in there and wipe the brains off the inside of the
turret. Vivid details. I must say I went along with it, putting in my
oar now and then, wanting, I think, to share some corner of Marrow's feeling that nothing nasty could happen to him on this earth;
little did I dream that our game of that evening would come home
to roost on my sickened conscience weeks later, in July, when Kid
Lynch had his immature but dazzling brain removed by part of a
shell.

By that time Marrow and Braddock apparently considered
their malice warmed up, because they excused themselves and,
with me and a couple of others tagging along to feel safe, wandered over to the enlisted men's Nissen huts and rooted around
until they found the new boys; found, in fact, a youngster named
Willis Lamb, whose last name appealed to Marrow.

I laughed that night. In those days I thought my pilot could
do no wrong, and flakking-up was an honored institution, the
dividing of a new man's possessions against his likely death being
a macabre burlesque of the conviction men held that disaster
would strike not themselves but others. But memory has altered
my point of view, and I wonder why I laughed at the sight of Marrow, with his eyes bugging out exactly as they did at the height of
his stories about making love, an officer razzing an enlisted man,
using death as a big joke to frighten a boy who had not yet faced it
for the first time: Lamb on his hands and knees with Marrow leaning over him, Butcher Lamb who was to be Marrow's own radio
gunner, with his pathetic store of possessions scattered across the
floor, his shaving set, his penknife, his flashlight ("Say, that's a
pretty keen flashlight, where the hell did you buy that flash-

light?"), right down to a snapshot of his girl, a pale stick of a city
girl in a cheap organdy dress that was like a whirl of spun sugar in
an amusement-park eatery—Lamb's upturned face, streaming
sweat and agony, as Marrow triumphantly lifted the snapshot and
said, "Well, look at Little Bo Peep! Hot s——! Lamb, when you're
shot dead I'm going to go home and put the clamps to Bo Peep.
Mmm—*mmm*. I bet she's got a tight crotch. Look at this, fellas.
You think this girl even knows she *has* a c——?" I saw a momentary
flash of hatred, of what might have passed for courage, on Lamb's
face, then its fading away into incredulity and despair as Marrow
tore the snapshot into tiny pieces and threw them, like confetti,
over Lamb's head, and shouted amid the laughter all around,
"Lamb of God! You ready for the sacrifice?"

As we walked back to our hutment we suffered a reaction. It
was obvious that the Group badly needed replacements, yet at
dinner we'd heard some of the new officers talk of having spent
three months sitting around with nearly a thousand other trained
pilots in a replacement center in Tallahassee, unable to get orders
cut sending them to the E.T.O., unable even to get up in aircraft
long enough to make good on their flying pay. The new men had
said, too, that they were positive they hadn't had adequate training
for combat. One of us brought these squawks up as we walked
through tall woods toward our quarters, and Marrow stopped on
the path, raised a fist and shook it toward Pike Rilling Hall, and
through clenched teeth he uttered a cry of protest, frustration, and,
I think now, yearning for the very authority he hated: "The bastards! The mother-f——ing bastards!"

But when we got to our room Marrow said, "I'm famished.
Let's steal us some eggs."

So we organized a foray to the enlisted men's mess hall, where,
we'd learned, we could pull rank if we were caught, and while
Braddock and I covered, Marrow and Stebbins broke a small pane
in the mess-hall pantry door and let themselves in and put about a
dozen real eggs and some butter in a helmet shell, and we took
them back and scrambled four at a time in a pie tin on a hot plate,
and while we were eating the second batch with spoons out of the
common pan, Marrow, with his mouth full of hot eggs, said, "Oh
Boman, letter for you. F'got to tell you."

"Where?"

He pointed with his spoon at our desk. "Under some that stuff." He turned to Braddock. "Good eggs, huh? Better'n that f——ing powder. Wonder where they'll send us tomorrow."

I dug down in the chaos on the desk and finally found the letter. It was typed. Addressed to Captain Boman at the base. A promotion and no first name. English stamp. Cancellation dim; try under light. Date four days past. Locus of origin Cambridge.

"How long this been here?" I asked.

Buzz was chewing. He shrugged. "Day 'fore yesterday," he said, "two, three days, I forget. Brought it over for you."

I tore it open.

"Dear Captain," it said. "It occured to me that neither you nor your friend has my address. It is Abbey Road, 24. If you could ring up before six you could get me at the office, Cambridge 7342. Ask for Section B. If that should be impossible try Cambridge 1476 after hours, and if you catch my landlady, Mrs. Coffin, in a good humour, she might fetch me downstairs to speak with you. Better tell her you're a colonel to offset your being a Yank. She's a bit of a lady, if you please. Place used to be digs for University Students. She had an Indian prince once. I'd love to see you both. Do ring up, or write to: Yrs., Daphne Poole."

Before I felt really good I had three quick thoughts: Of course she knew my last name because that was all Marrow ever used; and, Nice straight note, no fake excuses for being forward, and only one serious defect—that word "both"; and, The rascal, hiding the letter on me for three days. The worst I could think of my pilot then was that he was a playful rascal.

Braddock looked at my face and said, "Rich aunt die?"

4 /

On the hardstand, next morning, just before we boarded *The Body*, Clint Haverstraw said he had something to tell us all. He looked pale and earnest.

Haverstraw was one flier who never had wanted to be a pilot.

He had elected navigation because he had a long head for numbers and patterns. The one thing he lacked was a sense of direction, and it appeared that navigation was unnatural work for him; the worse he was at it, the harder he tried. When, getting a fix with a sextant to keep in practice, he shot the sun, you had the feeling he left it thoroughly dead. He did most of his navigational figuring in his head, and though he seemed quiet, steady, efficient, he made dangerous mistakes, not of computation but of application; formation flying saved us. He was rather submissive, eager to do a good job, though he had told me once that the idea of dropping bombs and killing people was deeply disturbing to him. Somehow he tickled Marrow, who seemed his opposite pole, and when others teased Clint, Marrow rose, often angrily, to his defense. Haverstraw was inflexible; hated change of any kind. His enemy was not Nazi Germany but dirt, and he uttered the word "mud" as if there were some of it clinging to his palate about to trip by counter-weight the sluices of nausea. He would not have dreamed of going on a mission without carrying his good-luck charm—a British swagger stick.

"Spill it," Marrow said.

"You won't like it," Haverstraw said. "Maybe I better not."

"P—— or get off the pot," Marrow said.

"I've been doing some figuring," Haverstraw said. Then he said we'd had a sixteen-per-cent loss on the Bremen mission, "but let's say, to give ourselves the benefit of the doubt, that five per cent is more normal." His calculations indicated, he said, that if you took an attrition rate of five per cent and applied it to the remaining ships in the case of each successive mission, only two hundred seventy-seven out of each thousand planes would survive the standard tour, twenty-five missions.

"Great timing, Clint," I said. "Perfectly calculated to calm the troops just before battle."

But Marrow gently said, "Lay off him, Boman." Buzz turned to Haverstraw. "Thanks, son," he said. "I tell you something. I don't give a s—— if only ten are left out of a thousand, I'm going to be one of 'em." He stared us all down. He seemed a great man in those days.

As we emplaned through the belly hatch, I happened to follow Haverstraw aboard. He paused at the mouth of the hatch, grasped his swagger stick as if it were a wand, touched lightly once with its tip each of the four sides of the hatch opening, then leaning and twisting his torso he kissed the skin of *The Body* just to the right of the doorway. After that he went up into the ship.

They had given us St. Nazaire, another of the U-boat bases on the Bay of Biscay, and after Bremen we were nervous without yet knowing enough to understand why.

Getting a mission started—that was when Marrow was at his best in those early days, for the wait before the take-off was the bad time, with so much idleness. He kept us all busy; poured out a stream of chatter. "All right, Boman, watch that number three. Is number three coming up all right? . . . Watch the cowl flaps." Then taxiing: "How are we on the right? O.K. on the right?" because if a wheel went off the hardstand into the mud the whole mission could be loused up. And he had similar jogs for all the others, keeping them on their toes.

That was a rotten mission. There were low-flying clouds and spotty rain at the base. The —th Group, which was supposed to lead the strike, left the rendezvous ten minutes early, and our people had to fly with our throttles wide open twenty minutes to catch up. Five ships aborted.

Over the continent we flew through a clearing, and below it was surprisingly hazeless so early, and we had reached base altitude, and looking down I could see a spread of France, flat, farm-textured, the faraway greens night-washed and yellowy under the morning sun. I saw a river that must have hated the sea, so much did it writhe in its reluctance to reach the coast. And there were towns, like splotches of gray fungus, here and there on the carpet of Brittany. Views like this from the upper sky made me feel, even in danger, a kind of calm that came from considering myself an insect, or a unit of virus, for the activities of men—I imagined a Breton farmer playing a game with greasy cards at a tavern table, wine at his elbow, a fat brute with pink skin, bloated and selfish, oblivious to war, his bloodshot eyes flashing as he raised a winning card and slapped it down on the table and bellowed his triumph— were reduced to a microscopic scale, so that a whole city of such activities was no more than a stain on the earth, and a whole province of them was only a splash of cartographer's green. It was comforting to think of men as being so small as to be invisible altogether, and therefore of the self, too, as utterly insignificant: a poor target.

Yes, I had begun to watch my own reactions very closely, and I decided that there was not, in the mission, the sensation of personal danger I'd experienced in more intimate conflict, such as boxing, which I'd doggedly done in school. Flying at high altitude in extreme cold, unnaturally masked and strapped, depending on oxygen for survival, forced to communicate with my fellow creatures mechanically (I had to remember to press the button at one end of my half-moon wheel to make myself heard), above all seeing the earth so far below as a mere pattern, a palette, gave me a feeling of severance, of being cut off, of being, as I was in an English pub, foreign. I think I'd have been very surprised at the connection with humanity that would have been involved if *The Body* had been hit; and I guess I would have reacted automatically with a further disconnection—by bailing out. I decided that the battle on the ground between missions was much more hazardous than combat itself, and up there I felt a kind of numbness, an alienation. All that changed later.

Over the target, where there was eight-tenths cloud, the enemy met us strongly. Prien exclaimed once on the interphone, with distinct accents of enjoyment, over the sight of one of our planes going down asmoke. I had an uneasy feeling about him, for he with his bad stomach seemed to regard combat as a kind of game.

Flak was heavy ("We could've let our wheels down," Handown said afterwards, "and taxied on the stuff"), and just before the bombing run there was an incoherent bit of jabbering on the interphone from Bragnani, but soon Farr broke in on CALL, saying, "Don't pay no attention to him."

Those two. The crew of a Fort was supposed to be a big happy family, its members all willing to die for each other. Our crew was not that. We had individualists and cliques aboard our ship, and lots of bickering and hard feeling, even when we were in danger. Another thing. According to the poop you got in the movies, all enlisted men were supposed to have hearts of gold, and all officers were supposed to be f——ups. I couldn't see it that way. A sergeant waist gunner was the trouble-maker on our ship. Farr. For my

money he single-handedly justified Marrow's insane war on sergeants. Farr and Bragnani, the two waist gunners, were willing to
die for each other, so they said. They claimed they had made a pact
that if one had to go the other would, too, and I believe Bragnani
would have followed Farr, all right, into the jaws of a lion; the
other way round, I'm not so sure. At any rate, those two were
surely allied against the rest of us; I still remembered the practice
flight when I'd stumbled into the waist compartment with those
flare pistols aimed down my throat.

Farr was aggressive, always known as an irascible and difficult
character, and consequently he was our lowest ranker, tech-three;
he'd been demoted twice for brawling. Bragnani was not so much
his friend as simply fastened to him, imitating every moment Farr's
loud gripes. As Haverstraw's enemy was dirt, Farr's was the U.S.
Army. "You'd think they'd give us some consideration. All this
bull s— they put out! They never had it so good. I'll be f—ed
if I'll brown my nose for those bastards."

On the bombing run Farr called in a claim that he'd shot
down a German fighter. Regulations required that such claims
should be reported at once to the pilot and be logged by the navigator. "I got one," Farr shouted. "I got me a ME-109."

"You lying bastard," Marrow said. "You never did. You made
it up."

Farr and Marrow ranted on the interphone until I shut them
up.

The Group's bombing was frightful. Visibility was poor, but
it was good enough to see that most of our bombs fell short, into
the sea. Going home the lead group turned north over Brest before the briefed point, and our formation had to take such a sharp
turn that it went to pieces. We became scattered in a cloudy sky.
The weather worsened, and Haverstraw had no idea where we
were, and our ships landed separately at R.A.F. airdromes all over
Southern England—at Warmwell, Potreath, Predannack, Exeter,
Portland Bill—but Marrow took us right through a front and, flying low with a chart in his lap, got us home to our own base; only
one other ship made it.

Upon landing we learned that our radio gunner, a timid,
conscientious boy named Kowalski, had frozen his hands over the
target. At altitude that day the temperature had been forty-five

degrees below zero, and in such cold as that, ninety seconds' exposure is enough to freeze a man's hands into solid blocks. The boy had been too afraid of a bawling out to report his condition; he just whimpered, when we found him in the radio room, doubled over. His gun had jammed; the electrically heated gloves we'd been issued were all right to push a throttle or turn a turret crank, but they were too cumbersome for clearing a gun, and the poor sucker had tried to work too long with naked hands.

Marrow was gentle with Kowalski, who was, as Marrow said, "one of my boys."

At the interrogation Farr pushed his claim of having shot down a German, but Marrow obdurately suppressed it.

Farr was pale with anger, and unexpectedly he turned his rage, as soon as we were dismissed, on his pal Bragnani. Farr declared that before the bomb run—when we'd heard that burbling on the interphone—Brag had panicked and had wanted to bail out. Farr said he'd restrained him by force.

Marrow promptly made a joke of it. "What you doing, Brag, testing your death pact with Jughead?"

Bragnani was absolutely enslaved to Farr from that time onward.

We were all depressed after that mission. Gross-Error Brindt was so hacked about the bad bombing that he began to say that the whole heavy-bombing campaign was a farce, and that the Allies were losing the war. Marrow valiantly teased us, to keep us game. But when Marrow learned that Kowalski had serious frostbite and would have to be grounded indefinitely, Marrow himself became morose. "The stuff those sergeants get away with," he said.

After supper a stand-down was announced for the following day, and I called Daphne, and, though she did not sound particularly excited to hear my voice, she agreed to meet me at noon, at the Bull.

"Will your friend come, too, Captain?"

"Marrow? He's all tied up tomorrow. By the way, I'm only a lieutenant. Leftenant to you."

"Couldn't matter less," she said.

5 /

The next day was the second of May, and the sun arrived
in a brand-new sky as cheerful and strident as a milkman. I waited
for Marrow to leave the hutment before I got slicked up, and afterwards I went to the PX and drew hospitality rations—one of the
parcels of G.I. goodies with which we were allowed to spread
among our English cousins the ill-will arising from gratitude. I
hopped a liberty bus at ten, and driving across the base in the glorious morning we passed first a rectangular place where workmen
were laying down four tennis courts, and then the five plowed acres
of the station's agricultural project, the dream and stubborn fixa-
tion of a patriotic major from Ohio in Group Headquarters who
wanted us all to eat good American golden-bantam corn in summertime, if it would only grow in this lousy rainy swamp of a country. I felt completely engulfed by the life of the Group, and I was
sharply struck by the intermittency of my war: high hell at noon,
a warm familiar sack at midnight; briefing at three in the morning,
tennis-anyone at three in the afternoon. One day the sight of poor
Kowalski's dead-looking hands; the next the sight of Daphne's
delicate fingers lighting a cigarette. Braddock had gone on one
raid in his dress uniform under a flying suit so he wouldn't be late
for a date in London that night. My war was only in the air. I felt,
as a shudder, my luck that I was not a foot soldier forced to sleep
on the ground night after night, never able to get clean, my
Daphne an impossible fantasy; my luck that at this moment I
could deny with all my heart the existence of danger. I had only
one idea: to go to bed with a girl I liked.

There she was, before I knew it, in the dusky lobby, in a
printed cotton dress with a sweater over her arm.

"How come you got the afternoon off?" I asked.

"My dear auntie"—a very broad *a*—"in Bury St. Edmunds is
ill."

I laughed with her, and a question went lickety-split through
my mind: If she'd lie for me, would she lie to me? Then I held the
parcel out to her.

"Oooh!" she said. "Snacks?"

I nodded.

"Then we must picnic." Her delight was unaffected and sincere. "We'll go out along the river."

"You ought to save that junk," I said. "We can eat somewhere fancy. I'm loaded." I put a hand in my pants pocket and jingled the bulky half-crowns and florins and pennies there. I guess I was playing the rich American to the hilt, and I got my come-uppance.

"Why save?" she said. "To feast alone?"

She flooded me with a sense of the importance of that single day—a feeling I was to get often from Daphne. Sometimes she would speak freely of the past, but she seemed to prefer the present. Talk of the future made her secretive, taciturn, gloomy.

We went on foot through a soft noontime across Christ's Piece and Midsummer Common to a raised footpath along the Cam, opposite a row of boathouses, and soon we were in a countryside of lanes, coming down to the river, that Constable might have painted, where firethorn and viburnums had spread out their linens, and cattle broke the greenness, and the shade was bluish close at hand. Daphne was evidently elated at the way I stared at her. I could think of nothing except touching her, and though her body walked sedately on the riverside path, her mind moved like the feet of a child playing hopscotch. I couldn't follow what she was saying; she didn't seem to care.

We came to a meadow full of daisies, and I spread my tunic for Daphne, and we opened a can of I forget what and tasted it. "Should have brought some beer," I said. We couldn't eat.

For some crazy reason I talked about Janet, my so-called fiancée. "She's on the chubby side," I said, "and she's got a very long tongue, she can touch the end of her nose with her tongue. Also, double-jointed thumbs." I told Daphne that Janet had been the most—what should I say?—libidinous girl, judging by appearances, in Donkentown, and I got the habit of going around with her, even after I found out that appearances could be deceptive, and if there hadn't been a war I might have gone ahead and married her.

"Did you love her?" Daphne asked.

"With an adolescent tomcat love," I said. Janet and I were at loggerheads from the start, though, because I wanted her to be Ingrid Bergman, and she wanted to be Virginia Woolf, and we were both stuck with her being Janet Spenser. She was a tease. She'd lead you on, and then, whammo! Put it on the basis that

That Was Sacred To Marriage. I kept coming back for more and never could figure out why we argued so bitterly—whether Vivien Leigh made a good Scarlett O'Hara, and whether a third term for F. D. R. was a good idea, and whether the British pavilion at the New York World's Fair was stuffy. I mean, we really fought. I recalled one time with her at a Robin Hood Dell concert while I was at Penn, when we shouted at each other all through one of those Stokowski transcriptions of Bach; around us the shushes were louder than the music.

"I'm finished with her," I said. "When I got over here she wrote me two letters in two weeks, and the second accused me of being unfaithful to her—when, hell's bells, I hadn't had a chance to figure out the best way to walk through the mud from our hutment to the officers' mess—and then she quit writing. Haven't heard another word. You know what I think? I think she's come as close as she can to being unfaithful to *me*. I was sore for a while, but to hell with her."

The marvelous warm sun made me drowsy.

"You look ninety years old," Daphne said. "Here. Put your head here." She patted her lap.

I gladly took her suggestion, and I slept like a baby for two solid hours.

I awakened grumpy, perhaps somewhat humiliated that I had put Daphne' patience to such a severe test on our first outing— bored her with Janet and then folded on her. She was tranquil; she waited out my bad humor. "Big deal for you today," I said. "Bet you wish you were back in Section B." But she wasn't going to indulge my self-pity, and she silently stood up and brushed off her dress, and then, with the first tiny pain in my chest in her honor, I recalled the feel of her thigh under my cheek. "Where's the fire?" I said.

When we started back, however, I felt refreshed. We struck out across country through tawny green fields and into a shadowy woodland, along a tiny path, and, with a last stab of my bad mood, I thought: How come Daphne knows about this path? How many guys has she led along it? So quickly, so subtly had she taken possession of me by making me feel possessive of her.

As we walked along, with the sunlight drawing a fragrance of renewal out of the damp earth, I remembered a vivid mood I had

had just before I had fallen asleep with my cheek on Daphne's
leg, the back of my head pressing against her ungirdled abdomen
—a mood of restlessness and dissatisfaction with myself, for I had
thought of a few of the many things I'd left unfinished back in
Donkentown, of the books I'd planned to read some day, the arti-
facts I'd intended to make. Next time. There'd never be a next
time. If I lived, I'd be older, different. "We must come back to our
meadow some time," I said.

"Love to," Daphne said. "It's wizard out here, isn't it?"

"I'll bring a couple beers next time." But I knew we'd probably never return, and if we did, we'd be different: we wouldn't be
total strangers, anyway, trying by random words and apparently
casual touch to find the other's innermost secrets.

We dined at the University Arms on the dull fare of English
austerity: whatever it was, it was breaded and cooked as if cooking
were a type of punishment. And we asked about each other in a
rather challenging way, almost saying: What's the matter with
you? There was something here about being foreign to each other,
our ideas at variance and our goals for life, though unexplored,
probably far apart. But on my side there seemed to be more: I
wanted to know why Daphne had preferred me to Marrow, yet I
could not ask, and I wondered whether, now that she knew me,
she really did, or would, and I had begun to doubt my intention of
taking her to bed. Of all this I said not a word. I see now that perhaps we were both steeling ourselves to unnatural and immodest
animal haste, for I suppose we both could see that no matter how
strong my doubts, I would surely try to go to bed with her before
the evening was over. I guess I assumed that my risking my life as
an aviator gave me the right to do that.

This certainty produced a curious perversity in me. I did not
try to be as attractive as possible; to the contrary, I ran myself
down.

I told her I'd been a boxer at Penn, had become Eastern in-
tercollegiate runner-up in the one-hundred-thirty-eight-pound class.
I told her I'd hated it; I'd stayed with it, I guessed, in order to
prove something to Janet and to myself about a man of my small
stature—although I'd always done all I could to avoid being a typical cocky shorty. I'd never hit anyone hard enough to knock him
out, never really roughed it up, partly, I suppose, because I'd used

to play the piano, and I was concerned about what my mother had always called my "piano hands," and I was also worried about my ugly nose, whose shape I wanted no worse than it already was, but also because I didn't enjoy hurting people, and I'd come to see that to be a good boxer one really had to enjoy dealing out pain. I stressed to her that I had always been a runner-up; a co-pilot.

Daphne asked me what had been my field of interest in college.

I kept right on depreciating myself; said my sole interest had been dean's-list marks, which I'd achieved by writing long essays in such a scrawly, semi-legible hand that the instructors had thought there must be *something* hidden in that underbrush. "History. I was hot for everything remote. Want to hear an example of my examination prose style? 'The Merovingian dynasty, ruling iron-fisted over the Franks, helped Actius stem the barbarian wave at the battle of Mauriac, on the Catalaunian fields, the Frankish *foederati* under Meroveus gnashing in the forefront of the fray.' "

"Gracious," Daphne said.

"That's me," I said.

I even went to the trouble of dragging Marrow into the conversation. "Funny guy," I said. "He talks about new pilots being rookies and he's only been on three missions himself."

Daphne, I was discovering, was tactful in a painfully feminine way: She took a position only after finding out exactly what yours was. Her answers often took the form of questions. "Is he a good flier?" she asked.

"The best," I sourly said, and dropped the subject, lest it become interesting.

After dinner she asked me, with a direct look in my eyes, if I wanted to go with her to her room.

The answer to the question was obvious, but I had to say, "How does your landlady feel about your having visitors?" I couldn't even say what I meant but had to use a sardonic euphemism: visitors.

"Mrs. Coffin? As I told you in my note," Daphne said, playing upon my churlishness with an absolute innocence of expression and tone, "she takes a dim view of Yanks."

"You make the traffic sound pretty heavy," I said.

"Not really," she said, and she put it directly—but there was a sadness in her eyes as she spoke. Pitt?

What a heel I felt! I was gratuitously giving a hard time to this girl whom I barely knew, almost calling her names—for what reason? Maybe to justify my having gone to the PX to buy those condoms before I had even learned where she lived.

6/

The first thing Daphne did when we reached her room —Mrs. Coffin may have heard my heavy shoes on the stairs, but she didn't make herself known—was to close the door and shoot the bolt. She sat down with the oddest expression before a mirror on a tiny single-drawered dressing table she had, for her face seemed to say, "Look at me! Did you ever see such a clever girl?" She seemed uncommonly pleased with herself.

Then that expression passed, and she began brushing her hair, and sitting on the edge of the bed I was struck again by her obvious liking of herself. It was almost as if she were sneaking hungry looks at herself while she pulled the brush through her hair.

The packet of hospitality rations was on the edge of her table, and she began taking the things out, one by one, and when she came to a bottle of hard candies she behaved like a child. She jumped up and brought it to me and asked me to open it, and while I made a show of being strong, she jiggled impatiently in front of me. She popped a sourball in her mouth, and, speaking thickly, asked me if I wanted her to tell me a secret. She was like a kitten. She sat on the opposite side of the bed from me, pulled her legs up, threw her shoes on the floor. I said, sure, I'd like to know all about her. This secret was an embarrassing tale, told with the too-big candy in her mouth, about Major Silg, who had showed his appreciation for her at an earlier dance on the base in a distinctly unorthodox way. "You're the only person I've ever told," she said. "Swear you won't repeat it to anyone." I solemnly swore, and a week later I heard the same story from Stebbins at the bar of the officers' club. The bottom almost fell out of my stomach when I heard Steb begin to describe Silg's pathetic technique of attack; then I realized that Stebbins might have had the account from Pitt, and I felt better.

I asked Daphne about Pitt, and it was obvious that she had overestimated him. But she said, perhaps as a comfort to me, "He wasn't really right for me."

During this time I was torn, for Daphne's face, as she talked, was suffused with a pinkish warmth, and I was drawn toward it with a painful yearning; but at the same time I was more and more impressed with her air of child-like innocence, and I had a queer feeling that I must not take advantage of her.

It was a foregone conclusion that my desire, the deep, lonely hunger of a death-risking man for the life-giving act, would triumph over my scruples, which were dissolving. In the back of my mind, no doubt, as a goad, was the thought of what Marrow would be doing while I sat there talking.

Somehow, at any rate, I decided to compromise, to experiment—to see if I could kiss her a bit and then opt what to do. I thought I was leaving myself a free choice!

As my desire grew stronger and I came closer and closer to touching her, I began to feel a need to be attractive and I began to experience powerful and painfully sweet emotions, akin to those of my adolescent years, and suddenly I was talking about those years. "In the eighth grade I was a good boy, I was Class Monitor, and that meant I had an important job—clapping the erasers at the end of the day." The clouds of fragrant dust, the hoarfrost on my sweater. I told Daphne about Miss Davis, who wore short sleeves and had fascinating ambushes of hair up them. In Assembly we sang under the direction of a Czech refugee, and I recalled my brilliant tenor swipe, "in the mo-o-o-orning," in Do Ye Ken John Peel? I took great interest in Marion Swienkoski, a tall girl at the next desk, who was said to be fast. No luck; I was unable to bring myself to speak to her. I described basketball knee pads to Daphne, and I told her how embarrassed I had been about the shape of my hands, which were stubby; I used to try to spread my fingers on my own thigh in a sophisticated, relaxed manner. The steel legs of my desk in class were like those of an old-fashioned Singer Sewing Machine; I wished for a treadle.

Civitas, civitatis, civitate, civitatem, civitate. Was that right? I remembered, walking home, Mr. Watkins' cherry tree completely covered with cheesecloth to keep the birds out. The workbench in my room was cluttered with strips of cardboard, ready to be assembled into a model, let's say, of Melvin Vaniman's peculiar triplane. Already hanging by threads from the ceiling were the Wrights' primitive kite, the *Spirit of St. Louis*, the *Winnie Mae*, Bellanca's *Columbia*, a Gee Bee Sport Racer. . . .

I shifted my weight, to quite a clanking and squeaking of the brass-framed bed, and I put my cheek against hers. She did not draw away; to the contrary, she moved as if slowly melting. This soft, yielding acquiescence, on top of her many other signs of acceptance of me, stirred an overpowering flood of feeling in me, and I took her in my arms.

7 /

I was eased yet unfulfilled. Never in my young life had I experienced anything like what this extraordinary girl had given me, yet I was far more aware of what she had withheld. There had been no resistance, no difficulties. What I had seen of her delight in being admired, her pleasure at being hungrily watched by many men at the dance, had had its counterpart in something that had made her, here in her yellow-walled room, seem readily conquered. I felt I had been treated to the easy surrender of very much. This was not a cheaply used girl. Yet instead of feeling like a lion, arrogant, boastful, and exultant, I felt, instead, somehow embarrassed and locked out. She had sweetly given in, but she had yielded only her shell, not her self, for I sensed that she still wanted to be fought for and truly conquered, and that she still awaited her defeat at my wooing hands in joyful agitation. This had not been what she wanted. It had not been what I wanted, either. I had great obstacles to overcome before I would have access to the enormous treasures I now knew were deeply secreted in Daphne.

Her underclothing was shabby and frequently mended. As

we dressed I handled some of it, passing it to her, and she gave me
the look of the poor, called pride, which is hard to distinguish from
resentment.

Yet she spoke with a generous voice. "Leftenant Boman,"
she said, with a comical look in her eyes, when we were half
dressed, "don't you think it's time you told me your first name?"

"Charles," I said. "Some people call me Bo."

"Bo," she said, cocking her head to one side as if listening
with a thoughtful ear. "Yes, I like that. Bo." Then she took me in
her arms and pulled me to her. "My dear Bo," she feelingly said.
I was as gentle as I could be. I saw that I had much work to do, to
fathom the surely marvelous depths of Daphne.

8 /

We were checking over the plane after a practice flight,
and Marrow told Red Black that he might pass as a mechanic but
that he looked like a chimneysweep—couldn't he neaten up? His
whole ground crew, Buzz said, was filthy.

Black then had a temper tantrum, shouting at Marrow that
the mechanics had been issued exactly two suits of coveralls apiece,
and that the return of their last batch of laundry had now been delayed for over a week; he strode off, quite audibly calling Captain
Marrow a f——ing Captain Bligh.

Marrow said to me, "This is on those bastardly desk pilots up
at Wing." Wing had long since become our favorite target for
gripes. "Come on, Boman, let's get our bikes and go on up there
to Wing right now and blast 'em about this." Sergeants in clean
clothes were bad enough.

We rode out through the Wing gate to Pike Rilling Hall.
Wing Headquarters was in a placid Georgian house set in a formal
park designed (Lynch told me much later) by André Lenôtre.
From wide parterres the vistas extended down avenues cut
through woodlands of towering beeches, and at the end of the
principal one, running toward the eastward, there was a Temple
of Love sheltering a marble figure of Aphrodite. "Great climate to

be bare-ass in all year round." In one of the reception rooms of the house, where Marrow and I were kept waiting for half an hour, there was an early eighteenth-century print of the house, and out the window we saw that certain trees in the print were still living—notably one linden, which, after two hundred years, had become a noble giant overvaulting one whole end of the house. Lynch observed, when I later spoke to him about the great tree, that the house was now occupied by men whose country was younger than the tree.

Marrow, of course, had asked to see the General, and it goes without saying that we saw, instead, his aide, a Major Hunert, who was notorious for riding to hunt foxes in a pink coat with a local pack. He led us through the Wing Operations Room—the Bubu Factory, as it was known to us fliers—a high-windowed parlor with a huge celotex sheeting over one wall, on which there was a vast 1:500,000 situation map of most of Europe, under talc, splotched with red measles representing flak areas, decorated with toy airplanes showing where the Hun fighters were based, webbed with lines and circles marking the locations of radar channels and splasher beacons, and dew-dropped with bright-headed pushpins. There were blackboards and desks with WACs at them, and Marrow's eyes rolled in lightning flirtations.

Major Hunert sat us down, and he was polite to us, in the way a man of the world is polite to waiters, and he got rid of us quickly, and nothing ever happened about the laundry. But something happened in Marrow.

On our way back to the base, as we rode near the Temple of Love, Marrow stopped, dismounted, examined the alley of enormous beeches that lined the vista, and, after a brief calculation, said, "You know, Boman, I bet a Fort could fly up this split in the woods. You could fly lower than the treetops—straight at those windows up there. Bet you something else, too. If that Major Hunert was standing in the window, he'd really p—— in his pants."

9 /

  We met after Daphne's office hours in the lobby of the Bull on Trumpington Street. It was pouring outside. The morning—it was Wednesday, the fifth of May—had broken cold and disagreeable. A huge truckload of mail had arrived at the base; we had been starved for mail for three weeks, and it turned out that this whole shipment was a month old and had been dispatched by mistake to the Twelfth Air Force in North Africa. Situation normal: all f——ed up. No letter from Janet. I was actually glad. I had taken off for Cambridge on the afternoon liberty bus, carrying with me some candy bars I had saved from a scrubbing and a mission we'd had in preceding days. I handed Daphne the candy, and she kissed me on the cheek, to thank me, and said, "How you Yanks must eat!"

  I said, "No, listen! We have a guy named Prien in our ship, our tail gunner, he gets gas on his stomach, you ought to hear him bitch about the food they sling us." Monotony. Powdered eggs. Grease and starch. Pancakes just before take-off—in the face of the law of gravity. Beans and cabbage just before an evening alert—a bellyache and morale all shot. I told her Prien's whole song and dance. "I want milk. I need milk." Filthy mess halls. KPs shoving the food off spatulas with dirty thumbs, black fingernails. What a way to start off a date with a girl!

  "You poor dear," Daphne said, as if Prien's complaints had been my own, seeming to know exactly what had made me talk that way, seeming to take such talk for granted. "I'm going to fix you a high tea in my room, but we'll have to get some buns. Do you have some of that famous money?"

  "Cash is my middle name," I said.

  We went shopping. She had an umbrella. She scolded me for not wearing a raincoat.

  The first thing she did in her room, again, was to lock the door.

  "Why do you lock up?" I asked. "Snoopers? Mrs. Thingumbob check up on you?"

  "No," she said, and she shrugged. "I guess I just like secrets."

Her room was our secret place; the rain tapped at the window. Everything was different from the last time. We wanted to please each other, and I felt happy, and I wanted Daphne to know that. She brewed some tea that would have flown a Fort, and she put out some cakes, and we talked about our childhoods.

She had had diphtheria, she told me, when she was four or five. She remembered that she was supposed to be taken to the hospital, her father had been summoned from his office to carry her there, but he was delayed, and he didn't come and didn't come. He was a civil servant of some minor kind, she said, a versatile man, humorous, kindly, and well read, but not born or educated a gentleman; he'd come of working-class people in the Midlands, so despite his evident talents there had been a ceiling to his career. This had not, however, by Daphne's account, embittered him, but had turned him to a life of the mind, and to his children. Anyway, the day she fell sick, it got later and later, and her mother was upset, and finally her father came—and why was he late? Because he had been to Regent Street, to a shop much above his budget, and he had bought her a nightgown, and a bed jacket, and a comb, for her visit away from home.

"He sounds like a kind man," I said.

She told me he was dead. She said she remembered being led by his hand to art galleries; she spoke of her vivid response, when she was about thirteen, to Bouchers and Fragonards in the Wallace Collection, and she spoke of the "burning Turner sunsets" that her father loved in the Tate.

"I'd like to see those," I said. "Anything to do with the sky."

"I'll take you one day," she said, as if an understanding had been reached between us that we would have a great deal of time together.

I tried to tell her about the sunrise we'd seen flying out on the Antwerp raid the day before—a clear, lemon-yellow sky ahead, and behind us the dim blue of the part of the heavens still in the earth's shadow, and far below us an upside-down sky—a vast sheet of cirrocumulus with its tidy mackerel pattern seen from above.

"I like to look at the sea," she said, and she told me about a childhood trip to the beaches of Devon.

"I love the sky," I said. "I remember a mackerel sky, when I was maybe twelve, as if it were yesterday, out of my window in

Donkentown." I remembered it so vividly! There was a foretaste
of dry days—a few sweeping mare's tails off to the northwest. They
made me think of Apollo; I thought he must have had huge horses,
and I began to daydream, looking out the window, about chariot
races, and I was a driver, and I hooked the wheel of the copper-
sheathed chariot of the Hun villain, on a skidding turn, and his
wheel came off ten feet before the torches of the finish line, and I
looked up at the Emperor, and the crowd was roaring, and overhead—I saw it so clearly in my memory!—overhead, above the
Circus Maximus, there was a mackerel sky, tinged with the first
pink undertouches of the end of the day.

"Did you ever have cambric tea?" Daphne asked me.

"No, what's that?"

"It's really only hot milk and water and sugar with the least
suggestion of tea. . . ." Daphne pictured to me a tiny summer-
house in a tiny garden, and something about her brother, who was
meticulous, had a model railway outdoors, the L.M.S., a perfect
replica. . . .

But I was not listening to her too carefully, for I was thinking
of what I could tell her next to impress her with my sensitivity, my
kindness, my warmth, the ideality of my parents, my high regard
for everything fine. Daphne was trying to impress me in the same
way, I guess, and probably she was not really listening to me, either. But strangely enough, each of us, so concerned with our own
excellent qualities, came through that conversation to appreciate
each other more than before, even though we took in little of what
was said.

This feeling of self-love, the first step toward the love of someone else, was a source of inner strength for me, and I wanted to
let Daphne know that ever since I had been in this room with her
the last time, I had felt stronger, more sufficient to my tasks. I told
her that, thanks to having been with her, I'd been, ever since, a
friend to all mankind. I told her we'd lost our radioman, Kowalski,
to frostbite, and that I'd gone to call on him in sick quarters, and
I'd cheered him up a lot.

Now, through my exultation in my own goodness, I was paying a tribute to Daphne, so what I was saying was partly about her,
and she therefore had begun to listen attentively to me, with her

head a little on one side and her eyes looking at me with profound understanding and approval.

I was quite off-hand about a raid we'd flown to Antwerp the day before. It was a funny war, one joke after another. Our new radioman, Lamb, on his first mission, had begun by talking volubly over the interphone, but later we hadn't heard a word from him, and he was supposed to be firing a gun on a sliding bracket mount in a slot back of the top turret, so Handown had gone back in the radio room and had found the guy sound asleep. Thought he'd passed out but he was just taking a nap! I laughed, and Daphne laughed, too.

I even grew magnanimous about Marrow. "He's amazing," I said; "flies by intuition." An FW-190 had dive-bombed us, air to air, from about four thousand feet above us, and Buzz had waited to the very last moment, and then . . .

"I'll bring him along the next time I come to see you." I was so dazzled with myself that I'd lost my mind.

"All right," she said.

The hours fled from our happiness, and the time came to leave. "I don't know," I said, "you've sort of given me a whole new slant on things." I kissed her once, and that was all.

On the liberty bus going back to the base, I looked at the faces of our fliers, and I thought, What decent men! How fortunate I am to be one of them!

10 /

On Saturday, May eighth, I called Daphne and arranged to meet her the next day for lunch in the town of Motford Sage, which was about halfway between Cambridge and Bartleck. She could take a bus there. I asked Marrow later if he wanted to go with me.

"Hey, neat," he said, like a kid. "We can ride bikes."

And that was what we did, though it was a sad, drizzling day.

Part of the time we rode side by side. Willows lined the highway
for a stretch. Buzz began talking about after the war. According to
Haverstraw's Law of Probabilities, there wasn't going to be much
chance of surviving the war for any of us, but Buzz, I guess, believed that the law couldn't be proven without some exceptions,
among which he planned to be one of the most prominent. He
said, "Jesus, I got a stack of back pay just rotting. It's rotting till it
stinks." It hurt his feelings to think he'd have to wait until after
the war to spend it. A few minutes later he said, "You know something? After this war they're going to retire me to stud. I'll popu-
late a whole new heavy-bombardment group for 'em." He pumped
some more and said, "No, I guess I want to be a padre after the
war. Those f——ing chaplains lead a nice life—not too much work,
just listening to a bunch of guys spilling their guts about their
troubles, same as a bartender, you know? Only a padre can sit
down while he listens and a bartender can't. And then he picks
out some hymns and thinks up a sermon and maybe cleans up
five bucks marrying somebody: 'We are gathered together, breth-
ren and sistern, to unite this man and this woman in holy matri-
mony. . . . Will the fellows from the glue factory please take the
back pews, near the windows? . . .' Jesus Christ, Boman, now,
you know, that's a *good* life. That's for me."

We met Daphne in time for lunch, or maybe it was tiffin, at
the Old Abbott Inn in Motford Sage, and I watched her operate
with Marrow over breaded veal and brussels sprouts and boiled
potatoes.

It seemed to me that Daphne was one of those women who
keep a close eye on themselves, who think hard about why they do
things, and so have a powerful apparatus for understanding other
people's actions and motives. Daphne appeared to have Marrow
absolutely taped. It was as if his inner mind and feelings were her
own. She gave a striking impression of warmth and sympathy toward him, because of this capacity of hers.

She knew, right off the bat, that the only proper subject of
conversation with William Siddlecoff Marrow was William Siddlecoff Marrow. He laid it on with a trowel.

She got Marrow going on the thrill of flying. "Why," he said,
"it's like nothing can stop you. Sometimes I just want to yell up
there. You see," he said, approaching a serious face close to Daph-

ne's, "that whole machine is part of you. You're the most powerful creature that ever was."

Daphne seemed to shrink a tiny bit, in deference to the might of which Buzz spoke. This was undoubtedly what gratified him the most.

"What about death?" she asked in a small voice.

"Phooey!" Marrow scornfully said. "Do you know the biggest discipline problem among pilots?—I mean pilots that are *men*. It's they can't resist thumbing their noses at death. They take chances that would turn your hair white. . . ." And Buzz showed that he was angry with death. He spoke of death as "that bastard in the sky" and "that God-damn sergeant."

"You know what I'd like to do?" he ferociously said at one point. "I'd like to kill death."

He banged the table, and the ladle jumped in the soup tureen.

Marrow was twenty-six—a strange age at which to have given death so very much thought.

When we had finished the main course Daphne said to Marrow, "Tell me about your life."

"My life?" Buzz said. "Hell, I've flown thirty-one hundred hours and never cracked up a plane."

"No," Daphne said. "Start at the beginning."

"Oh, Christ!" Buzz said.

But Daphne looked at him with that air of close concentration of hers.

Marrow lit a cigar.

11 /

"O.K., I'm twenty-six years old," he said. "I was born in Holand, Nebraska, and was raised up there. It's in the corn country sixty-four miles from Omaha and fifty-six from Columbus, between the Elkhorn, Loup, and Platte Rivers. Population nine hundred and three. They have sidewalks but nobody uses 'em.

"Right away I'll say my old man was my hero. He did a little of everything and not much of anything—real estate, and a bit of insurance such as there is in a hick town like Holand, and he had the Chevvy agency for the county for a while. He wanted me to have all the opportunities he missed. His name was Frank, and he was a man's man. He's dead now. Sometimes I suspect maybe he was a blowhard, but I loved the old son of a bitch.

"I'll never forget the first night I stayed out all night. Me and some other guys took some girls over to Columbus, and you know, one thing led to another, nothing much in a crowd like that, only all of a sudden the sun was coming up. It was the Fourth of July on a Saturday—or had been when we started out. I got home at nine thirty Sunday morning, and I knew the old man was going to get after me with the hammer and tongs. I had a story made up, but I didn't bank on it to help me much. When I went in the house I didn't see anyone, so I went in the dining room, and there was the old man, eating breakfast. 'Why, son,' he said. 'I didn't know you were up yet. What are you doing up so early Sunday morning? Sit down,' he said, 'have some breakfast.' So I did. I thought I'd split a gut from not laughing.

"I went two years to Creighton University in Omaha. I was going to take premedical. I wanted to be an obstetrician. I don't know, women just naturally fascinate me, and"—Buzz turned an ego-maniacal grin on Daphne—"and vice versa. And sister, I mean vice.

"The first woman I ever went to bed with, I was thirteen years old, and she was so old she had a daughter ten. I don't know what pleasure she got out of having my little body on top of her, I swear I don't. But she made me do it. Afterwards she was ashamed and made me promise not to tell anyone. Well, by the time I got to be a sophomore at Creighton, her daughter was seventeen and I was going on for twenty. That girl was stacked, I mean, she had talent. Vacation time, I noticed whenever I used to call on the daughter, her mama would go right upstairs and leave us alone. One night I said to Dottie, "Let's go to the movies over at Columbus.' Columbus was an hour's drive, and our town was strict—you know?—so when a fellow wanted to take a girl to Columbus, the girl needed notice, she had to ask permission, and you always had to double-date. So Dottie said she'd have to ask Mama, and I said, 'It'll be all right,' and she said, 'Why, Bill'—I was called Bill in those days—'I couldn't go all the way to Columbus alone with you, without I even asked Mama.' So she went over to the stairs and shouted, 'Mama!'

" 'Yes, dear.'

" 'Can I go to the movies in Columbus tonight?'

" 'Who with, dear?'

" 'Bill Marrow.'

" 'That'll be perfectly all right. Yes, dear. You go right ahead now with Billy.'

"We drove over to Columbus and I took her to the movies, and one way and another I kept her out real late. I went to see her the very next night, and Mama raised no objection to me taking her to Omaha. So that second night Dottie said to me, 'You know, Bill,' she said, 'I don't get this. Mama won't let me go out with anyone else alone, and two nights in a row! And with everyone else she gives me a definite time to be home, and when I come in, she asks me: what did I do? and was I a good girl? But last night she didn't even call me in her room, and when I went in there she just rolled over and made out she was half asleep, she only groaned like. I don't get the picture.'

"So I said, 'Maybe she just trusts me, Dottie.'

"And Dottie said, 'That's a hot one.'

"And I said, 'Yeah, it is.'

"Junior year I transferred to Georgetown, in Washington, D.C. Christ's sake, I just had to break away and get to the Eastern seaboard. I arrived in Washington with a portable radio and a brand-new set of golf clubs; I must've thought I was joining a God-damn country club. I soon found out.

"My roommate was Maxwell Gorse Ervin. We called him Plankton, he was so little, he was littler than you are, Boman. He was the hundred-and-fifteen-pound wrestler on the team, and now he's wrestling the controls of one of those huge PBYs, those flying barges they have in the Navy, you know? He's a lot smaller than you are, Boman, and those planes, Jesus, they're huge. I have to laugh when I think of him flying a PBY. Almost as silly as you flying a Fort, Boman.

"The first time I ever flew, I tell you, it was so much better than going to bed with Dottie's mama—or anyone else. It was really keen. It was one day Plank and me went out to look around

at Anacostia, and while we were looking the planes over we asked
if we could hop a ride. And one of the fellows said, 'Sure.' It was
an old Navy O2U he took us up in. We just flew around Anacostia.
God's teeth, I couldn't wait to get another ride.

"Then, vacation time, Plank said to me, 'Thug,' he said,
that's what he called me for a while, he said, 'The hell with the
train, let's go over to Bolling Field and catch a lift in a plane.' So
I said I was game, and we did, and after that we both wanted to
be fliers.

"I lasted out that one year, then I flunked out. That place
wore me to the bone. End of that year I weighed a hundred and
forty-eight pounds. At the present time I weigh a hundred eighty-
six. So you can see. At the present time, by the way, I wear size
nine shoes and a size seven and a half hat. Did you ever hear of
such small feet going with such a big head? It's the girls that gave
me a swelled head.

"I wasted two years working in a grain dealer's office in
Omaha. I never did anything except what they told me to do, not
a God-damn thing more. I was like a God-damn sergeant. All I
could think about was learning how to fly or else getting in there
with some girl. But I didn't do anything about the flying—and the
other: hell, those girls were so easy it turned your stomach.

"Then I got this letter from Plank, he was in Worcester,
Mass., and he said he was taking flying lessons, so I packed a suitcase and went out there and got a job, and me and Plank learned
at the same time from this old guy that was a boozer from way
back. The reason I'm such a good flier, he was drunk all the time,
and you could say I was obliged to solo the first time I ever
went up.

"Seriously, though, I was a natural. My reflexes are fast.
When a doc hits under my kneecap with that little rubber hammer to test my reflexes, that doc has got to be a well co-ordinated
man to duck my foot, I kick like a God-damn bullfrog—know
what I mean?

"I couldn't afford a plane, so I just bummed rides whenever I
could. I built up pretty good hours that way. Then I finally got a
job testing for Mildress—I lied like a Eyetalian hoor about how
many hours I'd had, and they liked the way I handled a plane, so
they put me to work. They'd broke a test pilot's neck two weeks

before, so it was in their minds that they wanted me more than I wanted them.

"It took me exactly twelve minutes to test a plane, they made these stodgy little trainers—remember, Boman? Twelve flat, to get up, give it a slow roll, a snap left, a snap right, and a dive. Those dives were my meat! I used to give the *hoi polloi* a thrill, believe me.

"Then the time came when you could be blind as a mole in the ground and still see there was going to be a war, so I got myself lined up to pretend I had to learn to fly, and from Spanner Field on it was one long rat race. You know that, Boman.

"That's about it, except I failed to mention the women in my life, only don't think I forgot 'em. I never forget 'em for a minute. I'll *never* forget one, I called her the Filly from Philly, she came to deliver an album of records, wanted to make me a present of this album—Dwight Fiske; remember Dwight Fiske, Boman?—and she stayed seventy-two hours. The Girl Who Came to Dinner.

"I don't know my secret, me and my ugly pan, unless maybe if you treat a hoor like a lady she'll do anything for you, and you treat a lady like a hoor she'll either do anything for you or haul off and bop you one, which is a time-saver in the long run.

"No, seriously, I'm just nice to 'em. I make an effort. I remember when I was working at Mildress, I used to make a point of diving right down over the houses of each one of my best girls daily. To let them know I was thinking about 'em.

"Some people say I talk too much. That gets me real sore, because I'm just making an effort. Once a girl in Denver, she'd heard I was a blowhard and she came up and she said, 'Are you this famous Guff Marrow?' I didn't talk for two days. Man, that struck a nerve.

"I didn't get my name of Buzz until I was at Spanner Air Base, getting my so-called flight instruction when I was already a hell of a flier. In my bunch of cadets, we had two Smiths, two Days, and two Turners, and no less than ten guys named Bill, which was always getting everybody screwed up on exactly who they meant, so they just doled out a whole new bunch of names. They looked at me and said I was going to be Buzz. So I'm Buzz.

"Let's see, what else?

"Oh: cars. I've had a slew of cars. The only thing that used to pass me out home was the Streamliner. I clocked it at a hundred and five near Grand Isle, once. My last car, you know, I left it in the parking lot at Bennett the day we flew over here. The key was in it and everything. I just drove up and got out and went on board the plane. It was a second-hand Olds convertible, only cost me two hundred and thirty bucks. Who knows, John Q. Public may be honest after all, the damn thing may even be there when I get back. But if it's not, hell, I'll just figure I lost it in a crap game. I've lost more'n that at one sitting. But God damn it, I *am* sore about leaving my electric razor in the car. It was Haverstraw's fault, the son of a bitch. I told him to put it in the back, in my suitcase. He just left it loose. I'd a lot sooner lose my car than that razor. I have a very tough beard. Have to shave at least twice a day to be presentable.

"And, let's see. Wherever I go, I always carry two fifty-dollar bills. I call it my mad money. Case I get in any kind of trouble.

"Well, you asked for the story of my life."

Buzz folded his arms on the table and leaned on them, and stuck out his jaw at Daphne. He looked pleased with himself.

"But what about the war?" she said, using again the very small voice of someone intimidated by such masculine vitality as his.

"Never had it so good," he snapped out.

"What do you mean?" she asked.

"I like to fly," he said. "I like the work we're doing."

"Work?"

"Listen," he said, with flashing eyes, "Boman here and I belong to the most destructive group of men in the history of the world. That's our work."

Daphne looked at me questioningly, as if to ask whether I associated myself with these statements, and I believe I gave my head the slightest negative shake. Her look, then, of only a moment's duration, dissolved me altogether. I had from that instant onward no question in my mind that Daphne really did prefer me to Marrow, and that I was quite lost to her.

I had an odd, uncomfortable feeling about my pilot. For the first time, I sensed a serious lack in him, and, also for the first time, with Daphne, I was conscious of a gap of nationalities. I felt apologetic about my American colleague. I determined to explain to

Daphne, at a later meeting, that . . . But what would I explain?
There was something wanting in Marrow's education. He was un-
cultured, crude. . . . No, that was hardly it. . . . Ours was a
people who liked what money could buy; we were blunt, open,
aggressive. . . . No . . .

But I did not need to explain, because already Daphne understood far better than I myself did about Buzz Marrow.

12 /

Dunk Farmer, the tech-three bartender in the officers'
club, was trying to worm his way onto Apollo Holdreth's crew.

A number of us were loafing in the club, playing acey-deucy
and shove ha'penny, or just standing at the bar and throwing the
bull. It was May twelfth, and by then we had gone more than a
week without a mission, for chilly, cheerless, damp weather had
kept the Fortresses on the ground, and the combat crews, particularly those that had nearly completed their tours, were increasingly
nervous and bored. Many of the men were drinking, and Marrow
and I were at the bar having Scotches; neither of us was the least
bit tight. I was still oppressed by the shadow of doubt about Marrow that had come over me the previous Sunday, when we had
lunched with Daphne.

You could tell who was considered the hottest pilot in the
Group at any time by watching which man Dunk was trying to do
a snow job on. Dunk was a Florida swamp cracker who in peacetime had been a shouting sort—a carnival barker, a honky-tonk
singer, a small-time auctioneer. Night after night, in the club, he
proclaimed, in his rapid, penetrating, assertive voice, a crude fa-
talism that went down well with the fliers. "I figure I'm a goin' to
die, see, but I don' reckon it's goin' to be till my number's up. I
don' give a damn what happens, like I might be in a Flyin' Fortress, or in a boat, see, and it crash, and if it ain' my time, hell, it
cain't kill me. Might to cripple me, but it cain't kill me, not if my
number ain' up."

It was Dunk's everlasting complaint that he couldn't seem to

get sprung from bar duty to combat; he couldn't seem to talk anyone into taking him on as a gunner.

"Hell, I ben pullin' treggers ever since I was knee-high to a
rabbit tick," he was saying to Holdreth. "I can shoot real nice."

"All right, Dunk," Holdreth said. "Tell you what. If my tail
gunner gets shot up, I'll take you on."

"Gee, Major, that's the nuts," Dunk said. His voice was delighted but his face was curiously crestfallen.

"What makes you want to fly with him?" Marrow asked
Dunk, jerking his head in Holdreth's direction. Holdreth turned
his face quickly toward Marrow and saw that Marrow was grinning
at him. "He don't fly a Fort," Marrow said. "He flies a f——ing
windbag."

Holdreth could have made a fight out of that crack, but he
chose to turn away.

Marrow had been like that for several days—edgy, provocative. But there was always a grin balanced on the edge, and it
was hard to tell how serious he really was.

Doc Randall, our Flight Surgeon, came slouching up to the
bar for the first of his invariable pair of nightcaps. Doc was a big
man, who carried himself with a stoop, sagging as he walked and
never standing up straight, as if he thought it wouldn't be polite
to be too big. He had a free-flowing mustache and a number of
warts and moles, and the lines running down by his mouth were
deep, and his brown eyes, under thick brows, were like a judge's
pardon. He had huge hands on thin arms, and his gestures were
demonstrations of the law of centrifugal force, for once his hands
got moving they swung right out to the limit. It was not a bad
idea to stand beyond his reach, when talking to Doc, so as not to
be clouted by uncontrolled flying objects with fingers on them.
Doc mumbled, especially when on the border of being tight, and
this made him seem undogmatic, which we fliers liked in a flight
surgeon. It was a basic rule of Air Force life that officers of field
rank, desk warriors, chaplains, and flight surgeons should be
closely watched for signs of cowardice, effeminacy, hypocrisy, or
moral turpitude; Doc was free of all that. He was sturdy, masculine, aggressive, and he had an eagle eye for goof-offs.

Right now Dunk Farmer, as he poured the Doc a shot, apparently began to face the possibility that Apollo Holdreth's tail

gunner might in fact be killed. "Say, Doc," Dunk said. "I get a bitch of a pain in my chest when I breathe. Anything I can do about it?"

"Stop breathing, Dunk," Doc shortly said. "That'll relieve the pain."

Marrow barked out a laugh. Marrow, I have come to think, was afraid of Doc, and because Buzz was driven to show the world that he was afraid of no man or thing, he took a fierce line with Doc. "Listen, Doc," he said. "I'm horny. I get horny after we get all these stand-downs. Why don't you set up a nice clean hoor house for us fliers? I got to get me a girl—or else get up in the air."

Doc just stood there looking at Marrow. The placid friendliness in Doc's stare must have been profoundly upsetting to Marrow, who was itching for a fight.

"Flying's the same as saltpeter," Marrow said. "It kills the sex urge—right, Doc?—in any guy who's got a lot of it. If you bastards are going to keep me on the ground all the time, why don't you give me some relief?"

Doc gave Marrow an unmistakable brush-off. He turned to others at the bar and began discussing with them news that had come over B.B.C. earlier in the evening, of the Axis collapse in North Africa. Von Arnim, Rommel's successor, had been captured.

"Where's the relief in that?" Marrow truculently asked.

"My office hours begin at six a.m.," Doc firmly said to Marrow. "At sick quarters. You know where it is."

I saw Marrow blanch. I expected him to say that there was nothing the matter with *him*, he didn't need a God-damn psychiatrist; but he held his tongue. Buzz was silent, indeed, for half an hour, but he had a couple of snorts, and he was as tense as a racehorse in the starting chutes.

Doc finally left. No sooner had the door slammed on his exit than Marrow started a meaningless argument with Braddock. Buzz knocked over Brad's drink. They had a short tussle. Through some extraordinary alchemy, their first angry clinch turned into an embrace, and they wheeled on the rest of us, malevolent, leering, crafty. They became collaborators in stirring up violence; they played on the restlessness of the old hands. Calling for a celebration of the Axis defeat in North Africa, they fomented instead a

riot that had no joy in it. It was the worst brawl I had ever wit-
nessed—or rather, assisted. Marrow and Braddock began firing
glasses at the club stove. Dunk Farmer shouted for a halt, and he
was rewarded by being carried to the door and thrown out. Others joined the disorder—began tearing magazines to shreds, throwing darts at the ceiling. We overturned tables and broke up chairs
and smashed bottles of coke and soda, and we tore down the curtains at the windows. Braddock lit fires in three metal wastebaskets, and the smell of burning paint was acrid and strong. Marrow
got down a heavy-duty fire extinguisher with a long rubber nozzle
and made as if to fight fire by the issue of urine; he squirted the
walls and tables. There were fist-fights and sounds of splitting
wood and the crash of glass, and three men were carried to bed
with serious head injuries.

"I got my relief," Marrow said, as we were going to bed.

13 /

I couldn't seem to hold formation. I'd put on a lot of
manifold pressure, trying to catch up and pack in tight, then I'd
get afraid I was going to overshoot, and I'd chop it off and nearly
throw my turbos, and I'd practically lose an engine or two, and
I'd have to pour it on again. My feet felt frozen solid; they hurt
like the devil, but I was certainly not going to admit it. I remember, more than anything else, my feeling of helplessness.

When I had got up that morning, I had had a distinct impression that I must have been one of the fellows carried to bed with
a cracked head; my mouth had tasted like the inside of one of
those wastebaskets Braddock had fired. I had been so foggy that I
had put on a pair of badly shrunken wool socks, and long before
we had reached altitude the blood had stopped pumping to my
feet, and they had grown colder and colder.

As soon as we reached the enemy coast the German fighters
whom we called the Abbeville Kids, in yellow-nosed FW-190s, reacted against us, with attacks from ahead, split-assing right in front

of us at two hundred yards, or going on through the formation. I was nervous, and my feet were torturing me, and I flew badly. The target was the airplane factory of S.N.C.A. du Nord at Meaulte, not too deep in France, and somehow we got there and home again. My flying was atrocious, there was no doubt of it, and, hung as Marrow was, his was superb.

No sooner had we got down than Marrow started eating me out. It was the first time I had ever been the object of one of his verbal attacks. He said I flew according to poop. No imagination. Everything I did was in the book.

Gradually it got worse. "You aren't thinking about anything but yourself," he said, "and you know how that hurts everyone back of you in the formation. Other words, you're just flying along and any correction you make, it's just for yourself, you're not thinking it's got to be smooth and help the other jokers in the formation, doing it gradual—you know? You got to remember that whole formation out behind. You're going to start the whole God-damn thing accordioning."

The condescending tone in his voice crushed me—as if he were lecturing a flying cadet who still had his diapers on. I guess he was making good on his claim of being one of the super-destructive men of this world.

To me the most interesting part of all, looking back on it, was the extent to which I *allowed* him to be destructive. I took what he said to heart and fed his madness; my slipped morale let him see what he could do.

After the interrogation I rode out alone on my bike and lay on my back in a meadow of feed grass of some sort that was already two feet tall, so that all around me there was stockade of slender green shoots, tipped with the fuzz of half-formed seed scales, fencing me in from the sunny day.

What was the matter with me, anyway? Was it all because I was small?

My bad flying couldn't be just because I was short. I'd been over that plenty of times. Being short made a lot of people sorry for me, and others despised me, and others thought they had to take care of me when I wanted it least, and others kidded me to make themselves feel bigger—and I knew all these things, and I knew they had an effect on me. They put me on the defensive and made me try to show what I could do, on my own. But I wasn't going to let them make me cocky. I wasn't going to be a typical shorty—noisy and pushy, declaring myself all over the place.

With two minutes of his belittling talk, Marrow had set me right back to the refrain of my teens.

A breeze stirred the grass around me, and I began to study the swaying, juicy tubes, crisscrossing against an unusually crisp blue sky, and I forgot Marrow, and I thought of Daphne, and I was vividly conscious of being alive; intense gratitude fell on me, like a cool shower.

I remembered images from a certain day: the somber steel bascule railway bridge, near home, with its massive concrete counterweight on the far side of the river, and my dog, Lad, a more-or-less collie with a reddish tail curving up and forward over his back, the tail incessantly fanning; a perfect sky; a crazy towhee in the sweet birch in our yard, shouting, "Trick or treat! Trick or treat!" And my gentle father, who had never spanked me, looking at me with a pained expression, saying, "Son, this was supposed to be *your* job." He did the job himself, before my eyes, whatever it was.

Yes, I assumed on slightest provocation a disapproving attitude toward myself and readily took the blame for things that were not my fault. How shrewdly Marrow sensed this! And moved in. And, moving in, opened the way to crippling himself, because his appetite for destructiveness was insatiable, insatiable.

14 /

The others had gone, and we had been left behind. Buzz and I stood on the hardstand, looking at *The Body.*

Buzz made a show of being sore at his ship. "The bitch," he said. "The first time she stood me up. I feel like I caught some guy in bed with one of my girls."

It was May fourteenth. The Group had taken off on a mis-

sion for two big submarine-building yards at Kiel, Germania Werft
and Deutsche Werke, but we had been crossed off the list because
the previous evening our crew chief, Red Black, had found some
trouble in a turbo and had grounded *The Body*.

Black was up on a wing, opening up the cowling of the ailing
engine. Marrow approached, and he called up, "Sergeant Black!"

A screwdriver was put down on the wing with more energy
than was necessary, and a dark-haired, pale-faced head appeared
over the leading edge of the wing.

"Listen to me, Sergeant," Marrow said . . . and out came a
tirade, for Marrow could not stand frustration—least of all, frustration of his urge to fly.

Our crew chief was a strange bird. He was subject to lightning
changes of temper. Immediately after having been talking with us
on the hardstand, early any morning before a take-off, in an obviously jolly mood, beaming like a seraph and going off trolling
snatches from *I'm Dreaming of a White Christmas* or *Waltzing
Matilda* in a loud voice, off key, he could suddenly be heard to
have switched, with no apparent cause, to a high pitch of fury,
swearing blue flame like a blowtorch and banging tools down on
the skin of our poor ship. "And he's a bastard, too, a second
f——ing lieutenant of a bastard." Black was a small man in his
early thirties with a big pocked plow of a nose. Not at all a standardized G.I., he went around in coveralls but swung the upper
part off his shoulders and let the loose folds and sleeves hang
down from his belted waist, and his dead-white arms were always
streaked with black grease marks. I don't know why he was nicknamed Red, unless as a tribute to his temper. He was outwardly
servile toward all officers from the rank of first lieutenant upwards, but he seemed to consider second looeys like me some spe-
cies of schoolboy, to be hazed and gulled at every turn. Under his
fawning manners there lurked a tyrant. Let a corporal from the
motor pool make a false move on our dispersal point, and Red
would land on him like a hod full of mortar. "*You!* Where you
going? Get that p——pot of a jeep out from under that wing!" But
the other members of the ground crew swore by the chief, whose
meticulousness as a mechanic and whose worship of *The Body*
were unbounded. He was a dedicated workman—and this was
precisely the point on which Marrow attacked him.

Our lives depended on Black's carefulness, yet Marrow accused him, in vile, insulting terms, of being too cautious.

Black appeared to be in an agony of agreeableness as Marrow undermined his talent, his triple-checking cautiousness. Marrow said Red should have let the turbo go another day, so *The Body* would not have missed a mission; if we'd lost an engine—so what? Ships came home every day on three. Marrow made it out that Black's care was a kind of timidity, and that such timidity would lose us the war.

In the end Marrow made Black's finest quality as a mechanic seem traitorous.

15 /

We played in a pickup ball game with some ground-grippers while the mission was being flown, that day, and Marrow was ecstatic, again, about Haverstraw's throwing arm. Funny: that made me sore. I guessed I was as bright as Haverstraw, taking aptitudes for number concepts and for verbal concepts together. It was just that I wasn't a lousy *idiot savant*. Your mathematical nut (Haverstraw) would always be flashier than your all-round, socially adjusted, intelligent high achiever (Boman). And when Buzz found out that Haverstraw could remember his dames' phone numbers for him *and* peg a ball like Peewee Reese, he went all the way off his conker. Phooey on that.

Later that afternoon I felt low. I wanted to quit the whole show. I sat in our room, alone, and I could hear test-firing at the clay bank, and as I looked through the window at the meadow on the near side of the flight line, an English farmer crossed in the middle distance, plodding behind six Guernsey cows, oblivious, apparently, to the firing; he looked neither to right nor left but simply kept on walking with a heavy plowman's stride. I wanted to go to Daphne. My chest ached for Daphne.

16 /

At the interrogation after a mission we flew the next day, May fifteenth, we caught, as our interrogating officer, an apple-cheeked captain from Wing Headquarters, who wore an unconvincing mustache, more a plea than a declaration. This mother's boy got off on the wrong foot with us right away, by asking which mission this had been for us.

It was our sixth.

"Oh," he said, on a groaning note, which had the effect of dismissing us as beginners, and therefore unreliable. We had thought ourselves rather seasoned.

The interrogation was held in the briefing hut, into which a number of small tables had been moved. An interrogator sat at each table, with a stack of report forms before him, and he took on one crew at a time. When our turn came, we of *The Body* gathered around the pink-faced young captain's table, some sitting and some standing; we were still in flying gear, with our jackets unzipped, our flying helmets flopping on the backs of our heads, and several of us held white mugs of coffee.

Well, our child captain began giving us a hard time. It seemed that neither he nor any of the other interrogators, even our own from the Group, were too well satisfied with our day's work. They didn't quite believe we'd been where we said we'd been—or that we knew where that was.

By rights, the mission should have hiked our morale, because, having been briefed for some sub yards at Wilhelmshaven, our Group had led the mission out over the North Sea, and we hadn't climbed to altitude until twelve minutes before the target, so we had been comfortable and warm all that time, and not even on oxygen. The primary target, besides throwing up considerable flak, which Handown now called "iron cumulus," had been under ten-tenths cloud, so, with no briefed secondary target, we had wheeled full circle and had gone out to sea and had bombed what Colonel Whelan had taken to be the Helgoland Naval Base.

What made us think it was Helgoland?

Under pressure from the baby captain, Marrow grew ugly, and he began to jump his own crew.

First he piled into Haverstraw, of all people—teacher's pet; asked for his log of the mission right there at the interrogation table, to check it and prove we'd been to Helgoland, but it turned out from his record that Clint had had no idea whatsoever where we'd flown.

"I figured the Colonel knew what he was doing," Clint lamely said.

Marrow took off on Brains; really scored Clint for a mental defective.

Next it was Farr's turn. In the background of the anxious cross-examination, we could hear the Jughead muttering about Wing's having sent us to a target covered by solid cloud, without a secondary target, and so on; all in Farr's nastiest whine. Jughead's complaints about what he considered to be the futile and suicidal missions the bicycle generals had been devising for us were getting on our nerves. Farr, who talked so tough, was like a spoiled child. He made outrageous demands on all of us, and alternately exploded with dangerous rages and wheedled for sympathy, irritated us and charmed us, abused us and flattered us. He blew up over nothing like a child and saw reality with the clear eyes of a child. Indeed, his complaints were largely justified; he railed against conditions the rest of us were doing our best to ignore.

Marrow, in a white heat of defending himself against the baby-face, turned on Farr and told him to shut his big mouth before he, Marrow, pasted it shut.

Farr fell silent, but after the briefing he rounded up several of the crew and, in a barely audible murmur, said that Marrow was too weak to carry legitimate beefs to Wing.

It took our breath away to hear Marrow called a lily-liver, and Handown spoke for all of us when he told Farr he was only bellyaching because Marrow had shut him up. He reminded Farr that Marrow had in fact been to Wing to grouse about the enlisted men's laundry problem—and that was more than lots of other pilots had done.

17 /

It had been a very early mission, and we were all through by lunchtime, and we had just turned in for some luxurious afternoon sack time when a voice on the Tannoy ordered all combat crews to report to the tower in olive drab on the double, to be taken to the dispersals to stand review by some personages.

I had to wake Marrow up, and he was so mad he was speechless.

We got out there and stood around for an hour, and then a batch of about six Rolls-Royces and Bentleys whizzed by on the perimeter track, and we could see the procession stop a couple of stands down, at *Angel Tread,* Wheatley Bins' ship, for about ten minutes. Then it sped on and ducked in by the hangars and hurried past the Admin building and cut out the main gate.

When we got in, we were told we'd been visited by Their Undoubted Majesties, the King and Queen of England, together with their retinue of gentlemen-in-attendance and ladies-in-waiting, and, to add insult to this injury of cursoriness, Generals Eaker, Longfellow, Hansell, and several other unidentified U.S.A.A.F. officers of whom we hadn't seen hide nor hair in all those dangerous weeks.

Marrow reacted to this with a crazy fury that Their Royal Jackasses, as he called them, had stopped at *Angel Tread* rather than at *The Body.* He went on with an elaborate, carefully detailed, and quite devastating analysis of Wheatley Bins' flying technique. Buzz made a convincing argument that he was a far better flier than Bins. I think, in justice, that he was.

18 /

Through the dance Daphne sat at a table with me in a corner, wearing around her bare shoulders a scarf of pale, blue-gray, gauzy material, something I could have reached out of the cockpit and grabbed on the way to Helgoland that morning, and

with her eyes rather heavily made up, she looked as if she had
been weeping, though in fact she seemed happy in my company.
We talked about the King and Queen. I felt a peacefulness such
as I had never experienced before. I was attentive to her; she was
acknowledged to be my girl, and I did not have to worry about her
drifting off with some guy (Janet's trick: she used to get me hot as
a firecracker at a party and then disappear, just leave the party with
a total stranger), and I called fliers over to meet her and talk with
her. I danced with her now and then just to have my arm around
her; she was responsive, and I felt unhurried and extravagantly
alive.

Marrow hung around, but he was plastered. He kept singing,
What Shall We Do With a Drunken Pilot? The answer, in successive stanzas, was, "Put him in the nose of a Flying Fortress, so
earlye in the morning," and, "He will bomb the blind and pregnant . . . he will bomb their homes and churches . . . he will
bomb their turnip patches. . . ." Marrow had a cherubic expression as he sang these macabre lines, and Daphne and I laughed at
him too hard.

During one of the times when we were alone at the table I
said I'd heard she'd had some sort of tragedy—lost her first important man, supposed to be a Spit pilot, or something. I thought
I was being sympathetic; the illusion that Daph had been crying
was strong at that moment.

"Don't ask me about other men," Daphne said, and the way
she put it made her seem not self-pitying but instead inclined to
spare me pain. "Let's try . . ."

But impulsively she told me a little about the man. She called
him only Dugger; whether this was a last name or a nickname I
never asked. He had been a great R.A.F. bomber pilot who, she
said, couldn't get enough, and upon the completion of his regular
tour he had transferred to night fighters, and he had grown more
and more daring, or suicidal, until, it was said, he had led his entire squadron in pursuit of German bombers, in darkness, too
deep into Germany to return to their airdrome in England. Word
had come home through prison-camp escapees that Dugger himself had been killed. Then, with a somber expression, Daphne
said, "He was like a blood brother to your pilot."

"Marrow?"

"As like as two peas in a pod. In character, I mean."

I wasn't sure I relished that likeness, but Daphne stared at me with a sort of helplessness; she looked as if she were skidding and couldn't stop. "My father was killed in the Blitz," she said, "too."

"I'm sorry," I said, and I knew at once that that was a stupid response.

But Daphne went back to talking, half-heartedly, about Dugger, and then her voice drifted off, and she looked as if she had forgotten what she wanted to say. So I laid off the subject of other men, and she never came back to it until the day we went to Hampton Court.

Soon I forgot where I was. All experience, all purpose, and all meaning seemed to be encompassed in each moment's perceptions. An edge of Daphne's scarf against the white tablecloth, an ash tray with our crumpled cigarettes (Daphne's butts were short, frugal), my Scotch with a ring of shining soda bubbles around the glass at the surface, a sensitive trembling of Daphne's mouth at the beginning of a smile: I had the impression that each image was immensely important—that the enjoyment of life, which might end some early morning soon high in the sky, could not be more than a savoring of these glimpses. I had seen that Daphne always experienced every moment with deep and easily available emotion, and my own feelings were greatly heightened. I responded strongly to absurd trivialities. Our bar used plastic swizzle sticks embossed with the phrase, BUNDLES FOR BERLIN; some pilot's old man manufactured such things and had given us a trillion gross of them, though as yet we had by no means the capability of carrying anything as far as Berlin. I studied the shiny red globe on one end of such a stick, as if it were a marvel of nature, a salmon's egg or an immense dewdrop on a rose petal, and I experienced a kind of ecstasy; then I felt with my finger tips the sharp edges of the thing, and I took extraordinary pleasure in my sense of touch. I bent the stick. It broke. I felt intensely sad, as if I had snapped something of great value.

At about midnight there was a drumroll and up stood General Minott, himself, our Wing Commander, and in an unbecoming manner, almost groveling, he vindicated us for that morning's mission; acknowledged that strike photos showed that we had, in truth, hit the Helgoland base and had done damage to naval installations.

The din in the place was deafening; our joy—not at having hurt the enemy but at having bested Wing—was unbounded.

While the celebration of the announcement was still going on, Marrow showed up in the doorway, with a fierce grimace on his face that I didn't like, holding in his hand a lighted candle. "Hey, Braddock!" I heard him shout. "Get your ass over here."

When Brad joined him, Buzz climbed on his shoulders and rode pick-a-back out onto the cleared place that served as a dance floor. Daphne was convinced that he was going to set fire to the mess hall. I said he was a crazy goop but not that far gone. Waving the smoking taper and shouting incoherently, Buzz rode to the center of the floor and, with many a hitch of his balance on poor Braddock's shoulders, he wrote in smoke on the ceiling: TO HELL WITH HELLAGOLAND.

As the message unfolded, men standing with girls around him cheered him, and the cheers seemed to make him wildly happy.

As usual, some pilots from the —th Group had crashed our party, and Marrow got into an argument with one of them over which group had dropped its bombs more accurately that day, killed more Krauts, and Marrow proposed that they settle the argument with a bike race right there in the Senior Officers' Mess, so four or five guys ran out for bicycles, and others pushed tables around to make an oval track, and Marrow and Benny Chong were selected to compete for us.

As the desperate, aimless wildness of our men grew, with Marrow in the forefront of the restlessness, I found that I was becoming more and more embarrassed, in Daphne's presence, over the behavior of my companions. It was national pride again; it was because she was English. I felt sure an R.A.F. party would not have turned out like this. Australians would have been like this, yes, but not Englishmen. We were crazy frontiersmen.

"We don't know what we're fighting about," I said. "Our people haven't been hurt the way yours have."

I got talking with Daphne then about how badly prepared I'd been for war. I said I'd waded through translations of both *Mein Kampf* and *Das Kapital* but hadn't got wet while wading—was, in fact, poorly motivated for combat, though I should have been, perhaps, better than most. I had had at best a passive acceptance of my country's part in the conflict. I washed my hands of responsibility, saying that Grew and Hull should have been better aware of the true intentions of the Japanese, and should have avoided conflict by diplomatic means. I guess this was all college stuff; Janet stuff. I regarded war as a struggle between the haves and the have-nots, and I said, "You can't really blame the Japanese and Germans and Italians for wanting to live as well as we do." I brushed aside the notion of the Axis threat to our way of life, saying, "There's plenty that's not so hot about us." But even about "us" I was unclear, unsharp. I told Daphne that my father used to talk about the Depression; being at the time engrossed in geography (for there couldn't have been a sky without an earth), I thought of the Depression as some sort of geologic deformity, a lowered place in Pennsylvania, not exactly a valley but rather a kind of crease where there was unfamiliar misery and want. I was too young for it, and anyway, my father, being a doctor, escaped the worst of it, because sickness did not fall off along with jobs, and enough people could pay their bills so that my brother Jim and I always ate.

Daphne said she didn't think that wars were started on account of economics.

"That's what all the books say," I said.

She said something about men like her Dugger . . . but then the bike race began, and we lost that thread.

The four cyclists rode a couple of laps, and everyone was shouting, and Benny crashed (accidentally on purpose?) into the bar, and scores of glasses were broken. People began throwing glasses then, and Marrow got into a fist-fight with one of the crashers and wound up with a shiner and a bad cut on his knuckle which came, he later said, from breaking a front tooth of one of those uninvited wisers.

I suggested to Daphne that we get out of there. Outside it was a fine May night, and we found Daphne's bus and sat in it, holding hands. I had no thought of where our feelings would lead us. I was caught up in the widespread delusion that men who exposed themselves to death had no moral responsibility, and in my self-centered haze I felt that Daphne asked nothing of me except my

company, my good manners, my absorption in her, my strong
erotic desire for her. I would have sworn that I had never been so
happy, and that the same went for her.

19 /

We had an alert the following evening, and after it,
Marrow suggested that we ride our bikes out to say good night to
the ship.

He was still in his combative mood. We'd had a critique of
the Helgoland raid that morning, and Marrow had got into a
pointless squabble with Wheatley Bins, over a technical point—
how our intervalometers had been set for the bombing. It had
been obvious that Marrow was wrong and Bins right, but Buzz
had hung onto the quarrel with a tenacity that exposed his true
feeling about Bins. And as we rode out to *The Body* under a partly
cloudy night—it looked as if great uneven fields of stars had fallen
to the ground, leaving black holes where they had been—Marrow
railed in a monotone about a group in Bins' squadron that he
called "Bins' clique." But I could think only of Daphne—of the
pressure of her knee against mine under the table the night before.
I felt a joyous pain in my chest. . . .

The Body loomed, gray and dull, in the darkness of the blacked-
out base.

Marrow slapped the side of the fuselage. "Good night, baby,"
he said.

And I said, "Good night," too, but my message had some distance to fly in the night.

20 /

We were in the low squadron of the lead group, and
Braddock was flying the lead ship of the whole attack, with some
freshman general from Eighth Bomber Command riding along as

a tourist, and they were perhaps two hundred yards above us and ahead of us, the craft a glinting silver tube against a midday cat's-tail sky.

We were coming home from Lorient. It had been an early mission: up at two forty-five, briefing at three thirty. Since we had been to Lorient on our very first mission, we had felt a blasé detachment about the assignment, and indeed, the morning had seemed to go easily. After sunup the sky had been a pale semi-globe of sapphire, flawed only by a thin sheet of frosty cirrus over Europe. There had been no ground haze; no contrails had formed; the target had been visible from forty miles away. Enemy opposition had been relatively light and had concentrated on formations other than ours. The bombing had been fair. At the rally point Marrow had suddenly asked Haverstraw, in order to check up on Clint's alertness, what the bearing would have been to the secondary target. Haverstraw, apparently having thought his day's work virtually over, had been daydreaming and hadn't had the faintest idea how to answer, and now Marrow had just finished eating him out.

Braddock's ship was named *Bull Run*. Braddock was Marrow's good friend, but I scarcely knew him, except as a ton of prime meat, a big, tall, fat man, about whom I had heard it said that he was incredibly cool and steady in the air; his nervous system must have been primitive, like a whale's. I had not even stopped to think who else was in his ship besides the tourist: eight nobodies; to me, the plane was simply Braddock up there, *Bull Run*.

We were going along all right. We had flown through some of Handown's "iron cumulus" over the target, but none of our Group had been knocked down, and it was good, leaving the rally point, not to have any fighters around, and to have such a clear sky, with home and rest ahead, and we were all socked in close, a good formation, and nobody was saying a word on VHF about fighters, though the general, being new, was chattering a lot of nonsense. On the whole we were comfortable, with another mission, *The Body's* seventh, practically under our belts; it was really wonderful up in the sky streaking for England.

Then Marrow was pointing. Up there, Braddock's ship. And I thought, Look out, Brad, look out, look out, you're smoking, number two's smoking.

I could not take my eyes off the thin gray telltale of smoke, more than exhaust but less than peril as yet; it did not blow out. Someone came up on VHF to tell Braddock he was burning, and at that the whole Group was alert to his danger. Suddenly the smoke went black, and there were visible flames, pale against the sky, and it seemed to me that the ships of the formation edged in closer (it was a fact that Marrow pushed up the manifold pressure) to watch, like insects crowding a night light.

Braddock pushed over from his position above us and began a shallow power glide to try to blow the fire out, and just then Max Brindt shouted on our interphone, "Look out! What the f—— is that?"

What was it? What was it? Something had come off *Bull Run* and went flipping past us. I realized it was the little rear hatch door; the tail gunner must have kicked it out. No, it wouldn't be the tail gunner in the lead ship with a tourist aboard. It would be the co-pilot, because under the circumstances he would be back there flying tail-gunner observer, watching the formation and reporting everything up to the general, so the general could make a fool of himself with a full supply of information; it would have been myself back in that tail position if we had been leading the Wing. I had a moment's fantasy that it was I who had kicked out that small flipping plate; I was getting out. I remembered then with a shudder that Braddock's co-pilot was not I but Kozak, a pale fellow who never seemed to speak a word—an impression of white, white skin with a heavy black stubble of beard, a face immobile and silent. There came a leg, and another, and Kozak was squeezing out like a creature being born, and I almost shouted on the radio, "Look out, Kozy! Christ, there are over a hundred ships here, we're all coming at you."

Surely Kozak had thought of just that, or surely he would not have done what he did. He ripped his chute the moment he was out. He was too excited. His body, fresh from the speeding Fort, was going through the air at more than a hundred fifty miles per hour. I saw a flutter of shining nylon, flaglike at first, then what seemed to be a big loose bunch of feminine understuff, and we were all coming up at it—he'd been small before and now, with the breaking parachute, he seemed massive; he was too excited. Then the snap. Every bone in his body must have broken, he just—his

back—we were right close under him—when the chute filled, his
back arched and flapped like a ribbon snapping out in a wind; it
must have killed him on the instant, the way he—Kozy, he jumped
to save himself but he was dead, because of the speed we were all
going up there, and he didn't wait. He just snapped, mind and
body. What he thought would happen, with all those ships, he
must have thought someone would run into him, that was the way
I judged it, and he bailed out and did not hold his count, he must
have been afraid of all those props, because we were coming all
around him, and he was going to drift back through the formation, and he must have thought that if he could just get his parachute open right away, we'd all see him and could evade; but that
was the wrong idea in every respect.

I coolly thought: I'd be alive. If I'd been the tail-gunner observer in the lead ship, Kozy, I'd have dropped and dropped, a
delayed jump, clear down to those newly forming white fluffy
clouds on the edge of this high-pressure area of sparkling blue, a
long, long drop, more than fifteen thousand feet; way down. That's
what I'd have tried to do. Arms against the sides. Knees up . . .
But you're dead, Kozy, from trying too hard to be alive.

I had thought it was easy to get out, no problem, just get out
and wait and pull and float down; that's what I had thought.
Maybe it wasn't so easy. I had never let myself think about that.

Braddock's plane was quite far ahead and below, now, perhaps a thousand feet down, going very fast and pulling forward
and down and away, but the smoke was worse than ever and flames
were pouring back off the wing, not blowing out at all but fanning up, it seemed, glowing like coals in a camp stove blown on
with a deep breath.

Braddock started to climb. As he got halfway back up to our
height I noticed that Buzz had begun to climb in key with him,
and I looked out and saw that we were all climbing, we were all
flying formation behind and above Braddock's black plumes. We're
going up with you, Brad, don't worry, we're sticking with you. No,
not like that, we can't climb like that. Hey. Hey. Don't climb that
way. You're out of control, you're going right up to the top. What
an impressive sight!—a big Fort shooting straight up, ahead of us
in the sky. Your smoke. Such a clear day . . . No! No!
No!

He blew up. Right at the top, right in front of us, the whole thing. That smoke—why didn't you all jump?—that smoke—fire, it must have been your number-two engine and a wing tank and then everything. Two or three flashes . . . He blew up.

Buzz! Look out for all that crap!

Twenty, thirty tons of bits, we're going to fly right into the stuff. Look at it. Look at that big piece of metal. Head down, cover eyes, don't look. Nothing's happening, we're diving. It's past us.

Marrow, good work, Marrow.

What an explosion that was! I even heard it, I think I heard it, and that would be unusual at altitude, in all one's gear, and that far away; it made such a big thud I think I heard it in the cockpit.

Now it was quiet. A minute before everyone had been chattering on VHF, everybody making his big remark, we had been talking away and then everyone stopped. It was such an impressive sight. Now there wasn't a sound, and there were more than a hundred Forts around us, but not a word, they all had something to think about; no one was saying a word, not even an exclamation. Why didn't somebody speak? It was so quiet. I wished somebody would come up and talk. There. There it was. High squadron. "Well, form on me. We'd better take over and do something." There, that was better.

Junior Sailen called in. He hadn't heard anything, you understand. Only Buzz and I and Lamb in the radio room could hear the VHF, and Buzz had only pointed at Braddock. Just that one remark of Max's. Sailen cut in on interphone from the ball turret, down under the plane, asking, "Say, what was all that junk that went past us?"

Marrow answered. "Braddock," he said. "That was Braddock."

"Any chutes?" Junior said.

"Anybody see any chutes?" Marrow asked.

Max Brindt in the nose said, "One out of the tail. The guy ripped too soon."

"That was Kozak," I said. "That pale guy."

Then little Junior Sailen, down in the close cocoon in which he flew, said in a low voice, icy dead cold, "I knew it. I knew it. You can't get out of these God-damn crates."

It hit me. Nobody had got out. Not one. They all died. Kozak died. Braddock died. That general. Ten men dead. I had always thought you could get out of a Fort, it was so big. Plenty of hatches. But maybe you wouldn't get out. You'd just sit there and get killed. You couldn't escape.

I thought: I'm scared. Somebody's got to help me. Look at Marrow, maybe he'll help. Oh, Jesus, look at Buzz, he's smiling at me. He can see I'm scared. I see his eyes smiling behind his goggles to buck me up. He wants to tell me something, his eyes are bulging out as they do when he talks about getting a piece of tail, he's going to speak to me, he's pushing the interphone button on his wheel with his thumb, he's going to say something to all of us.

"It can't happen to this bucket, boys, not while I'm in it!"

21 /

I was in rough shape when I got to Cambridge.

We went to a pub and drank quite a lot, and to my amazement I blurted out, "Why do you love someone as short as I am?"

There had been no mention of love.

Daphne hung her head and said, "Everything's so mixed up." I understood that she was not really answering my question.

There was a woman at the next table, a pretty but hard-looking blonde, a working girl, waiting for a man, or hoping for one. She was getting drunk and angry. The owner of the pub cross-examined her about her expectations. Stridently she insisted that someone was coming to meet her, though she kept looking over toward the bar, alongside which a pair of young Americans, one in a leather flight jacket and the other in a crimson nylon basketball windbreaker with the nickname of his unit applied in cursive script across the back, were playing darts. The owner managed to hustle the girl out of the place, but not before she had drawn a great deal of attention to his inhospitality.

Stirred by the sight of the blonde's loneliness to an awareness of my good fortune in Daphne's company, I began to recite some sentimental verses: "I dreamed I stood in a valley of lovers," and "Wine comes in at the mouth," and "I whispered: I am too

young," and I was carried away on a flood of emotion, so that at
certain lines my voice caught in my throat because the words
seemed so valid for Daphne and for me. Her eyes had a way of
melting, her lids sagging down, when I came close to a truth about
her, and I was half choked when I spoke the phrase, ". . . cloud-
pale eyelids falling on dream-dimmed eyes. . . ."

Daphne had a curious trait. She felt things deeply, I knew,
and when she was moved her face would soften and grow pink,
full of warm, warm blood, and her eyelids would droop in that way,
and sometimes a hand would move spasmodically toward me, but
suddenly her mouth would say something that seemed to me quite
out of key: that seemed to me almost harsh. This time she abruptly
began to recite:

> ". . . Here, said she,
> Is your card, the drowned Phoenician Sailor.
> (Those are pearls that were his eyes. Look!)
> Here is Belladonna, the Lady of the Rocks . . ."

I suddenly felt cold and gloomy. The Channel! Each time we
went out, and each time we came back, I dreaded crossing England's moat: just to think of that choppy, frigid stripe of water gave
me a chill.

But one glance at Daphne's face relieved me, for she was
blandly looking at me, with a faint smile curling her lips. These
lines she had spoken were simply nice words she liked; she was not
trying to say anything, except perhaps that I had let my batteries
get overcharged. My verses and hers—there was the gulf between
us. Naïve sentiment; powerful irony. A nice clean-cut American
boy; a woman on the edge of a Europe in agony. But I insisted
on being serious in my own way. I reached out my hand and
touched Daphne's cheek, and with the slightest movement of her
head, pressing her cheek against my palm, she acceded to my seriousness and confirmed her surrender. "Dear, dear Bo," she said.

"My darling!" I said. It was the first time I had used that word,
the first time I had claimed her.

Daphne gave me her liquefied look, and her cursed little
mouth changed the subject. "Your pilot," she said, "has a wild
look in his eye."

For a moment, driven back from my intimacy with Daphne, I saw in memory the blinding burst that had been Braddock's plane that morning, and I said, "Remember, the other night, when Buzz was burning those words in the ceiling, the guy whose shoulders he was riding on?"

Daphne, obviously having sensed the intensity of my question, nodded and searched my eyes with hers.

"This morning . . ." I began, and then the bottle of my feelings broke, and I put my forehead down on the edge of the table and cried.

"Steady, steady," I heard Daphne say. In the midst of my dramatics I felt a startling sharp amusement that she had fallen back on a standard English response to a public show of emotion. Stiff upper lip. Must dress. Pip pip. I had to laugh. The realization that I was on the edge of hysteria quieted me at once, and I sat up. "Good man," Daphne said.

"What the hell's it all about?" I feelingly said. "Why do we do it?"

At that Daphne said, "I just try to get from day to day without too much fuss." As if to say: she was a girl, she had nothing to do with war except to endure it.

I had a feeling of utter helplessness, almost like what I had felt in the nose of the ship that time on our first raid, when Marrow had suddenly pushed over and I had hung weightlessly floating in mid-air along with some inanimate objects. I was being carried along toward death through a life over which I had no control.

I remembered experiencing at the dance the previous Saturday, if not happiness, at least an approach to it, through close attention to momentary impressions: seeing small things with a clear eye. I now tried to recapture that observant and receptive state, but all I saw this time was banality: a glass of warm and soapy stout; a half-eaten and anyway barely edible piece of cold kidney pie; the owner of the bar, savoring his triumph over the blonde, muttering out loud and flicking a dirty napkin at bits of lint and bread crumbs that seemed in his mind to be aging prostitutes trying to trump up trade on his decent premises. And even Daphne: her sleeve was shiny at its cuff; from an American point of view there was something shabby about her.

"Bo," she said. "Dear Bo. You don't like me very much just at this minute, do you?"

Startled at her perceptiveness, I said, "It's not you, Daph."

She took me to her room and sat me down on the edge of her bed and urged me to tell her about what had happened that morning, and I did. She made no attempt to comment, but I had a curious impression of a deep satisfaction she had from listening to me. What I said was less important to her than the fact of my saying it. I was spewing out bitterness, retching; she seemed profoundly happy. What a way to court a girl! Yet it was, I think, exactly appropriate to that place and time, and to her and to me. And, gradually, hearing me out with big reflective eyes, she instilled in me a feeling, not exactly of strength, but at least of resiliency; a hide in tanning grows flexible.

CHAPTER FIVE

THE RAID

1356–1404 hours

1 /

We crossed the Dutch islands at 51°35′N–03°40′E, at four minutes before two o'clock, flying at twenty-one thousand feet, and of course Marrow had taken back control of the ship before our penetration of the enemy zone. My rage at him, over what Clint had blurted to me of his lying tale of having mounted my Daphne, had ebbed away, but I was still aware of him, across from me, as a kind of adversary, along with the German, on this long day's flight which was now entering its dangerous phase.

Yes, Marrow was my enemy, just as surely as the Nazis were. One contest was a matter of life and death; the other, against Marrow, whose life was bound with mine to our common ship, was one of inner tensions, of all those personal values the survival or loss of which would make the rest of life, if life remained, worth or not worth living. For Daphne had shown me the truth about Marrow. He was a destroyer. He was in love with war. I could have no peace—the world could have none—if men like him were indulged in their passion.

Being now convinced that Marrow, whom the Group considered my closest friend, was in fact my most intimate enemy, I became alert for signs of vulnerability in him, and here, as we crossed over the huge islands of man-made land at the edge of Europe, I began thinking there had been indications all through

the morning of something which in many men would have seemed
to be strength but in Marrow could only have been weakness. I
mean caution. In a superb flier like Marrow a certain carefulness
was inbuilt and natural, and his indifference to inspections and
checks, during the period when he had become a hero and had
gotten his D.F.C., was abnormal for him; but an excess of caution in Marrow was bound to be a danger signal, and this morning he had been checking up on things too much.

Now, out of the blue, he came up on interphone to the engineer. "Listen, Handown," he said. "Did that son of a bitch Black
say anything to you about changing the hydraulic fluid?"

"Negative," Handown said.

"He was supposed to change it," Marrow said.

"Didn't say anything about it," Handown said.

"I forgot to ask him," Marrow said. "Meant to ask him."

"The pressure was O.K. this morning," I said. "I checked it in
the preflight. Both accumulators were O.K."

"It was O.K., huh?" Marrow said. "He was going to put new
fluid in."

I knew all about that kind of worrying. During the July Blitz,
when we had flown so many missions so close together, I had
done plenty of it. I used to begin at the beginning—wondered if
the designers had known what they were doing. I wondered if
they'd figured all the stresses correctly, if the wingloading was
right; and I'd heard somewhere that if you dived a Fort at more
than three hundred miles per hour the de-icing boots on the leading edge of the wing would begin to rise slightly, and then more
and more, and would begin to flap and then tear and then . . .
And when I'd finished with the designers, I'd wonder about the
people who put *The Body* together. Workers in a factory had meat
rationing and gas rationing to worry about, poor bastards, and after
dozens and dozens of planes, performing the same operation, they
could have gotten careless, wondering where their next sirloin was
coming from. I used to think there might have been an inspector
whose wife was having a baby the day he inspected *The Body*, and
he wasn't concentrating the way he ought to, and he missed a
whole seam that was supposed to have been riveted but hadn't.
Once, during the first Le Mans mission, the day Farr and Bragnani
had called me "teacher" because I had been so finicky about in-

spections, I actually went back in the plane, on some excuse or other, and began looking for places where the rivets weren't right. . . . Then, when I got through with the workers at the plant, I'd start in on the ground crew. There was *so* much they could go wrong on! Four motors, each with a million parts. A hydraulic system as complicated as the water-main system of Donkentown. A wiring system like that of a big building. Radios. Tires. Brakes. Cables. They *couldn't* check everything. What had they forgotten? What had they skipped? What had they got in the habit of skipping? If Red Black had worked twenty-four hours a day, he couldn't have begun to check *The Body*. I used to spend hours up there cataloguing the things he might have missed.

That obsessive concern for details of *The Body's* health was all very well for me, because I had been conscientious to begin with. That was my way. But when it began cropping up in Marrow, it was time to stop fussing about the plane and start watching him.

2 /
Ahead of us, now, the layer of cirrus that I had seen from over the Channel was building up, and its base at the edge of the cloud, which was perhaps ten miles away, was no higher than we. The formation therefore had to make one of two choices, neither good. The first was to trust that deep into Europe this was only a thin sheet of mackerel cloud, as it seemed at first to be, and so to rise above it; the risk in this alternative was that the cloud might thicken and tower too high for us, and that the whole formation might be forced to plunge into it and inevitably scatter—or that the target might be obscured. The second possibility was to abandon our briefed base altitudes, between twenty-three thousand and twenty-six thousand five hundred feet, and duck below the cloud mass; here the risks lay in our becoming sharply silhouetted targets against the clouds for flak and fighters, our providing the fighters with cover above our heads, and our possibly having to descend ever lower, to altitudes unsafe for our special sort of work.

I spoke of the cloud to Marrow on interphone, partly, I sup-

pose, to probe him, partly to seek reassurance. "How about that
cirrus ahead?"

"Keep your pants on," he said, giving me no comfort at all.

3 /

"Check in," said Prien from the tail, and he began to
count us off, and as he did I visualized our plane, and the men in
it, and this gave me comfort, for I worried about *The Body* and
loved her, not in Marrow's erotic way, but because she was familiar, and reliable, and her interior walls curved about me, cup-
ping me as I took life-giving nourishment from her oxygen tubes;
perhaps because I had entrusted my existence to her so many
times.

"One!"

"O.K.," Max said.

Max Brindt would be in the bombardier's seat in the very
nose, leaning forward in his tense way in the air, bathed in greenish light. Before him, source of that light, was a conical plexiglass
windshield with a lozenge-shaped panel in the middle of its
lower part, through which the concentrated sightings for bom-
bardment, the aim and point of our missions, were made. There
were also low windows in the plane's walls on both sides of Max.
Just now Max would be ready at the handle of a hand-held fifty-
caliber machine gun with a post-and-ring sight which was poked
out through a kind of nipple up near the center of the nose; in
action he might also have to jump to another gun farther back in
the left side of the nose. To Max's right, on the side wall, were his
oxygen regulator, suit-heater outlet, interphone jackbox, and
brackets to stow the nose gun. To his left were his instrument
panel and bomb controls: a round-knobbed handle which, along
with a switch, worked the bomb-bay doors; another handle, which
could either lock or salvo the bombs, or set them to be toggled out
at electrically controlled intervals; and a release switch, covered by
a protective guard, for this toggling. Fastened to the curving wall
above these controls was a goose-neck lamp that might have been

on an office desk in some peaceful place. The bombsight was still stowed, for freedom of action, back in the navigator's space.

The navigator's area was directly behind Max's at a somewhat lower level, but with no physical barrier between the two so-called compartments. Clint Haverstraw's province was lit by two pairs of windows in the sidewalls, by the navigator's astrodome overhead, and indirectly by the plexiglass nose. Clint's desk, with a dial of the radio compass recessed in its right side, stretched across the back of the bombardier's seat and ran to the right side wall; on the left was Max's passageway forward. Along the side wall to Clint's right were a bulbous driftmeter, a storage box for the bombsight, an aperiodic compass, and Clint's suit-heater and oxygen outlets. On his left, beyond the narrow passageway, were the radio compass and its control panel, Clint's map case, his interphone jackbox, and another oxygen regulator. Everything was neat as a pin; Clint had even installed a set of grip holders on the wall over his desk to hold a comb. Just now Clint was manning, doubtless with distaste, a fifty-caliber gun that poked out of a large covered window on the right side of the nose, at the forward end of his compartment. A corresponding gun on the left side was Max Brindt's alternative weapon.

Aft of the navigator's compartment was a section of the plane that was divided into two levels. The upper one was the pilots' cockpit, and to reach it, one had to climb up through a trapdoor between Buzz's seat and mine. The space of the lower level, which was only about four feet high, was in part for the storage of large oxygen bottles, but it also provided access to the forward escape hatch of the plane, in the bottom of the ship.

Buzz and I sat at the top of the plane, looking out through a windshield which ran across over the nose; we had side windows, too. We were, it seemed, embedded in instruments. The main panel spread like a swollen dashboard before us, while the power-plant controls—throttles, turbo levers, mixture levers, and propeller-pitch handles—were in a central stand between the two flight columns; below that stand, forward of the trapdoor on the floor between us, was another block containing the automatic pilot with its many knobs and switches; each of us had a pair of side control panels, on the wall and floor beside him; radio-tuning apparatus was on the ceiling above us. Altogether there were more than a hundred and fifty dials, switches, levers, indicators, handles, cranks, knobs, buttons—any one of which might, at a moment of crisis, save or lose the plane and all of us.

Directly in back of the cockpit was the engineer's working space; Negrocus Handown's. Now Neg was in the upper turret, above it. This was a ribbed plexiglass dome, shaped something like the gun turret of a tank, with room for Handown's head and shoulders in it. From it extruded a pair of fifty-caliber guns; the whole dome could revolve, under power, on a cogged track, while the guns, which Neg fired through an automatic computing sight, could be elevated and depressed by an electrical mechanism. It was a pity Neg had only two hands. There were two handles with which to charge the guns with ammunition; a pair of hand grips to control the azimuth and elevation of the guns; triggers on them; a range knob between them; and the usual gadgets for heat and oxygen and communication, as well as hand cranks in case the power failed—all to be manipulated at once, it seemed, in response to lightning reactions under the threat of death from an attacker.

The engineer's compartment ended at a bulkhead, in the center of which was a door leading into the bomb bay: a windowless cavern containing a big vee of racks for the bombs. One had to step down two steps from the doorway to reach a narrow catwalk to the rest of the ship; I had gone in there one day—it was on the Hüls mission, on June twenty-second—when the bomb-bay doors, like great longitudinal jaws, had been jammed open by a wedge of flak, to help Neg crank them shut by hand, and we had nothing between us and the good earth but twenty thousand feet of air. It took us an hour to fix it. Another time, over Kassel, Max had leaned way down off the catwalk into space to fuse some of his bombs by hand when the arming mechanism had failed.

Next, going back, was the radio compartment, Butcher Lamb's place. This was the only self-contained room-like space on the ship, a kind of cabin, where Butcher, at a table on the left side, operated, as needed, the main controls for the VHF and liaison sets, interphone, marker-beacon equipment, radio altimeter, radio-compass recorder, and homing set. The receivers and transmitters were disposed around the room; in one corner there was a stack of five transmitters which looked something like a high layered office file. Besides Lamb's seat, there were two others, where Brag-

nani and Farr, the waist gunners, commonly sat on take-offs and
landings. Behind one of them was lashed a portable emergency
transmitter, for use in case of a ditching in the sea. At the end of
a mission Butcher's compartment was littered with pencil stubs,
butts, scraps of paper, and, above all, Westerns and comic books in
which he immersed himself at crucial moments, sometimes reading
while supposedly manning his hand-held gun which pointed rearward out of a slot at the top of the cabin. Handown caught him
doing that once—firing when a fighter took a pass at us, then reading a few sentences, then firing again, absent-minded, dreamy-
eyed, like a certain kind of man fussing with a pipe he is smoking
while he reads.

Moving aft out of the radioman's room one came next to the
ball turret, set like a knuckle in its socket in the bottom of the
plane. The ball turret differed from the upper turret in one vital
way: Junior Sailen had to let himself down into it and sit in it,
hunched up like an embryo, firing between his spread legs, with a
door locked above him, and with the whole turret revolving not
only in azimuth, as did the upper turret, but also in elevation, as
the upper turret did not. In other words, Sailen, locked into the
ball, spun and tilted with the motion of the ball, which he controlled himself by power as he aimed at the enemy. His mechanisms were even more complicated than Neg Handown's; in order
to adjust the reticles of his gunsight for range he had to use a left-
foot pedal, and to press the talk switch of his interphone he had to
use his right foot, while he tracked the target with hand grips and
fired with switches on top of the grip handles. The door of the turret could only be unlocked if the ball was properly upright. It was
no wonder that Junior had repeatedly made his crewmates swear
that they would get him out of the turret if it ever got stuck.

Abaft the ball turret was the waist gunners' post. Here one was
in the long tube of the naked fuselage, its walls honeycombed with
ribs and frames. Farr on the right and Bragnani on the left would
be standing with their guns on brackets pointing out the two large
open waist-high windows; the main entrance door of the plane
was to Farr's right, and beyond that a chemical toilet, which was
the center of much kidding of Prien with his bad stomach.

Prien himself was beyond a doorway in a final bulkhead; his
station was in the narrow wedge of the very tail of the plane. He

sat perched on an oversized bicycle seat, and when he was actually firing he heaved his body further to the rear and kneeled on a pair of knee pads. He fired twin-fifties hung on pulleys and cables, with a ring-and-post sight.

Now Prien completed his oxygen check with Farr, and switching to VHF I heard some chatter among the command pilots of the first Schweinfurt task force, up ahead. Various ones of them were calling "Croquet"—trying to get in touch with the Spits that had been supposed to rendezvous with our leading force over the Dutch coast. The fighters' radio channel was jammed by the Germans; the answers were unintelligible.

"Sounds like the Spits didn't show," I said to Marrow, having cut back to interphone.

"We weren't supposed to have any," he curtly said.

"I mean up ahead," I said.

"All right," Marrow said. "Let's keep our eyes peeled."

4 /

In battle, under attack, I was supposed to be in charge of fire control and interphone discipline, though of course no one man could really be in charge because no one man could see all the sectors of possible attack; and there was the added fact that Marrow could not stand letting anyone else be truly in charge of anything. Each gunner was assigned a definite segment of the sky, corresponding to the zone of fire of his gun or guns, and he was supposed to cut that piece of sky into small sections in his mind and to search those sections systematically for enemy planes. Neg Handown in the top turret searched ahead and above—from ten o'clock to two o'clock, high; Junior Sailen in the ball turret searched ten to two, low; Butcher Lamb searched (if he could tear his eyes from his book) four to eight, high; and Prien, in the tail, four to eight, low; Farr, at the right waist window, searched two to four, high and low, and Bragnani, on the left, eight to ten, high and low. From time to time each man might take a look outside his sector; Neg Handown and Junior Sailen, for instance, intermittently made.

three-hundred-sixty-degree sweeps with their turrets. The officers, having other duties, were not assigned definite sectors to watch, but of course we scanned the sky as much as we could. When a man sighted an enemy fighter in his sector, he was supposed to call it in at once, and generally speaking I was supposed to co-ordinate our firing, but in practice Buzz often jumped in ahead of me, and in the heat of action the gunners often called directly to each other, the man who sighted a fighter in his sector alerting another who was apt to get a good crack at the attacker as he passed. The greatest menace to our efficiency was everyone's talking at once, and here I was supposed to ride herd; though, again, Marrow couldn't keep his big mouth shut for long. Since our mutual safety was at stake in all this, no one stood on ceremony. We were eager to help each other and were not jealous for rank or duty, and occasionally, singing out at the sight of the enemy, calling back and forth to save our skins, we had (or at least I know I did, and I believe the others did) a feeling of the close brotherhood of crewmates, so that we who were so diverse, gentle Sailen, thug-like Farr, tidy and compulsive Haverstraw, cold-fish Prien, and the others, all of us, who got along rather badly as human beings, some of us bearing deep hatreds for others—all were drawn together under attack by what, for most of us, was the second strongest love on earth, second only to self-love: the love of those upon whom our lives depended.

Now, passing beyond the coastline, our searching began in earnest. All we had seen up to this point had been a few black puffs of flak—the erratic, inaccurate anti-aircraft firing we always seemed to catch at the rim of Europe, where the batteries either had had insufficient alert or were not of the quality of those ringing many of our targets.

At any moment enemy fighters might come up. We had no way of knowing to what extent, if at all, the Regensburg strike had disorganized or exhausted the German defenses. Nor could we know when they would jump us, for sometimes they held back and concentrated on trying to break up our bombing runs on targets, while on other days they began to ride us a few minutes beyond the coast.

"Anybody see anything?" I said.

"I see the sun and the moon," Negrocus Handown said.

5 /

        As I searched, as I monitored the bands of sound and
scanned the dials in front of me, I was trying also to work out in
my mind whether what Daphne had told me the day before about
Marrow was as much a revelation as it had seemed at the time of
her telling. It had come to me that I had dimly seen the real
Marrow all along, that I *must* have, and now I was trying to place
a turning point, if there had been one, in my attitude toward him.
I realized that such a turning point, if there had been one, had
come not from anything Marrow did that was new in him but
rather from a growth in me, an enlargement of my understanding, and undoubtedly this was something Daphne had helped me
to achieve, along with Kid Lynch; this must have come some time
in June, about halfway through our tour, before Marrow became a
hero. I now had glimpses of him in that period: at the throttle of
that railway engine rolling to a stop in King's Cross Station, his
ugly face creased with his delight over our amazement at him; his
homicidal eye as he roared his disapproval of John L. Lewis in a
London bar, and his sentimental expression standing in the review formation listening to the vainglorious Senator Tamalty rant
about "the blood of arr Amarrcan boys"; the clench of his jaw
during that split-second nightmare thundering up the alley of
noble beeches leading to Pike Rilling Hall at a hundred and seventy miles an hour, when Buzz took his pass at Them; his tender-
ness with his pet dog; the tumbling of his wit, and his happy
grimaces, at that squadron party at Lady Minsdale's castle; furious
expressions on his face on several occasions—when he found the
bicycle he had ridden to the Blue Anchor in Motford Sage missing, and when he got the news of Wheatley Bins' having been
awarded the Distinguished Flying Cross, and when he started
that near riot between the active pilots and the Happy Warriors,
the men who had completed their tours and were hanging around,
dangerously idle, waiting for new orders; the telltale hesitancy of
his head and hand as he turned *The Body* toward the act of courage (so it was considered) that made him a hero among us. I saw
him as shrewd, adaptable, moody; a natural aviator; bellicose and
noisy; growing wiser and more exhausted, like all of us. But did

I see deeper, and more? In retrospect I thought I could mark the
gradual change in him, and I knew I could follow the gradual
change in myself. At some point the two curves must have crossed,
and at that point, it seemed to me, my attitude toward Buzz must
have changed.

On VHF I heard Colonel Ewing, the commander of the
strike, say, "Windbag Red to all Windbags. Dropping altitude
two thousand. Repeat, dropping altitude two thousand."

So we were going under the cloud cover. I indicated this to
Marrow with a gesture.

"The son of a bitch," he said.

"What gives?" Handown asked, his curiosity aroused by Marrow's curse.

"Mind your beeswax, sonny," Marrow said. Then apparently he relented, for he added, "Colonel Chicken S—— is going
to tuck us under that cloud."

"That's ducky," Handown said; he understood the dangers
in going close under the cirrus.

I supposed that my getting to know Kid Lynch had been
the turning point—the unself-conscious prattler, so naïve and un-
formed; yet serious, too, always groping, between wisecracks, for
some reason for all this we were doing. He provided the foil to
Marrow that I guess I had needed. But of course it was Daphne
who had brought me to the stage of needing a dose of Lynch's
curious blend of skepticism and idealism, to offset Marrow's repeated assertions that we had never had it so good. It was Daphne
who had opened my eyes, had made me love my life and want
some purpose for it. I remembered sitting on the ground, one
June afternoon, under the huge elms of the Backs across from
King's and Clare in Cambridge, while a cluster of students spiced
the bland air of a good day with bouncing madrigals. "You call
that music?" Marrow said. He got the giggles, like a child. But I
remembered Daphne's calm. She looked at me and filled me with
it. We were sitting near the Clare bridge, whose pale gray stone
seemed alive in the moving, dappled shadows, and the slow Cam
reflected the bridge and the sky, and I leaned close to Daphne and
saw the delicate down on her cheek and the sweep of shining
light-brown hair back over her ear. She was leaning back on her
elbows, and I saw her breast pressing the soft cloth of her dress,

and in a moment of wanting to touch her, with my life force stirring and swelling, I had very strongly a curious yearning—for
idealism. My physical want soon drowned that out, but I remembered it. The singers stood on the far bank of the stream, young
men frowning as they opened the wet caverns of their mouths
and reached for high notes, then ducked their heads to the low;
and beyond them was the silvered rectilinear repose of the Clare
courtyard, and beside it, as if Clare had been built to set it off, the
breathtaking note of optimism, hope, and yes, stolid idealism of
King's Chapel, which Daphne had told me was the most beautiful building in England, and I believed her. Then that yearning,
which was a kind of dissatisfaction, passed, and I wanted to be
alone with Daphne, I wanted to hold her—she had a way of
turning her head on the pillow, looking at me each time as if she
had never seen my true value before—and I glanced at my watch,
and it was fighters at four o'clock low, fighters at four o'clock low
. . . and crackling.

Marrow was bolt upright, gesticulating. He was craning over
toward my side, and I started up. Earphones, it had been in my
earphones. Four o'clock. I turned my head around as far as I could
to the right and looked downward and saw them. The yellow up-
sniffing noses. Farr came up on interphone, "Sweet Jesus! Here
they come." Marrow was pounding my left arm. I slowly pivoted
back toward my pilot and raised my gloved hands as fists, then
stretched out my fingers, then clenched again, then stretched: ten,
twenty. There seemed to be about twenty.

And off there to the right, on a level with the bombers, well
out of range, was their guide plane, the one we called Coach, throttled back and idling along like a fox terrier at the same speed as
the Forts. And lower down, there they came! They were swinging out in a wide, climbing arc, to rise as usual outside the reach
of our guns and go up to a kind of dumping point where they
would break off to come in at us. They liked to come from the sun.
They were flying smart formation. How beautiful the day was!
The school of yellow-heads swam up in a long curve, and beneath
them the peaceful farmland spread out and out to a place where,
in thin haze and smoke, earth gave way to sky, not so much with a
horizon as with a kind of emptiness, or uncertainty, and now the

school of enemy planes was crossing that indefinite zone in the line of my sight. They flew much faster than Forts, and their angle of climb was astounding.

While still struck by the beauty of what I saw, I felt my heart begin to hurry. For a moment, in a corner of my mind, I saw a flicker of a picture—reclining on the bank of the Cam near the bridge, Daphne stirred, turned toward me, so the far breast rose and moved and the near one leaned my way. I could hear the chorus of students in full outcry. I wanted her; my heart was pounding.

On the interphone Marrow began to shout reminders. For a moment he was like his old self on the early missions, meddlesome yet keen, quick, happy—only now did I know how grotesquely happy. "All right! Let's not forget they might split ass and pull up ahead of us, or either push on under and loop back up for a traverse shot from under. So Junior, you be ready to open the second they get under, if they go under. Max, you be ready to tell us soon as they break. Say, 'Down,' or, 'Up,' whichever. And Boman, I want you to watch the . . ."

Boman, it was always Boman. Nicknames for the others.

And Daphne wanted me, too. Her melting eyes, cloud-pale eyelids.

What was it Marrow had wanted me to watch? I realized I hadn't listened at all. My belly muscles began to shake.

The Messerschmidts were rising against the blue, now, abeam, a close march of them, twenty or thirty planes. Now and then a whole cluster of the fighters' props would catch the sun just right, and there would be a sudden constellation of silvery yellow-centered roundels; then the shining shields would fade.

I recoiled as a shout rattled in my earphone. It was Marrow, upon catching his first view of the enemy procession off to the right. "Hot spit!"

Slowly I turned my head and looked at my pilot. Behind the flat glass parabolas of Marrow's goggles I saw a frightful sight: the green pupils of his eyes completely surrounded by porcelain laced with lightning-shaped veins. The eyes of cattle with the lids pulled back, unripe grapes being forced out of thin skins; the eyeballs might pop right out and splatter against the glass.

Almost choking in a resurgence of my rage against Marrow,
I tore my eyes, with a convulsion of my will, from Marrow's eyes
and looked at dials.

"Tighten up, people. Tighten up. Pack it in." In the phones
it was Colonel Ewing, commander of the attack, in the lead plane,
wanting to get the poisonous bristles of the huge formation as
compact as possible. I did not need to relay the word. Colonel
Bins ahead of us was already chopping the speed down so the
long files behind could push in closer, and Marrow, responding
automatically, had eased the throttles back ever so slightly. I
looked out at the Germans. Their small swarm was up at ten
o'clock and perhaps five hundred feet above the level of the Forts.
It would be only a matter of seconds now.

I tried not to let go of the memory of Daphne in the shifting
filtered sunlight. Her dress was pale yellow. Why did I cling to
the memory of desire, when I could have thought of a passage of
fulfillment? Deepest peace of all . . .

I started to hum a tune that I guess I considered protective, a
kind of armor-plate spell I had often used in the air. A slow
melodic line from *There's Nothing in This World*, the way I'd
heard Kenny Sargent treat it once with the Casa Loma band, slow,
souped up. I'd make a string of pearls out of the dew . . . Over
the highways and over the seas . . . It had come to me once, for
some reason, on a raid, as the music of safety, magic music that
would keep me out of trouble. Marrow was shouting something;
I didn't get it. I looked up into the sky ahead. Suddenly four German planes skidded up and over out of the chunky parade in a
beautiful simultaneous peel, and in no time they were coming
down four abreast. Then Marrow began his customary war whoop
at the first joining, a guttural scream, not words at all, a howl of
defiance of death and delight in killing, a kind of primitive elated
expulsion of a chestful of breath of a spear-thrower, and I
hummed as loud as I could, because the vibration of the hum, with
that of the plane, blocked my ears somewhat and helped me not
to hear that familiar nightmare shriek of Marrow's. I gripped my
knees. I had for an instant a feeling that everything had stopped—
the Fort, the oncoming fighters, my heart, my humming, our
war; only the scream persisted.

CHAPTER SIX

THE TOUR

May 22 to June 25

1 /

Enough of us to fill two ordinary locals horsed around on the platform of the tiny railroad station at Bartleck, with three days ahead of assured life, and of freedom from being bulldozed by Them. It was May twenty-second and fine. Our crew stuck together. The station was a wrinkled wooden building which put me in mind of the Toonerville trolley in the funnies of my childhood, and under its wide eaves on a notice board was an advice of change of fare, thenceforth to London the first-class tariff rising to ten and threepence, with a faded date underneath, of my thirteenth year. The fare was still the same. The platform was raised and fenced and it swayed under our stamping feet. More men were arriving on bikes from the base, and the old biddy in a ragged sweater who took sixpence to keep the wheels in a stall was growing muddled and had begun to whine at the fellows' crude jokes with her. A narrow, curving alley came up a slope to the station, and across from the city-bound platform two ancient men, twisted like old storm-broken willow trees, were unloading lumber from a dilapidated lorry; the planks must have been heavy for them, and Benny Chong said, "What say we help the old goats?"

The two toothless grandpas never knew what happened to them. There was a rush of perhaps thirty of us Yank fliers, and a

lot of whooping and clattering ensued, and in a jiffy the whole
load was neatly stacked at the side of the street.

It surprised me to see that Marrow had not joined us, and
when we got back to the platform he said, "You do-gooders really
got those old f——ers confused. They planned to spend all day unloading that crap. Look at 'em. Never pays to meddle in other people's lives. Just makes 'em sore at you."

The old men were puttering around the tidy stack. They
would lift a plank, and put it down just where it had been, and
look testily across at us, and lift another plank, and put it down.
They went round and round the stack with little senile steps,
wringing their palsied hands.

"Come on, Haverstraw," Marrow said, "let's have a catch."

There was a chipped and rusted enamel cup for thirsty way-
farers hanging from a tap against the station wall, and Marrow
grabbed it and pegged it to Clint, and then Buzz ripped one of
the half-rotten pales off the platform fence, and assuming a bat-
ter's stance he called, "Come on, son, see if you can get it over."

Haverstraw threw the cup. Marrow swung and missed, and
derisive shouts went up—shouts, I believed, with such an edge to
them of vindictive glee over my loud pilot's having whiffed that
I felt a bristling defensive anger. The cup went back to Clint, and
he took a big caricatured windup and threw it again, and this time
Marrow connected, and the picket dustily broke, and the bottom
fell out of the cup, and everyone, including Buzz, laughed.

Then the train came in, a tiny soprano engine with two
cylindrical bumpers like "a nice pair of boopers," as Marrow said,
pulling a line of old-fashioned four-wheeled cars along whose sides
ran rows of metal-handled doors.

Marrow latched onto one of the handles, and he shouted,
"My crew rides first class, by Jesus," and he brushed all comers
aside, and he shouted, "Come on, Boman, drag your ass over here.
Haverstraw! Farr! Come on, get the lead out of your pants."

The ten of us pried ourselves into the compartment along
with an elderly dominie in a backwards collar who had already
been sitting inside by the window, facing forward. Marrow, seating
himself opposite the preacher, was subdued into a Sunday-school
docility by him, and he chatted politely and quietly with the old
man while the rest of us silently stared out the window at fields of

turnips and wheat and rye, and at hoardings in praise of Bovril and
Bile Beans, and at the towns along the way—Royston, Hitchin,
Knebworth. Marrow and the curate got friendly over Marrow's
appalling lies about our life, and I noticed that my pilot had the
gall to eat half of the old boy's picnic lunch. "Just did it to please
him," Buzz said later.

I shook the rest of them at King's Cross Station and headed
for Leicester Square Underground, where I had a date to meet
Daphne at ten o'clock.

She was there ahead of me, by the news kiosk where we had
said we'd rendezvous, and at the sight of her I took a deep breath
and felt as if I were diving into a cool pond of peace.

We decided to ride around, having nothing but time to kill,
and we mounted the stairs of a shiny red double-decker bus, to the
upper level, and it felt to me as if I were seeing London for the
first time—a beleaguered place long after the worst of the siege,
with vast stretches of barbed wire and barriers of cheveaux-de-frise
and pillboxes with menacing black gun slits, and boarded-up
houses, and sandbag walls with the burlap rotting and weeds
growing out of the sand, and Anderson shelters, and signs pointing
to refuge in the tubes, whose stations were still lined with triple-
decker bunks. We passed a troop of soldiers singing as they
marched, and I reckoned myself fairly cynical by then, but those
full throats and jaunty exaggerated hand swings made my scalp
tingle, and I held Daphne's hand, thinking of her father killed in
a night raid.

We had hardly touched each other since that first night I'd
gone out with her in Cambridge, and when she squeezed my arm
between hers and her side, I had a flood of ideas.

"Would you like to go up the Thames?" she said. "It's such a
wizard day."

"Does time go slow up the Thames?" I asked. "I'll go, but
don't rush me."

I wanted a big stretch-out; I wanted the day to drag. I wanted
to be with Daphne for a long, long time.

"Let's take a look at Big Ben," I said. "A clock that big ought
to have real enormous hours."

So we did, but I could see the minute hand moving, and I
said, "Uhn-uhn, baby, that clock gives me the heebie-jeebies."

We went to a dock where there was a big flat steam barge with an awning and seats like park benches, and I thought I'd bust a gut when I said through the purser's grille, "Two tickets for Maidenhead," with Daph poking me in the ribs.

It was Saturday, and sunny, and mobs were out on the river. The only thing that spoiled the day was uniforms—Britishers, Canadians, Australians, Poles, Czechs, Frenchmen, Belgians, Dutchmen, and far too many Yanks. The river water was dirty, but under the open sky it tried its best to be blue. The river diminished and became just a stream, narrower than the Shaushohobogen at Donkentown. It was hard to take that in, because the whole world had heard of the Thames, and a couple of my own crewmates didn't believe, to that day, that there was a grand, wide watercourse in the U.S.A. called the Shaushohobogen.

The barge docked, and the passengers filed ashore, and Daphne and I sat on the grass in a kind of park beside the river and watched the boating parties, some in small launches which glided silently along, propelled by storage batteries. "Petrol shortage," Daphne explained. I thought of Marrow joy-riding in a B-17 with three nurses, and I estimated that he'd burned enough gasoline on that self-indulgent mission to keep boating parties going at Maidenhead till the war was squeezed into history books. Waste. I thought of the rows and rows of garbage cans, outside our messes on the base, full of leftover mashed potatoes and half-finished hunks of meat and jillions of slices of perfectly good white bread.

"Hungry, Daph?"

She gave me that melted-eye look and said, "For you."

For the second time in my life I lay down and put my head in Daphne's lap, but this time I didn't sleep. She stroked my temple and sang old music-hall songs in a furry, droopy voice.

It is not surprising that my foremost memory of that hour—and it was an hour that I called up often for review in the subsequent weeks—was of the absolute peace of lying on my back, looking up at Daphne's bosom and at the underside of her face as she dreamily stared out across the river, and concentrating my entire being into the few square inches of my skin that Daphne's finger tips caressed.

Thinking back more painstakingly, however, I realize that during that time we talked quite a lot about Marrow.

To begin with, I said, "Daph, do you remember I told you how I lost one of my big illusions on that Lorient raid—I mean, that you can always get out of a Fort? Well, I lost another, going to Kiel the other day."

Daphne's fingers seemed to hesitate; I think perhaps there was a delicate tremor in them. "What this time?" she asked.

"That nothing can happen to Marrow's ship. I wanted to believe it. Seemed better than having insurance to believe it. But I got shed of that idea."

I told her the story.

2 /

"I'm afraid that mission didn't do much to win the war, or to reflect credit, as your military chaps say, to our branch of arms. I don't know, it seemed to have a deliberate plan of chaos and error about it. They got us up at two forty-five, but there was a bad ground haze, and we had two postponements, and by ten o'clock we were so sure the strike would be scrubbed that we were mentally relaxed and let down—and then they sent us off, at ten fifteen, in the wrong frame of mind.

"There was a period of about ninety seconds on the bombing run, Daph—it was just a distillation of confusion. There was a heavy smoke screen around the target, and nobody up ahead seemed to know where the aiming point was, and a formation of twin-engine German fighters was in the act of bombing *us* from twenty-seven thousand feet, and about forty single-engine jobs were coming in, head on, at our level, and you could have walked on the flak. Any jerk could have told that the lead group was so far off its course that it couldn't have bombed accurately without a three-hundred-sixty-degree turn, but it let go anyway. Listen. We later learned that not a single bomb of the five attacking groups landed within four thousand feet of the aiming point; in other words, the bomb closest to the target was four fifths of a mile away from it.

"But let me tell you, darling, some brilliant lug in the planning section at Wing had worked out a nice little surprise for us.

"The group going in on the target immediately ahead of us, and higher than we—they'd been loaded with a considerable quantity of five-hundred-pound clusters of incendiary bombs, and when they toggled, a lot of the clusters opened at once, and the individual incendiaries—each one was fused to splash flame on anything it touched at the instant of contact—these things floated slowly down directly in our path. Marrow really has remarkable reflexes; he saw this and he knew in a flash what had happened, and what might happen, and he took evasive action as if his finger had touched a hot stove.

"The trouble was, some other pilots in our Group were alert, too, and they dodged, every which way, and *wham!* We hit prop wash.

"*The Body* wung up onto her right ear, and I was sure we were going into a spin. Handown, who'd been operating the upper turret, came sprawling down out of it and somehow landed against the right-hand wall of the cockpit above my head. . . ." I closed my eyes. It made me dizzy even to think of those moments. Being in prop wash is like being in the water in the wake of a ship; the turbulence has an elemental ferocity, and in the air only the long fang of a tornadic squall can match it. "I couldn't have told which end was up, tail or teakettle. But Marrow righted us within seconds— only the prop wash had thrown us right into the mess of incendiaries; they were as thick as a flock of starlings.

"I heard Marrow holler to Max Brindt to toggle, and I guess Max whacked his bomb-release handle—and that was our ship's contribution that day to what is known as high-level precision, or pin-point, bombing. Rather large pickle barrel.

"Anyway, I looked out the right-hand window and saw a flame going like a big match-head on the leading edge of the wing close against the nacelle of number three.

"I rapped Buzz on the shoulder and pointed out my window.

"By the time Marrow had stretched his neck enough to look out my side there was a nasty streak of black smoke pouring out behind the number-three engine. I had one thought: Braddock. Otherwise I was blank.

"Somehow Handown had got on his feet and was plugged in on interphone, and he growled at me, 'Cowl flaps.'

"But Marrow said, 'No, wait a minute.' He wanted to run the r.p.m. up on that engine first, to see if he could blow the fire out. At the same time, incidentally, he was pouring on the coal to catch up and hook back onto the formation, because if there's anything lonely in this world it's a straggler just after the bombing run. He really was on the ball. I was really impressed by his presence of mind, and Handown's, too. I couldn't have scratched fleas, myself, at that moment.

"Nothing happened when Buzz ran up the engine, so he nodded to me, and I closed the cowl flaps: that's like closing the damper on a stove. I was really just reacting to Neg's growl. I saw Marrow close the fuel shut-off valve to number three, so as not to feed the fire. But though the smoke thinned out, it persisted.

"My heart, Daph, it seemed to be going with a double thump: Braddock Braddock Braddock Braddock Braddock.

"Handown said, 'Set your fire-extinguisher selector valve.'

"I was gazing at the smoke, you know, like somebody puzzling out the flames of a fireplace fire on a winter evening.

"Handown kind of sang, 'Lieutenant Bo-o-oman.'

"At that his message about the selector got through to me, and I jumped to it, feeling like a jackass.

"'All right,' Marrow said, 'pull the God-damn charge.'

"I pulled it. The fire went out. I felt as if I'd done something important, as if I'd been a resourceful fellow. Like I thought you'd be proud of me, Daph.

"Marrow nipped this by saying—and he said it as if he'd been ordering some step of familiar routine, 'All right, let's feather.'

"By this time I was fairly rational, and I moved the mixture control of number three, above the throttles, to engine-off, and I flicked a little bar like a metal light switch on the central control panel which cut three's booster pump, and then I reached over below the bank-and-turn indicator and gave the feathering button for number three a good thorough mashing.

"All this seems like nothing to tell, Daph, but to me it was impressive. My heart was going Brad-Brad-Brad-Brad, and what seemed like six billion switches and buttons and levers were bristling all around me—and I reached out and eased the right lever, flipped the right switch, pushed the right button. It really wasn't bad.

"Now that the crisis was over, the fire out, the prop standing up stiff and cutting the wind, the fog in my head finally blew away, and my mind became unbelievably quick and clear. . . ."

I remembered it, too, with utmost clarity: For a few minutes, as I had worked with Handown, this time on my initiative, to transfer fuel from the tank of the dead engine, no extraneous thought had intruded, and in the command centers of my mind all had been swept away in favor of action and reaction. Thanks to Marrow's steady hand, we had held our place in the formation on three engines as rigidly as if we had been attached to the Group by struts, bolts, and rivets. When we had got down to twelve thousand, Marrow peeled off his mask, and he threw a look my way that seemed to say, "Well, you jerk, you thought we were in trouble, but *I* got you out of it."

But I was thinking, *The Body* could be hit. There was nothing sacrosanct about Marrow's ship. I wanted to puke. I decided to move around a bit, so I said I was going to use the relief tube, and I got unstrapped and went back in the ship. In the radio room, Butcher Lamb was pretending there wasn't a war, for he had his mask off and, using a clipboard and a Form One, he was writing a letter to his mother.

"What are you thinking?" Daphne asked me.

I was thinking, *The Body* was not inviolate after all. "Nothing," I said. "I was just thinking that Marrow isn't magic. I really guess I'd thought he was."

3 /

"All the same," I said, "he's *grown* in my estimation, too."

I told Daphne that his coolness in moments of stress, and his ability during those moments to keep track of many complex threads of action—these were truly remarkable. Whereas for me there was a dangerous gap in time, of a kind of stunned amazement, between the shock of an untoward happening and the wonderful clarity of mind and speed of reaction that finally supervened, in Buzz's case this turnover was instantaneous; the same was apparently true for Neg Handown. I told Daph that to achieve combat efficiency I must narrow that time gap. But I realized, too, that this narrowing was not something I could accomplish as an act of will, or by autosuggestion, by repeating, as in prayer, "I'm getting braver and braver."

"The day after the fire," I said, "I did get a hint of how the gap could be closed, and of course I got it from Marrow.

"No mission was scheduled that day, but Marrow was up early, and he went to Operations and arranged to borrow a ship, *Betty Grable*, since ours was on the line having her dead engine hoisted out, and he rounded up our crew, and he took us up high, so we were on oxygen, and he sounded a mock alarm—fire in the number-one engine! Then he re-enacted with us everything that had happened the previous day, and he had us all rehearse, not once, but several times, exactly what to do if such a thing ever happened again. And while he was at it, he started imaginary fires in other parts of the ship, and we practiced putting *them* out."

This was the toughening process, which Buzz understood. The threat to his life was not a monolith called Danger; it was a lot of bits and pieces of trouble and potential trouble, and his secret of gaining internal strength was to recognize them, and deal with them, one by one. It had dawned on me that Marrow broke off little fragments of Danger, put them in compartments, and took them out from time to time to dust them off in his mind. He evidently mastered every possible separate minor mishap, and every possible major breakdown, too, by going over it many, many times in imagination, till his defenses were second nature. Thus there seemed to be very little about flying that was unexpected or unknown to him, and when something nasty happened, the event was not just a blank empty wall in his mind, against which cries of vague inner fear echoed; it was rather a familiar-shaped reality, it was itself, and it stirred up in his mind other realities—consequences, remedies, preventions, counter-measures.

I talked about all these things with Daphne, but I realized something else, too, and this I did not discuss with her—that in our kind of warfare one had to have an almost infinite capacity for toughness. At the beginning we had had an amazingly efficient substitute for strength—ignorance. On our early missions we re-

acted well to danger because we couldn't see it. But now, as we
were learning how to atomize danger and master its fragments, we
were also learning, with giddying rapidity, that there were ever new
pieces of peril to be overcome: experience brought both the attrition of danger and its expansion. The race between these two was
a race for our lives, and, I must say, Marrow's intuitive grasp of the
way to grow tough was a help to me—something that, ironically,
helped me in the end to outlast even him.

4 /

I began talking then about our all too frequent inaccu-
racies, gross errors, what they must have meant twenty-odd thousand feet below us, when our bombs, intended for some visceral
center of enemy industry, landed instead in housing. I guess I still
had Daph's poor father on the edge of my mind, and all the
boarded-up windows and shells of homes we'd seen on our bus
ride that morning. I came right out and said I was getting scrupu-
lous about killing people. When it was Germans it was bad
enough; with Frenchmen, Belgians, Dutchmen, it was even worse.
I said I'd been brought up with moderate middle-class strictness,
nothing exceptional, for my people were nice but not so nice as to
be nasty—and I had had what had seemed to me a more or less
average social self, I'd had a sense of decency, much like that of
many of our officers and enlisted men upon the inception of their
military lives. In the service, in the face of the standardized debase-
ment of all values that went with an army existence, where toughness and self-centered amorality were the popular things, and consideration for others and any form of propriety were considered
chicken s——, I had rather easily given up a great deal of what
came under the general heading of square behavior, and I took for
granted and, along with my associates, indulged freely in obscene
language, drunkenness, sexual promiscuity, and a certain ruthless-
ness in looking out for one's own comforts. But there were some
taboos—and killing was foremost among them—that were harder
to shake, even under the persuasion of a good cause. With my com-

rades, I could live and let live; it was not so easy, with my enemies, to live and let die. I hadn't been truly persuaded, before I'd got into the fight, that the Germans were a threat to my life or my way of life; I'd heard a lot of *talk* about the threat, and I'd read about it in the papers, but none of that had been real to me, and it still was not—even after touring the wreckage of London that morning. I tried to express some of this to Daphne.

"You're lucky," Daphne said. She had begun again the gentle movements of her hand across my face, and I guess that for a minute I took this massage, as I had taken so many dull, badly organized lectures of indoctrination in the Air Force, to be a deliberate lulling of my qualms, for Daphne, being English, and having lost a father and a lover to the Germans, had a vested urge to keep me in fighting trim.

"How come 'lucky'?" I truculently said.

"You're not like some of the others," she said.

All of a sudden I wanted to make a little argument. "What the hell do you mean by that?" I asked.

"For some of them war's a license," she said.

"Like a hunting license?" I said, meaning to be ironic.

But she said, "Exactly. Makes what they want to do legal and even respectable."

"Who's 'they'?"

"Oh, I know them," she said. "I made the mistake of falling in love with one of them." At that she stopped rubbing my head.

"Hey!" I said, protesting the stoppage, and the automatic fingers began to move again, and I realized that their warm friction was more important to me than all the bellyaches and gripes on earth. I gave up interest in our exchange and pressed my head against Daph's resilient abdomen and half lost what she said next.

"You ought to know one of them."

She meant Marrow, of course. So my Daphne, having already sized up my pilot, had dropped a hint about him, to which I wish I'd paid better attention. Had I thought through what she had said, had I not been transported, put half to sleep, by that stroking of my temple, I might have seen Marrow whole much earlier in my tour, and I might have been spared the full force of the disappointment, shock, and revulsion to which I was treated so near the end.

5 /

Time glided along like an electric launch, and too soon
we had to board our barge, and we rode downriver, and we were
famished. There was supposed to be a five-shilling limit on the
price of meals all over England, but Daphne knew of a place called
the White Tower off Soho Square where, for a heap more than the
limit, we could get some fine crackling bootleg roast mutton.
("Nothing like beating the system," I said.) And afterwards, in
mid-afternoon, we took a room at one of the best hotels, and when
a stiff clerk asked where our luggage was, Daphne held up her
purse, which was a big one with her nightgown and fixings in it,
and without batting a lash the clerk said, " 'Nk yaw," on a rising
inflection, meaning thanks, and didn't even ask me to pay in advance, because of war and allies and all that, I supposed; perhaps
he was thanking me for Lease-Lend. And I took time to think:
Americans call it Lend-Lease, the English, Lease-Lend—a nice
exercise all around in self-congratulatory self-deception.

A very old porter—for all the young men were otherwise engaged—with a single key on a huge ring led us to our room. "If you
please, sir," he said, standing by the door and pointing with his
elbow (in order, I suppose, that only the gentleman would get it)
at a sliding bolt with which one could lock the door from within.
At that I tipped him too much, and when he was gone I loudly
shot the bolt and Daphne and I, laughing, embraced.

The sack was superior. We were in it, awake most of the time,
for twenty hours.

6 /

Daphne had to go back to Cambridge on Sunday afternoon to be able to return to work on Monday morning, and I took
her to the King's Cross Station and then hopped a cab to join Marrow and the gang at the Dorchester, where they had said they would
be. Marrow had a room, all right, but no one answered the house
phone, and I bribed an old boy to take me up and let me in, and

no one was home, so I lay on the bed and gave myself over to the best glow I'd ever experienced.

Daphne was really mine! When we had first approached each other, the previous afternoon, it had been with a deep shyness yet an overpowering yearning. What ensued seemed our first touching and joining, for this time Daphne truly gave herself to me, and I found that I had not been mistaken: deep in her there were surprises, storms of feeling, extraordinary furnace fires, bottomless spasms, tender places, changes, quiets.

At the end she had anxiously asked me, "Do you still love me?"

I had not made any formal declarations; I was not sure what love was. But I was sure that I was the king of the forest, and I was amazed at her question.

Then she had wept. She had sobbed in my arms, and I had been stirred all through, because I understood that her tears, her wrenching, heaving sobs, stood for an enormous gift to me—of her whole self. I understood that something that had happened to her in the past had made her want to hold back large parts of herself; she would allow herself, perhaps, to be more or less raped, as I had, I guess, violated her, with her acquiescence, the first time we had been together in Cambridge, but she would not dig deep and make, as the expression goes, love. But now she had done just that, and she wept out her overwhelming joy. I dried her tears with a new access of passion. All night and all morning we made new discoveries.

I fell into a sleep such as I had not had since our arrival overseas—a velvet blackness, a sleep of my innermost soul; but this healing rest was interrupted, because Marrow, half tight, came blustering in to take a shower before dinner. He got me up and recruited me for a pub crawl. It seemed that the mighty swordsman had nothing definite to do. We went out and moved from bar to bar. Marrow may have crawled; I floated. I was high. I didn't need a drink. But I took one. And another. We lapped up wine; tried gin; had a Pimm's; found some so-called whiskey. Sang down the Mall.

We tied up with some Dutch R.A.F. pilots in the Berkeley Buttery, where, through some inadvertence, we decided to have some chitterlings and champagne.

After we got talking, the Dutchmen started ripping Hitler's stomach with vengeful hearts ("Daph! Daph!"—I kept floating off into reveries), and suddenly Marrow said to those two guys: "You know whose guts I hate?"

Marrow lit into John L. Lewis. The Dutchmen, who had lost homes, families, and livings to Hitler, were astounded at Marrow's vehemence, for they didn't even know who Lewis was. Marrow started by describing Lewis' enormous head, and the great contempt-swollen flap of his upper lip; he gave a vivid picture of Lewis —and, oddly, of a physical being such as he, Marrow, might one day become: gross, aggressive, toad-like. At the end of April Lewis had taken his soft-coal miners out on strike in Alabama, Kentucky, and Pennsylvania; he had thumbed his nose at the War Labor Board; Roosevelt had had to seize the mines. Men were dying overseas! Marrow's tirade began with animal epithets: skunk, pig, horse's ass, and it moved through scatology into demonology, until it appeared that Hitler was only a petulant, troublesome urchin and John L. Lewis was the true scourge of the earth. Really, the Dutchmen began to look cross-eyed, and I must say that I was surprised by the virulence of Marrow's invective; sergeants had never had it so bad from him. I wondered why. Perhaps the physical picture, or caricature, that he had drawn of Lewis was a clue, for there was surely some self in it; perhaps Marrow's own long battle with cold and discomfort, back in March and April, which had involved him in that theft of coke from the stack for the enlisted men's showers, was preying on his mind.

The Dutchmen went off shaking their heads, and pretty soon we got on the move again. In the Savoy we found Max Brindt hooked up with some fancy Army desk types in gabardine uniforms which they'd had made, they told us, in Savile Row. They were fighting a hard sartorial war; had to buy new uniforms all the time to keep the seats of their pants from getting shiny.

"Boman," Marrow said while we were drinking with them, "what the f— has got into you? You look like you got a snoot full of hasheesh."

I think that what bothered Buzz was my being, because of daydreaming about Daph, aloof; he demanded, and usually got, close attention.

I said, "Girl name of Daphne."

Marrow said, "You gone soft in the head?"

One of the tailor's dummies, slightly soused, said, "What's a matter, big boy, don't you like name Daphne?"

"Listen, Mr. Gabby Dean," Marrow said, "I've screwed more women than you'll ever shake hands with in all the Embassies and all the Duchesses' palaces you'll ever worm your way into, but I'm a *flier!* No woman is ever going to come between me and flying."

Max, bless him, chimed in for me. "Who said Bo was going to quit flying?"

"Look at him!" Marrow said, holding a hand up toward my face.

"Captain," the soldier said, "you sound like you can't stand for anyone to get onto Topic A except yourself."

This soldier-boy was too perspicacious for my comfort; I expected Marrow to blow sky high. Instead he said, benignly, "Listen, Mac, Topic A may be women in the suit-and-cloak branch of the service. In the Air Force, Topic A is flying. Topic B is s——, which is just another way of saying bombs, huh, Max? Topic C is women. Right, Boman?"

He had allied himself with me, with us. Fliers against the world.

We took off once more. We got around that night. At the Captain's Cabin we wound up at a big table of Eighth Air Force staff johnnies with some Mayfair girls who were out slumming, and a funny thing happened to me. I got flirting with one of them, and I danced with her, and I felt all arrogant, and I damn near asked her to go to bed with me; I felt sure she would. Yet all I cared about in the whole world was Daphne. It was some kind of momentum in me, I guess, and the spirit of the crazy twilit zone we lived in.

I turned in at the Dorchester as a saffron dawn seeped in behind the barrage balloons to the east. The last thing I heard as I dropped off to sleep was the sound of some hard-heeled British boots striking the pavement outside our window, going away, echoing, fading.

7 /

I slept some more of that innermost sleep until the middle of the following afternoon, when I got up and went out to an old-fashioned photographer's studio and smirked like a man who has just won a war single-handedly while the widow who ran the shop ducked under a black cloth behind a big box camera, and squeezed a rubber ball, and I paid for the picture, sight unseen, and told the lady to send one copy to Daphne's address and one to my mother's.

8 /

Our whole crew rendezvoused at King's Cross to catch a train out to the base. As we were waiting, a cocky littly shunting engine kept puffing back and forth, and when it started up once, Marrow jumped aboard, and the mighty mite pulled out of the station altogether, going much too fast.

"Runway ain't long enough to take that thing off," Handown said.

Our train time approached. We began to worry about our pilot. About fifteen minutes passed. Then in came a crack express from the north, the Scottish Queen, or something like that, and the majestic black and red engine came to a stop and exhaled, with a contented cloudy hiss. A huge head, topped by a coal-dusty English engineer's cap, poked out the cab window, the ugly mug split by a magnificent grin—Marrow's, of course. Behind him in the cab we saw a dignified elderly English railroader in an Air Force cap with the wire ring taken out.

Marrow never would tell us how he had managed it.

9 /

On the train on the way out to Pike Rilling (Marrow still in his new hat) we learned that during the leave Handown had attempted the worldly education of Junior Sailen, had procured for the tiny man a tiny woman and had rented for them a tiny room with a tiny bed in a tiny house, but at the last moment, as Handown was offering instructions for the tiny operation that was to ensue, Junior had put on a demonstration of unexpected spirit and had thrown Neg the hell out. It further developed that after bolting the door the ungrateful little bastard had poked some toilet paper into the tiny keyhole.

"How was it, Junior?" Marrow asked.

"Big," said Junior, grinning in a fairly good imitation of his pilot.

10 /

Back at the base, as we checked in, we took a lazy look at the C.O.'s bulletin board, and we saw a notice which read: "The intensity of operations has permitted an accumulation of various kinds of trash, waste paper, scrap lumber, and other debris on various parts of the airdome. Commanding officers of all units at Pike Rilling are warned that they will be personally responsible for the cleanliness of the areas they control." Immediately under that information was another typed page: "A deplorable laxness in discipline, and especially in military courtesy, has been noted on the station. All personnel are advised to improve their personal appearance and to adopt a more soldierly standard of behavior. All officers and enlisted men will observe the ritual of the salute with the greatest possible precision and propriety."

"The Colonel's cracking up," Marrow said. He meant Whelan, the Group C.O.

"S——," Haverstraw said, "that's just to depress us in case we had a good time on our leaves."

But Marrow was dead serious. "No," he said, "you watch. He's off his chump. Any fighting man who gets the regulation book on the brain"—and Buzz kissed his finger tips and threw the kiss away.

For the next two days we were breaking off salutes as if they were wooden laths. After that we returned to normal.

11 /

Having checked in I went to our room and had an hour alone there, because Marrow felt compelled, I guess, to go to the officers' club and give a full (presumably invented) account of his ravishing of metropolitan womankind during the long stand-down. I thought I wanted to think about Daphne, but when I got to the hut and tossed myself on my bed, I found that all I wanted was to savor the familiarity of my room. The stove. The muslin blackout curtains, faded from black, in places, to yellow-green-gray by sun and dampness. The acrid smell of dirty Army blankets. Every detail of it was familiar to me. This was my home. I closed my eyes and visualized the contents of my metal locker, the crammed, rather orderly array—a place for everything and everything, if not in its place, at least accounted for. In time I was thinking about Marrow—the inanimate Marrow scattered around our room, disorderly, positive, maddening, distinctive. I despised and admired his sloppiness. He parked his towels, wet or dry, under his bed. He raided my locker often for socks or handkerchiefs just because he was too lazy to dig deep enough in his own tangled haberdashery to find what he needed, which would surely be there. He had the upper half of a human skull—said it was a woman's—on the desk for an ash tray, and it always brimmed with cylinders of cigar ash. His eight-dollar pillow. Stringless ukulele. Pin-ups neatly covered with transparent talc: Danielle Darrieux, within reach; Paulette Goddard, twisting rear view, about to take everything off; Eleanor Holm, demonstrating her flotation mechanisms in a racing suit; Betty Grable ("She is able," Marrow *always* said); Simone Simon, leaning dizzy-makingly forward. ("How do you suppose she

squeezes that *e* in between those two See-moans?") One Varga.
One Petty. Only one nude—picture of a dame, said to be a starlet,
named Carmen Lundquist. Swedish tits, Spanish ass, Marrow said.
Strictly his. For a while he had a laundry shirt-cardboard hinged
over Lundquist, so that he, and only he, could lift the flap and look
at her when he felt the need. I remembered coming in the room
the second day after we arrived in England, and finding Marrow
at work nailing up these pictures. Where had he acquired them?
He hadn't had them during training, or in the phases. . . . On
the desk there was a precariously balanced pile of Marrownesses:
four cans of shoe impregnate—stuff we'd lugged halfway across the
world to protect our feet against poisonous gases—which Marrow
had found to be even better kindling than shoe polish for English
so-called stoves; one pair drop-seat long underwear in readiness to
take along when joy-riding nurses because (according to him) one
of the three on his early joy ride damn near came down with frostbite of the nates; fire-fighting bucket of sand used as ash receptacle
and cigar-butt douser; comic books and back issues of *Stars and
Stripes* and *Yank*, not for perusal but for starting fires, wiping up
spilled beer, and swatting the bees that kept getting in.

The Tannoy crackled outside, and I half sat up, then let myself down again when I heard the voice of the odd ball who called
himself Kid Lynch.

"Now hear this," the voice said, Navy-style. "Footnote on
morale:

> "Those that I fight I do not hate.
> Those that I guard I do not love . . .
> Nor law, nor duty bade me fight,
> Nor public men, nor cheering crowds.
> A lonely impulse of delight
> Drove to this tumult in the clouds."

He signed off: "Lieutenant Lynch reporting." Those lines
gave me a funny feeling; for some reason I thought of my mother.
Lynch didn't write those words, I thought; his stuff was doggerel. I
dropped off to sleep in my clothes and slept right through till ten
the next morning, something like sixteen hours.

12 /

An irony: Having some point to my life made my days seem intolerable. I became bored, impatient, jumpy; wanted to fly and hated flying.

On the afternoon after my long sleep there was a shake-up in squadron commanders, because two of the three in the Group had completed their tours. Bins was promoted to lieutenant colonel and given one of the squadrons, and one of Marrow's friends, Curly Jonas, was made Operations Officer of the Group. When these and some other promotions had been posted, Marrow went around with more than his usual swagger and bounce, but I sensed that he was feeling badly slighted, and indeed I myself felt hurt on his behalf. How could he have been passed over? New evidence that Colonel Whelan was off his trolley. Anyone with any gray matter knew that Marrow was the best flier of the bunch.

That evening in the enlisted men's mess some civilian, a real sharpie, gave us an exhibition of card tricks, magic, and sleight-of-hand, but with a new twist: He showed us *how* the tricks were done. He explained "strippers"—decks of cards shaved to a very slight wedge shape for certain effects; other decks with tiny bits of ends off certain cards. Very slowly, so that the eye was faster than the hand for a change, he showed a dozen ways to lay out a crooked deal, and how easy it was for experts to fool suckers. Coming out afterwards, the padre, Major Plate, a bald, heavy-bearded man who had been a saxophone player in a jazz combination before he got the call, happened to be alongside Buzz and me, and he said, trying to be a funny joe, "Anybody for a couple rounds of poker?"

Marrow, who prided himself on his poker winnings, who was indeed famous in the Group as a steady winner, tugged me by the sleeve to slow me down; the chaplain walked on. Marrow was burned up. "That bastard padre," he whispered. "He must think I cheat on 'em. God damn it, I'm shot full of luck."

13 /

The following day, May twenty-sixth, the weather was perfect, but we were stood down. The worst of it was that there was no advance notice of the free day; we didn't get the word until ten in the morning, and I was fed up at Wing and at Batty Whelan because an announcement the night before would have given me a chance to arrange seeing Daphne. The whole station was on edge, and the core of the restlessness was the band of thirty-odd men who in recent days had completed their tours, the Happy Warriors, so-called, only they weren't warriors any more and they certainly weren't happy. I watched the try-outs for the Group ball team in the afternoon, and Marrow was shouting so raucously, so childishly, for Clint Haverstraw that Clint was almost cut off the squad, but Clint's natural talent for scooping up grounders finally won out over the coach's exasperation at Marrow's rasping voice, and Clint was picked for the first club. You'd have thought Marrow preferred this choice to his own promotion to Squadron C.O. I felt stale and half nutty, and I was conscious of Marrow's having made a spectacle of himself, and I decided to take a bike ride alone.

It was already nearly six o'clock. I followed the perimeter track around to the Bartleck gate and struck out along some back country roads. The sky had a silken texture, the pale color of certain off-white hollyhocks we had had in Donkentown. Warm sunlight lit the hedges and fields of crops. I was fed to the teeth with everything. I rode back and threw myself onto my spine in one of the beer-smelling leather chairs in the officers' club and listened to Frances Langford and Ginny Sims and Connie Boswell on an American Forces Network program, and that just made me want to break up the place.

So I called Daphne at her lodgings, and I said, "Baby, you've got to rig up some emergency yarn so we can get together when they spring a last-minute stand-down on us."

"I'll think of something, Bo," she said.

I didn't sleep a wink that night, and they gave us a tedious Group practice mission next morning, to break in some replacements. And when we got back down there was this notice that

Loony Whelan had posted. Bicycle regulations. Lights after dark.
Left side of road, with traffic . . . And then *wham!* No individual
to ride bicycle more than fifteen miles from the station. That put
Cambridge out of bounds.

I went straight to a booth and called Daph at her office: "Listen, Daph," I said, "first chance I get I'm going to rent a room in
Motford Sage." So she and I could have some privacy once in a
while. Easy bike distance from the base. She could bus it.

"That sounds wizard, darling," she said.

My boiler pressure was getting mighty high.

14 /

Marrow came rushing into the room. Panting, he told me
they'd announced a blanket invitation to officers of our Group
from a certain Lady Minsdale, who had a big country place the
other side of Bartleck, to come to a joint R.A.F.-U.S.A.A.F. tea
party that afternoon. Marrow talked me into going with him. He
said this Lady Minsdale was probably a dark-eyed nymphomaniac
like lots of British noblewomen whose husbands were in the desert,
and there were bound to be bevies of local female gentry to entertain the troops. There would be sherry—famous aphrodisiac used
by English lady enthusiasts. I was so knocked out I went. We rode
in a convoy of weapons carriers, about forty horny fliers and I with
Daph on my mind. Snaking up Lady M.'s long driveway we saw a
troop of the Home Guard, the sorriest collection of lopchicks and
wheelchair reprieves you ever saw, out for their Thursday tactical
problem, on a stalk across Lady M.'s magnificent lawns after imaginary Huns with a lot of rabbit guns and crow irons. Truly it
was very touching, but our fliers laughed at the old boys and yoo-
hooed as if those earnest defenders of the realm were a gaggle of
high-school girls. When we got to the house it turned out that
Lady M. was seventy-three, and that she had a sister sixty-nine.
"That one's the nympho, Buzz," I said, and he gave me a sock on
the upper arm. Not a single girl had been invited, just a lot of chaps
from the Stirling base near Motford Sage. The two nice old duck-

ies treated us like schoolboys. Games we had. Tug of war. Lady M.
and sister Agatha sat nine limeys and nine Yanks in two rows
facing each other on the polished parquet, each man with his legs
spread holding the one in front of him around the belly, the lead
man in each line holding one end of a mop handle, then at a cry
from Agatha the two lines began to tug, the men inching and
squirming and straining backwards on their behinds, grunting,
yelling like wahoos. The R.A.F. won once; our team, with Marrow
holding, won once. There was a treasure hunt. Then the R.A.F.
fellows introduced a game called, "Are You There, Moriarty?,"
played by two blind-folded men on their knees, each grasping the
other by the left hand and holding in his right a rolled-up magazine for a cudgel, the purpose being to outguess the opponent's
evasive maneuvers and blam him on the head. The dear old girls
shrewdly saw violence brewing, and they trotted out the tea. We
snatched and gulped like wolves.

Toward the end, Lady M. stood in a chair and in a sweet,
fruity voice said, "I find I have just one biscuit left. What shall I
do? Which of you nice officers can tell me what to do with this one
last biscuit?"

Marrow spoke up in a marvelous imitation of Old Man
Whelan on his severe note. "First man," he said, "who tells the
lady what she can do with the biscuit gets thirty days in the guard-
house."

15 /

The next day Marrow was away down in the dumps. They
had alerted us for a mission to the ship-building installations at
Bremen, and Sully wakened us at two thirty in the morning, and
we went through all the preparations, and then they scrubbed us,
and of course we were sore as cats in the rain, and we went back to
our sacks. In mid-afternoon they mustered all the crews over in
front of the Admin building for a lecture by old Whelan—it really
seemed that Marrow was right, that the Colonel was losing his
mind—on security, not talking while intoxicated, not giving brief-

ings to Piccadilly commandos, but the thing I remembered of that assembly was being conscious of Lynch, on account of the bogus crew he had set up for Stormy Peters.

At the last moment, just as the roll was about to be called, Stormy and Doc Randall and some of the S-2 boys came tumbling out of the building, all in a heap, and formed up with us a crew; their mythical plane had been named the *Blue-Ass Baboon* a few days before, and Lynch had gotten Chan Charles to make a drawing of a monstrous ship, half airplane, half ape, and he had had postcard-sized photographs made of the drawing and had put them up among the recognition silhouettes and drawings in various offices all over the base. A ribald folklore was growing up around the *Blue-Ass Baboon*, and we all knew that Lynch was the instigator of most of it. After we had been dismissed I began talking about "this Lynch character," and Marrow cut me off really with a snarl.

16 /

I rode my bike to Motford Sage and rented a room. It was easy to do. I inquired of the bartender at the Blue Anchor about rooming houses in the town, and he asked some townsmen who were having late afternoon beers, and they told me of a Mrs. Porlock, on Stanley Crescent; this turned out to be a curving street of stucco houses behind stucco walls at the edge of town, a pathetic caricature of London pretentiousness, and Mrs. P. was a fat, stoical woman who, having been cleaned out of a husband and four sons (two men drowned on the *Repulse*, one dead in the desert, one killed at Narvik, one missing at Dunkirk), had nothing but room and memories, and for a weekly stipend that was less than the price of a steak and French fries in Donkentown she let me have an upstairs back room, with substantial privacy, that had been shared by two of her boys—still contained their civilian working-class youths' chattels: clothes of iron cloth, cleated soccer shoes, a box of spanners, a drawer full of marbles, cheap lead soldiers, a brass gyroscope, a wooden foot-rule, treasures of Mrs. Porlock's heart, which she took out for me, one by one. She understood perfectly the situation. She asked me, "Will she be livin' in constant, or intermittent?"

When I got back to the station, after dark, Marrow was tight and surly, and an alert was announced, and he said, "Come on and walk me, Boman. I got to sober up."

We struck out along the perimeter track under a quarter moon, and Marrow said in a disgusted tone, "I want to go to that God-damn track where they're trying to grow yellow corn."

We walked to the station agricultural project, and we saw that in the English drizzle and mugginess the corn, ten thousand stalks of which had been transplanted out in recent days, had poorly started, and only came to our ankle bones, and was puny-stalked, and this made Marrow, a Nebraska cornland boy, absolutely furious. "Muddle-headed bastards!" he shouted, and before I could stop him he was wildly running directly down the rows, kicking and trampling the tiny stalks. He had destroyed nearly three rows' worth of those seedlings before I could catch up and throw him down with a football tackle. "Crazy f——ing Whelan idiot," he was shouting, and he seemed to be whimpering, as he lay on the ground, and he said once, "They should've known there wouldn't be enough sun," and another time, "What ever made them think that Bins can fly an airplane?" Poor guy. Drunk as a coot. I was sorry for him.

17 /

Riding out to the ship in a weapons carrier on May twenty-ninth, we had a brand-new crew with us, and it might have been a college football team just before the first game of the season. The boys were chatty, eager, not sure they remembered all the plays. I thought: How innocent they are!

I was going on my ninth raid.

On the whole the crews were happy, for the briefing hadn't been until eight thirty, and the take-off was to be at five minutes to two in the afternoon. We in *The Body* worked up some apprehension about flak before the take-off, discussing that day's innovation—for our formations were to be joined that afternoon for the first time by a handful of YB-40s, Forts that had been converted from bombers to super-fighters by the addition of five extra fifty-caliber guns and some armor plate around the engines. These air destroyers were supposed to beef us up defensively. The only trouble was that their extra weight made them slow, and to keep them socked in we could only go at an indicated air speed of one hundred and fifty—and this, good old number-brained Haverstraw had remarked, would make the problem of the German anti-aircraft trackers simpler than usual. Furthermore, St. Nazaire was known as "Flak City," for the Germans had brought more than a hundred of their famous dual-purpose eighty-eight-millimeter guns and ringed the city's submarine installations around with them, and their crews were obviously superior gunners.

On top of all this, we saw, as we approached the initial point, that the Heinies had a JU-88 sitting up over St. Nazaire as a flak observer. On the bombing run I think every one of us on the ship, with the exception of Max, who was happily busy getting ready to "take a crap," as he called toggling the bombs—except for him we were all frozen at our stations waiting to get ours. There were no fighters yet. After spotting the JU-88, Junior Sailen said, "They must be using a predicted barrage." We all had flak on our minds.

The terrible thing was the enforced passivity. You could strike back against fighters, and under attack from them we shouted a lot on interphone to work together in our common defense. With flak we just had to sit there and fly through it and hope they'd miss. Before the actual bombing run we took evasive action with turns of ten degrees or so every twenty or thirty seconds; it had all been laid out in the briefing. But on the run we had to fly straight as a pool cue for ninety seconds, and that was when I felt most helpless. Neither Marrow nor I could even help fly then, because we had a gadget called Automatic Flight Control Equipment, which held you as if on railroad tracks, and on the run Max Brindt actually flew us, through his bombsight being tied up with the AFCE. There we sat, strapped down with safety belts, so a near miss wouldn't knock us out of our seats, and waited.

Max broke our tension after he let the bombs go. You could feel the ship tremble as they vacated her belly, and Max told us they were away, and he gave the controls back to Marrow, who began to swim us all over the sky, which wouldn't necessarily evade flak but made us feel better, and then, several seconds later, when Max saw the first bombs of the formation explode on the ground, he hollered on the interphone, with his babyish glee: "Voom! Clobbered the bastards! Voom voom voom."

We all began to chatter then, and enemy fighters hit us, and we felt lots better.

From that day onward, through all the raids leading up to the Schweinfurt strike, I was petrified by the sight and thought of flak, which once had seemed so harmless, so beautiful. And so—I happened to learn from Daphne on the eve of the Schweinfurt raid— was my great pilot, Marrow, who told all comers that he feared no man or thing, and who was soon to be regarded, in the world's eyes, as a hero.

18 /

The following day was Memorial Day, and a Sunday, and the weather was good, but no mission was scheduled, so I called Daphne and arranged to meet her at noon in the street in front of Barclay's Bank in Motford Sage.

That gave me plenty of time to go to a nine-o'clock service which was held out on the apron in front of the Admin block, in memory of the men who had died in our Group. Now Preacher Plate, as I have said, had been a saxophone player, and I guess he knew the power of a short musical line, and he had promised in his notice advertising the memorial service that at least it would be brief, and it certainly was, for he lined us up (a very large number of men showed), and all he did was to hold up a book and read these words:

"Remember now thy Creator in the days of thy youth, while the evil days come not, nor the years draw nigh, when thou shalt say, I have no pleasure in them: While the sun, or the light, or the moon, or the stars be not darkened, nor the clouds return after the rain: In the day when the keepers of the house shall tremble, and

the strong men shall bow themselves, and the grinders cease, because they are few, and those that look out of the windows be
darkened: And the doors shall be shut in the streets, when the
sound of the grinding is low, and he shall rise up at the voice of the
bird, and all the daughters of music shall be brought low. Also
when they shall be afraid of that which is high, and fears shall be
in the way, and the almond tree shall flourish, and the grasshopper
shall be a burden, and desire shall fail: because man goeth to his
long home, and the mourners go about the streets: Or ever the
silver cord be loosed, or the golden bowl be broken, or the pitcher
be broken at the fountain, or the wheel broken at the cistern. Then
shall the dust return to the earth as it was: and the spirit shall return unto God who gave it."

He lowered the book and dismissed us, and I rode off on my
bike to meet Daphne, thinking of Braddock, who was dead.

Along the road I stopped for a while on a stone bridge over a
stream on one of whose banks there was a thicket of gnarled osiers.
These trees had often been pollarded, perhaps in order to make
baskets out of their shoots; the eleven-o'clock sun was bright on the
trembling narrow yellowish leaves of the new growth.

I thought, without regret or fear, that the days of my youth
were far behind me. Flying was making me old.

There was a deep pool under the trees, and its water was
black and still, and it mirrored the lacework of the osier's leaves.

Hearing the words from the Bible that the padre had read, and
having had in mind the young men who were dead—very young
boys, some of them, who had died without having learned a single
thing about people or the world—I thought: Religion is of no good
to me.

My forebears were Presbyterian; my parents were what I think
of as automatic church-goers. I guess they believed. Our minister
in Donkentown was a prig and a bore. As soon as I was well
launched into years of understanding, I gagged at the notion of
predestination, perhaps because of the attitude of some members
of our congregation that they were among the absolutely elected,
while others in the world were not; they took baths on Saturday
night and put on irresistible grace for an hour or so on Sunday
morning. Some of them could be pretty un-Christian on week-
days.

I loved the language of the Bible—as literature—but religion was not much use to me.

Some of the men who patronized the Nissen hut on the base that the padre used as a chapel were doubtless devout, but most of them, I wagered, went for the purpose of lining up magic aids to survival; for them church was like tossing a pinch of spilt salt over the left shoulder.

I guess the best I could say for myself was that I had a vague sense of decency. I had tried to tell Daphne about it, a few days before, but I wasn't sure exactly what it was, or where it came from.

It wasn't a natural product of American culture, because the same culture, more or less, had produced some men, whom I intimately knew, who had none of the sense and no very great share of the thing itself: Marrow, Max Brindt, Jughead Farr—though Farr was to surprise me in time.

It was related, though, to a basic American notion, that anything that contained the spark of life should not be pushed around.

There was more to it than that. My time with Daphne had opened up in me a realization that part of what I meant by decency, or dignity, was the one aptitude, aside from higher intellection, that set men apart from animals—the greater faculty of self-denying love. I was for that. I doubt if I ever would have said such a thing out loud at the base, because I would have caught an unholy razz. In the face of a distinguished body of literary works to the contrary, however, I had come to think that my belief in the importance of this kind of love was widely, though secretively, shared by many of my colleagues in the military forces, and I think, indeed, that the vociferousness of the razz would have bespoken the depth, the life-saving depth, of the conviction.

This faculty was something Marrow not only did not have, but scorned. Perhaps this was why we came, in the end, to be enemies.

I grew cheerful as I pedaled on, and I waited for Daphne on the sidewalk in Motford Sage in a sunshine that seemed to soak into me.

19 /

The bus from Cambridge stopped across the way from
Barclay's Bank, in a square, at the center of which a stone horse
trough encircled a well. I held my ground, and Daph ran across the
cobbled street and stood in front of me, with her head on one side.

I said, "Mind walking?"

She said, "Not with you. Never."

"Might have to run a bit," I said.

"All right, darling," she said. "Let's hurry."

We got to Stanley Crescent pretty fast, and big Mrs. Porlock
took one look at my Daph and nodded her head at me, in approval. She said she'd been expecting us. I liked her. She fixed us a
pot of tea and brought it up to the room and said, using a minimum number of words, that she had to visit an ailing friend and
would be gone until six o'clock and hoped we wouldn't mind an
empty house. Slight smile gripping her dry lips. "She's a lamb,"
Daphne said after she had left. I said I was sorry the room wasn't
fancier, and I started to tell Daph about Mrs. Porlock's husband
and sons, but halfway through the catalogue of their deaths I
found myself in Daphne's arms.

Archie and Willie Porlock, rest their souls, had slept alive in
lumpy beds; we sampled both that afternoon, and we found that
we were deeply, joyfully, unreservedly given to each other. In quiet
interludes we laughed hard over nothings. I had never in my life
been so free, so proud, so quick. Daphne was offering me a
woman's innermost gift: identification. She seemed to renounce all
former convictions and poses and quite sincerely to take on, as
hers, my opinions, my prejudices, even many of my mannerisms
and turns of speech. All this was profoundly flattering to me, for
it gave me a sense of my own worth that I hadn't had before.

We had only to touch, finger tip to finger tip, for us both to be
consumed with our need for each other.

"Why did you let me make love to you that first night?" I
asked, because it seemed that a single kiss now gave more reward
than that whole first importunate grabbing had given.

Daphne ran a finger, at her own risk, down my nose, over my
lips, and back and forth across my chin. "Because," she said, "I'm

the sort who finds it hard to give up today's pleasure for tomorrow's much greater pleasure." That seemed to me a sufficient answer, and a pleasing one. But she added, "Besides, I thought you might leave me." I had just begun to revolve that in my mind when she further said, "Why should a man do anything he wants and a woman have to wait for . . . for . . ." I laughed, because her feminism was so weak. She laughed, too, but perhaps, in the outcome, something about this was to cause her pain and me bewilderment. Giving too much of herself to me had to lead to her trying to save some of herself, I guess.

I tried to tell Daphne of my new feeling about flak. "I want to *live*," I said, holding her close to me. But as I said that, I knew that it was not as simple as that; all my crewmates shared my feeling about flak, but they didn't share Daphne, my particular reason for loving life. I realized that our new attitude toward anti-aircraft fire must have been part of our growing up together in combat; we were wiser in the lore of survival—wiser, perhaps, in knowing that survival in aerial combat was largely out of our hands.

These thoughts got me started pouring stuff out to Daphne about some of my crewmates. I found myself unable to say enough in Neg Handown's praise, for this thirty-six-year-old boy, who behaved so peculiarly in London, was in the air as substantial and immovable as the Dover cliffs we loved so much to see on coming home from danger. During the previous day's mission Neg's massive solidity had really come to the front. Max Brindt had talked so much in early days about being hit by flak (Max, who delighted so in hitting with bombs) that we had all come to believe that such a thing might happen—all of us save Handown, who just seemed to go about his business. How he loved his small corner of the plane! He treated his guns, his delicate automatic gunsight, and his complicated turret as he might have treated children of his own. His preflight inspections of his gear were models of meticulousness; on missions his guns ran like sewing machines, and he kept checking the harmonization of his sight, and he constantly moved his turret to keep the hydraulic fluid warm and so have a lively turret. He had great stamina and a burning sense of responsibility, and it was he who called in by far the greatest number of enemy fighters first, many of them far outside his sector of search. And in the midst of our fear of the flak on the way to St. Nazaire he had struck in on interphone singing, "There'll be no promotion this side of the ocean." I had shut him up, but his steady, firm voice had bucked up my courage.

By contrast Farr was getting more and more sour. Though he had often said he liked the open waist window because firing through it was like shooting skeet, he had now shifted his unending torrent of complaint to the poor provision of armor plate for waist gunners. Whereas most men managed to utter their gripes and then master their feelings, Farr went on and on, gnawing his bitter bones, until at last he concluded he was being discriminated against, and he began to fume about grocery clerks who'd become ninety-day wonders in order to push him around. "I'd like to stand some of those so-called officers up against a wall and plug 'em." Farr was perfect firing-squad material.

Yet Marrow lumped all the enlisted crewmen, Handown as well as Farr, together for condemnation, not only in his crazy tirades against sergeants but also in his more reasoned talk. The career gunners, he said, were under-educated, and anyway, as infants they hadn't been fed enough cod-liver oil, or whatever it was that gave you the I.Q. to tell your ass from your ear. The only thinking they did was to figure out how to goof off, and the only reason they looked ahead was to see whether they could get out of a stint. "Boman," he said, as if it were a compliment, "I could make *you* a better gunner than any man on my ship."

Not our ship. "My" ship.

Yes, I see now that I was getting riled, that sunny afternoon in the squalid room of dead brothers with my only known love, about my pilot, Marrow. Daphne listened to me, in her quiet way, still and deep as that pool under the osiers along the road. She did not comment then, but she silently stored up, to be able to give it to me some day, her treasure of understanding.

20 /

During the inactivity of the first days of June, some of the more enterprising combat crews, including our own, inspired perhaps by the beefed-up YB-40s, designed and built gun-mounts for twin instead of single fifty-caliber machine guns at the waist-window positions. Farr and Brangnani had all but finished installing their new mounts when, on Memorial Day, an order came down from Wing ordering all such twin-fifties removed. Our crews were enraged. Wing, as usual, gave no reason for the command. Perhaps they thought we'd overload our planes and slow them down. Anyway, Marrow ran around trumpeting to everyone in sight about the twin-fifties, and after a few days he had worked up enough of a storm so that Group finally put in a formal application to Wing for permission to modify the mounts. Nothing happened, and nothing happened.

21 /

I was lying on my sack after lunch, one Tuesday, bored silly, reading a funny piece in a copy of *Stars and Stripes* that I'd scrounged from the trash drum at the end of the hut—only it wasn't funny—about how hard it was for this jerk of a 4-F who was making $65 a week just out of high school to get home from a vacation in Florida, when Buzz came in and said, "I got to *move*. Let's go for a ride."

I pointed out that it was drizzling.

"So when did it ever not?" he said.

We had had a spell of weather which made us think that someone had acted upon the standard G.I. query about the island on which we were stationed: "Why don't they cut the God-damn thing loose and sink it?" We felt as if we were sunk. The days had gone like this: May thirty-first, cold, wet, and windy; June first, beautiful clear dawn, cloudy by eight thirty, rain by noon, wind in afternoon, stoves going by evening to drive away the chill; June second, nine separate fronts, some bearing hailstones, and more to come; June third, electrical disturbances. And so on, day after day. We had begun to abuse Stormy Peters, as if the inclemency were his fault. By that Tuesday, June eighth, we were all three-quarters crazy. We hadn't had a raid since what we had come to think of as Flak Day, May twenty-ninth; I hadn't seen Daph since the thirtieth. All the excitement we'd had was one scrubbing (Caen), a visit from a Senator, and Farr getting blotto the day he was finally supposed to receive a promotion.

"I'm on," I said.

Marrow had no registered bicycle of his own at that time, because he had wrecked the front wheel of one machine, by wrenching it sidewise out of a bike rack, and he hadn't bothered to put in for another. Before we started out on our ride he hooked the best-looking wheel he could find in the racks at the Admin building.

Off we went in a gentle rain. We stopped first at the Star in Bartleck and had a beer, and I could see that Marrow's teeth were on edge. Old Whelan had posted a notice a couple of days before directing personnel to wear Class A uniforms when away from the base. But Buzz remembered that weeks earlier Whelan had classified cycling as an athletic sport, so this afternoon he had talked me into leaving my blouse at home and wearing a leather jacket; we were just going out for a "workout" to test the situation. In the Star Buzz developed the theme of Whelan's insanity, and said he just wished a bloody M.P. would come in and try to start something.

We moved on. We pedaled along the main road toward Motford Sage, and I thought with an ache in my chest about Daphne, and our sun-filled room at the Porlocks', and our drawing together there.

We stopped at the Cat and the Fiddle, at a country crossroads, and at the Old Abbott Inn in Motford Sage, where Daph and Buzz and I had had lunch that day, and that made me miss her all the more; and then at some other public houses in Motford Sage—the Wheat Sheaf, the Bell, the Sceptre, the Blue Anchor. We had one beer in each place, and in the Blue Anchor we had an argument about how many pubs we'd tallied. I think that I was right and Buzz was wrong. Anyway, we lost interest in setting a record and just stayed there, and we both began beefing about the missions Wing had been setting up for us. Publicity raids, Marrow said. Killing sheep, I said. Noball targets. S——ty bombing. Fighter bait. Marrow was furious at Wing, because of Wing's having put the kibosh on the twin-fifties.

Buzz railed at the brass for a while, then suddenly he said, "The thing I like about flying—it's like it used to be out of doors

when I was a kid, with your friends. Nobody to jump on your neck.
We had the best f——ing time. I remember once we had this firecracker fight. We took big ones, double-enders, you know, bombs:
they would go off on the ground and then go off in the air. We had
these brick forts, and we made these slanting troughs for the double-enders, and we'd shoot 'em off and they'd go over toward the
enemy fort and go off there; and the other guys were shooting at
us. It was keen." As he talked Marrow looked like a small boy.

But then he was suddenly sore at Jughead Farr. "Stupid bastard, getting soused the day he was going to get his stripe." Farr
had complained for weeks about not having that stripe, which had
been twice given and twice removed, after brawls. Took the line
that the officers were just trying to keep him down. "You want to
know something, Boman? I think Farr's one of those fake tough
babies that all he really wants is a swift kick in the ass. I mean he
asks for it. He whines and whines till you give it to him, and then
he's like teacher's pet."

After that I had one of my rare arguments with Marrow. I
guess I used to figure that the easiest way to handle him was to
keep the peace, give in and agree even when I inwardly disagreed.
But when he got going about Senator Tamalty I just had to speak
up. On Saturday, June the fifth, the Tannoy had announced in
the morning that distinguished visitors were expected on the base
that afternoon and that combat crews and base personnel should
stand by in quarters in uniform for a parade review at about one
o'clock. As always happens, the VIPs were late, and we'd killed an
afternoon doing nothing by the time a cortege of black cars pulled
in at Admin, and the Tannoy called us out on the double, and
they formed us in a three-sided box, in the drizzle, and Whelan
introduced a party of Senators and Congressmen, who were touring the battlefields, and presented "for a word or two" the Honorable Francis P. Tamalty of the U.S. Senate, who seemed to be the
dean of the group. He was a real man of the gravel pits, a primitive,
with bulging veins and a pronounced speech defect—a lisp which
he had, so to speak, furiously crushed, so it had become what he
must have felt was a manly thickening of words. He stood up before us and talked nearly as long as it took to fly to the Dutch coast.
The blood of American boys was as saliva in his mouth. You can't
trust allies; have to be strong enough to stand alone. Nations, like

men, had to be practical. "I know the Frenchies. I fought in their
mud in the First World War." (Later research by Kid Lynch developed the information that Private Tamalty never got east of a
camp near Fayetteville, South Carolina.) Amarrcan knowhow. As
it says in the book of Isaiah. Mothers by their hearth-fires. No
man's brother is as good a watcher at the gates as that man's self.

Self. Of course. That was what appealed to Marrow.

Marrow had never seen such a hero. Wanted to run the pa-
triot for President, get rid of Roosevelt, who only knew how to
give things away with his eyes closed. Cripple anyhow. Everything
from the waist down. When a man was paralyzed *there* . . .

Well, I finally said my say about the Senator. Marrow blinked
with amazement at my daring to speak out against both Tamalty
and Marrow. At one time Buzz had the gall to say, "Shush, son,
you're surrounded by English ears."

And so we were. Some elderly men, laborers of some kind,
with limestone faces and fingers beaten out on forges, were sitting
at the next table, and they had fallen silent and were listening intently to us.

Marrow talked louder than ever. Began to pitch in on the
Frogs. Suddenly he let out a peal of laughter. Martin Foley, a pilot
in our squadron, had announced that he was going to study French
in one of the language classes that had been set up on the base by
the Special Events Officer. "Imagine, Foley the F——up, trying to
parley voo." Marrow bellowed. The idea of trying to learn a foreign language, and French of all languages, struck Marrow as very
funny.

"He figures he stands a good chance of getting shot down over
France," I said, "and maybe getting to use his parachute."

"Let the sons of bitches speak English," Marrow said with
brutal force.

"Matie." One of the old Englishmen was tapping Marrow on
the shoulder. "Do they put up classes in the King's English at the
Yank aerodrome?"

Marrow got the point, and I saw the red rise in his face. "Your
King stutters," he said.

"Aye," the man said, very benign. He nodded happily, as if
stuttering were quite a feat.

"Let's get out of here," Marrow said. "This stuff tastes like p——."

"Aye," the man said.

"Listen, stupid," Marrow said, turning his chair full around, "what makes you think you'd be sitting here enjoying yourself at all if the Americans hadn't come over to fight your war for you?"

"Henjoying meself?"

"You'd be browning your nose on some Nazi's bum."

"Never!" the old man said, and he bounced two or three times with an odd laugh that came out of him at the absurdity of the young American's ideas.

Suddenly there were three R.A.F. enlisted men behind Marrow's chair. Marrow saw them out of the corner of his eye, and he turned and said to me, "Silly f——ing night raids, what the f—— do they accomplish? Kill civilians, I guess." He took a sip from his glass. "If that's what you want to do in a war."

One of the R.A.F. men grasped the straight back of Marrow's chair and gave it a single powerful shake which threw Marrow to his feet. I stood up. Marrow's jaw was sticking out like an engraved invitation.

"Hoy!" the old man who had been talking to Marrow now said with his face up to the R.A.F. men.

"This cheeky bahstit," the man who had rocked Marrow's chair said.

" 'Ere, 'ere," the old man said. "Let's 'ave friendly language."

At this the three R.A.F. men turned away from Marrow and started toward the bar.

"God-damn limey chicken s——," Marrow said, ostensibly to me but loudly enough to be heard all the way to the bar. "Come on, Boman."

You could see the control in those retiring backs. Not one of the heads turned.

As we went out of the door I heard the old fellow say to his friends, " 'Omesick, poor miserable bloke."

When we got outside to the bicycle racks we found that the bike Marrow had been riding was gone.

Forgetting altogether that he himself had swiped the machine on the base in the first place, Marrow began screaming about the sneaky British. God-damn limeys stealing an American bike. "Bunch of bloody crooks," he shouted. He was really teed.

He wanted to go inside and pick a fight with the three R.A.F. boys, but I managed to persuade him that it was quite unlikely that they had taken the bicycle, inasmuch as they were still in the pub.

For a while we tried to make our way by riding each other, taking turns at the pedals and on the bar, but we were both beer-logged, and we zigzagged and fell down often. At last we came to a fish-and-chips vender's horse-drawn van, and we ate some of his freshly cooked wares and persuaded him, a lean fox with a scarf wound round and round his neck, to drive us back to the base for two pounds—more than he could make in several days of selling fish and chips—and we put my bike in the back and rode, all three in the cab, to the clopping of an old gray's feet. Our heads were wreathed with the acrid smell of hot deep fat. A weather front peeled back the dripping clouds, and there was an apple-green sky over a sparkling landscape.

22 /

On Wednesday, June the ninth, we went to Cambridge and heard the university students sing madrigals on the banks of the Cam, and I lay beside Daphne among the listeners on the grass under the enormous trees of the Backs, full of desire in the warm afternoon.

Between numbers some Yank near us said to his pal that the concert was part of an annual celebration, which was, he said, called May Week because it was in June.

"These screwy limeys," the pal said.

I saw Daphne blush.

After the sing Marrow wandered off with some others, and Daph and I hired a punt and drifted on the narrow river along the Backs, under the marvelous King's and Clare and Garret Hostel and Trinity and St. Johns bridges, for an hour or so, and it was then that I worked my way, with Daphne's help, to some thoughts which foreshadowed my crisis of late July.

While the students had been singing their sixteenth-century

madrigals, about which I knew nothing, my mind had wandered, and I had spent some time thinking about girls back in the States. There had always been a girl. I had some very particular associations with the casual ones during the phases. With Penny it was a moving picture in Sikeston, Missouri, called *Here Comes Mr. Jordan*; with Sybil it was her old man's Buick, in the mountains out of Denver, parked in a turnout, not even necking, but listening to Tommy Dorsey on the car radio; with Marylee it was a tune, *This Love of Mine*, blaring out of a juke-box in a drugstore in Montgomery, Alabama. All through the whole time, like a theme, ran Janet, my home-town girl, who was official, who seemed inescapable, like an inheritance. The reward of this rumination had been to appreciate Daphne all the more, for with each girl, no matter how much of a yen I had had for her, I had always been conscious of some quality that grated on my nerves, and with Daphne I could find no cause for holding back.

I got the knack of poling the punt right off the bat, then after a while I just sat in the stern, and we talked.

Daphne was open with me. There was no language barrier. In some way we cut straight through our differences of nationality and experience.

I understood that she had seldom provoked aggressive behavior in men, for though she was fragile and feminine, she had, besides, the enormous inner strength of a woman at peace with herself.

"We never argue about anything," I said.

"Why should we?" she said. "I miss you so much when I'm away from you, how could I spoil the time when we're together?"

She loved longing; it was clear that she loved the suffering that a deep attachment could bring.

"What would you do for me?" she asked.

The things I promised to do were out of songs. Climb a mountain. Slow boat to China. I could write a book. Swim the ocean wide. I'll make a string of pearls out of the dew—my safe song. Yes, with Daph I felt, above all, far away from danger of any kind.

Then suddenly it seemed that Daphne was cross-examining me a little. "What do you want of me?" she asked. It was an anguished question and took me by surprise.

Bed came into my mind first, but I knew I must give a better answer than that. Comfort when I am in despair. Good company; good talking; good laughing. A way to kill dead hours between missions. I felt embarrassed, because it was clear that Daphne wanted to shake some kind of open-ended commitment out of me, a promise, a very big promise, and all of a sudden I was chary and evasive.

"There's a war on," I said, as if to explain my long pause. "I want this war to be over and done with."

"Why are you in it?" she asked. "I mean, what have you to do with war?"

Her question was oddly worded, and I should have known Daphne well enough by then to realize that she meant the question exactly as she asked it, for I suppose she had a woman's belief that wars could only end when men refused to fight in them, but I was rattled, and I probably would have scoffed at that belief as too namby-pamby, soft, because I certainly didn't think that conscientious objectors would bring a warless world, and anyway I chose to believe that she had simply asked me the standard question of those days.

"I don't know what I'm fighting for," I said. "Certainly not for Senator Tamalty's brand of patriotism. I don't think any of our guys are fighting for that—not even Marrow. I think they're fighting to finish twenty-five missions, period. I know that doesn't sound very good to somebody who's English, Daph, but I swear, I think that's the only war aim. Every mission you get behind you is one more mission toward getting finished. If you can just get through it alive, that's the thing." I think I was too embarrassed even with Daphne to speak of the sense of decency that had been on my mind.

I thought some more later on about trying to kill in order to stay alive. In school in Donkentown, when I had been about ten years old, I'd been interested in dinosaurs. Maybe it was because I was so small, such a shorty, that I was crazy about brontosauruses and stegosauruses and triceratopses and allosauruses and the greatest of all, tyrannosauruses, the kings. Those beasts took millions of years to adapt themselves to killing in order to stay alive—did it by developing spikes as tall as men, tails that could knock down houses, collars of bone as big as the sides of Sherman tanks, claws like axe blades. They had brains the size of walnuts. And seventy-five millions of years had passed and I, in my Flying Fortress, with my brain the size of a goodly grapefruit, might just as well be a tooth in a leather-winged pterosaur. It seemed to me that for civilized man, it was not enough to have as the central idea of life mere survival.

When I came to think more carefully about the question Daphne really had asked me—what had I to do with war?—I realized that fighting in the war was something I was doing simply because it seemed easier than not doing it. I was a member of a community in which flying and fighting were the only accepted ways of behaving.

It all seemed to come down to the proposition that I would rather die than behave in a manner that was not considered normal, proper, usual.

At the same time, looking at Daphne in her yellow dress on the green thwart of the flat-bottomed boat, I knew that I would far rather live than die.

What would I do for her? she had asked me.

At the end of July, at the height of the series of raids we called our Blitz, having put Kid Lynch's body to rest in the U.S. military cemetery here at Cambridge, I passed through a crisis in my attitude which came from trying to pull these confused and conflicting thoughts together, and it was not until the last trying passage of the Schweinfurt raid that I was to come face to face with what they all meant for me. On the day of the madrigal concert they were merely random, troublesome ideas.

When our hour's rental of the punt was over, we went to Daphne's apartment.

23 /

A bunch of us were sitting around in Titty's room, gassing about a mission we'd flown to Wilhelmshaven that day, June eleventh.

In walked a screwball character I'd seen around the station, who looked about sixteen years old, a flaming redhead, and I saw LYNCH stenciled on his leather jacket and assumed it was the jocko everyone called the Kid, who kept reading poems, ditties, doggerel, and wisecracks over the Tannoy—I guess with the acquiescence of the Special Events officer. The Kid would break into the middle of nothing on a rainy afternoon with a clean limerick. Always signed off, "Lieutenant Lynch reporting." Some guys thought him a nuisance, but I'd been for him, sight unseen, on the ground that he was a co-pilot who was said to be a much better flier than his first pilot. A man in a position like that *has* to disseminate screwy verse.

We in Titty's room got talking about the lone black Fort, the German spotter, which we'd seen again that afternoon. Following a briefing for Bremen and a leisurely take-off at noon, clouds had made an attack on the primary target impossible, and as the formation had turned at Bremerhaven for our secondary, the lead group, too eager or not poised enough, had swung too sharply, and the turns of succeeding groups had grown wider and wider, till ours, at the end of the line, like that of the outermost man in a game of Crack the Whip, had overswung so far that our bombing had finally been rushed and poor, and we had cut for home, disgusted, and then, in the evening sky, tracking us from a position to the rear and high above the last element of our Group, that unmarked B-17 had made its appearance and had stayed with us nearly halfway across the North Sea and at last had turned back and had flown, unescorted and incongruous, toward Germany.

While we were talking about the spotter, someone brought up the concept of the Germans as good fighters, good sportsmen. *All Quiet on the Western Front. Wings.* Kid Lynch kept quiet. Marrow said one of our crippled planes had pulled out of formation on one raid and had put its wheels down and the German fighters not only hadn't fired on it but had hovered around it, sort of mothering it down to the ground. The Krauts probably wanted another spotting ship, but Marrow had to believe that this was the Code of the Sky. Never shoot at a man in a chute. The Victory Roll. The fellowship of aviators. Fliers were different from other men; enemy fliers were more like you than Allied foot soldiers.

Then Lynch spoke up, and at first he rattled me, but I see now what he was doing. He wanted to show this self-deluded glory-boy that all the crap about the chivalry of the air was just a way to pretend everything was going to be safe and nice—for Number One, one's self. Of course the Kid had uphill going in our crowd. Humanity's abomination was not at all clear to us, for we'd been too young for Spain, and it was too soon for Auschwitz, and we thought we had, in the Fortress and the blockbuster (what a vaunting name that seemed then!), the greatest weapons man would ever hold in his fist—because of course our war was going to be the last war ever. There's too much idiocy at large about how we were disenchanted young men who'd been wised up by *A Farewell to Arms* and *Soldier's Pay* and *Three Soldiers*. We were up to our tallywhackers in illusions, slogans, shibboleths, belief in magic—mostly out of ads. We were ready to die to the last man for Dinah Shore, rare sirloin, a cold beer, and a Caribbean cruise. Maybe we didn't put much stock in the Four Freedoms; that was propaganda. But we really believed in *Time* and the *Post* and *Collier's* and *Life*. Anyway, the Kid said he'd heard from the boys in S-2 that this fellow in the spotting plane was known as the Black Knight, he was from the Black Forest, he wore a black onyx ring that Hitler had given him, he had taken pilgrimages to all the scenes of German heroism. Lynch was persuasive, he could weave a subtle web out of fantastic threads, and that night he took strands, I guess, from the *Nibelungenring* and from the Grimms and the *Walpurgisnacht*, and I tell you, it was creepy. He threw in a bit of Fainéant Le Noir for good measure. It was the first time I ever saw Marrow scared. After the session broke up he took me in our room and questioned me, with a kind of feverish desperation, about how much I thought Lynch knew, and whether all that could be true about the Black Knight. I had to face it that Marrow half believed every word the Kid had said. I think Lynch had Marrow believing that each evening the Black Knight drank a tiny silver gobletfull of blood drawn from the veins of captured R.A.F. and U.S.A.A.F. pilots. After that, when we saw the Black Knight on missions, Marrow would suddenly become cautious, and would start raising hell with me about manifold pressures and oil temperatures.

24 /

Lynch dropped into the seat next to mine at supper the following evening. "You and I have a pair of lulus for pilots," he said.

"At least mine can fly," I said. I'd heard about the clunk Lynch had drawn, Bessemer.

"I don't know which I'd less rather have," he said, "a born non-flier like mine or a bloody hell's angel like yours. Boy, that Airman's Code stuff!"

I told Lynch that Marrow was human, that he'd just adopted a pet dog—a half-starved medium-sized long-haired nondescript —and that he was pretty good to it, and the pup had taken to him at once. And about how Marrow felt about sergeants, and about his old man having been a sergeant in the First World War. And that just before I'd come over to the mess hall, Buzz had said: "Know what I'm going to do? I'm going to inject this mut with hydrophobia and let him go after some of these sergeants."

But Lynch got off that topic. "Hear about the zoot-suit riots in Los Angeles?" It seemed that beginning back in the winter hoodlums dressed in exaggerated pegtop trousers and long jackets and pointed shoes, and wearing enormous watch chains, had begun waylaying lone sailors in San Pedro, beating them up and sometimes stabbing them, and over the months had extended their crazy operations to the whole Los Angeles area. Lynch told me that there had been open warfare in the past week between bands of servicemen and gangs of zoot-suiters.

My eye had vaguely wandered across two-line items about the zoot-suiters in *Stars and Stripes*, but Lynch was up on all the details—the circumference of zoot pants at the cuff and at the thigh —and what interested me was the fiery intensity with which he talked. He wanted me to discuss with him the reasons for these outbursts—guilt over high wages and non-combat status, latent homosexuality, the pose of indifference on the West Coast; the Kid was full of theories. This was the first conversation with any meat in it that I'd had in a long time. Lynch was serious. He was fighting a war, in which he might lose his life, and he wanted to know and feel all he could, good and bad, about the country for which he might be asked to pay the ultimate tax.

This earnestness surprised me. The uninhibited Kid who broadcast doggerel and bad jokes on the Tannoy hadn't prepared me for this other man.

Lynch was pretty ugly to look at, yet he gave an impression of charm and even beauty. His hair was of an unbelievable redness— not russet or auburn, but the color of the undersides of stratus clouds in one of the sudden-flash sunsets we used to have in Donkentown; you expected the violent glint to fade off his head any moment, to give way to gray and night. His eyes had something wrong with them: the folds of skin and conjunctiva around the lids were somehow pulled tight, so his eyes seemed too small and piggish. He had not the usual redhead's creamy complexion but a pitted and thick-looking skin, like canvas or a fruit rind. He looked, despite these flaws, a fresh and childlike person. The rapidity with which his mind worked; the warmth of his feelings; his wit, heard on his tongue and seen in his queer eyes; and, perhaps most impressive of all, the passionate seriousness that underlay his flippancy—all these gave him more than enough to pay back the debt on his looks.

He was twenty-two, and he was a college graduate, a married man, and—hard to believe!—the father of two daughters. Maybe this was where the seriousness came from.

At the table in the mess hall, amid the crude jokes being passed back and forth like mashed potatoes, Lynch secretively showed me a snapshot of his "three women." The little fat girls were redheads, too—Ruby and Ginger (nicknames, he told me). I'll bet I was the only man on the base who knew that the Kid was a father.

25 /

We had a raid the next day, June thirteenth, our eleventh mission in The Body, to Bremen, and I couldn't wait, after it was over, to seek Lynch out and talk it over with him.

The mission as a whole had been a dud, because another wing, not ours, had cut off from its briefed course about thirty miles before the initial point and had headed straight for the target, and this short cut had put it on a collision course with our Wing, which had followed instructions, so we were forced to circle wide to avoid the others, and in the ensuing confusion most of our groups dropped their bombs a couple of miles from the city out in the sea. But I couldn't help telling Lynch that this had been our best raid in *The Body*. Fighter opposition had been stiff, and we had been hot. Reports of sightings by our crew had been quick and concise, and our interphone discipline had been tight.

Lynch and I, still in our flying suits, holding sandwiches at the Red Cross stand, talked rapidly back and forth and sometimes we put the food down and, with our two flat hands banking and angling, we illustrated maneuvers.

I seemed to want to convince Lynch that Marrow was a remarkable pilot. His evasive tactics that afternoon had been superb. Under head-on and tail attacks, he had devised a subtle, eccentric corkscrewing, a spiral path varying from four to six compass degrees out of the line of flight, which must have given the Germans exceedingly difficult targets, as their reflection allowances must have been continually varying; yet Marrow seemed to hold formation and over-all course as truly as any.

Another thing: We got a radio message, halfway home, that there were some VIPs visiting Pike Rilling and that upon returning to base we were to take one low pass over the field, flying smart formation, and I told Lynch that Marrow had turned the plane over to me for that run (having a puppy must've made him kind-hearted), and I'd felt great, supposing that Hap Arnold, or Clark Gable, or somebody else of consequence was down on the ground watching *me* hold *The Body* in there like a screwed-on attachment.

Lynch shrugged at that; later he came out with what he meant by the shrug.

Just then Marrow came over and tore down before Lynch all that I had built up about him. He was laughing hard. "Boman," he said, barely able to control his heaving and cackling enough to speak. "Boman, Jesus, the joke's on you, kid. Foley got shot down. Over Germany. Now that he can talk French. You and your God-

damn foreign languages." And he went rollicking off to tell someone else; I gathered later that he kept telling the story as a joke
on me.

That evening Lynch told me that he had heard about Marrow's having knocked the bottom out of the old cup at the Bartleck
railway station and that he, Lynch, had, a few days later, sneaked
a new enamel cup out of the mess hall and had carried it to the
village on his bike and had hung it on the spigot against the station wall, to replace the wayfarer's cup one of our men had destroyed.

Later he said to me, "I flew that pass over the field today, too,
but that was only because Bessemer may be a first pilot but he
can't fly formation yet. He's promised me he'd try to learn how.
But listen, Bo, what makes you think Marrow was being kind-
hearted to you, letting you fly that run? In his language that was
an insult. Marrow'll fly when it matters, Boman can fly for the
shiny-ass brass."

I stood up for Marrow: said he wasn't like that.

26 /

Doc Randall, his huge hands flailing, conducted a class
on venereal diseases. They had scrubbed Le Mans in the morning,
and now in the afternoon they had assembled all the officers in
the Number One Mess. Doc seemed embarrassed, and we guessed
that Loony-bug Whelan had put him up to it. Doc showed us a
movie on how to catch a dose. We got cheering for the microbes,
as if they were the Good Guys.

Lynch and Marrow and I walked back across "the campus,"
as Lynch, after our lecture, called the living area of the base.

Marrow said, "Any of you guys know how to dip a sheep?"

From a farmer near Bartleck, Marrow had acquired some
sheep-dip, so he could free his ever-scratching pup of vermin.

Lynch, who seemed to know everything, instructed Buzz.
"It'll be quite an experience for both of you," he said.

When we got to our room Marrow took one look at his pup,
really a sad apple, and said, "Watch out, fleas, here I come!"

Lynch and I decided we were not obliged to witness the slaughter, and we went for a walk. In the clear weather the day of the Wilhelmshaven raid, a dry and sparkling turn which had promised to hold two or three days, farmers had come out with horse-drawn sickle bars and had mowed the great golden expanse of grass within the triangle of the runways, and now, as Lynch and I strolled out across the airdrome we saw men with wagons taking in the dried hay and kerchiefed women gleaning behind them. It was a warm, sunstruck hour, and shadows on the stubble were sharp and nervous, like scavenging crows and grackles.

"Think of it," Lynch said. "People who can't afford to waste a few blades of grass."

"I know," I said.

Out of the blue Lynch made a prediction. "Listen," he said, "you may not think so, but you're going to outlast that tough guy you have for a pilot."

"I don't want to outlast him," I said. "I just want him and me to last exactly the same amount—fourteen more missions."

"Sure, sure," Lynch said. Then after a moment he said, "It's the man with imagination who suffers during a war. To imagine is to suffer. Really, it's very painful, but you get used to it. The man without imagination takes a lot, he doesn't even bat an eye. But when he does break, goodbye! He's gone and you can't salvage him."

I said, "That poem you read the other day, about not hating the people you fight and not loving the ones you guard—how do you get away with that stuff?"

"Oh, that!" Lynch said. "I told Whelan that was by an Irish-man, and it was about an Irish flier, and Whelan thinks everything Irish originally came from Boston and must be O.K."

That was why I had thought of my mother when I heard the poem. "My mother used to recite Yeats to me," I said, and I had a flood of feeling, remembering my childhood, my brother Jim, my father in his summer mood, my mother brushing her hair.

Lynch and I were in a turnip field beyond the end of the north-south runway, and the dirt was fragrant when we kicked it. In the woods around Pike Rilling Hall, beyond the wire fence, we could hear an argument of sparrows.

"Why did you get into this?" I asked. I would never have

dreamed of asking Marrow such a question, and even with Lynch I was afraid he might razz me to death on account of it.

"Well," he slowly said, "it strikes me that in this century something awful has been let loose among the so-called civilized peoples, something primitive and barbaric. I don't say the Germans have a monopoly on this . . . this regression. But I figure I'm here to help put down the Nazis because right at the moment they're the most dangerous representatives of this sort of throwback we're liable to. If I can do my part in keeping this worst side of mankind in hand, I'll be satisfied, whatever happens to me."

Lynch had spoken with such unaffected sincerity, such simplicity—very quietly, and answering as if he had given the question much thought—that I was deeply stirred by his words, but I think he was unaware of their effect on me.

27 /

The Le Mans mission on June fifteenth was a fiasco. It was an early one, with a take-off at five fifteen, in bad weather. The field order had stipulated a climb at six hundred feet a minute—too much for the Forts carrying their maximum bomb load of three tons. Nine of our twenty-three ships that took off couldn't find the formation in the mealy-mush sky, and they aborted. At altitude the temperature was minus fifty-five degrees Centigrade, and thick contrails formed that made formation flying dangerous. There was a solid cloud cover over the continent, and finally, when we were about ten miles inside the French coast, I heard on liaison a recall order from Wing.

I told Marrow.

At first he wouldn't believe me. He had started the day with a tirade at Wing, because an answer to the Group's request for permission to install twin-fifties had come down: Nix. Now, when he heard that we had been recalled, he took both hands off the wheel and formed fists and shook them over his head. He was apparently beyond speech with anger.

At safe altitude Marrow ripped off his mask, and he looked

very odd. I recalled at that moment an exchange that had taken place while we had loafed around on the hardstand waiting for stations time before one of our early raids. The enlisted men were discussing their pilot, who was in the ship and out of earshot. Junior Sailen, meaning to praise, said that Marrow ought to have been a fighter pilot. "Yeah," Farr growled. "I agree. No crew." From there on in, that June day, Marrow behaved as if he were alone at the controls of a P-47. We peeled off the formation and entered the landing circle as usual, but at the last moment, instead of swinging in and leveling off for the east-west runway, Marrow jerked us to the right out of our slow banking turn, poured on coal, and got us tearing along about fifty feet above the deck. The next thing I knew there were enormous trees flicking by on both sides, and I had just time to think that the crazy bastard was going to fly right in one of the windows of Pike Rilling Hall, and to hear Max scream on CALL, "Marrow! Have you lost your mind?," when I saw a slate roof loom up and then one of those fancy-brick fluted Georgian chimneys go past, close enough for me to have counted the bricks. As soon as Marrow had passed the house, he whipped us into a turn that was so tight you could hear the rivets squeak, and down we charged again on the slate roof, and we flew right back between the rows of stately trees. We were well beneath the treetops. Aphrodite had no pants to p—— in, but I bet something squeezed out of the stone. Whew! But Buzz wasn't satisfied. He took a vicious pass at the tower, shouldered into the traffic pattern, and landed.

First thing Marrow said in the interrogation, his chin jutting out like East Anglia, was, "Do I get a sortie credit from you f——ers for *that* one?"

I guess the interrogating officer, our tanned friend, Merchant, hadn't heard about *The Body's* passes. Very dryly he said, "All planes that got as far as the French coast get credit for a mission in spite of the recall."

"Well, that's very God-damn charitable," Marrow said.

28 /

Later that afternoon there was a wild hailstorm with so
much white in it that a whole crowd of officers and men ran out
on the line and had a snowball fight, and Marrow was among
them, laughing like a schoolboy.

But in the evening, when the sun's lemon-yellow rays were
tangent to the earth, I saw Marrow walking out toward the dispersal areas with the chaplain. His head was bent, his shoulders
rounded, and from a distance he looked old.

29 /

Daphne was already in our room at Mrs. Porlock's when
I arrived there the next Sunday morning, June the twentieth. She
was sitting on the edge of the late Archie Porlock's bed, and she
was fiddling with a long bead necklace; couldn't rush to greet me
because she had half the beads unstrung and in her lap. I sat beside her and offered to help her thread them back on, but she said
she could do it easier alone. As she worked she put one end of the
string in her mouth, and whenever I said anything, all she said
was, "Mmm." I watched, with enjoyment, the swift, dainty movements of her fingers as they handled the pieces of glass like tiny,
dark, faceted grapes, bits of cherry jello, fragments of sky. Her face
was so intense! No time for me.

I moved across on Willie Porlock's bed and set myself to entertain her—told her, of course, about Marrow's pass at Pike Rilling Hall. Mmm. Marrow taught his dog to beg and took him in
the mess hall at mealtime, and the C.O. happened in and threw
the dog out. Marrow was badly hacked; acted as if his spirit had
been broken. Mmm. Squadron practice flight last Wednesday.
Boring. Mmm.

Fist-fight on Friday. There were still about thirty Happy Warriors—men who had completed their tours—hanging around the
station with nothing to do, and since heroes are soon forgotten,
especially where there is a surfeit of them, we regarded them as a

nuisance. Marrow, who believed that flying and potency were equivalent, said, "Poor guys, they've had their b——s cut off." Sitting in the officers' club one night Tex Miller, a retired co-pilot, began to rail about having seen a Negro sergeant in a pub with a blonde English girl. "They'll try to lay a blonde ever' time," Tex said. Marrow let go—not because of Tex's ideas, I thought, but just because these castrated graduate students were getting on his nerves. He said in a loud voice, "I'm sick of this Texas bull s——." They wound up outside: Marrow, a cut lip; Tex, six stitches on the forehead, a shiner the color of that bed right there.

Mmm.

I was getting fed up with the mmm routine. Life was too short. I didn't say so, but I thought Daphne could have fixed the God-damn wampum on her own time.

So I stretched myself out full length on the bed of Willie Porlock, who went down with the *Repulse*, and I just shut my big mouth and waited. I had made the mistake of doing some very fancy daydreaming about love-making—astonishing prolongations, and modulations of gentleness and strength—that I had been going to enjoy with Daphne that day, for our relationship had been building and building; the pain of separation had been sharp but strangely sweet—sweetened by the certainty that our pleasure in reunion would be even greater than last time. But now all I was getting was this *clack clack clack*, mmm, nervous fiddling. I found I had a headache, just a malaise at first but gradually it grew into a real rock-crusher. It passed through my mind that I was about to have some sort of stroke. I was going to die. Humiliating. In bed with my shoes on.

At last she got that horrible string out of her mouth.

"Listen, Daph," I said, "is anything the matter?"

"No, darling," she said, "I just fell off the roof."

I sat up. "You *what?*" I was so used to assuming that people were crazy in those days that I really wasn't surprised or alarmed to find that Daph was, too. All that was happening, in truth, was that Daphne was talking to me in code, but I hadn't the key; my old fiancée, Janet, had been a secretive one. I pushed out a "Hunh?"

"My period," she said.

My headache vanished with one heartbeat; I felt gentle and

unselfish. We found a set of checkers that had belonged to the Porlock brothers, and we began a game.

I told Daphne about my new friend Lynch, and when I came to the part about Yeats I was revisited by powerful feelings about my childhood, and soon I was pouring out my heart about my mother and father and brother. My mother, I said, was mild and gullible. She firmly believed, and indoctrinated me with the faith, that everyone was Nice. My father did some mean things to my mother, but she insisted that he was all Heart. Two of my mother's closest women friends were malicious, gossipy bitches, but my mother said they were True Christians. She had a simple recipe for sugar cookies; they were white, with a raisin pushed in the middle. I took the raisin out first and ate round and round the cookie's belly button. Mother had long hair, which she brushed by the hour, holding a handmirror to reflect her profile in the mirror of her chiffonier; but I believe she was homely. She used to recite verse to me when I was a grown boy, at the stage when I was counter-rubbing the fuzz on my face in the belief that this would firm it up into shavable material. "Near to the silver Trent Sirena dwelleth. . . ." And, ". . . All day the same our postures were, And we said nothing, all the day." And she was crazy about Yeats. I used to scratch and want out (scudding cirrus, west-northwest wind, glass rising), but some of it stayed with me—not just the words and the taste, but also the emotion, the aspiration.

She had got me onto music, too. At first, when I was too young for it, she gave me lessons herself, and during them I, monopolizing her sweet and patient attention, banged at the keyboard, whined, miscounted time, and sulked, with exuberant, really ecstatic badness. Later she sent me to a Mr. Florian, who sat beside me on the piano bench, baring his yellow irregular teeth, like kernels of mutated feed corn, as he reacted with horror to my dirty, long fingernails, and he'd go off and get some manicure scissors so I wouldn't "chop up the keyboard," and I was convinced that one day he would plunge the curved blades into my rib basket because I hated practicing and him so much. But I think because of those hours my mother had given me, I kept a love of the sounds of the piano, though I gave up playing myself in college. I spent much of my time with Janet listening to records. My favorites were Teddy Wilson and Jess Stacey.

Daphne had never heard of them.

"I'll play them for you sometime."

I loved my father. He was a kind-hearted man who couldn't help being stern with my brother and me—and mean to Mother. It was supposed to be for our own good—and hers, I guess. There was a place across the street from our house where Sheehan, the builder, had scooped out a foundation and then quit, for some reason, and Jim and I played there; he, being older, took the lead. Jim was made for engineering projects. We had assembled an array of dead light bulbs, dead Christmas-tree bulbs, dead flashlight bulbs, and dead radio tubes—together with some light bulbs which were, I'm afraid, not yet dead—and we'd built ramps and banks, and we'd broken the bulbs and stuck their screw ends in the ground, with their filaments sticking up like radio masts, and we'd arranged cigar boxes and mud shapes, and the whole thing looked like a futuristic seat of big doings. It was muddy there, and we always got dirty. One Sunday afternoon (stratus overhead, the gray overcast sky a sopped sponge ready to be squeezed by the slightest wind, a day for mistakes, sorrow) we'd played there awhile and then wandered off, and we found in Partson's woods an abandoned, honest-to-goodness log cabin with a caved-in roof and one collapsed wall, probably some Boy Scout project but we were convinced it was a Colonial fort. We tried to repair the fallen wall, and Jim lost his balance, and a log fell on his hand and split a fingernail, and the blood was something awful, all over Jim. He cried. I gently sucked the place, to prevent fungus poisoning, a danger we had just invented, and we decided Jim had better not face Father, bloody and muddy as he was. We lay out in the woods till after dark and sneaked in by the slanting cellarway door, and Father caught us as we went up the kitchen stairs. He spanked me on the assumption I had hurt Jim, and he made us stay indoors two whole Sunday afternoons.

Now in wartime my brother Jim had a desk job in the Navy at Key West, with a wife, baby, small house, new refrigerator on installments; a tough war. Hard time about gas rationing. Sometimes actually had to walk to the beach. Got his wife to write me letters about it. "Bastard Roosevelt," I could hear him.

Father smelled of tobacco and occasionally of something I once, at the age of six or so, called medicine. "I can smell the medicine in your nose," I said, when he was kissing me good night. Maybe he was using it for medicinal purposes, but I doubt it. I could remember him best, when I was very small, on the beach at Pamonassett, to which he always walked from the summer house. Father had a floppy white cotton hat, like the one President Hoover wore fishing, and he took me by the hand, and we strolled along the lip of the tide, and he let me run around him like a sandpiper, and I believed that he was truly happy in my company, and whether he was or not, all that mattered was the belief. . . .

I guess that talking on like this was the only way I could find of telling Daphne about that obscure sense of decency.

We played several games of checkers, and Daphne went out of her way to let me win. We were closer than we had ever been, and more peaceful. This was surely the opposite, the ultimate opposite, of war.

"It's almost as if we were married," Daphne said at one point.

Only long afterwards, looking back, could I realize the intensity, the yearning, the beseeching appeal in that remark which seemed so casual and so apt at the time.

In wartime all the settled ways of peace seemed make-believe. Had I given the matter serious thought I would probably have told myself that a man whose daily concern was death could not think of life—of giving life, making life—in serious, responsible terms. And I lacked the understanding then to realize that for Daphne, nothing else could be serious. Had I possessed that understanding, I would not have been taken aback, and nearly crushed, by what Daphne chose to do, in the end, with Marrow.

30 /

On June twenty-second they sent us to Hüls. The raid provided a serious setback to the Group's morale. The enemy aircraft seemed to concentrate on our formations, and after the initial point there was a foul combination of flak—both a curtain barrage and continuous following fire—and altogether the Germans shot down four of our planes, *Pizza Pie, Lucky Lulu, Miss*

Manookie, and *Kilroy Wasn't Here,* and a fifth, *Straight Flush,*
ditched in the Channel, and four men drowned. We, in *The
Body,* had some special, rather tricky feelings. Before Hüls we
had had Bremen, when we had thought we were finally coa-
lesced as a crew, and the recall from Le Mans, when Marrow had
taken that hair-raising run at Pike Rilling Hall. Hüls was our thirteenth mission—the halfway mark on our way to twenty-five. Haverstraw, the number boy, whose life was getting more and more
routinized—he never entered the plane without his little ritual of
tapping the sides of the hatch opening with his swagger stick and
then kissing the skin of the ship—and who wanted everything to
be orderly, was absolutely insistent that we refer to the mission as
"Twelve B" and there be not so much as a whisper of the number
thirteen. We could call the mission "going over the hump" if we
wanted. Marrow seemed in pretty good shape, except that he
kept jumping Prien, and after the mission he said to me, "You got
to have a good tail gunner. That Prien's chicken. You can tell
from the sound of his voice on the interphone. Him and his stomach. He tries to give the impression he's rugged, what you might
call antagonistic, but I can tell his kind, he's got apron strings
coming out his ears. Remember how he used to joke about ships
going down? Now he knows the Heinies are playing for keeps.
He's scared." And perhaps he wasn't the only one. Over Hüls
there had been pink shell bursts of flak, apparently signaling the
fighters that there would be a lull and they could take a run on us,
then black bursts; a lot of us had that flakky feeling again. Our
people were very depressed after that raid, for they believed,
rightly or wrongly, that the Germans had had advance information of the target we were to hit. This conviction, which was bolstered by our having had a scrubbing of Hüls just the day before,
swept the base like an October meadow fire.

The Group was ordered out again the very next day, to Villacoublay airfield, not far from Paris. *The Body* didn't go. There
was cloud cover, and the mission was recalled, and most bombs
were carried home. This, too, was bad for the Group's morale, as
a follow-up on Hüls. We didn't go because we hadn't been scheduled. There was nothing wrong with the plane. We just weren't
on the list. Marrow raised the roof but was firmly told that he had
the day off. We couldn't figure out whether this was to punish us

for our pass at Wing, or whether Doc Randall thought we needed a layoff, or what. It made us very edgy, the more so because everyone got sortie credit for a recall on which there'd been no fighters or flak at all. We hated to miss that one.

Two days later Marrow became a hero.

31 /

On June twenty-fifth we were wakened before we had begun to get into the chugging part of sleep, at one in the morning, and we were briefed for Hamburg. We took off in the first dilution of night with dawn, at four thirty, and everything seemed out of gear from the moment we left Pike Rilling. The sky was a gray structure of clouds in several storeys, and the rendezvous was like the Covent Garden dance hall on a Saturday night: everybody was waltzing cheek to cheek with total strangers in a dimly lit setting. We finally got formed and then found we couldn't climb at the briefed speeds because of the clouds; out over the Channel the whole formation flew a twenty-mile circle in order to reach altitude before we crossed the German coast, and upon getting up there, we found that we were all swathed in dangerous contrails. We were very much aware that our big spiral had registered on the German radar and that it gave Jerry plenty of time to position his fighters to greet us.

All through this unhappy climb Marrow kept cursing and complaining on our interphone.

Over the Channel, I looked out once, I remember, and saw that we were in a great chamber of clear air between two layers of opacity, the one beneath us somber and greenish, the one above a sheet of hammered silver, while between the two strata, at some distance from us and all around, puffy, globular clouds with blackish centers and snow-white trim, like huge immobilized flak bursts, ringed us about, shut us in. We were passing through an empty room of one of the many houses of the sky.

Our mission that morning was being led by Walter Silg, but he was not in control of the strike, because he was carrying in his second seat a command pilot from Wing, a certain Colonel Trummer, who was said to be bucking for Whelan's job as our Group C.O., and who was famous for being bullheaded. This was his second mission; our fourteenth, so Marrow could be pardoned for thinking he knew more than the Colonel. For once Haverstraw was on the ball, and after we came out of our big loop Clint remarked insistently, five or six times, that we were as much as three degrees to the south of our course. Marrow flicked his selector switch to command and he had the nerve to tell Trummer that he was off course.

I was monitoring the band, and I heard the Colonel say, "Get off the air. I know what I'm doing. Who *is* that?"

And Buzz said, "It's Captain Marrow, and you're still off course."

It was crazy of Marrow to break code, and I told him so.

As we approached the target the cloud cover was pretty bad, and some fighters jumped us, and listening on liaison we could just feel that Colonel Trummer was getting the jimjams. He began asking Wing Headquarters, back home, what he should do if this and if that. Then he reported that both primary and secondary were under ten tenths. This simply wasn't true. The undercast was bad, but we could see the ground from time to time. Finally Wing gave a recall order—what Trummer obviously wanted, because he was on that radio verifying the order before the airwaves had stopped twanging from getting it to us. We weren't more than ten minutes from the initial point, and we were under constant attack from fifty or sixty squareheads.

The Body was leading the second element of the high squadron of our Group, with Gurvine up ahead of us in *Black Cat* as squadron commander—and incidentally as deputy commander of the Group in case anything went wrong with the Silg-Trummer ship. Just as Trummer came up on the radio to tell us all to follow him home, *Black Cat* suddenly stood up on one wing and flipped out to one side and, according to Handown on interphone, dived without smoke or sign of trouble.

Marrow poured on the coal and pulled our element through under Gurvine's wingmen and took over the high lead.

He took over a lot more, too.

Silg and the lead squadron had just begun to swing out for

home when Marrow, still on his command set, said, sticking to code this time, "Padlock Green to all Padlocks. Deputy command taking over. Anybody wants to bomb, form on me."

Apparently Trummer was back on liaison talking to England and hadn't heard Marrow, because, at any rate, he said nothing, and with no countermand from him, and considering that everyone knew how close to the target we were, the rest of the strike stayed with us. The low squadron dropped back and hitched onto us, and the other groups just hung on.

Clint sang out that we had reached the i.p.

I must say Marrow did a beautiful job of taking us through the briefed turns of the approach routine because he had certainly not expected (but then again, maybe he had; as a flier he seemed to have worked everything over and over in his mind) to be a leader.

Max kept muttering. You could tell he wasn't ready.

We were about halfway down to the start of the run itself when Handown reported that a clutch of Forts, six or seven, that had apparently turned out to follow Trummer and then had changed their minds and decided to attack, were straggling and were under severe attack.

"Tough s——," Marrow said. He was having a big time. "Come on, Maxie," he said. "Come on, Baby."

For weeks Max Brindt had been griping about having to toggle his bombs on signal from the lead bombardier—giving the impression that on the average he could do better setting his own sights and bombing independently. Now he was having his chance. "Wind, wind, wind," he said, evidently trying to build the drift into his sight.

We were in the run. Max had us on AFCE. Suddenly with forty seconds to go, he said, "S——! I've lost it."

"What's the matter?" Marrow shouted.

With amazing speed our rock, Handown, said, "If we went around again we could give those stragglers a chance to tack on."

"You stupid mother f——er!" Marrow shouted at Max.

Fifteen, fourteen, thirteen, twelve . . .

"Clouds," Max said. "It's covered with clouds." But you couldn't tell whether to believe him.

Of what I did, I remember only that I pretended Neg was

standing behind me, as on take-offs and landings, so I was sort of drinking in his casualness, and that I looked over at Marrow and saw him looking at me, and that suddenly I was rip-roaring mad, and that I grabbed the wheel and put my feet on the pedals and put a very decided amount of pressure on the controls in favor of a left turn.

Then I heard Marrow say, "All right, Max, get yourself straightened out, we're going around." And he flicked his band-selector switch and told the other ships: "Three six oh turn. Repeat. Three six oh turn."

If there's anything an outfit hated to do, it was to take a three-hundred-sixty-degree turn for a second run on the target, because one Fort going around alone takes time enough, but with a formation you almost had to multiply that time by the number of ships, and you had to multiply the agony by plenty, too, because you'd thought the worst was almost over, and the fighters were still there, and the flak was still coming up, and it took forever. Oh, it was a nasty thing to have to do.

I don't know, I'll never know, whether Marrow would have done the same thing if it hadn't been for Handown's remark and my push. I never told anyone about that little hint of mine on the controls, and you can bet your bottom dollar that Marrow never told anyone—until he told Daphne.

At any rate, it all turned out O.K. I'm afraid the formation lost three ships on that big turn, but the rest of us got around, and the stragglers hooked on, and this time Max had had time to get everything straight in his head, and apparently the clouds didn't bother him, and he did a good job—the P.R.V. photos the next day showed that he did a creditable job, which is not to say that we schmoozled the whole German war effort, but there wasn't any Gross Error, anyway.

We hadn't reached the rally point when the ships began to call in to congratulate Buzz. They called him a horse's ass, and the f——ing mulberry bush was mentioned, but it all stacked up as grudging praise for having done a tough thing.

As for me, after we got away I turned my electric suit off, but the perspiration still poured off me.

When we landed it turned out that down in the ball turret Junior Sailen had been so busy tracking Jerries that he never had

understood what had happened, and when I told him, just before
interrogation, he leaned against the side of a door and began to
blubber: "He's a good egg, Captain Marrow is, he's my friend, my
friend," he said. "He's like a buddy, you wouldn't think he was a
captain. I got to get him out of my head. I don't want to think
about him. He has ahold of me, and he'll never let go. Never,
never, never." Junior sobbed as if he'd just heard of Marrow's
death.

That evening in the bar at the officers' club, where there appeared to be extraordinary unanimity about the notion of tying
one on, Whelan, who hadn't gone along on this raid, came up to
Marrow and told him he'd put in for a D.F.C. for him. I believe
Marrow thereupon took a new look at the question of our commander's sanity.

A few minutes later Dunk Farmer, the bartender, sidled up
and said, "I been tryin' for three months to get shet of this job and
get on a combat crew, and I was just wondrin', Cap'n, if you
might find a slot for me."

Yes, Buzz was on the top of the heap. "Sure, son," he said,
"just as soon as my boy Boman, here, drops dead, you can have his
chair."

"I ain't kiddin'," Dunk said.

"I know it, son," Marrow said, serious now, benevolent, oozing *noblesse oblige.* "I got a tail gunner I may have to wash out. I'll
bear you in mind. You don't get gas on your stomach, do you?"

"No, sir," Dunk said.

"I'll bear you in mind," Marrow said.

CHAPTER SEVEN

THE RAID

1404–1455 hours

1 /

Marrow's scream persisted until that first wave of four fighters had committed itself to go above us and comb through the high group.

The relief then was twofold: of the end of Buzz's terrible battle cry, and of the knowledge that the main force of the day's first blow, at least, was to strike a formation other than ours.

The Body trembled as Handown fired at the planes passing overhead.

We were near Antwerp. Looking down through air as clean as a washed window I saw the city. A thin, steam-like smoke screen lay over it, eddying on a gentle southwest breeze that was moving down there.

At our altitude the wind was west-by-north, two hundred eighty degrees, almost precisely a tail wind, at fifty miles per hour.

Our squadron, at the apex of the huge slanting wedge of the task force, was about a thousand feet beneath the plate of cirrus which, so far, was thin and translucent, so the color of the sky came through it as the color of my grandmother's grape jelly used to come through the film of candlewax she melted on its surface to seal it off from mold before she put it in the cellar.

Ack-ack came up from Antwerp, meager, fairly accurate, evidently a predicted concentration. It was quickly ended.

The second and third waves of the Hun had run in on the high group, and on the far side of it the enemy planes turned now to come in from every rearward direction. Our gunners began to call in individual planes that might attack our Group.

Then Bragnani saw a formation coming in from above and behind.

"Look out," Marrow said. "They might be Spits."

"Christ Almighty," Handown said, "they look like P-47s." You could hear elation in Neg's voice, a kind of pressure on the underside of his larynx, near where the beads of the throat mike lay against his neck.

And yes, they were Thunderbolts, which we had least expected, but they did us no good.

I tuned in on the "C" channel, which was reserved for communication with the fighters, and I could hear Colonel Ewing, up at the front of the first task force, seventeen minutes ahead of us, holler on it in an attempt to reach the 47s. "Croquet! Croquet! Do you hear me? This is Windbag One calling Croquet." But the band was jammed, and that was all I could hear. It was enough to gather, however, just from the urgent sound of that call, that the forward task force was catching it bad.

Our bombers were disposed to take advantage of the usual P-47 tactics of sweeping over us in a column of squadrons at two- or three-minute intervals, furnishing what was known as corridor support. In other words, we expected all three squadrons to keep weaving back and forth over us in turn, and to jump German formations that came up. But after two or three passes overhead both of the P-47 squadrons pulled away and flew on to the forward task force of bombers and did not return. I was sure from this that there must be heavy going ahead, and at the same time I became apprehensive about our own situation, because I knew the Germans' habit of pouncing on unescorted formations.

Junior Sailen saw two Forts going down from the high group. Farr reported a new flight of German fighters swinging up from below.

2 /

I looked at my wrist watch. It was two twenty-one. We were supposed to reach Eupen, in the southeastern reaches of Belgium, a city once German which had been given to Belgium for her sufferings in the war that had made the world safe for democracy, at two twenty-six, and there we were to change course and go more southerly, so we would miss the dreaded flak areas of the Ruhr and fly over relatively open country. There was no promise that anything would change at Eupen except our direction of flight, but in my mind I clung to that turning point as the most important goal of our trip. It was only five minutes away. I had to get through those five minutes. After Eupen I would set another goal and strain to reach it—but that was not to be thought about yet. Eupen was everything. Five minutes.

I had learned thus to break up danger, not only into its component individual hazards, but into temporal fragments as well. I could not have borne the thought of the entire three hundred and twenty-two minutes from this point until the moment when, if we were fortunate (as we were not in fact to be), we would recross the English coast in safety at Felixstowe, but I could face getting through the next five minutes—and that I set myself to do.

I saw a stolid pack of barrage balloons off to the left, over Aachen, fat pigs of the upper air.

3 /

The second attack of FW-190s came in and again, not surprisingly, concentrated on the high squadron. The German tactics of those days were highly co-ordinated, not only as between ships in a flight but also as between flights, and once they started bearing down on one of our formations they usually did their best, in consecutive swoops, to tear it to pieces before turning on another.

The first German attack had not broken off but was still

working on our high group of Forts, and the second attack simply joined in.

But something new turned up in that second attack—and in those five minutes. Prien was the one who saw it and told the rest of us.

He called out first a fighter coming in at our group from dead astern, then a few seconds later said that from the way its tracers were going it seemed to be after our low squadron, not us.

"Mother of God!" he said next. "It blew up. . . . No, it didn't. . . . Look, it's got a big cannon or something. . . . It was a flash. . . . A very big flash on the fighter . . . It hid the whole plane." Prien gave these garbled reports in his familiar cold, flat tone of voice, which made their staccato rhythm and startling content seem the more eerie. "Wait till I tell you," he went on. "I could see the damn thing, like a shell, it came out after the flash, only it went so slow I could see it. The burst was in our low squadron, black, like flak, only easy twice as big. The thing is, the plane split-assed up behind us and I could see this tube, this cannon thing, fastened under the fuselage. I could see it plain as anything."

"All right, Prien," I said, "give somebody else a chance."

Thus I kept so-called interphone discipline. I wished, for all our sakes, that I had cut him off sooner—not that the new weapon he described frightened me, or would frighten my crewmates, in itself. No, it was the newness that was upsetting, the fact that there was some new, unknown weapon at large in the sky, not fearful because it made bright flashes larger than the airplanes that carried them, and bursts as black and twice as large as flak, but fearful simply because it was new. The Germans were constantly throwing new things at us: timed bombs dropped from above us on little parachutes, rockets, air-to-air dive bombing, flak bursting in different colors. And always it was the novelty that frightened us more than the device itself. What was it that frightened us so about the newness of new weapons? Was it some prescience in us—the fateful fear of true prophets? Yes, I think we were afraid, even so long ago as that, that the enemy might suddenly produce a newness that would be final. End us, the war, the world, all at once.

We were over Eupen. I had made it.

"All right, let's have some chatter, here," I said. "Call in your sightings."

"Ten o'clock, high," Handown said, and stopped.

"Give," I said.

"Friendly fighters," Handown said, masking in formality the depth of his feelings, "returning to base."

'The sons of bitches," Farr said, as if the Thunderbolts had no limit to their range and were simply betraying us.

4/ My next compartment of time, until we should reach our next goal, a course change at 49°45'N–08°20'E, roughly between Darmstadt and Heidelberg, was to be twenty-nine minutes, and I can only say that in those minutes we were under the most vicious and prolonged attack we had ever seen, and in that time there began, subtly but unmistakably, the transformation in Marrow that I had expected, hoped for in shame, and feared.

Within seven minutes of the departure of our escort three new German attacks came up to us. The first two were still with us. Some seventy fighters were honoring us with their attention.

"Coach" was still out there, an ME-109 jogging along, out of range, telling his colleagues what to do.

Just beyond Eupen he began engineering a series of frightful pack attacks, supported by smaller waves. First we would get as many as twelve FW-190s or ME-109s, flying abreast, attacking on nose or tail, from level or slightly above or below, and this pack would spray us with twenty-millimeter tracers and other calibers, firing continuously on approach, passing through the formation, and, if from the rear, flying straight on to hit the forward task force. This sort of attack had an effect as of a concentrated barrage, and it was supported by free-lance assaults by flights of two to five fighters, which came in from three, nine, and eleven o'clock, level and below. Individual planes attacked, meanwhile, from wide angles at the nose and tail, high, level, and low, and from directly above. The packs abreast alternated with charges made by entire squadrons of fighters in line astern, and there were nose attacks by from seven to fifteen aircraft in javelin-up formation—coming in, that is,

in succession in a line staggered upwards in altitude, each following plane higher than the one before it. While the pack attacks
were being made, the solo attacks, often by cannon-firing or rocket-
firing planes, swerved away just within the range of our fifty-
caliber guns, so it was hard to get a crack at them.

By this time the cirrus had thickened, and at the end of a pass
the fighters would pull up sharply and disappear in the cloud
cover, and I guess they'd re-form above it, because in a few seconds
they'd come screaming down through it, all set for a new swipe
at us.

I have told all this as if I had clearly seen and understood the
intricate teamwork at the time. No, at the time it was only a series
of glimpses, vibrations, whiffs of powder in our plane, shouts about
the great sky-clock, curses, and exchanges about roller coasters,
swoopers, triple threats, split asses, and, alas, falling Forts.

"Oh, Jesus"—Junior Sailen, who, being underneath, saw so
many go down—"there goes *Rats Wouldn't Stay*." Chong. Benny
Chong. The Minnesota menace. A great kidder; eyes as still and
remote as the lakes in the forests of his own north country. Benny,
gone down. So many jokes in the hutment with Benny Chong.

A long silence before the next word was called in.

Then Handown. "O.K., watch it. . . . Three o'clock high.
You take it, Bragnani. I got one up here."

5 /

I saw a plane with a yellow nose and a bright red spinner.
At a distance the fighters were skidding shapes—profiles from the
recognition cards; the FW-190s, ME-109s, ME-110s, and JU-88s
were easy, while the less familiar ME-210s, DO-217Es, and
HE-113s were harder to spot, but they were all there, all of them,
the entire battery. A Focke-Wulf with one wing black and one
wing white. Mostly the fuselages were blue, gray, and green.
Orange nose, and spinner, too. They whisked by, and I understood
them to be menacing, yet still they were somehow unreal. Red
and yellow noses. I was used to the skidding, now. I took the skid-

ding as a matter of course, but the concept of purposeful, murderous enmity was still, after twenty-three missions and part of a
twenty-fourth, hard for me to grasp. One plane was checker-
boarded all over. The ME-210s were painted silver, and the
JU-88s were gray, black, and silver. After our fighters left I saw an
FW-190 painted like a Thunderbolt and an ME-109 with R.A.F.
markings. A flight, abreast, of ships with wings striped black and
yellow, like the bodies of bumblebees.

These exotic markings were disquieting, because they spoke
of individuality, differentiation, and not of machines but of men
within. I thought for a second of the dead German boy in the
crater that day of the field games at Pike Rilling.

Did the Germans see, as they flicked by, the sultry nude with
her legs bent and spread on *The Body*? Did they have a disturbing
sense, seeing her, of the man Marrow in our ship?

6 /

He was pestering the gunners.

Six minutes after Eupen the first two groups of German fighters broke off. I could see the ships peel out, wherever they were,
and dive down.

But the minute they were out a fresh batch pounced on us—
and that was the way it was going. As we flew we could see the
fighters coming up from fields miles ahead of us, and when any
had to fall out and land for gas there was always a new flock coming along to take their places.

Prien started an oxygen check.

"Hurry it up," Marrow said. "Snap out of it, boy."

That was the fastest check we ever had. All ten men responded.

Everywhere I turned my eyes something was happening. I
chanced to look out my right window, down to our low group off
to the right, and just then I saw a Fort, afire all along its fuselage,
flip up and over like a griddlecake and go out of the formation;

fire seemed to be pouring out of both inboard engines, or maybe
gas tanks.

"Who was that?" I sharply said.

Prien, knowing what I'd meant by the question, said in his
flat, cold voice, "Leader of the high squadron of the low group."

Curly Jonas. We all knew that was Curly Jonas, our Air Ops,
in *Baggy Maggie*, Buzz's partner in the intrigues of the Group,
Buzz's special friend, next to me. I waited for Marrow's reaction,
for I expected him to lash out at the mother f——ers in Wing who
were trying to kill us all all all.

But Marrow seemed not even to have registered that last exchange.

"Farr," he said, "get on the ball. Get that gun going."

Farr was truculent. "What the f—— you think I'm doing—
playing checkers with Bragnani?"

"All right, all right," Marrow said. "On the ball."

He was bothering the boys. It was not like him.

The sergeant gunners were maintaining continuous watch on
their assigned sectors and firing when needed, and they were talking back and forth with the best discipline we had had, I'd say,
since the Bremen raid on June thirteenth, when we'd felt that
everything had clicked for us. Far more was happening now than
on that day, yet the interphone didn't rasp with overlapping shouts.
The gunners in whose zones of search the planes were sighted
called out what they saw and notified the positions that were
most apt to get a shot at the passing fighters. We even heard from
Lamb once in a while. Handown was alert and cool. Prien talked
in his flat voice like a man watching and describing flights of birds
or the descent of leaves in the autumn. Farr was surly, and
Bragnani, like a dumb wall, echoed him. Sailen was quiet, soft,
small, but he was very much there. And up forward Brindt and
Haverstraw, on the nose guns, talked on interphone with the assurance of the officer class. Only one thing was uncommon. Marrow was ragging us all—not with the zestful abuse he had so often
dealt us, of a powerful man bursting with his aggressive vitality,
but in a monotonous, hounding, thoughtless, steady drumming of
naked impatience.

I became very worried, for I felt as if responsibility were coming at me like a flight of planes abreast in the sky. I dreaded it because the kind of responsibility I saw coming was in direct conflict with the vow I had taken to myself, about combat, about war, some three weeks earlier.

"Come on, Handown. Come on, come on."

7 /

The dangerous quality of caution I thought I had noticed in Marrow in the earlier phases of the mission, an over-carefulness which then had had to do with the workings of our ship, now appeared to be spreading in him, and had begun to be evident in his handling of *The Body's* defensive tactics.

One aspect of Marrow's genius as a combat aviator had showed up, especially in the middle missions of our tour, in the subtle, intuitive, rippling movements with which he endowed *The Body* in order to make her contribution to the defensive fire system of the formation as great as possible. If he was flying wingman, for instance, stacked lower than the leader of the element, and to the leader's right, and an enemy plane dived down from above and to the left, Marrow would almost imperceptibly slide out from under the leader and hike up alongside him in order to uncover as many of our guns as possible to fire at the plunging enemy. Or if he was leading the low squadron, and it began to receive level head-on attacks, Marrow would ease and ease and ease all six of his ships upward and across until they were more in trail with the lead squadron, so that the butting Germans would be forced to pass closer to the other formation's guns.

Now, however, as we flew down the green corridor south of the Ruhr and north of Luxembourg and the Saar, under attacks which seemed to have an ever-increasing complexity, and which were still aided by the now thinner plate of cirrus overhead, it seemed that Marrow was piloting us not so as to make a flexible and honorable phalanx with Bins' element but only so as to keep us—himself—alive. The fact was that he was using *Angel Tread*, *Erector Set*, and *Gruesome Twosome* as a triple shield. Rather

than opening out to uncover our guns he seemed to want to huddle
us under the mothering wings of the first element.

A ship had been called in at ten o'clock high. Handown had
claimed it. "I can't get at it, Major. Give me some air."

This happened more than once—crewmen asking Marrow, as
they had seldom needed to do, for room to fire without hitting
friends.

Marrow did not answer these calls but instead discovered the
means of finding fault with other crewmen, as if he were changing
the subject in an argument that was going against him.

Our men saw that two planes had fallen back out of the high
squadron, after those first terrible passes, and from the positions of
the gaps, before the formations filled in, they figured out that
the cripples were *Big Bum Bird* and *Miss Take*, Perl and Stedman.
They were as good as gone. Perl, the thinker. Dopey Stedman, always saying, "Hunh?" As good as lost. What the Germans wanted,
above all, was to knock us singly out of the formation, for stragglers, wanting the mutual support of the group's many guns, were
easy prey. Prien saw one of the straggling Forts turn away and dive
down, evidently in the hope of hedge-hopping back to our base, or
at least into France, where, if the men bailed out, civilians might be
helpful.

And so the roll call of casualties was growing. *Rats Wouldn't
Stay, Baggy Maggie, Big Bum Bird, Miss Take*. Chong, Jonas,
Perl, Stedman. And thirty-six other men. And we were only about
two thirds of the way to the target. No planes had yet been knocked
out of our own squadron.

8 /

Prien ran an oxygen check. Lamb didn't answer.

Ordinarily Marrow would simply have tapped my shoulder
and given me the thumb, pointing backwards to indicate that I
should get back there and see what the matter was. But this time
Buzz called out on interphone, "Lamb! Lamb! Come on, boy,
speak up."

There was a note of incredulity and appeal in Marrow's voice,
and for a second I thought how different this was from Marrow's
voice the night he had hazed Butcher Lamb, flakked him up—
Butcher on his knees on the concrete floor of his Nissen hut, marrow standing over him with eyes bugged out, tearing up the snapshot of Lamb's girl.

I arose from my seat without being told and hurried back to
look into Lamb's silence. To be truthful, I was glad to get to the
curving, shut-in parts of the plane, where I could not see the sky.
I paused in the dark, cramped space on the catwalk of the bomb
bay, but then thinking what might happen if there were a direct
hit on a bomb, I scurried, rodent-like, aft to the radio room.

I found Lamb at his radio desk, with one gloved mitt holding
his log book, closed, and the other pressing a novel open on the
table. I saw that his headphone was not plugged into his jack. He
was bending over the book, squinting at it through his flying goggles; his oxygen bladder expanded and contracted like a bullfrog's.
As a reader he looked very far out of his element—a man from
Mars, or a deep-sea diver, trying to peer through some viscous, unfamiliar element to see if he could discern the meaning of life on a
printed page.

Lamb did not stir as I entered through his bulkhead door, and
I moved close behind him, and holding my walk-around oxygen
bottle high I leaned over his shoulder and read:

". . . We have too much on our hands and Black Carlos,
though his radius is small, is king of this particular quarter. Apparently he is using his position to pay off an old score. . . ."

Poor Lamb! Poor Lamb!

He had come down from his gun, I could see, probably to
check his circuits and make an entry in his log, and he had become
engrossed in an open book on his table—*Hell Let Loose*, it was
called—and here he was, a million miles from war, on a roan horse
moving on a sun-drenched landscape as the tallies of frontier hatred, revenge, lust, and justice were crudely, simply paid. It was
better, I guess, than being on the way to Schweinfurt, Germany,
and I had to press myself rather hard to tap him on the shoulder.

He came back to the war with a pronounced jump. He looked
up at me and as if by reflex held up the log for me to see. He wasn't
goofing off, he was making an entry, see? Indeed, he whipped off

his right mitten, dexterously split the book at the right page, grabbed a pencil, and wrote:

"1430. Time check."

So he had been there since before two thirty. It was now two thirty-four.

I returned to the cockpit, plugged in my oxygen, my suit heater, and my headset, and I told Marrow that Lamb was O.K., had just left his gun to make an entry in his log and had been disconnected.

9/

During the time I had been in the radio room, the sun had come out. We had flown beyond the enormous flat cloud that had caused us so much grief, and we had broken now into the uncovered day. Now there was nothing above us but pure, dry sky— and the wonderful sun that splashed its light so fiercely on our silvery ship. I looked out on the wing and saw a dizzying pool of glare between the engine nacelles. The sun was somewhat behind us, but its being out made me feel warmer and more relaxed in my seat.

Blessed sun! This zone above all clouds, where the sky gave hints of its interstellar blackness, had always been for me even more beautiful than the myriad forests and caverns of weather that one traversed nearer the earth. This high, clear area had seemed to me, since my first tropospheric training flights, the place where twentiety-century man was destined to explore—as near to freedom and the life-giving sun as he could so far get. For emotion: Up, up, up! The thrust of Chartres, the steel-boned towers on the rock of New York, *Sequoia sempervirens*—these things, the sight of which in photographs had moved me deeply as a young boy, were upward reaching, and the uppermost place of all, during the years in which I flew, was this clear cup of crystal in the teen and twenty thousands of altitude. Yet that afternoon, for the first time, I inwardly shuddered at these thoughts which I had nurtured so long. With Daphne I had for the first time come face to face with life on the

earth; in my terrible, wrenching interview with her the day before
about Marrow, and about ourselves, I had, for the first time in my
very young years, been forced to look life right in the eye, and I
had seen the possibility of doing something more than pretending
to be alive, with or without her. The *illusion* of being alive that
she had so intensely given me all along, even before this shatter-
ing talk, when I believe I had had little more to give than pretense,
made me realize that life on the earth contained possibilities of
heights I'd never imagined, and that my thrill in climbing the sky
had been flight, in the sense of escape, from the real life on the
earth that I had not been ready to live. I had been free up high
because I had not had the understanding or the generosity to be
alive on the earth below. This was a spurious freedom, and in that
first moment under the open sun, that afternoon, a desire for life,
real life, a life in which I faced truths about myself and could therefore be able to give myself to others, began to seize me.

I do not say that I thought all this through, or consciously
realized what was happening. All that I experienced at the time, I
guess, was a momentary shudder and a sharpening of my perceptions.

But this was, I believe, the point at which the curves of my
destiny and Marrow's might be said to have crossed.

10 /

For what happened in the next few minutes, however,
neither Marrow nor I—Marrow in his inner climb toward death,
I in my settling down toward life—was quite prepared.

Squadron after squadron of enemy fighters came after us. At
two thirty-five, two new flights joined the attack.

Handown said, "Oh, the bastards, they got bombs coming
down on parachutes up ahead."

I think that a few minutes before I would have reacted to this
by pretending it hadn't been said, perhaps busying myself with a
check of pressures and temperatures on the instrument panel, but
now I ducked my head forward and looked up at the chain of small

glistening hemispheres of synthetic fabric, which stood out clearly against the blue-black infinity beyond. They were quite far ahead; they were floating downward, and we were flying into their field. And German fighters were charging obliviously through them.

"Come on, Handown," Marrow shouted, and again there was that unfamiliar sound of appeal, of pleading, in his voice, "watch out for planes, will you?"

For some reason I thought of Buzz's claim—one of his most boastful stories, which he had repeated often, only to have it collapse on him in recent days, turn out, like so much else, to have been falsehood—of having left his car at the airfield with the key in it when he had left the States. It seemed to me pathetic that a man had to make up such a lie as that about his indifference to things.

The parachute bombs had been dropped too low and exploded below us.

Now I saw another way in which Marrow was off, way off. Customarily, on nose attacks, Max Brindt would call them out first to Clint Haverstraw, they'd divvy up the shots, and if the planes were coming in at an angle that wasn't ideal for either, Max would tell Marrow to drop the nose, or turn a little, or skid us; on skidding turns our gunners would get some very good shots. On one attack a German came in from ahead who was so obviously green that his rawness showed in everything he did; he turned in too close and overshot and never brought his guns to bear, and he evidently tried to pull the nose through with the rudder, and it stuck and got up and just stalled and shuddered up there.

Max shouted, "Give me some right. Oh, he's just sitting there. Right! Right!"

But Marrow didn't seem to hear, or else he had completely run out of right turns—something very peculiar.

"Buzz!" Max cried in dismay—but now it was too late. "What the hell! He was easy as pie."

There was another time when a plane was called at ten o'clock low—out Buzz's window, and he got watching it, and Sailen quietly said, "I think that's a decoy," which (for Sailen's understated warnings were like sirens to us) would ordinarily have been enough to make Marrow smartly swing us into the best spot in the defensive fire system to meet the main punch which was sure

to follow. But this time, after Sailen said, "Six o'clock, low," Buzz
flew woodenly on, and we were awkwardly positioned with reference to our wingmen when the attack came, from the tail.

Bragnani saw a German fighter hit as it flew forward through
our group, and he shouted that the pilot was jumping. "Look!
Look! Nine o'clock. He's right out there."

I saw Buzz's head turn, and I peered beyond him and saw a
yellow chute filling. I felt a surge of apprehension, for I remembered having seen a yellow parachute break out once before, on
the Nantes mission, in July, and something awful had happened
that had been a kind of turning point for me—and now I knew
from Daphne that it had been one for Marrow, too.

"That f——ing bastard Silg!" Marrow now said, with a kind of
groan. "Him and his big mouth." It was Silg who, after having
parachuted down, was rumored to have been captured and to have
taunted Goering, so that Goering was supposed to be out personally to get our Group. What a strange response, coming from
Marrow! It was as if he felt that the Germans were laying for us,
for him.

11 /

Handown called in a pack attack from twelve o'clock
high. "Coo, blimey!" he said. "A whole blahsted squadron."

I saw them. Twelve? Fifteen? Flying abreast, wingtip to
wingtip.

Marrow saw them, too. I noticed out of the corner of my eye
how he lowered his head and took them in.

The next thing I knew—we were closing with the fighters at
a terrific rate of speed, theirs plus ours—our element was tucked in
tight under *Angel Tread*, *Erector Set*, and *Gruesome Twosome*, so
snugly that it was almost as if we were in a hangar in order that
rain and hail couldn't fall on us. I couldn't even see the fighters
any more. We were simply hiding.

Handown had time for two yelps to Marrow. "Clear me!
Open up!"

Then we were not covered any more. The three Forts that
had been above us were gone. The first element was completely
wiped out. The fighters had gone on through. I saw nothing of it.
I don't know what happened. They were shot down. *Angel Tread,
Erector Set,* and *Gruesome Twosome* were shot down in one pass.

Handown said, "My God, did you see that?"

At this point Junior Sailen called in and said in a quiet, calm
voice, "Guns are stuck. What'll I do, Neg?"

There ensued a perfectly logical conversation, only it seemed,
at that minute, quite mad.

"Burnt out?"

"No, hell, it ain't hardly hot."

"Try taking the back plate off. You can manipulate the trigger
bar."

A few seconds later Sailen said, "Fires all right, but it mashes
my thumb."

Handown said, "Use a screwdriver, you dope. Christ, they left
the brains out of your chromosomes."

"Repeat, please."

"Use a screwdriver. *Scarew-dariver!*"

"Roger."

The first thing that occurred to me was that Marrow wasn't
badgering the gunners any more, or he would have had something
to say after those little formal touches of Junior's. No, Marrow
was silent.

My second thought was that there was some meager, inaccurate flak bursting around us—from where? Koblenz? Wiesbaden?
Mainz? Vividly my mind recalled Feather Merchant's bronze lips
naming those cities, to the left of our line of flight, shortly, he said,
before our course change.

Only then did a third thought burst in on my consciousness,
like the beam of Sully's flashlight blazing out of the darkness: We
were the lead ship of the task force now.

12 /

I guess Prien didn't know what had happened. He kept calling in fighters.

I looked at my watch and saw that it was twenty-three minutes before three. "Clint," I said, "do you think you better check—"

I hadn't even finished my question when he said, "Sixteen minutes to course change. We're two minutes ahead of flight plan."

Old indefinite Haverstraw was ahead of me. People certainly gave you surprises.

"Did you get that, Buzz?" Clint said.

"I heard you, son," Marrow said, but his voice was dull, passive.

Just about then three separate clumps of German fighters dropped away from us. That helped, but there were still plenty around us.

Our gunners were all chattering again now.

We were plodding along all right, I guess, but the thing was, Major Holdreth, in *Round Trip Ticket*, the leader of the high squadron, jolly, big apple, he was supposed to take over in case anything happened to Bins, he was deputy lead of the task force; *Round Trip Ticket* surely should have come up and taken it away from *The Body*. Not if this had been on the bombing run, or just before it, because it would have been standard operating procedure for us to carry through under those circumstances. But we were half an hour from the target, and Holdreth should have come up. He certainly should have.

Any doubt I may have had whether Marrow was aware of our position was removed now, as he said to me on interphone, "Get on command, Boman. See if you hear anything."

I flicked my selector switch, thinking: The old Marrow would have got on the pipes himself and would have trimmed Holdreth, or would have been glad to assume the lead—felt it belonged to him, anyway. In fact, Holdreth's reason for holding back was undoubtedly that he and everyone else remembered the way Marrow had taken over, that time when Trummer had chickened out on the way to Hamburg, when Buzz had earned his D.F.C. Here Buzz was asking me to carry water for him.

And of course I didn't hear a word from Holdreth.

What I did hear was some other ship, which opened up and broke code. "Marrow. Marrow. Are you leader?"

I didn't check with Buzz. I just said, "I guess so. Close up. Tighten up."

I have to say that I did not feel elated. I think I must have had fantasies about this kind of situation, about saying words on the radio like that on my own hook, but it wasn't any good. I felt rotten bad.

At two forty-four another group of Germans broke off contact, and that left only about ten ships plaguing us.

Clint was on the ball. He gave us a minute's notice of the course change and reminded us of the new compass reading.

Marrow, it must be admitted, made a fine easy turn which the whole task force had no trouble following.

We now had fifteen minutes to the initial point.

CHAPTER EIGHT

THE TOUR

June 28 to July 30

1/

Here was a paradox: I was skeptical of Marrow's heroism,
yet I was proud of being his co-pilot.

After the Hamburg show Buzz was the hot aviator of the
Group, and I wanted to be near him, to bask in the light that reflected from him, and I suppose this is one of the reasons why
June twenty-eighth was almost the worst day of my whole tour—a
day on which I remained on the ground yet felt deeply endangered.
The Group flew a mission in St. Nazaire that day, and I had to
sweat it out. I was left behind. Operations wanted Marrow to
carry Louis Maltitz along as co-pilot, in order to check Titty out
on combat before letting him command a plane of his own.

The mission was a comfortably late one. The briefing wasn't
until nine in the morning. I sat all the way through it under the
impression that I was going along; suffered all the pangs, was satisfied at being given the old milk run to the sub bases, knew the
flight, had been there on our third and ninth missions, this was to
to be our fourteenth, all downhill now to the end of our tour. Familiar visceral sensations. Then, at the end, when the formation
sheets were handed out, Curly Jonas announced that three co-
pilots would give way to three men who were ready to be checked
out as first pilots—a new routine that Mad Whelan, who was leading this mission himself, had obviously devised—and I was to be
one.

I watched the take-off, at two in the afternoon, from the balcony of the control tower, and I gripped the railing there, and clenched my teeth, as if my vitals were being torn out of me.

It was strange. I had nothing, really, in common with any of the nine other crewmen in *The Body*, and toward some of them I was genuinely antipathetic. In civilian life I would never have willingly passed an hour of my life with a man like Jughead Farr, nor, indeed, would he have chosen my company, even for a minute. But now, hearing the head-splitting roar of the four props of my ship, *our* ship, beating the soft air of a cloudy afternoon to get away from the ground and me, my heart yearned for those nine.

What if they got it on this mission?

I would kill myself. Die with them. I would shoot myself out of remorse, guilt. Why hadn't I fought for my right to fly with them? I had let them down. I should have jumped at Curly Jonas' throat, torn him apart rather than let him separate me from my crew, my family.

I can't remember how I passed the hours that followed. I do remember walking out to the empty dispersal area, and on the way I had a passage of homicidal thoughts about Colonel Whelan, whose idea it must have been to leave me behind. I was burned up at him about the previous day, anyway. Whelan had posted a notice, some time before, announcing that combat officers would take their turns at desk duty, checking enlisted men in and out on passes and doing various kinds of paperwork, and I had caught mine the day before, on a Sunday, just when our Group ball team was going over to play at Kimbolton, with Haverstraw holding down third base. Everybody from *The Body* went but me. I sat at the lousy desk with nothing to do, reading *Yank*, seething at Screwy Whelan on account of this desk-duty invention I supposed to be his. (We later learned that it was actually the idea of a softhead up at Wing who, I suppose, felt so sick about having shirked combat that he wanted all combat officers to know how arduous desk duty was.) Whelan walked in while I was fuming there, and he made me sorer then ever by piling into Marrow. He said he'd put in for a D.F.C. for Marrow on account of the Hamburg show, but, "Personally," he said, "I've got some doubts about your pilot's great deed."

"He took 'em around, didn't he, sir?" I said.

"A better pilot would had had his crew and ship ready to drop accurately the first time."

"Christ, sir," I said, "there were clouds. You can't ask a mere captain to control weather conditions at the target."

"He'll get his decoration," the madman said.

I wondered, walking out on the perimeter track, whether my half-sassing Whelan was the reason I'd been left behind today. That really didn't make sense, though, I told myself, because two other co-pilots had been left at home. Still, there were a lot of co-pilots to choose from.

At *The Body*'s hardstand I found Red Black sitting on a tool chest, chewing a dead cigar, talking with one of his crew. Black was transformed; I scarcely recognized him as the irascible prima donna whom we handled with such care and respect around the ship. He had become fretful and fidgety, and he seemed to have shrunk, and though the mission had only been in the air two hours, he kept glancing at his watch and then at the sky, across which broken clouds were driving toward the southeast, as if pursuing our absent companions. Red was in a state of near-collapse over an oil line he wished he'd checked more carefully. "I did check it once, but I meant to get Captain Marrow to rev up the engine again while I watched it. Or you, sir."

Sir! Me, a second lieutenant? Had Red lost his mind, getting respectful to a second looey?

And, by the way, why wasn't I a first lieutenant? I was overdue by several weeks. Up to that moment I hadn't ever worried about my rank; I'd supposed some dizzy WAC in the Pentagon had stuffed the wrong card in the IBM machine that controlled the destinies of officers overseas. It would get straightened out, and I'd get a suitcase full of back pay. I was at the front, I hadn't cared about such things—until this moment, when, standing by Sergeant Black crouched on his tool box with that lick-spittled wad of a cigar butt in his pale pink lips, and conscious of a cloud-shade chasing the sunlight along the perimeter track, I suddenly had a terrible sinking feeling. I was no good. I had been passed over on purpose. They'd left me behind because I was a failure. I was never going to fly again with Marrow. He would see what it was like to have a real flier along in the second seat. He wouldn't want me again. Clint! Max! Neg! Junior! My friends!

2 /
 A full hour ahead of the E.T.A., I was back on the rim
of the tower, straining my eyes to see, in the rare breaks in the
clouds that were still scurrying southeastward, the distant specks of
a formation, and straining my ears, too, to hear the thunder that
sometimes overran the sight of a flock of planes.

 While I was waiting I managed to get in some worrying about
Kid Lynch. In one way Lynch had an Asian look—that is, in the
strangely shifting impression his face gave of his age. In some lights
and in some moods he looked sixteen, seventeen; naïve, unused,
a fellow aptly nicknamed the Kid. At other times you saw the pits
in his skin and the drawn lids of his eyes, and there appeared a
fated look of the kind one associated with old men, because it
spoke of a close approach to the end, of acquaintance with, and
acceptance of, death; the expression I remembered having seen,
and having been deeply moved by, on the young faces of the soldiers in Brady's photographs of the Civil War.

 What if both *The Body* and *The House of Usher* were shot
down? Perhaps they were already lost. I was alone. My friends were
gone.

 The E.T.A. had come and passed. Maybe the headwind was
fierce up above. The weather was foul and getting worse. I kept
ducking downstairs into the control room, where the disciplined
silence itself seemed a kind of excitement, and where the slightest
crackle of a radio made heads turn, and there was nothing new,
except some talk of a weather front in the south, and finally they
told me to stay the hell out; I was a nuisance.

 This intensified my feeling of uselessness, and of failure. I was
a nervous Nelly they couldn't stand having around.

 I returned to the balcony. The long, lingering dusk of England was settling down, with a mean-looking sky—scudding clouds
and gaps of wind-filled purple. The station disregarded all blackout precautions and kept the field ablaze; the flare-path lights were
a soft hyacinth blue, and the enormous red eye of a mobile beacon
on a trailer at the east end of the runway winked a welcome in
code. You could feel the worry in the men who came out into the
cold breeze from time to time. The vigil seemed endless. I kept

thinking I heard a roar, but it was only my own blood cascading in my ears, or the wind eddying in them. Twice we thought we saw flares dropped at a distance from the field. An enlisted man ran excitedly up to the control-tower balcony, where five or six of us were standing, to shout that he had seen a strange orange glow in the eastern sky—"like it was a ship on fire," he said, his teeth chattering. We all pushed toward the east rail, and there was a faint something, and then the clouds parted and we saw the round disk of the rising moon just above the horizon. We went back to our watch toward the south. Fifteen minutes more were swallowed by the night.

A door opened and slammed below us.

"Boman! Boman! Boman!"

I ran down. Major Fane, the Flying Control Officer, whom we all disliked, was standing at the foot of the concrete stairway. He led me into the control room and handed me a yellow strip torn from the teletype machine.

"X27B 628 2208 EXPEDITE EXPEDITE PROBOMAN PIKERILLING EXMARROW PORTNEATH URGENT QUOTE MADE IT WITHOUT YOU COMMA YOU GOLDBRICKER UNQUOTE END"

"We'll jolt Marrow for this," old F—— Face Fane was saying. "We'll bust him to second lieutenant." This sad, hated man was rankled because Marrow had made light-hearted use of official lines of communication.

I was so happy—not just that my ship was safe, but that Marrow had somehow contrived to get a message through to me even before the official reports on the mission—that I turned on Fane and said, "Say, Major, you better check with the Colonel before you break Captain Marrow. The Colonel thinks he's a hot patootie —just put in for a D.F.C. for him, account of Hamburg." Oh, I was extremely jaunty. But really, Fane was so *straight*.

The reports were coming in. The Group had hit a front and had been scattered. Seven ships at Portneath. Others all over the south. Four planes unaccounted for. Whelan believed lost back at the target. Front passing; the Forts would be hopping home soon.

I went back up on the upper deck, and suddenly, in the wind and my exultation, it seemed really a deck, the bridge deck of a ship, and I a sea captain. Overhead scudding clouds at three thousand hid the moon except for blurred glimpses. The feeling of motion was overwhelming. It seemed that I was alone on the bridge of a great aircraft carrier, and the long rectangle of the flare path was the flight deck, and it was not the clouds that were moving, but I, my ship, our flight deck, the movable beacon sailing along with us blinking our recognition signal in crimson flashes. Far from being a failure, I was in charge, and the ship, the night, the planes were mine.

"Stand by to take aircraft aboard," the sea captain murmured.

"Aye aye, sir."

And in they came, singly, in pairs, weary stragglers.

I was waiting in the interrogation room. I clapped Marrow on the back and tried to thank him for his message, but he was wising around with Maltitz and didn't even notice me. They were all giving each other the customary razz about the mission. Whelan really had been lost. I went back to the room alone. I thought I'd turn in, but pretty soon Marrow came in with a bunch, had a case of beer in cans, said they were going to play some poker. There were seven of them; the deal was full. Maltitz was in the game, and so was Brindt, and so was Haverstraw, and I obviously wasn't. The only thing Marrow said to me was, "Prien got another gut ache. Should have heard him holler." And Buzz threw out a peal of laughter. I went down the hall and crawled into a sack belonging to a guy named Quinn, quite a new man who'd been shot down that afternoon in a plane from which no chutes had appeared. I couldn't sleep at all, because I didn't feel like the captain of a great ship any more, and I was in a dead man's bed, and the poker game got rowdy.

3 / Lynch and I were throwing horses on one of the low oaken tables in the officers' club, and for a while nothing passed between us but the rhythmic *korrowp-rowp-rowp* of the dice in the leather cups and their clattering falls on the table, *krakatakaka*. Lynch looked all knocked out. We had flown to Le Mans that afternoon through rotten weather, and the Kid had had three missions in five days.

"F—— this," he said. He was fed to the teeth with our habits of life. "Let's go over to the room. I got a letter I want to show you."

Lynch's room was one of the dirtiest pigsties on the base, because Bessemer, his pilot, besides being unable to fly a plane, had apparently never learned how to take care of himself. The place was knee-deep with wearing apparel; Bessemer just walked out of his clothes. "I bet he never learned how to wipe his own bum," Lynch said once. "I know for a fact he doesn't know how to get a drip of snot off the end of his nose, I mean without a handkerchief. He uses the *front* of his hand. I tell you, I'm on the verge of throwing up half the time."

Lynch wasn't exactly a fuss-budget about tidiness, but his side of the room was not disgusting; it was a cleaner heap of dirt.

The Kid dug down into an orange crate he and Bessemer kept on their desk for personal treasures, and he pulled out an air-mail letter and scaled it to me.

"Dear Ambrose," it began.

"Know something?" I said. "All this time, I never knew your moniker."

"Ambrose," he said. "From the Greek. Means 'immortal.' Great name for a birdman."

"No wonder they call you Kid."

"The hell with it. When the war's over, I'm going to turn it in for a new model. I'd like to be called Hephaestus. That's a hot name. Hephaestus Lynch. I'd like to be a fireman. Sit around the firehouse in your slippers. Slide down the pole. Steer the back end of the hook and ladder. Read it," he said, sticking his chin out at the letter.

It was from his wife.

"Paul, you know him at the market, makes it perfectly clear that if you are willing to pay extra, he'll disregard your sugar coupons. I feel like saying, You crook, do you know where my husband is? People just stare at you with a glazed look when you get emotional about the war. Sometimes I think I'm a plain sucker for going without the extra sugar, and extra meat, and extra gas, because of you. I had a slight accident backing out of a parking place in that lot in back of the bank, but Fred's Body Shop said they could fix it for about fifteen dollars, I guess I'll wait, it doesn't look bad. Millicent finally got her license. It cost her about two hundred dollars at the driving school. Time before last she quit because the instructor lost his patience with her. 'I'm not paying you to shout at me,' she told the man. What made me think of it was my having the accident backing. Millicent couldn't learn to back, she couldn't get the idea of turning the wheel the opposite way. Her last instructor got so disgusted he made her pull over, and he got right out of the car, and he said he was going to walk down the square, and when he came back he wanted her to be backed into a driveway that was there. He left her cold. She tried six times, and finally she got in catercorner, and when he came back, she said, 'Is that good enough for you, mister?' You know her sharp tongue. 'It's not for me, ma'am,' he said. 'It's for that other fellow that gives the tests.' She finally got her license. I rode with her once and she just went smack down the middle of the road, straddled the white line. This fellow behind her about honked himself to death, and she kept saying, 'What's the matter with him anyway? Man driver!' This morning she called and wanted me to ride over town with her, but I had to go to the church. I was glad."

"What's the point of all this?" I asked.

"The point, you'll come to the point. That first part is a smoke screen."

I came to the point, all right. After three pages of closely packed trivia, in the next-to-last paragraph of a long, gossipy letter, Mrs. Ambrose Lynch made the point unmistakable. "Darling, darling," she wrote, "I don't know how I'm going to do this, but I feel everything rising up in me, and I have to make a confession to you. Please try to understand that the whole reason for this is I love you and I miss you so much I kind of broke down. I couldn't stand missing you. I cried myself to sleep every night and I used to gnaw my knuckles. I've been seeing Tom. Millicent is so wacky and trusting. It started at the Masquers' dance. Darling, you have to believe that you come first, I've been trying to stop it with Tom. I don't love him. He's not like you. I swear, I swear to you . . ."

I couldn't read any more. "Nice of her to tell you," I said.

"Ruthie's an original," the Kid said. "Marked originality all through school. You could be fully confident that she'd find an ingenious new twist. Just being a whore in the boring way of all the rest of the poor wives who've been left at home to gnaw their knuckles by their mean husbands—that wasn't good enough for our Ruthie. You see, she's got a real good twist, has it worked out that it's not only good for her to confess, it's good for me to hear confession. Makes me a priest. That makes celibacy easier for old Father Ambrose. Get it?"

"Who's Tom?"

"Millicent the Woman Driver's husband. Junior executive in an aluminum-tube company. He's essential to the war effort and a famous tail hound in our town. Listen, Bo, if you only knew the irony of Ruthie saying she doesn't love him!"

Now *I* have a confession to make. Lynch's trouble made me feel good, and I think this is why: That morning, while we had waited out at the dispersals for stations time, I had suddenly discovered that several members of our crew seemed to regard me as a strong, giving, and supporting person. I'd have expected this from Junior Sailen, because we all took care of him, but Prien, the cold fish, came up to me on the Q.T. and said, "Boy, are we glad to have you back, sir!" I remembered that Prien had had a gas attack going to St. Nazaire, and I mentioned it, and he said it was because things were in such a mess without me. This, mind you, was when Marrow was at the peak of his career as a hero. Later Handown banged me on the back and growled, "Wasn't the same without you, sir." Max and Clint both said something that seemed to me more than formality, and finally even Jug Farr said, "You shoulda seen the time we had with those two apple-knockers yesterday"—meaning Marrow and Maltitz. I found it was true that Marrow was wearing his heroism as if it were a dramatic costume; he was dangerously close to being funny, and his self-importance was even further inflated by the fact that he had been assigned the leadership of a squadron on this mission. With Whelan missing, Colonel Trummer, the ape from Wing who did the bubu over Hamburg, had been given temporary command of our Group. We knew he wouldn't last, because even those myopic goons at Wing must have been able to see that he was a horse's ass. His motive for letting Buzz lead a squadron had been pretty obvious to everyone except Marrow, who had assumed that it was his due. Marrow had been cavalier about preflight checks and all the mundane preparations of groundlings, and this had given me a chance to take myself pretty seriously, too.

And so when Lynch, in his dry, caustic, understated way, threw the horror of his life into my lap, I had begun to regard myself as a pretty helpful fellow, a boulder. While he was talking along about his wife, I had freight going on two tracks in my mind, for besides trying to sympathize Lynch into a stupor, I began thinking about how I was going to rescue Daphne from Section B, get her a room in Bartleck, spring her from her slavey job, and set her up, let her enjoy herself and me. I had sensed the passionate, dissatisfied yearning in Daphne our last times together, but I guess one would have to call my attempt at a solution for it an example of Gross Error—only I didn't know that until much later. At the time I was The Helper.

But a curious thing happened as I was handing out the comfort to the Kid: Somehow things got turned around, and all of a sudden I was pouring our *my* most sincere and terrifying worries to Lynch. I had had my bombing-and-being-bombed dream for the first time, and I began talking about the destruction of the City around St. Paul's, and all the boarded-up houses, and Daph's father knocked off by a direct hit while he was working as a first-aid stretcher bearer. I didn't want to kill, I didn't want any part of the destruction of civilization, I was looking for a way to eliminate myself from the slaughter squad, I was interested in the survival of mankind; yet when these thoughts began to go through my head in the night, I told the Kid, I wondered whether they were simply rationalizations for efforts to find a way of saving my own skin, and I worried whether there could be virtue or safety in being passive in the face of German aggression, and I thought that my yen for a larger allegiance than to the land of Senator Tamalty and of Colonel Whatshisname who wanted to stuff us with golden bantam might be unpatriotic, might be based on my love for a foreign girl, might be just another way of looking for the nearest exit.

I can see now, better than I saw then, that I was also on the edge of expressing to Kid Lynch my deep inner battle about Marrow—whether to regard him as a hero, or as something quite different, and how to serve as his co-pilot in either case. And this undoubtedly lent an edge of reality and personal emotion to my worrying about the abstract question of passivity in the face of aggression—concretely, mine in the face of his. But it remained for Daph to make me see this openly.

And about Daphne, too. Did I have a right, since I might be killed any day, to entangle Daphne deeper and deeper with me?

Well, the Kid began answering my questions, giving me advice, and I didn't realize then, but I know now, that what he said made me angry.

But instead of arguing with him, I read my bad feeling as misery over *his* trouble, and I switched the conversation back to that.

I managed to end the evening with a very comfortable view of myself as Humanity's Helper. After I turned in I began thinking about how I'd talk with Doc Randall about the Kid. Try to get the Doc to get behind him. I felt so good then that I dropped off into a dreamless sleep.

4/

On the last day of June, Marrow's ego, already stretching its seams, took in two new pump strokes.

His promotion to major came through.

And Wing Public Relations ordered him to go up to London and take part in a Special Services broadcast to the States, on a program that was part of a series designed to let the home folks get acquainted with their heroes overseas.

Marrow, who didn't want to be thought an unripe major, bummed a set of second-hand, tarnished gold maple leaves from, of all people, Wheatley Bins, a wearer now of the more elevated silver leaves of a lieutenant colonelcy.

Then Buzz talked Trummer into letting him take his co-pilot, bombardier, and navigator along to London for moral support, and into authorizing our driving up to London in a little British weapons carrier from the base motor pool.

All our sergeants—Handown, Sailen, Farr, Bragnani, Lamb, and Prien—came out to the gate to cheer Marrow away.

Marrow drove the little British truck pretty fast, but in broad daylight it wasn't too bad, for Clint, Max, and I could see, if not feel, that we were on solid ground, and we could gang up on Buzz to make him slow down when it mattered most.

All the way Marrow rehearsed what he would say on the program. He was going to tell the people back in the States what conditions were *really* like over here.

We three kept egging him on.

I was still suffused with the glow of my helpfulness, and I daydreamed of yesterday's preflight, during which the enlisted men had come to me with their questions and complaints. My banquet of self-congratulation was cut off short, however, by the thought that all of us in the crew, and especially the enlisted men, had restored to Marrow his glow of magic. "Old Untouchable," Handown called him. He was a hero where it really counted—in the eyes of his own men. There was, to be sure, some mockery in their worship of him, but that was only because the invincibility with which they had endowed him was so important to them, so vital to their survival, that they dared not show their true reliance on it and openly made fun of it.

Junior Sailen had kneeled on the hardstand before the raid the day before, with his flat hands pressed together like those of an altar boy, and his innocent eyes had turned up to the threatening stratus above, and he had said, "Our Buzz who art in heaven. . . ."

We all took strength from the myth of him just when the real he was going soft.

A bevy of P.R.O.'s, the most humble of whom wore, with less self-consciousness than Marrow, the golden maple leaves of majors, took us from Eighth Air Force headquarters in a pair of khaki Buicks to a loft building, and they led us up some metal fire escapes into a chilly, brick-walled room with a number of partition-like baffles on wheels which stood around a heavy wooden table. A couple of mike booms hung their globes of ripe fruit over the table. Max, Clint, and I, whose uniforms looked wrinkled, mildewed, and napless alongside the crisp outfits of the headquarters johnnies, were pushed behind one of the baffles when it had become obvious that every time one of us cleared his throat, our huge-shouldered hero looked over at us and giggled.

The broadcast turned out to be a farce—a bitter one, considering the appalling sincerity of Marrow's conviction that he was going to tell the world The Whole Truth. He had taken strength from his own myth, he felt the inner power of a hero. He had a message to tell: that our Wing Headquarters was full of horse s——. He thought the taxpayers of the United States would be interested to know that.

Clint and Max and I, watching the broadcast, which was really only a recording session for a broadcast that would come later, could see nothing except the hypocrisy of institutionalized heroism. It was sickening.

The broadcast was to last six minutes, and there was to be another star on the show. What with introductions, a trailer for the next broadcast in the series, and a short fight talk to the home front by a chicken colonel from Public Relations, Marrow was to get two minutes, really not quite time enough to tell The Whole Truth. Anyway, they had handed him a script.

The other star of the show, Marrow's Co-Hero, was a sergeant gunner from a Liberator who was said to have shot down two German fighters on the same run. He could barely read.

Marrow's two minutes consisted of a description, in the form of a first-person narrative, of how he had led the strike against Hamburg around for its second bombing run. The tale as he read it had been written up at third hand from the interrogation report by a former news-magazine writer who was working as a P.R.O. at Eighth Air Force. This wasn't what had happened at all; it was a tense little over-simplification; it was a two-minute lie.

From behind the baffle we heard Marrow, as he finished stumbling through his reading, slap the script down on the table.

At the end of the session we could hear the rank crowding around Marrow and the poor semi-literate sergeant and congratulating them for the wonderful work they were doing to win the war.

We heard Marrow say, "Where'd you hide those three aviators?"

We came out from behind the baffle board.

"Let's get out of here," Buzz said. "I got to get drunk."

But they weren't going to let him off that easily. There was to be a reception for Major Marrow and the retarded sergeant in the Gondoliers' Suite of the Savoy. The brass was eager to meet them.

"Christ Almighty," Marrow said, "you got more brass than *this*"—waving his hands at the majors, lieutenant colonels, and full colonels clustered around him—"at your headquarters?"

They had. We met brigadier generals, major generals, and a lieutenant general. Chicken colonels were fawning around the

Gondoliers' Suite like real-life corporals. It turned out that the
brass wasn't actually dying to meet Marrow, and it certainly had no
desire to touch palms with three raunchy lieutenants who smelled
like damp Army blankets and happened to be named Haverstraw,
Brindt, and Boman; the brass was dying to meet the bartender.
This gave Marrow and the three odoriferous lieutenants plenty of
time to stand in one corner of the room and get drunk.

"Your mother sure would be proud of you," Brindt said to
Marrow.

"*My* mother," Haverstraw said, "was a religious fanatic. She
used to beat the hell out of me. *You little basket, whomp whomp.
I want you to live by the Golden Rule, you hear me? Whomp,
whomp, whomp.*"

They finally liberated us, and we went to a toney place called
Manetta's for chow, and Marrow just about paralyzed his right
cheek winking at dames in fur coats.

5 /   The light little British weapons carrier we were riding was
one of several our Group had swiped or chivvied from the R.A.F.
to be, more or less, mascots to our heavier American transport, and
the vehicle seemed, like so many British machines, to have been
put together over a period of years by a watchmaker. It ran fast and
bounced to beat the band. Marrow leaned forward over the wheel,
holding it, as he held that of our Fort, in his finger tips, with his
pinkies lifted, as if it were a bouillon cup, and the reflected light of
the headlamps and of the dashboard instruments came up like the
glow of dim footlights, picking out his magnificent hulk from in
front and below. When we got out into the country Buzz *flew* the
little lorry. There was an ecstatic look on his face, and the rest of
us thought, with creeping scalps, that we were on our last merry
ride on this earth. The highways were blacked out; Buzz was determined to get to Pike Rilling, "in time," he said, "to get a drink
at the club and forget that s—— they made me say."

Along the road we passed an English soldier thumbing a ride.

Buzz slammed on the brakes so that Max and Clint, on the plank seats in the back, were thrown forward against the cab.

"Let's give the poor bastard a ride," Marrow said.

"Let's ask him where he's going," Brindt said from the back.

"He didn't ask us where we're going, did he?" Marrow said. "Tell him to hop in the back and shout when he wants to get out."

It was misty now, and trucks ahead of us made the fog swirl and flee and thicken, yet Buzz got up speed again and passed whatever blocked him with a rush and a long bleat of the genteel British horn.

We passed three trucks in quick succession. Each truck seemed to spew out a cloud of roiled fog, and when we got into the worst of the opacity the first time, Buzz put his head down and looked at the dashboard, and then he jerked his head up again and said, "Christ, I went to get on instruments."

We skidded and nicked something, a culvert, perhaps, with a hub cap.

I said, "Easy, fella."

"The ancient Greeks," Buzz said, "used to believe in moderation in all things, that's what they told me in school. But not me. I'm no Greek. I won't stand for anything mediocre."

Caution was mediocrity.

"I like to drive a thing with wheels," Marrow said. "It gives you a kind of a change. Only thing I don't like, these British cars, they put you on the co-pilot's side."

The tiny engine emitted its steady, high-pitched whine, like that of an electric cake-mixer.

"I've had a slew of cars," Marrow said. "You know, I left my last car in the parking lot at Bennett the day we flew over here."

"Yes, I *know*," I said with weary emphasis, for I'd heard this boast a dozen times.

"The key's in it and everything. I just drove up and got out and left the key in it and got on the plane. Hell's bells, only cost me two hundred thirty smackers. But it sure ran smooth."

Vehicles were going by in the opposite direction now and were crowding us on the road. Buzz said, "Looks to me like we only got one headlight."

I leaned out and told him I could only see the glow of one light in the mist, on my side.

Buzz fumbled on the floor and picked up a flashlight he must have seen earlier. "I got to get me some road," he said. He held the lit flashlight out to his right at arm's length, and the next car that approached gave us plenty of room. "Ah, there's my road," he said.

A big brown American eight-by-eight passed us, lurching and swerving, and Buzz shouted, "Why, you son of a bitch." The truck cut close in front of us, slowed down abruptly, let us pass, then hurtled by us again. Leap frog. This time a soldier leaned out and whooped at us as the truck passed. "It's a shame the way some people abuse Government property," Marrow said. The truck swayed away from us into the mist ahead.

Less than a mile further along the road we came to a British soldier standing in the middle of the road waving a lantern. We stopped, and he said to Marrow, "If you please, sir, I 'appened on 'em 'ere. They was precisely as you see. I didn't 'ave nothing to do wiv it. I just 'appened onto 'em, so 'elp me."

The open truck was on its side on the shoulder of the road. One of the two soldiers was behind the truck vomiting and gasping for breath. The other was out in front, lying still on his side, with blood trickling out of his mouth.

The soldier who had thumbed a ride with us disappeared; I guess he figured he'd get away while he still had his life. He'd told Brindt he'd been at Tobruk.

Soon other trucks and some cars had stopped. Marrow took charge. He felt the motionless man's pulse and found that he was alive. "All right," Buzz shouted. "Let's have eight pair of hands here. This man's back may be broken, carry him careful, that's it, right in there, easy, all right now . . ."

We asked our way to the nearest American general hospital, and found it, at last, in a big country house in a park a few miles off the main road. The conscious man cried out in pain as we drove. Marrow shouted back from the cab, "Shut up, you stupid son of a bitch, we're getting you there as fast as we can. It's your own f——ing fault to begin with."

Marrow made a report to a colonel. There was a lot of palaver about whether the hospital could admit men from a service unit, and while this was going on the unconscious man died in the back of our truck. Marrow raged at "the horse-doctors they have in this mother-f——ing sergeants' army" as we left the hospital, and when he reached the main road he drove even faster than before. "Christ, what a waste of manpower!" he exclaimed. "You can't be too careful in a war."

We reached the Bartleck gate of the airdrome in an hour and three quarters from Manetta's. "That's not bad time," Marrow said, "considering the delay for those stupid jerks."

6 /

The first of July was a calm blue day, and we were free, and I waked up early and called Daphne before she got away to her office, and she agreed to meet me.

She asked what I wanted to do.

"Let's go see something old."

"Why old?"

"To see that things don't end."

She suggested Hampton Court, and I asked what that was, and she said it was a country house on the Thames where kings used to live; we had passed it that day on the way to Maidenhead. I didn't remember it, but it sounded fine to me, and we met in London and went by Tube to Richmond Park, whose huge overhanging trees enclosed us in such a mysterious darkness that I began to think of Daphne as Rima; then we took a river steamer a few miles along the Thames, and I recognized the buildings when I saw them.

We walked first in the gardens of the palace, through an orangery, and a wilderness, and a maze. The air was heavy with a scent of flowers and breathing leaves that lay like a fogbank around us. Daphne had an infected finger. She seemed preoccupied; perhaps her finger throbbed. I was still haunted by the image of her as a wild, Rima-like creature, for her cheeks were flushed and her hair seemed insubstantial.

"You think I'm weak, don't you?" she said.

"On the contrary," I said.

"You think I'm easily influenced."

"I think you're the most accommodating person I ever met."

"Yes, but I have a mind of my own."

"You don't have to tell me that." But perhaps she did. Perhaps I should have listened more carefully. Perhaps I was drugged by the warm sunlight and the fresh smell on the air, and by Daphne's marvelous soft look.

"I can take a stand," she said, and then she blurted out the story of having broken off her relationship with her R.A.F. ace, her Dugger, because he could only love himself. She said she had been powerfully attracted to him. As she talked I remembered how she had once told me not to ask her about other men, and I had an uneasy feeling she was trying now to tell me something, warn me, put me on guard, but I was lazy-minded and charmed, and I listened without thinking, until she said, "He was like your Major Marrow in many ways."

At that I began to feel grouchy, and I said, "Listen, you're getting gloomy. Let's talk about something else. I told you I didn't want to think about endings today."

I clumsily tried to take her hand, having forgotten about her finger. She drew back. I felt hurt.

But at once her agreeableness to my wishes came out, and she forced herself to be light. We went into the palace buildings. She showed herself to be mine, and I felt a wave of gratitude. She told me that Cardinal Wolsey had given the palace to Henry the Eighth, and we went through Anne Boleyn's gateway into the Clock court and saw the colonnade and the staircase built by Christopher Wren, and in the huge hall I pictured Charles Laughton as Henry the Eighth, an obese tyrant gnawing on lambkins' drumsticks and tossing the bones over his shoulder to a pack of great Danes.

She hooked my arm with her good hand and pulled me against her and murmured, "My monarch! You're *my* king."

My chest expanded. I felt the weight of the crown on my head. "Listen, baby," I said, "we'd better get moving."

"Darling," she said, and gave me another of those provocative squeezes.

I said, "Wow-wee!" and shook my head and grinned.

We were famished, and we had a huge tea in the garden of the Mitre. Chewing a heavy sesame cake I told Daphne that a pilot had gone up on the Le Mans mission drunk; many of us knew that he was carrying a bottle, but no one had stopped him, and his

plane had been shot down. I told her that when Marrow had
heard about the loss of the plane, he had said, with what seemed a
lack of feeling, "That's just tough titty. Any aviator who'll take intoxicating liquor up in the sky just isn't an aviator. Why, Christ,
man, the sky's intoxicating itself. What does he want?" And I told
Daphne that one of our crew, Jughead Farr, often took a pint of
brandy along with him in the inside pocket of his flying suit; I
knew that but Marrow didn't. Farr said it was in case of loss of
blood, but I also knew that he'd taken more than one practice in-
fusion from the bottle on missions.

But then I said, "Don't let me talk about flying."

Daph said, "But it's your life. Can't you see that I want to be
part of your life?"

Then without a transition Daphne was talking about her earlier relationships again. Her first deep love, she said, was for a married man. She had been less than twenty, he had been in his late
thirties. He was bald. She said she had never minded his baldness,
had never noticed it. He had sensitive eyes. He had courted her
with tragic ferocity, and he had seemed to take his only nourishment from her growing love, yet he could not break his tie with a
wife he professed to hate. His wife dominated him, and to Daphne
he complained about her tyranny, yet he kept going back to it. The
passion had lasted two years. Somehow the image of his painful
yearning for Daphne and for freedom, and her own suffering, her
uncertainties, her suspenseful absences from him, her terror of being found out—all that had provided a more profound joy for
her, she knew, than the fulfillment of their love could have.

She looked at me, as she told this story, with, at first, merely a
kind of trustfulness, but as she went on, and as the stirring of her
emotions brought its usual train of exuberance and quickness in
her, she began to gaze at me with passionate longing, and finally
she said, "With you, Bo, it's different, it's different."

With me, it seemed, she wanted the full fruition of our love,
and at once I took her up on what she seemed to be saying—but
my response, alas, was narrow and self-serving, and it missed her
point altogether. "I've been thinking," I eagerly said. "I want to
get you a room in Bartleck, and you can quit your job and come
and live there all the time, and we can be together constantly. I've
got back pay just rotting"—Marrow's phrase, I now realize, which

he had uttered that day when we cycled together to Motford Sage
—"just rotting until it stinks, and there's no reason in the world
why we can't do it."

My accommodating Daphne said, "Ah, Bo, that would be
wizard, wouldn't it?" But there was a want of ecstasy in that answer
of hers. It was a sweet accession which she pushed out by main
force.

I, however, was so taken up with the pleasantness of the prospect of being with Daphne almost every day that I managed to
brush off, though I heard, the flatness of her voice giving me her
consent.

We rode down the river on a boat that was crowded with children, and their squeaking and impulsive rushes were delightful. I
realized how much I had missed the presence of kids. I felt as if I
hadn't seen any for months. The world had seemed not to be re-
newing itself.

7 /

On Independence Day we flew a mission to Nantes, and
on the fifth I went into Bartleck and rented a room for Daphne.
Being so near the base, the village was better set up than the
larger town of Motford Sage with lodgings and rentals, and I
found quite easily a clean, small room close under a roof, which
contained a bed, a chest of drawers, and a tiny closet, in the doorway of which hung a mustard-colored curtain. I wrote Mrs. Porlock
to tell her I wouldn't need her sons' room any more; I sent her an
extra week's rent. On the sixth Daphne quit her job, and on the
eighth she came to Bartleck to live in the room, bringing with her
two large suitcases of things. The rest she left in her flat in Cambridge, for which I was now to pay.

I spent the afternoon and evening of the eighth with her in
our new home. The hours of that day and night were, from my
point of view, imperfect in only one way: they sped too fast.

Being kept in this room was not (I know now) what Daphne

wanted, but she made it seem her life's desire, because it seemed to be mine.

There came over me that afternoon, happy as I was, some precursory signs of the crisis I was to go through later in the month. These took the form of flashes of disgust—with my lot, with myself, and with my closest companions. I guess I was about to come down with a bug, a nasty short-term vomiting-and-diarrhea bug that had hit many of the fliers in the last few days, I suppose because of the general conditions of filth and carelessness in our kitchens which had bothered clean Clint Haverstraw so long. Prien, our stomach man, had come down with the ailment first, and Marrow had said Prien was sick because he had a yellow streak as wide as a necktie along his spine, and six hours later Marrow came down with it himself, to his chagrin. But I had to tell Daphne about some other things that had thrown me.

The Nantes mission had been a milk run, "the Fourth of July Picnic," Marrow called it—though I was to find that his speaking of it in such off-hand terms was partly a cover-up. He was so far gone in his big-shot role as a hero that he had been positively slap-happy, on the fourth, about inspections and checks. "What the f— is a crew for, anyway?" he grandly said, as if we were his servants. I compensated for Buzz's laxness with what was probably too strict a conscientiousness.

I reminded Bragnani of something he was supposed to do.

"Yes, teacher," Brag said.

That one walloped me. Teacher. I tried to pass it off with a crack. "A little more military courtesy here, men."

"Yes, ma'am," said Farr.

Now that was what you could really call hitting below the belt.

Another thing I told Daphne: On the fifth, when Prien had begun to be sick from the bug but hadn't yet realized what it was, he sought me out and mechanically presented, in his cold, matter-of-fact voice, a complaint that Dunk Farmer, the bartender in the officers' club, apparently a trouble-maker, had told him, that he, Farmer, was going to get Prien's berth in The Body because Marrow had no confidence in Prien. Prien said to me, in sentences that were like metal strongboxes, so tightly was all emotion locked away in them, "My old lady was against me flying. I was glad to come in the Army and be out of the house, but she wouldn't sign my papers, or in other words I could've been a pilot myself and not take any crap off Marrow, see what I mean? I was scared at first, but I'm not any more, it's just this God-damn gut of mine. We got a wonderful crew, I want to finish out with them, but I can't stomach any more of this stuff from Major Marrow." I responded to this by praising our pilot, and Prien unexpectedly endorsed my views with wooden enthusiasm, and he went off, placated, so far as I could tell.

Lynch, too, had upset me. The Fourth of July Picnic had really been an outstanding attack, as reconnaissance had proved, for of the sixty-one ships that had gone over the target, the S.N.C.A. de l'Ouest aircraft factory at Nantes, eighteen had made direct hits from twenty-five thousand feet on a single building only six hundred fifty feet square—a real pickle-barrel job, for once. Yet after the raid Lynch had had nothing but beefs: Our Group had started its take-offs late, and there'd been confusion on the climb, you couldn't tell which group was which, and our formation had been endangered by a cloud-bank over the Channel, and apparently the altimeter settings of the various groups hadn't jibed because the high squadron of the low group and the low squadron of the high group had gotten all mishmashed together, and at the initial point the high group swung in on a collision course with the low group and had to turn off at the last moment and its bombs fell wide, and there was trouble with the VHF—and it just seemed as if he couldn't do enough to take the steam out of the best job we'd done. At that point I was too fussed to take into account the fact that Lynch was wearing the horns that his wife had so thoughtfully sent him, and I came out of the session with a feeling that we were booting the war, just getting ourselves killed fumbling around with expensive equipment. But there was more to it than that. My friend Lynch, whose acuteness and speed I admired, and whose dominance of his pilot, Bessemer, I envied, had begun to hand out free advice to me about how to conduct myself in relation to Marrow—something that was none of his business.

Then I told Daph what was really on my mind.

On the Nantes raid we'd received a mild fighter attack over the target, and I had seen a German pilot bail out, far ahead of us, and a little above, and I had watched his yellow parachute open out, and I'd felt pronounced relief at his safety, but then I'd seen, before he had, that his chute was on fire, and then he had seen it, and he had begun clawing at his shrouds, and that was the last I had seen. The picture had given me, worse than ever, the feeling I had often experienced, of helplessness. Seeing death—on the beach at Pamonassett, or of a waxen Nelson in a make-believe ship, or in a crater near Pike Rilling—was disturbing enough; to see a live man doomed was far worse. I suffered in two ways: imagining myself him and his killer.

Daphne comforted me—how thoroughly! Just to purge myself of these accounts would have made me sounder, but she with her gift of losing herself in me, and with words, and with actions of her body, lulled my fears and doubts and made me feel all new.

I walked back to the base exulting in the knowledge that thenceforth I could be refreshed by Daphne nearly every day.

8 /

At ten the next morning I learned that our whole crew had been ordered to rest homes, the officers to one, the enlisted men to another, for a week. We were to leave on July tenth.

The news threw me into a panic, and I hurried, without telling Marrow, to sick quarters, to protest the order to Doc Randall. We didn't need rest! We were at our peak!

Doc leaned back in his swivel chair and pulled at his pipe and looked out the window. Most men, he said, couldn't wait to get to a rest home.

This, I knew, was true. The combat crews who had gone and come back had not had to mention the element of reprieve in their stays at the rest homes; they had simply ticked off a few symbols—beds with sheets, steaks, cold beer, movies, softball games. There hadn't even been much talk of women. Most fliers, as Doc said, couldn't wait to go.

I began to talk about Marrow. I said he was one of the best pilots in the Group, if not *the* best. After fifteen missions he was at the top of his efficiency. He was a major now. He was about to get a decoration. He might be promoted any day to be squadron or even group commander, as it was obvious that Trummer wouldn't last. How could the Doc jeopardize Marrow's chances this way?

Doc Randall looked straight at me with those well-diggers he used for eyes and asked me if Major Marrow had sent me on this errand.

No, he hadn't.

"I have reason to think," Doc said, with a finality that lifted me to my feet, as if I were being dismissed, "that this would be a good time for your pilot to have a rest."

I made to leave, but Doc said, "Wait a minute, Boman. What itches thee?"

A man can hide a lot from himself, but even I knew my real worry. I had had very bad luck in timing Daphne's move. For her, a week alone in Bartleck, or even a week idle in Cambridge, might mean . . . I could not think what it might mean, but I had a feeling of dread.

"I just don't think I need it," I said, and then I felt such a stab of fear that I knew I needed something.

Doc Randall stared at me for a long paragraph's worth, but then all he said was, "Major Marrow needs it. And when a first pilot goes to the flak house, his crew goes, too. That's the way things are in this crazy Air Force."

I guess if I could lie to Doc, he could spoof me as well. Anyway, he got me wondering why Marrow needed a rest, and what he had said allowed me to blame my bad fortune on Buzz.

I went back to our hutment and started vomiting.

That evening, with a queasy midsection, I walked out to Daph's and told her the news. It seemed there was nothing that girl wouldn't accept for my sake. After having given me a deeply moving gift, which even in my weakened condition I was able to appreciate, she quietly packed her bag and took a bus to Cambridge.

9 /

Marrow, Brindt, Haverstraw, and I, and the officers from *Torch Carrier* and *Ten Naughty Boys*, flew next day in a bucket-seated DC-3 up to Lancashire, and by early afternoon we were installed, along with about a hundred and fifty other fliers, in what had been a luxury hotel in the seaside resort of Southport, outlooking on the Irish Sea.

We had a fine American supper at six o'clock. I was in bed at eight fifteen, and I slept until four thirty the next afternoon. That was Sunday. I had six drinks after supper and went to bed at ten and slept until Monday afternoon at two. Marrow slept longer than I.

By Tuesday I was all slept out.

I had to admit I liked it. There was nobody to tell you what to do. Every day, when I waked up, there was an earth-shaking problem, and I had to roll over on my back and grapple with it: What amusement am I going to pursue until it's time to get some more sack time in this sack that is like the womb that Mother used to make? Ping-pong? Acey-deucy? Tennis? Movies? Radio? Books? Swim? Walk? It was hard to decide, and sometimes I had to lie on my back as much as two hours making up my mind.

On Thursday a bad thing happened.

We had had so much shut-eye that I was wakened by the complaints of a sea gull at ten o'clock in the morning. Marrow, who would never get enough sleep, was still breathing like a hippo. There were no rules about eating meals, so I decided to skip breakfast. I read a Nero Wolfe mystery from beginning to end, and then thought about the day for a while.

Marrow finally roused himself, and we went out to look for dames, and incidentally to take a swim, on the beach in front of the town promenade, and the water was cold, and the few girls we saw were made of dough that was lumpy because it was still rising, so we went back to the hotel for a big late lunch, and Marrow saw a notice that there would be a horseshoe-throwing tournament the following day, and he signed up with a flourish and talked me into a practice session with him.

I beat him three games running. I couldn't miss. I got five ringers and seven or eight leaners.

Marrow said that he could only throw real horseshoes; these fake, rubber-covered ones that were made for men, and not horses, gave him a pain in the ass.

Later in the day I noticed he had scratched his name off the tournament list, and I, who had not signed up in the first place, felt smug, and I called Marrow on his loss of enthusiasm for that

fine American test of skill, and he became cranky—and this made
what happened later even worse than it would otherwise have
been.

I wanted to cheer him up, so I suggested sampling the cure at
one of the baths in town; maybe the baths in Lancashire would
be like those in Japan, men and women together.

This expedition, too, turned out badly. The place we chose
was a grim hydropathic institution, not for laughs, where the only
other customers were a few wrinkled old crocks trying to purge
themselves of despair and decay. The dressing rooms were filthy;
the cockroaches were as bold as sergeants.

We got out as fast as we could and went for a walk in a park
where there was an observatory, and I said observatories always
made me think of the helmets of Roman soldiers, and Marrow
said, "Boman, you're too educated for your own good. You're
like a limey." I didn't need to answer that I could, nevertheless,
trounce him at horseshoes, because that was all too obviously on
his mind.

We walked back to the hotel along a wide boulevard, Lord
Street, where stiff-legged working people on vacation from Liver-
pool strolled in the late afternoon sunlight, and where there were
many men in the uniforms of several nations. I remembered something Marrow had said on one of our leaves in London: "Too
God-damn many foreigners on our side."

We met Max and Clint for a drink before dinner. There was
a tacit understanding among us that we would seek no new
friendships in the rest home. In general, all the aviators there stayed
with their own. These men, and we ourselves, had seen too many
friends go down to want to make new ones to lose.

Lynch! Was Lynch all right? Would he get through this week?

In spite of our determination to keep to ourselves, we were
drawn by curiosity into talking with some new arrivals from the
—th Group. We were sitting in a big parlor that was full of creaking white-painted rattan furniture with soggy chintz-covered cush-
ions.

What had been going on since last Saturday?

Two missions and two scrubbings. The newcomers thought
our Group had been involved in both missions, and probably in
both cancellations, too.

Say! Had we heard about Silg and Goering?

We knew, of course, that Walter Silg, one of our squadron commanders—the big, mild-mannered fellow who had tried a low-down approach to Daph at one of the dances when she had been Pitt's girl—had been shot down on the Hüls raid. What about Goering?

It had come over the German radio—Lord Haw-Haw—that this Silg had parachuted and been captured, one of the men said, and in prison camp he had taunted Goering, said our Forts were going to shoot down all that fat idiot's toy planes, and Goering had taken a vow to avenge himself on Silg's Group of Flying Fortresses. That was us.

Had any of these fellows heard this program themselves?

No, but they knew a guy who'd heard about it from a guy who had.

Someone brought up the news of the Allied landings in Sicily, and there was not a man among us who could bring himself to say that these might help end the war; we could only gripe about the drain the new Mediterranean campaign would put on replacements and reinforcements for us.

This was getting too depressing, and I had just suggested going in for chow when one of the new arrivals said, "What do you guys think of your new C.O.?"

Very quickly Marrow said, "You mean Trummer?"

"No. No. The real throttle-jockey that just took his place. What was his name, Ed?"

"Short name," the man addressed as Ed replied. "They say he's a real good joe."

"Yeah," the first one said, "it was a short name. Kind of like Silg, really."

"Would it," Marrow said between his teeth, "be a name like Bins?"

"That's it! Bins. Huh, Ed?"

Marrow got up and said to me, "Well, Boman, I guess we know now why we needed a rest," and he walked out of the hotel and didn't come back in until four in the morning, when he waked me up in our room. He was crazily cheerful, said he'd had it from a hoor who weighed three hundred pounds, said being on her was like swimming in Great Salt Lake. He laughed himself to sleep.

10 /

I got up early next morning and kept to myself all day. I went to a small zoo they had in the town, and watched the monkeys behave like happy people, and I felt listless, apathetic, indifferent to everything that had seemed, a few days before, to matter.

Pike Rilling, finishing my tour, Daphne—all that seemed far away, unreal. I realized that I had spent surprisingly little time here in Southport thinking about Daphne. Now, when she came into my mind, I had an automatic reaction of warmth and gratitude, but it seemed to me that she was not so much part of my real life as part of what I had just characterized as "all that." I was not in a position to choose my company and the steps of my destiny. Daphne could as easily be ordered out of my life as I out of our Group—or as Marrow out of his hopes. I did not hate those I fought, and I did not love those I guarded. I was overwhelmed by a feeling that was becoming familiar to me, one which resting did not dispel—of helplessness, of utter helplessness, like that of a pilot suspended from a burning chute.

11 /

The entire personnel of the base was gathered for the presentation of decorations in a hollow square on the apron in front of the tower. On one side of the square was a cluster of Army nurses drawn around four men in wheelchairs and one lying flat on a high hospital cot on wheels. The formation as a whole was ragged, for we in the Air Force were notoriously sloppy in ceremony and drill of any kind; we were arranged by crews. I watched Marrow's face, and he watched the nurses. A big C-54 transport, which looked fat and awkward compared with our slender Forts, chewed its way around the approach circle and came in and shot a beautiful landing, and a staff car hurried out to meet it, and pretty soon one side of our square opened its mouth and admitted our new C.O., Wheatley Bins, talking a mile a minute and chopping with his hands, and, beside him, General Eaker, and some other officers of his suite. They passed closed to us, and I saw the General's hat with its wire ring taken out, just like a lowdown flier's, and his pale skin, but Bins and some clean-shaven staff men were between the General and me, and my view of the great man was brief. I hated him because he represented the cold, dead hand of military authority, yet I was thrilled to be near him and craned to see him, but Bins was in the way.

I recognize now that I was sharply torn about Colonel Bins. We had been back from the rest home for a week—this was July twenty-third—and, though we had had no action except a scrubbing and a Group practice mission, we had had ample time to see that the fliers were well satisfied to have Bins as C.O. Marrow detested him, and I wanted to be loyal to my pilot, but I was drawn to Bins. He was a tall, thin man of twenty-nine, with a blood-drained face and prominent eyes over whose rolling orbs heavy lids drooped down, cutting across the gray irises just above the pupils; his dark hair was cropped short and flat on top, and his mouth, even when relaxed, curled up at the corners in what looked like a bitter smile. Wheatley Bins was an ascetic—didn't smoke or drink and had nothing to do with women. "Whole Wheat" Bins, the boys at the bar called him. When he was off guard his face looked haunted, almost anguished, and he habitually sat hunched forward, with his arms crossed, his hands pressed against his ribs, squeezing himself, as if suffering from cold, or fear. Though curt and anti-social, he had always had a circle of close adherents—what Marrow had contemptuously called "Bins' clique." With his pallor and his brooding eyes he looked like a scholar, or even a poet, but among the fliers he was known to be the hottest of the hot pilots. "Bins? Why, man, I seen him do a perfect chandelle in a B-17 out at MacDill Field—like to scared me to death."

Bins had done one fine thing in recent days. We had returned from the rest home to find the Group's morale sour. Trummer had been a bust. The story of Silg's taunt of Goering had spread like a virus, and the men believed it. Goering was out for us. Though Bins—the Great Granite Jaw—was too inarticulate to speak to the aviators about the worries that were galling us, he had gathered us in the briefing room one afternoon earlier in this week, and had awkwardly said that he felt men could fight better with their eyes open than closed, and he'd let Steve Murika loose on us with an analysis—the first I had heard in all this time of risking my life—of what we were trying to do. Steve told us that the missions we flew were not, as we might have imagined, capricious and uncoordinated but were part of a plan, then about a month old—the Combined Bomber Offensive—under which the American Forts, Liberators, and Mediums, by day, and the R.A.F., by night, were going after carefully selected targets in order to prepare for an invasion of Europe. Though we would still occasionally hit submarine installations, the primary objectives henceforth were to be German aircraft manufacture, beginning with fighters, and certain bottleneck industries, such as ball bearings, oil, synthetic rubber, and military motor transport.

At the end of Murika's talk Whole Wheat got up and uttered one sentence, a triumph, one could see, of thought and rehearsal: "In addition to the information you have heard, gentlemen," he said, "you will appreciate that our associates who were unfortunate in parachuting into the hands of the enemy, these associates, now incarcerated, would certainly not appreciate our inactivity at the present juncture, inasmuch as each effort, of course, it may be small, nevertheless each effort shortens their restriction."

He fell back exhausted by the delivery of so many Latin-derivated words, which he must have considered fitting for an appeal to our emotions, and we marched out of the hall silent, calm, and rather fierce.

12 /

Bins led the General and his staff officers to a trestle table not far from that side of the square in which the injured and the nurses were stationed.

The General made a short speech of a sort he must have made many times. We got from it a sincere feeling (not his, perhaps, so much as ours) that no one was fighting the war the way we were.

Then, with utmost simplicity, Colonel Bins began to call forward men to receive decorations at the General's hand. At first we had the automatic decorations—Purple Hearts and Air Medals. There were so many Air Medals, which fliers earned simply by having flown a prescribed number of missions, that they were handed out in sets of boxes, crew by crew, to the first pilots of the ships. Men stepped forward for Purple Hearts with a definite crispness of step and straightness of back not often seen among aviators. The General murmured a few words to each, and each would come back to the ranks with a flaming face and proud eyes. The General went to the men in wheelchairs, carrying the medals to them, and he stood for some minutes chatting with the man on the hospital cot.

All this, under a broken sky, in a seasonable breeze which made the shiny nylon flag above the tower's water tank slap and chatter, to a profound silence all around us on the parade ground, broken there only by the murmurs of the Colonel and the General—all this moved me deeply. I cannot say that the emotion was one of happiness, for there was a sharp sense of pain in it, yet I felt, all in all, very good about life.

We had returned from Southport the previous Saturday; Daphne had come at once to her room in Bartleck, and after our separation our pleasure in each other's company had been almost unbearably strong. She had stayed on until Thursday; we had been peaceful together. Just that morning she had gone back to Cambridge to settle up some things she had left unfinished on her job. Lynch had worried me, for I had found him, on my return, pale, drawn, and apathetic, and he no longer read poems and made odd announcements on the Tannoy. I felt, by the very measure of his decline, refreshed by my own rest, but I felt that he should have such a rest, too. It had been exciting to see the sergeants of our crew again, after a week apart. Prien had come back with what seemed a chronic diarrhea, and I had visited him in sick quarters, where he was on sulfaguanadine, and he had wept, gripping my hand, because his physical symptoms were going to keep him from flying any more with the greatest crew in the E.T.O. It had done me good to see that Marrow seemed to have recovered some of his old pepper. Four or five days after our return he had discovered that Butcher Lamb had salvaged a big piece of armor plate from the current Hangar Queen, and Butch had screwed it onto the

bulkhead of his radio room, for his own sense of well-being, and
Marrow had ordered him, with beautifully mordant language, to
rip it out, and he had stood over Lamb and watched him take the
nut off every bolt. Another day we had been handed instructions
for loading leaflets in the bomb bays—the boxes should be attached
to the uppermost bomb racks, and to inboard racks when possible,
and so on—and Marrow had shouted in the briefing room that *he*
was one pilot who was never, never going to carry a lot of crap
paper in *his* bomb bays.

Above all, I suppose, I felt on top because we of *The Body*
hadn't flown a combat mission since the Fourth of July Picnic, and
this was the twenty-third.

After the Purple Hearts and the Air Medals (I sneaked open
the blue velveteen box in which my own Air Medal had come and
read with a hurrying pulse the mimeographed form which spoke
of my courage in action), a few men were called forward who had
really earned their decorations. Bins himself got a D.F.C., and
when Silg was given a D.F.C. in absentia a kind of shudder ran
along the sides of the square. Braddock got a posthumous Silver
Star. All this was in a continuing silence; where I stood we heard
only the sounds of blowing cloth atop the tower.

Then something happened that I'll never forget. Marrow was
called forward for his decoration. As the General's hands went up
to pin the ribbon to Buzz's tunic someone in the back of the ranks
—not in our crew; it was off to one side—gave out, in a subdued
voice, so it sounded distant, as a kind of ventriloquist's lob of a
sound, a small and perhaps sarcastic "Hurray!" Then there were
other shouts, a bit louder, and gradually an amazing roar of approval, laughter, and deep feeling came pouring out from all four
sides of the square. The nurses began waving their white caps.
There were ear-piercing whistles, like those Bob Hope had received when he had played one night with a U.S.O. group in the
enlisted men's mess. I found that I was shouting and that tears
were gathering in my eyes, and I was thumping Max Brindt on the
back.

Marrow came back to us grinning the way he had used to do
in the early days, and he leaned over and said in my ear, "See
those nurses wave? I'm going to clamp it to 'em, one by one."

Was all the hullaballoo in Marrow's honor? Was he so much

admired? I don't know. I think that the very first hurray had had a lot of mockery in it; indeed, so had the whole outburst. There had certainly been a great deal of laughter. Perhaps the men had been trying to tell Marrow they were sorry for him because he'd been passed over in favor of Bins—though now, dispassionately, from a distance, I can see that Marrow never had had a prayer of being given the Group command; I doubt if the higher-ups ever considered him. Perhaps all the shouting was simply because Marrow was a character, the sort of man who would holler in the briefing room that he wasn't going to carry leaflets. Perhaps the great shout was simply an outpouring of the kind of good feelings I myself had felt standing there—rare feelings which wanted expression and were bound to find some excuse for ventilation. Or perhaps it was a deep, raucous protest against the absurdity of this formal show, for we knew who was durable and who wasn't, among us, and each man knew in his own heart whether he was sound or not, as of that day. We wanted no part of portentous words like bravery, gallantry.

Marrow himself took it very simply: It meant that he was the best aviator in the Group.

"Did you hear any cheering for that mother-f——er Bins?" he asked afterwards.

When we broke up, Marrow showed his gong, as he called it, to all comers; a formée cross on a square of rays, and superimposed on the cross a four-bladed propeller, all in bronze. On the back was engraved, "For Gallantry in Action—CAPT. WM. MARLOW." So, as usual, someone had goofed off, and the Great God-Damn System had got its hero's name wrong.

13 /

I spent the evening with Lynch. I asked him what he had felt during the cheering.

He said he had felt a wild elation, a kind of ecstasy, a strong pressure in his chest, a desire to weep. He had shouted loud. It had had nothing to do with Marrow, for him, he said, except that he had sensed a grim yet somehow comical incongruity—the boastful, foul-mouthed Marrow, with his huge head and tiny feet, receiving that small symbol of man's never-ending holding of bridges and forts and hills against his worst enemy, himself. Lynch said he thought that for him the shout had had to do with trying to tell the General to go back to his plush life in London. It had definitely had to do with the snapping of the flag. "It was very mysterious," Lynch said, in his strained, tired voice. "It was as if something had had hold of my throat."

Later in the evening we tried to talk to each other about courage, and suddenly Lynch said he suffered phobic terrors on missions. "Oh, yes," he said, in the voice of an old man, "I've had them since my first strike." Even when he'd been his most light-hearted self—"back in the Tannoy days." He was convinced that hatches might fall out of the plane, and he with them, or that the ship would blow up any minute, or that the walls of the plane would collapse. The dread ebbed and flowed; some days there was much, others he was nearly free. "Now I've told you," he said, and he looked at me as if ashamed.

I determined to go and speak with Doc Randall later that very evening, before turning in, to urge Lynch's grounding.

When I left Lynch's room I was flooded with a sense of how well off I was. Daphne! Darling! I was lucky! For some reason— perhaps because an alert for a raid sounded as I was walking home —I decided to wait till morning to speak to Doc about the Kid.

14 /

Far into that night I had a terrifying dream—particularly terrifying because it was an auditory dream. I did not see pictures but heard sounds. The sounds broke into the catacomb silence of what seemed to be a dreamless sleep. A voice spoke, and I could not tell whether it was mine or someone else's speaking to me, and if it was mine, I couldn't tell whether it was speaking to Lynch or to Marrow or to me or to whom. Somewhere at the outer edge of the dream there was a sense of Lynch and of Marrow, and of certain other aviators, too, I think. Daphne was not in it. The voice had great force and authority, and it spoke only one sentence.

"You are going to die tomorrow."

I found myself fully awake at once, with a hammering heart.
At first I was sure the voice, even if it was mine, was speaking to
me, and I leaped out of bed and stood in the middle of the room,
feeling doomed and lost.

Then, as if the dream had been reality, and as if everything
were logical and rational, I wanted to know which day would be
tomorrow. If it was before midnight, tomorrow would obviously be
Saturday, the twenty-fourth. But if it was after midnight, it was
already the twenty-fourth, and I might be spared—or someone
might be spared—until Sunday.

I patted the desk near the head of my bed and found my
watch, and I tried to make out from its luminous symbols what
time it was, but I couldn't see, so I walked down the hall, still
trembling with what seemed to be a quite practical and proper fear,
and went in the latrine, where a light was burning, and squinted
my eyes and saw the time.

It was one seventeen.

It was already Saturday. That meant Sunday. Yet perhaps not
Sunday. Perhaps the voice in the dream had talked with a simple
tongue; when one stayed up all night, one spoke, even into the
small hours, of "tomorrow" as the day that would follow the darkness.

I got back in my bed and lay shivering for a long time. At
last I fell into a deep, deep abyss of sleep, only to be wakened almost at once, it seemed, by the anticipation of Sully's flashlight.
Yes, he was there. "Out, boy. It's nearly three thirty. Briefing at
four."

For a time the dream was only a vague memory; those few
minutes of black oblivion just before Sully came on his rounds
had apparently almost wiped it out.

But it hit me again at breakfast. I got the shakes.

On the way to the briefing I ran into Doc Randall. I stopped
him. I think I meant to speak to him about Kid Lynch, but I said,
"What about Prien?"

"He's out. He'll fly," Doc said. "His stools were negative for
amoebas. No specific diagnosis. You might suggest to Marrow that
he mollycoddle Prien a bit."

"That's a laugh," I said. I wanted to ask Doc about my dream.
What it meant.

"Then *you* mollycoddle Prien," he said, and he started to walk away. Then he turned his head back and said, "And while you're at it, mollycoddle your pilot, too."

There was too much confusion. I was too bothered to think about what he was trying to say.

15 /

They briefed us for the longest mission the Eighth Air Force had flown up to that time, the target being the magnesium, aluminum, and nitrate works of Nordisk Lettmetal at Heroya, Norway. Steve Murika told us the plant had just been completed by the German chemical trust, I. G. Farbenindustrie, and had only been in operation for three weeks; our visit would give the Krauts a surprise.

When we took off there was haze and medium cloud in our part of England, and visibility was only a couple of miles. That day for the first time we assembled through bad weather by homing to a splasher beacon for Group rendezvous and then running along three splashers for force formation—and the newness of this procedure compounded my fright. As we went out over the North Sea, low cloud cover built up and we had ten tenths under us for hours on end. Above us the sky was clear. Happily we'd been briefed to fly just above the clouds, mostly at about five thousand feet, until immediately before the target, so we didn't have all that long time on oxygen. I was fearful all the way. I did not question the validity of my dream. I only wondered which day the voice had meant. I thought a lot about the cold sea hidden beneath the clouds.

Stormy Peters had promised that the clouds would abruptly break just before the Norwegian coast, and they did, and over the target we had thirty miles of visibility. Some of the groups—nine were out that day—apparently had trouble identifying the aiming point and had to go around a second time, but we bombed on our first run. Results were good; the plant was shut down, we later learned, and the Norwegians were impressed by pickle-barrel bombing. Anti-aircraft fire was meager. Only about forty enemy aircraft jumped the formation on the entire trip, and our Group was flying midway along the bomber stream, and we were never touched.

It was, in other words, a milk run, though a long one, but you couldn't have proved it by me, for I sat stiffly through it all, wondering when my dream was going to come true. I was too busy being afraid to notice how Marrow behaved all that day.

I was weary that evening, from lack of sleep the night before and from ten hours of rigid, self-centered flying during the day, and in the club after dinner I could barely keep my eyes open. I was looking forward to a splendid session of sleep.

An alert was announced, and we in the club greeted it with boos—not exactly a high point in the record of man's expressions of his patriotism. But little did we know what we were in for, because the fact was, as things turned out, we had launched only the first of a series of attacks which we were to come to know as "the July Blitz." *The Body* was to fly six missions in seven days.

After the alert I telephoned Daphne and told her how tired I was, and that we were going out again the next day, and that she might as well stay in Cambridge until we were stood down and I had had a chance to recover. I would call her. By then I had come wide awake, and though I hurried to bed, it was not to sleep. I had worked my dream over so much all day that I guess my head was sick of it, and this night I managed not to think about it much. From time to time a memory of that loud and assured voice forced its way into my mind, but each time I was able to push it down without becoming badly frightened. During the night I prepared, in full detail, a discussion with Doc Randall of Kid Lynch's problems, and for some reason, in the hazy half-thinking of the night, I grew angry with Doc; then I was angry with Marrow; then I was angry with General Eaker, who seemed at times to be Marrow. I told the General we needed more thorough briefings; that methods of assembly needed improvement, and that time spent in assembling should be shortened; that the wait between briefing and take-off should be cut down. He (he looked like Marrow) seemed deferential; eager for my opinions. . . . I got a lot off my chest, and perhaps I slept more than I thought I did.

16 /

I was awake when Sully came in to get me up, and I arose convinced I hadn't slept at all; I was exhausted.

Nevertheless, I had a curious feeling of coming out of myself that morning, of noticing much more about the outside world. The day before I had been shut into my own skin, a captive of my fears, and now I felt more open, and I heard what people said, and I reacted to my surroundings. Above all, to Marrow.

It seemed to me that Marrow must have been taken quite drunk by the queer applause during the award ceremony two days before, and that now he was having a dreadful, protracted hangover. He was in an ugly mood. At the same time, he evidently felt compelled to act the part of the slickest pilot in the Group; his maneuvers in the air, particularly evasive ones, had suddenly become flamboyant. "Christ Almighty," Handown said after we got back, "he thinks he's winning the war single-handed. In a single-seater airplane."

The attack that day was on the Blohm and Voss submarine factory at Hamburg. Our Group was Tail End Charlie, and we made a poor showing. The weather worsened as we approached Hamburg, the cover closing from five to seven tenths, and when we looked down on the city we had no idea where our target was, for besides the clouds there was a mass of smoke. Murika had off-handedly told us that the R.A.F. had hit Hamburg the night before with one of its devastating Katastrophe raids, but we had never seen the effect of an R.A.F. attack the morning after, and we were, in our various ways, amazed.

Marrow's way was to jump his crew. "You on it, Max, you on it?"

"I can't see anything only smoke."

"Get on it, boy."

I thought of what Doc Randall had said about mollycoddling Marrow, and I said, "You did a great job getting us here, Buzz. You can't help it if there's smoke."

Marrow answered, "You kiss my ass, Boman. We've come out here to drop bombs." His voice rose through this last sentence, in both pitch and volume, so that the word "bombs" was uttered in a tone very much like his scream at the first contact of each strike.

It was at this moment that my dream came rushing back into my mind, and with it a rush of terror. I was to die that day, or Marrow was to die. I was certain of it.

But we got home, and neither of us died.

I was too tired even to feel much relief at the realization that my dream, like all dreams, had not meant exactly what it had said.

After dinner we got our third alert in a row. I called Daphne. She said, "I wish I hadn't given up my job."

17 /

I had had a headache ever since our awakening at three o'clock in the morning. In the briefing, when Murika started talking about Hamburg for the second day in a row, I had a queer, paramnesic feeling that precisely what I was experiencing at that moment was also a whole set of memories retreating down my past like images within images in opposite mirrors; Hamburg Hamburg Hamburg Hamburg fading away in echoing cries. At the ground check I was listless and sloppy—gave the tires a swift kick and turned the switches on and let it go at that. I didn't care. There was an argument about the target, but I didn't care.

Junior Sailen, with a shrillness unusual in him, said Hamburg had had enough from the R.A.F. and from us. "I don't believe in spite bombings," Junior cried out.

"Aw, s——, Junior," Farr disgustedly said, "that's up to S-2. They know what has to be knocked out."

Bragnani, with his inverse way of speaking, seconded Farr by saying, "Farr, you sure are full of crap." That meant Farr knew what he was talking about.

Neg took Junior's side. "What's the use of bombing sub factories? I thought they told us we were going after German airplane factories now—synthetic rubber, oil—all that stuff old Tinhead told us." I had never heard the enlisted men's nickname for Murika —evidently given him on account of his metallic-looking forehead.

I didn't care. My skull pounded. My arms and legs felt heavy.

We flew up through and over a six-thousand-foot layer of haze which made us seem, at altitude, nearer the earth than usual.

This was the mission on which Max failed to fuse his bombs, and on the way to the rally point Marrow gave Max a short lecture over interphone. All he had to do on a mission was three things. Arm. Open. Toggle. Marrow really cut into Max about wanting to lose the war.

Then I saw *The House of Usher* hit.

Just after the rally point, when our formation was pulling together, I looked out and down to the right, to check up on Lynch's plane, as I had done many times on the flight, for we were in the lead squadron, and he and Bessemer were in the first element of the low squadron, about two hundred yards from us, visible most of the time just aft of the trailing edge of our right wing but tucked out of sight under it part of the time. Although fighter opposition had not been too strong on this raid, our Group was flying last again, and this time Jerry concentrated on us, and when I turned my head I saw *The House of Usher* chugging along in fine shape, well back of *The Body's* wing, as the formation pulled around on the turn for home. But I also saw, out of the corner of my eye, an ME-109 flick past on the right, and, looking down a second time, I distinctly saw a flash in the face of Lynch's plane.

Junior Sailen saw it, too. "Lieutenant Boman!" he said on interphone. "Lieutenant Lynch's plane just took a shell or something." It was like Junior to know, and to speak up, when a man's friend was in trouble.

"Keep your eye on it," I said. "Give me a call if they fall out." I couldn't watch.

All that interminable way home I sat there, with my throbbing temples clamped in a vise, unable to turn my head and look again at *The House of Usher*, depending on brief bulletins from Junior Sailen, to the effect that the ship was slipping back a bit—and I knew that once a plane straggled it was extremely vulnerable to concentrated attacks by enemy fighters—but then, no, it didn't seem to have lost more than one engine, it was coming in and holding formation, it was erratic, would lag and then pull up, it was catching some fighter attacks, but it was still with us, it was tucked in, it was coming along.

We lost two planes, *Alamo* and *This'll Slay You*, over Germany, and *Loony Bin* ditched in the Channel, and *Royal Straight* split off and landed at Scolthorp, and *Torch Carrier* broke off for Polebrook, but *The House of Usher* stayed with us all the way.

She dropped into a slot opposite us in the landing circle, and at last, just as we were banking for our approach to the field, I was able to look at her, and at that instant out came red-red flares: wounded or dead aboard, give way for an emergency landing, get the meat wagons ready.

I said to Marrow on interphone, "Bessemer's put up flares. Let's get out of the way and let him land."

Marrow glanced at the planes in the circle. "Which ship?" he said.

I pointed out *The House of Usher*.

"He'll take two, three minutes to come around," Marrow said. "I'm going in."

Then I said something the boldness of which, flying in the face of Marrow's mulishness and of all regulations, surprised even me. "Let me out at the end of the runway."

"O.K.," Marrow said, with complete indifference.

With an icy lump of fear in my belly, I fumblingly did my part of the work of getting down: watched the pressures and temperatures, dropped the wheels and saw the green signal light under the tachometers flash on, checked that the tail wheel was locked, made sure the cowl-flap valves were locked, and began calling the decreasing air speeds off for Marrow. I heard him cut through me to ask Junior if he was all set in the ball turret—with guns horizontal and pointing to the rear.

"One fifty-one. One forty-nine. One forty-eight. One forty-six."

"All right," Marrow said. "Flaps."

I lowered them, and Marrow, with gentle touches, adjusted the trim tabs. I kept giving him the speeds. I had a moment's flickering impression of the black tire streaks at the head of the runway. I didn't even feel us touch, but then the tail was down, and the tail wheel was bouncing. I raised the wing flaps. Our brakes were screeching. We rolled to taxiing speed, and I raised the lever on the floor to the left of my seat to unlock the tail wheel. I was already unhooking my belt. Marrow pulled off onto the taxiing strip and stopped, and I dodged down through to the forward escape hatch and dropped to the ground in the fierce wind of our four idling props. I ran out to one side, and then forward, to wave Marrow on.

Planes were coming in, but I had lost track of which *The House of Usher* was. I saw the ambulances and a fire truck on the other side of the runway, and between ships, after *Chug Bug* turned off to follow *The Body*, I broke every rule in the book by tearing across the runway to join those who were waiting to help. Among them, like a monster from the outer regions, was a fire fighter in a white asbestos suit topped by a tube head with a mica window in it. The sight of him reinforced a feeling that I had of being in a dream.

The House of Usher rolled to a stop at the extreme end of the runway, beyond the taxiing exists, and I could see she'd had bad trouble. There was one hole in the skin, near the astrodome, that you could have shoved a sheep through, and there were a couple of big holes back in the waist through which two gunners had stuck their heads; they were grinning like monkeys, and heaven knew what suffering there was inside their plane.

I was the first aboard. I had fought for the right to enter first. I had kept saying, "A guy I take care of is on that ship." Doc Randall was the one who let me climb up first, and he was right behind me.

They had dragged him into the radio room. I cannot describe what vomitous horrors I saw in there, or the trail of my friend leading aft from the cockpit.

You can re-create for yourself what I saw by reading, as I did that night, the Flight Surgeon's diagnosis, which, out of a sorrow of the sort I know Doc Randall felt, started with the least of it:

"1. Fracture, compound, 1st and 2nd metacarpals, left hand.

"2. Wound, penetrating, of chest, right.

"3. Fracture, compound, comminuted, of skull, caused by large piece of 20 mm. penetrating skull ½ in. above right orbital ridge; complete evisceration of brain."

It was that last which was unbearable. I thought of the Kid's sad humor—those marvelously improbable connections this brain had made, as fast as the switchboard of a great city's dial phone system; and of how this mind must have struggled in the dark of bed-

time to understand the letter he had got from his unfaithful wife;
and of its remarkable memory for verse—"Just a trick," he'd said
once. "Anyone can do it." But how many did?

"Let's get this out of here," Doc said, throwing a leather jacket
over what was left of the head, and I was so shocked at his speaking
of the remains of my friend Lynch as a "this," an object, that I
looked, frowning, at the doctor's eyes, and I saw, to my surprise, a
grief that challenged my own on that deep-lined face with its warts
and flourishing mustache. It was clear to me, then, why the men
trusted Doc Randall. A man can't mimic accessibility.

"Come on, Boman, grab ahold," Doc said. He wouldn't let
any of the men on Lynch's crew touch the remains.

Slowly there was growing in me a sickness—not simply nausea
—of feeling that I was responsible for my friend's death. I had
meant to speak to Doc about Lynch. I should have. It was my fault,
my fault, my fault. *I had killed him.*

We had got the leather-hooded "this" out the main hatchway,
and we started across the grass toward the ambulances. I began to
tremble.

"Not far," Doc said. "Keep going."

I tried to tell the Doc I'd killed my friend, but all I could say
was, "If you only knew."

"I know," Doc said. "I know very well."

But he didn't know. I was the only one who knew. I dropped
the dead legs and ran sobbing across the open field toward my
room.

18 /

After suppertime—I ate none, stayed in the room—and
after the announcement on the Tannoy of a stand-down for the
next day, I was sufficiently in command of myself to go and see
Doc Randall. I felt more and more guilty; I had a sensation of
slipping. I had a fierce desire to tell Doc Randall what I had not
done, and what I had therefore done. To kill a German from
twenty-five thousand feet, with a soldier's sanction for doing it, was

one thing; to kill a friend, with reckless carelessness, as I was certain
I had done, was another.

It was still broad daylight. The station sick quarters, three
Nissen huts joined by enclosed hallways, stood on a hill away
from the flying line, and apart from the huts in which we lived, in
a thicket of trees, which stirred now in a dry evening breeze of
summertime. At the edge of the grove was a tremulous aspen, its
leaves, lighter on one side than the other, turning this way and
that in the last sunshine of the day with an agitation not shown
by the more phlegmatic oaks and beeches, and I stopped stock
still on my way and gazed at the marvelous, delicate, continuous
coruscation of the one tree. It calmed me, not because I had any
grave or important thoughts as I watched it, but, to the contrary,
because the silently vibrating leaves seemed to drive all other pictures and motion out of my mind.

I walked on. I could not tell the doctor, I would wait and tell
Daphne.

There were many things Doc Randall might have said to me,
when he had sat me down in his office: consolations, rebukes for
running away from the body, trite salutes to death and deprivation.
Instead he sat and waited for me to take the initiative.

"Who tells his family—his wife?"

"She'll get a telegram in due course, after the machinery
grinds a bit. Maybe a week. No reason you shouldn't write her."

"I don't want to."

"Then she'll get the wire."

"What about—him?"

"He'll be buried in the American military cemetery in Cambridge, probably tomorrow. Why don't you go?"

I decided I would; I'd see him lowered, and I'd see Daphne
and tell her I'd killed him. Doc had the papers on Lynch on his
desk, and he showed me the diagnosis—in order, he said, "to put
things in perspective." Maybe he thought those factual, medical
phrases would help wipe out the memory of what I'd seen in the
radio room of *The House of Usher*, but when I came to the part
about the brain I began to shake, because I'd blown Lynch's brains
out, I'd done it, I was careless, it was my fault—and I stood up to
get out of there.

"Wait a minute," Doc said, and he went to a cabinet and got

some yellow capsules out of a bottle and reached them out to me.
"Take these when you turn in tonight."

I was more scared of pills than I was of being shot down in a
Fort. "I don't want to get hooked by those damn things."

Doc gave me a short lecture on sedation.

"All *three?*" I said.

"All three," he said.

I went to Bessemer's room and, to my extreme annoyance,
found Marrow there. What was he doing, butting in on Lynch's af-
fairs at this late hour? The possibility that Marrow had gone to talk
with Lynch's jerk of a pilot out of consideration for me never entered my mind—was driven from reaching it, furthermore, by what
they were saying. They were arguing about what to do with Lynch's
possessions. Bessemer wanted to bundle them up and send them
home; Marrow wanted to divvy them up among his friends. There
was, I should say, precedent for both ways of disposing of a dead
pilot's goods, but all I could think was that property was more important to Marrow than human life. He wanted some of Lynch's
things.

I broke out in anger at Marrow, saying, "You just want to get
your filthy hands on that Swiss knife of his, don't you? You tried to
buy it from him."

Marrow turned a look on me I'd often seen—his eyebrows
raised, his cheeks warming—when he took up some kind of chal-
lenge with a bully's first adrenal bristling. "Why, you low-minded
bastard," he said, "I was just trying to think what would be easiest
for his family. They don't want a lot of personal crap arriving on
their doorstep."

"How do you know what his wife wants?"

I was sore at Lynch's wife, and at Marrow, and at Their war,
and—cruelly—at myself, myself.

I told Bessemer about the probable trip to Cambridge the
next day and asked him if he wanted to round up his crew and go,
and he said he did. I said I'd check with the padre about time.

"And what's more," I said to Marrow, "you're not going. If
you want to get laid in Cambridge, you can take the liberty run."

"Up yours," Marrow said. "Listen, Boman, you're behaving
like a God-damn sucking crybaby. This is a man's racket we're in.
People get killed flying airplanes in a war."

At that I really did regress to childhood. "You think you're pretty tough, don't you?"

"Yes," Marrow said, and he stood up, and his chest seemed to swell and swell, "I do."

19 /

I made my contact with Preacher Plate about the next day's plans, and I arranged, through him, to procure a square piece of fabric cut from Lynch's parachute, which I wore from then on as a scarf.

Then I called Daphne. I told her about Lynch's death, and about coming up to Cambridge for the funeral, and I broke down on the telephone.

Daphne knew me through and through. "You mustn't blame yourself, Bo," she said.

I was too full of emotion just then to respond to her extraordinary understanding, and I said, "I'll tell you about it tomorrow."

We drove to Cambridge next morning in a six-by-six. Preacher Plate, who had gone on this errand many a time, rode in the cab with the driver. I sat on one of the hard benches running along the length of the back, in a dark cavern under a canvas cover, and with me were the nine men in Lynch's crew, strangers to me, all but Bessemer, and they had obviously been more terrified than saddened by what had happened on the way back from Hamburg, so as we drove they nervously cracked bad jokes; you couldn't blame them. My friend was laid out on the floor of the truck between the benches in a plain black box which was almost wholly covered by a big American flag.

The cemetery appalled me by its rawness, its newness, at the edge of a city of antiquities. I thought of Lynch's having pointed out that the great lime tree overshadowing the bulk of Pike Rilling Hall was older than the nation of the men inside the building. There were so many graves! White crosses, far more orderly than the ranks of life, marked a crowd of Lynches. Many graves were already under close-cropped grass. About a dozen new, open holes stood at one end of a row of officers' graves, for even here the ranks had separate quarters. A compact backhoe, clattering and roaring, was digging yet another hole beyond. A crew in coveralls slid Lynch's coffin out of the back of the six-by-six onto a sling suspended from a raised mechanical loader, and this contraption, driven by a jaunty-looking heavy-set sergeant, chugged alongside the first of the empty holes and parked there. The sergeant asked Preacher Plate if he was ready, and the padre nodded.

"Hey, Wallyo!" the sergeant called to the man operating the backhoe, but the engine of the digger drowned out the shout. The sergeant put two fingers in his mouth and gave a piercing whistle, which caught the backhoe operator's attention. "Knock off!" the sergeant shouted, waving as if to send the operator flying. The roar abruptly stopped. The padre murmured the service. Bessemer stood there with his mouth open. One of the gunners, a tall, thin guy, began crying. The coffin was still suspended over the hole from the loader, on the driver's seat of which the sergeant sat, holding his floppy workhat in his lap, and although his face was lowered with a practiced look of reverence and grief, his eyes, barely slit, alertly scanned the faces along the rim of the hole. Preacher Plate nodded again to the sergeant. A self-starter ground, and the loader's engine caught, and the sergeant lowered the sling, and his assistants cut it loose, and the sergeant backed away, and the engine died again. The padre bent over and picked up a handful of damp earth, and with the last words over Ambrose Lynch, speaking in tones that made one think of everlasting loneliness, sprinkled the dirt, and I could hear it hit the box. At once there was a roar of several engines, as the loader pulled away, the backhoe began digging again, and a miniature bulldozer crept up to fill the grave.

20 /

Daphne was waiting for me in her room. I had held back my feelings at the graveyard, expecting to weep freely in the privacy of her arms, but when I saw her I was dry-eyed. I took her in my embrace and felt a strong thrust of physical desire, and I drew back. I could tell by Daphne's eyes that she would be willing to accept whatever I felt. I think she had a secret grievance against me; she had given up a valued job for me, only to find herself left high and dry in empty rooms, in Bartleck and in Cambridge, first by my being shipped off to the rest home, and more recently by a series of raids that had taken everything out of me. At the very least, she must have been bored. Yet now all her attention, really all of it, with nothing held back for herself, was given to me.

She did not let me have a chance to blurt out my feelings of guilt, but said at once, "I never met your friend Lynch, but I felt as if I knew him, from all you told me. There were some things about him that I loathed."

I was shocked by her speaking of my dead friend in this way; the dirt had not even settled on his coffin. I told myself that Daphne must have resented my having any tie except with her. "Look," I said. "He was my best friend on the base. He was the only flier I knew who talked my language—or yours, for that matter." I acted hurt and more angry with Daphne than I had ever been—or than I actually was. Underneath, deep down, I must confess that I felt pleasure at what she had said, and relief. There was a distinct tickle of delight hidden beneath my indignation, and my proper and heated defense of my friend was hypocritical. As I talked about him my praise of him gradually shaded toward a slightly whining tone. "He had such a good mind, I almost never had to think when I was around him. He always had suggestions of what to do—'Let's go to the U.S.O. show.' . . . 'Let's go get some chow.' Or he'd say, 'Your eyes are bloodshot, you ought to rest your eyes.' He would eat breakfast with me, and he would try to make me eat some powdered eggs."

"Why do you think I said there were some things about him I loathed?" Daphne asked me.

"I wish you'd tell me," I said.

"Because you hated him," she said.

I wanted to be angry, but a laugh burst from my lips, a laugh not at the incongruity and absurdity of what she said, I am afraid, but one of embarrassment, recognition, one that brought to fruition that earlier tickle underneath. It was awkward. I felt I should be crying, working off my horrible guilt. The least I could do—and I did it—was to pretend that I was laughing at a ridiculous point of view.

"Are you crazy?" I said. "He was the only guy I got to know

who had the courage to question some of the military poop we get. He wasn't like Marrow, he saw things as they are. He was like an older brother to me."

Gradually, though, it came to me that I had, in truth, resented some important qualities in Lynch. More and more, in recent weeks, he had been interfering in my life, telling me how to do things; how to stand up to Marrow, how to conduct myself as a co-pilot, how to understand a book he had loaned me. A hatred had surely been building up in me toward my friend, even though I depended on him—or, more likely, *because* I depended on him—so much.

The more I recognized this unpleasing truth, the more I felt I had to quarrel with Daphne. I poured out all that I thought I had felt about my responsibility for his death, and I told her how I had meant to speak to Doc Randall about the Kid's condition. But even as I talked I felt the hollowness of what I was saying. I truly felt less guilty than relieved. Yet (I remembered the curious pleas-antness of my sobs as I ran across the field the day before) it was hard for me to give up my generous self-reproach, and as it slipped away from me I tried to make Daphne pay for my loss of it.

She was serene. She was wonderful to me. This made me rant all the more.

Soon I saw that I was using the loss of my friend to make Daphne baby me, and I began to be sorry that I had quarreled with her, and I told her so, and then I began to feel more like myself.

First Daphne said, "Dear Bo, one thing a woman learns in wartime is that combat doesn't make soldiers into strong, tough men, rather it makes them, the more of it they have, into children who want to be consoled and petted. Even your Marrow."

A few minutes later she said, "Don't let the pendulum swing too far, Bo. Don't forget the side of him you liked."

As I began to think then of other parts of Lynch, of the best of him, I experienced a new kind of grief, one that was centered on him rather than on myself, a sadness which, like my sobs, had a pleasant aspect, but this pleasantness, too, had to do with Lynch and not me. This sadness was his memorial, his life after death. Through its growth in me he would help to keep me going; I would remember him and so give him a little immortality, not very much, but more than some people get.

21 /

On the liberty bus on the way home, I found I had a strong repugnance for anything that might hurt or destroy human beings, or any life at all—a disgust so strong that it frightened me, because I had a tour to finish. I was one who had always tried to do my duty well; I couldn't simply quit. I was in the Army Air Force; I had responsibilities. I *had* to try to kill, and that was revolting, sickening. I rocked back and forth with the motion of the tiny bus, full of fear, heat, and nausea.

In this mood I thought again of what I had seen the previous afternoon in the radio room of *The House of Usher*.

I was quite calm when I reached the base. I guess the only way to forget is to go through the agony of remembering.

22 /

Just before Sully reached my bed at a few minutes before two in the morning, I rolled over and found that I was a new man. Or perhaps I should say a different man, for I was in fact much older. I was for life, and against death. A kid doesn't need to take a stand like that. So far I hadn't figured out what to do about anyone else's life, I'd have to think about that later, but one thing I knew: I was going to devote every ounce of my energy from here in to my own survival. I'd need luck, but I was going to push my luck in every way I could.

To begin with, I ran a rigorous ground check that morning. I really made sure. I was so thorough that Farr said, "Teacher's gone off his rocker this morning."

Bragnani said to Farr, "So have you." Meaning, "You said it." They didn't bother me.

Prien had a tummy ache, on account of the length of the mission they'd ordered—all the way to Kassel, a hundred and twenty-odd miles beyond the Rhine—and he wasn't saying so right out, but it was obvious he wanted to be excused from this raid. Please, sirs, just this once. He didn't *say* that, but his sniveling did.

Marrow listened to Prien's whining awhile and then he said, "Listen, son, if you don't go with us we'll have to take that God-damn bartender along."

That shut Prien up, and the new Boman was glad. I wanted a gripeless crew, I wanted alertness, I wanted life.

The long hour between stations time and take-off gave me leisure to think, and one of my thoughts was this: In some ways Ambrose Lynch had been a fine man, and now I remembered his goodness, while the rest of him, the hateful side, I had already blanked out, and with it my crazy self-reproach. His goodness was in me now; I was going to remember it and protect it, keep it alive like a coal in a poor man's fire.

We took off at six, and shortly after take-off we ran into scattered clouds varying in altitude from three to seven thousand feet, and it grew hazy, and there was another cloud layer, two- or three-tenths cover, at about fourteen thousand. I was sharply struck, as I had not been in some time, by the labyrinthine beauty of the sky. The Kid would have liked these sights. We came to a place where cloudlets seemed to be arranged in rows, as if on streets. Maybe my travels had brought me at last to Nephelococcygia. As we went out over the North Sea the intermediate cover increased, until it was a solid mass, over which we climbed. The top of this second slab was at twenty-three thousand, and above us, almost obliterating the blue, was still another layer, a broken one, at about twenty-five thousand. We flew in the mysterious flattened chamber between the layers, in a soft haze.

Suddenly into the chamber from above plunged our escort, some P-47s equipped, for the first time, with jettisonable belly tanks, so that they would be able to go thirty miles deeper with us than ever before. The belly tanks made them look even chunkier than usual, like fat bumblebees, but what gave the display a staggering beauty was that the planes drew along behind them in the misty air long gauze veils of condensation. We began forming them ourselves, and we seemed to be entering a dream world.

Marrow, however, seeing the contrails, grew cautious. That condensation, he said, was bad. One day, in a diversionary raid in weather like this (we had been in the main force and hadn't, thank heaven, seen it), an entire element had become engulfed in a combination of fighters' contrails and prop wash, and all three planes had collided and fallen in ruins. The new Boman liked Marrow's special carefulness—not realizing, yet, that it was the beginning of a danger sign in him. Buzz kept urging a particular watchfulness upon the crew; kept calling on me and on Handown to check various things about the ship.

Gradually the clouds thickened, and three quarters of the way to the target our task force turned back. I could hardly contain my relief and delight at our recall, for we were surely far enough to get sortie credit, and we would drop no bombs. But Marrow, even though he had been extra cautious for an hour, was furious at being frustrated from carrying through the attack.

The weather grew worse and worse, and two of our ships, *Income Taxes* and *Flak Sack*, plunked down at Ridgewell, and another, *She Can't Help It*, dropped out at Sutton Bridge. Marrow was in a filthy humor as we worked our way, through the beginnings of a fog, with less than two miles of visibility, into the landing circle at Pike Rilling. He had a nasty argument on the radio with Major Fane, the Flying Control Officer, about what slot *The Body* should fall into in the traffic pattern.

After the landing it was my turn to get burned up, because Marrow hopped a ride in from the plane as soon as we were parked and left the dirty work to me. It took a long time to get all the grouses about the airplane written up on Form One, all the guns unslung, and all the chutes and people into the truck.

On the way in I saw Handown literally lie down with his beloved machine guns, with his arms around them and his cheek against one of the perforated cooling tubes.

23 /

Marrow was waiting for me at the briefing room. He took me aside. He was fit to be tied.

Now, the concept of security was all very well, but in actual fact our base was one big chatterbox, and the latrines and hangars and offices and hutments had ears hanging on the walls like pictures, and there wasn't anything you couldn't pick up if you stayed awake. Marrow had a hot bulletin, and he was furious. He had had it from Curly Jonas, our Operations officer. Curly and Bins had been called the afternoon before, along with the key officers of other groups in our Wing, to Pike Rilling Hall, and there the Wing A-3 had outlined the plans for a real stinker of a mission. The fliers had been given full details, including altitudes, routes, timings, maneuvers for each group between the initial point and the target, directions on reassembly of the force—everything but the date and time of departure. Then they'd been taken in another room and had been shown something only British patience could have constructed—a sand model of a big piece of a city, with the projected target at the center. And what was the target? Schweinfurt. "It means in German 'In a Pig's Ass.' Honest. That's what Curly says." Marrow's fury was at the distance. "It's clear the other side of Germany," he said. "God-damn near to Czechoslovakia." Buzz said they were a bunch of murderers up at Wing.

A couple of hours later, when word had come in that out of six groups, some of which had gone through to their targets, twenty-two aircraft had been lost that day, Marrow said excitedly to Clint Haverstraw, "Jeez, son, look at the way the —th Group and the —rd Group have been hit the last few days. Now if the —th Group would lose a few ships, you know, get thinned out, we'd win the Inter-Group League in a breeze. They're bound to be losing some of their good players." Baseball!

24 /

In the club that night a handful of the pilots started talking about Lynch. Doc was in the circle, as it happened. Perhaps because of the Kid's having read poetry over the Tannoy, one of the men said he'd never been able to figure out whether Lynch had been a fairy.

Marrow hotly denied this. "Fairies don't fly," he said, dead serious. "Do they, Doc?"

Doc Randall raised his sad brown eyes and said that it was true the Air Force doctors hadn't run across any overt cases. Plenty of fliers indifferent to girls—maybe temporarily—and plenty of pronounced rivalry between the men; but overt, no, none to speak of.

"A flier," Marrow said—and he spoke with distinct pride—"can't really go for anyone except himself."

"There," Doc said, "you could be wrong. Though there's an element of truth in what you say."

25 /

There wasn't time to sleep, even for men like Marrow who were able. They briefed us shortly after midnight, and everyone in the briefing room looked more dead than alive. We were for the Heinkel aircraft factory at Warnemünde, and we were numb, we were moving like automatons, we were convinced we were going to be sent on an air raid every day for the rest of our lives.

Well! It was at the very end of the briefing that a piece of news came that wakened me all the way, and that made me want to stand up and cheer.

Two ships on this strike were going to carry leaflets instead of bombs. *Finah Than Dinah* and *The Body*. Stebbins, Marrow.

Marrow, next to me, did get on his feet and holler. "Not me!" he shouted. "None of that bumwad for me!"

Bins looked at Marrow with a trout's cold eye. "Orders, Major." When Bins called you by your rank, it was as if he'd done a very personal operation on you.

"F— orders," Marrow shouted. "I'm a bomber pilot. I take bombs."

Bins just waited him out, didn't say another word. There was some snickering around us. I tugged at Buzz's sleeve. He sat down muttering.

But he didn't give up. He rushed up after the briefing and raised hell. Delighted as I was, I do believe that Colonel Bins had been vindictive, and had assigned leaflets to Marrow precisely because Marrow had on a previous occasion so loudly objected to the idea of carrying them.

Marrow was still arguing at stations time—though by that hour, having failed in an attempt to put a call through to Wing, he was down to a journalist who worked for the O.W.I. or O.S.S. or something, in a uniform without insignia, a big tall fellow with a Poonah mustache and a German accent, who was trying to explain to Marrow that die ideological varfare vas pozzibly more important dan die uze of violenze.

"You can't tell me," Marrow said, "that bumwad is going to win a war."

But we took the leaflets in our bomb bays, and all that day I felt, along with intense sleepiness, a serenity that I'd never experienced on a raid before. Over Warnemünde, from the initial point to the rally point, the flak was extremely hot, particularly at the bomb-release line, where we flew through a storm of puffs. On the way out nearly a hundred fighters hit us, driving in to within seventy-five feet, from all directions, while some twin-engined craft arched rockets at us from eight hundred yards away, out of reach. But after the bomb-release line, as we swung for the rally point, I looked out and back and down, and I saw that our boxes of messages had broken open, and the paper began to flutter, like many pigeons' wings, downward.

26 /

My God! They gave us another raid the following day, and again the briefing was just after midnight, and once more the mission was for the Fiesler aircraft-component factory at Kassel—a city for which we'd been alerted six times. We somnambulated out of the briefing and dozed on the truck going out to the dispersals, and by the greatest effort of will in the world I carried out a thorough ground check, and at four thirty we took off, this time into a marvelous cloud-soft dawn the color of peaches going from ripe to over-ripe, and there were heavy clouds over Europe, but before the target they cleared, and we dropped our bombs. We had a rough time coming home, with the Hun using air-launched rockets again, and co-ordinated attacks of four abreast coming from the rear. Several of our ships were damaged but none was lost; *Big Bum Bird*, *Expendable* VI, and *Little Girl Blue* landed at Boxted, *Queenie* at Great Ashfield, *Voodoo* at Martlesham Heath, and *Miss Manookie* at Little Staughton.

Riding homeward, feeling drugged, I thought hard about Daphne, to keep myself awake. And for a second, just after we had sighted our runway, and I could feel the flood of certainty that we had made it again—just then I was overwhelmed with gratitude to my Daphne, who asked for nothing and gave me everything. Her understanding of me was greater than my own of myself. It struck me that I had loved her—as I had at first grieved for Lynch—all for myself, far too selfishly, so what I had offered her could hardly be called love at all. I wanted life, and peace, and a chance to give her better than I had given, and at that moment, as the wing on my side lifted, and we banked, pulling out of the formation to go around to settle back on the earth, I made an unauthorized separate peace with the enemy. I was going to find a way to quit killing.

CHAPTER NINE

THE RAID

1455–1604 hours

1 /
    Two minutes beyond our turn toward the initial point the last group of German fighters dropped away, and none came up to take its place.

It was five minutes to three, so I had been awake for thirteen hours, and we hadn't even reached our target.

Now that the fighters had left us, I expected Marrow to give me the controls, but he sat there, leaning forward, holding the wheel not in his usual light way but in a pair of fists.

"Want me to take her awhile?" I asked him.

He was a long time answering, then he said, "Suit yourself."

"Wait a sec," I said. "I've got to get me some relief."

I unplugged and unstrapped myself and went back to the bomb bay and unhooked the tube and managed to get everything unzipped, voided, and zipped again without any freeze-up. I opened the aft bulkhead door, and Lamb was at his gun without any literature in hand, and I went through past the ball turret and took one look at Farr and Bragnani in the waist compartment. The deck was littered with spent shell casings. Each was at his gun, scanning the sky so intently that I could back away and secure the door without having been noticed.

So far as I could see, *The Body* had not been touched. I remembered the sight of the plane at the hangars, after the Kiel raid when we'd run into trouble with our own incendiaries, with an engine pulled out and hanging by chains from a derrick; she had looked so mutilated on the one side, like a turkey half carved. And I remembered how wild Marrow had been—because the idea that his ship was untouchable had been taken away from him. As I went forward to my seat I thought how much I would have liked to believe in that old Marrow magic again.

When I got myself established I took the controls, but I soon found that it was a mistake, because at that point idleness was poison for Marrow.

Max, who was going to be the lead bombardier for the whole task force, began to try to get all his ducks in a row, so he would not be the cause again, as he had at Hamburg that time, for a three-hundred-and-sixty-degree turn. He wanted to check some of his data a good long stretch ahead—dropping angle, disk speed, drift —with Holdreth's bombardier, Colfang, who was supposed to be deputy lead bomber for the task force and for the Group, and should have been in Max's shoes.

Max knew that I had the controls, and that Marrow was just sitting there, but he now called Lamb, not Marrow, on interphone and asked whether the command set was tuned in so he could talk with Holdreth's toggleer.

"I'll do that talking," Marrow said.

"I want to talk straight with Colfang," Max firmly said.

Marrow yielded; or rather, he said nothing. This was certainly not like him.

I was flying along through the windowpane sky. Instead of holding position in a formation, it was now my job, as lead pilot, to clamp onto our course as if on steel rails, and to make quite sure that our indicated air speed did not vary. I had never had the sensation before of stepping out ahead of a whole procession of Forts. I was too tired to feel good about it, but I didn't feel bad, either. Of course, having the pressure of the fighters off us was a big help.

Brindt and Colfang were calling back and forth. Max was the best I'd ever heard him in a squeeze: steady, orderly, calm. But Marrow kept butting in, harassing Max in the monotonous, nasal, nagging tone we'd heard him use all morning.

I thought about reminding Brindt to fuse his bombs after he

got all his information checked, but then I remembered my determination not to take any part in the killing process, and then I
thought of my compromise on all that, and that made me think
for a moment of what had led to the compromise—to begin with,
the mix-up with Daphne over our meeting in London; or had it
been a mix-up? . . .

I couldn't let myself think about any of that, because it only
led to my thinking about Daph and Marrow, and about what she
had told me about him.

I looked at Buzz. He was sitting tensely straight, with his right
hand on the wheel and his thumb on the call button. I was worried about him; I had to help him last through to the target, because I wanted him to be in charge of the bombing. The least I
could do was to keep to the terms of a poor compromise with myself.

"Target surface pressure?" Max asked on the radio.

"Two nine point five two inches," Colfang said. He was coming in as clear as B.B.C. in the officers' club.

Marrow broke in. "Come on, Max. Get cracking. Don't forget
you got to arm your bombs."

"Get off here and let me get finished," Max said. We weren't
used to having people talk that way to Marrow on our crew. Not
without a word of answer.

But there was no answer. I saw Marrow still sitting up as
straight as if he had a poker in his vitals; very tense, but silent.

I figured he was better off flying than sitting there like that,
and I said, "How about taking it back, Buzz? We're almost at the
i.p."

It was two minutes after three, and we were due at the initial
point at eight past.

Marrow took the controls without a word.

Max had finished his verifying, and he called me and asked
me to arm the bombs for him. Of course I'd been checked out on
how to do that; we all had to be able to fill in for each other, because, as Marrow said, this was a man's racket, people got bumped
off.

I said, "O.K.," before I realized what I was agreeing to do—
to fix our bombs so they could kill.

I began unhooking myself again, and I was thinking: I could

go back there, and fiddle around, and not set the fuses. Nobody
would ever know.

"What settings?" I asked Max.

The five-hundred-pounders were to be one-tenth nose, one-
fortieth tail.

"Rajah," I said, my tone broad and jaunty.

I went back there and stood on the catwalk in the bays trying
to decide what to do. I couldn't take too much time. A lot was
going through my head: duty; thou shalt not; Hitler; Daphne;
months of training; my dream, with Max in it; the radio room of
The House of Usher; the rockets' red glare, the bombs bursting in
air; what Marrow really loved; Daph's father killed while trying to
rescue the wounded; Nelson in wax; the burning chute . . .

I saw a mouth. (My eyes were closed, and my forehead was
leaning against the bulkhead at the forward end of the bomb bay,
and the vibration of the ship was getting into me.) It was
Daphne's, and it was shaping words, and it came to the part about
what the rest of us have to do. . . .

I found myself arming the bombs. I worked fast. There were
ten bombs to fuse.

I went back to my seat, and I had been re-connected only a
few seconds when Clint Haverstraw announced we were at the i.p.

At that Neg Handown produced, with a zany cheerfulness not
the least forced, a falsetto anouncement: "This is your stewardess,
Miss Candycrack. We are approaching Newark. Please fasten your
safety belts and observe the no-smoking signs. Thank yoohoo."

Then another voice—was it Farr's? "Ram it, Negrocus."

Marrow came out of his lassitude with a sudden fury at this,
demanding, in a shrill, snapping voice, that we keep interphone
discipline.

We did in fact fasten our safety belts here at the beginning of
the approach to the target, because of the possibility of the plane's
being thrown about by near misses of flak.

At the initial point the great combat boxes broke up into their
component groups, three to a box, so the groups, after following
each its own briefed zigzag course to the target, could cross the
target on different courses and bomb independently, one by one.
The planes of each group would toggle their bombs on signal from
its lead bombardier—at the moment when the other toggleers saw

the first bomb fall out of the lead plane. Max, in other words, was to be responsible for the bombing pattern of our whole Group. After the target the groups, again following briefed routes, would rejoin each other in the vee formations of combat boxes at the rally point.

Brindt was silent as he worked, and I assumed that this meant he was calm and doing the best he could, but Marrow began to prod him, with a running fire of heckling questions.

We had gone onto Automatic Flight Control Equipment at the initial point, which meant that Max was flying the plane through the bombsight, and this left Marrow idle and impotent, and he gradually worked himself into a rage.

It was to take us eight minutes from the initial point to the bomb line, and we were following the prescribed zigzag, for both timing and flak evasion—straight on for thirty seconds, a fifteen-degree turn to the left for thirty seconds, a thirty-five-degree turn right for forty seconds, and so on, back and forth, until we would hit the actual bombing run seventy seconds ahead of the bomb line. I saw that we were not getting any fighters, but the flak looked pretty bad. During all this Max was flying us through the AFCE, and Marrow was getting louder and louder.

When we were about three minutes out Max finally blew up and said, in a grim, level voice, "Listen, Buzz, shut your big God-damn mouth. I'm doing O.K. We're going to bomb good—if you'll stop bothering me."

Thinking back I realized then the significance of a whole series of challenges to Marrow on this day—my own during the preflight, Lamb's about the tuning crank, Junior Sailen's startling one when he had called Handown, and now, for the second time in a row, Max's.

This time Marrow did not fall silent but began a torrential monotonous spewing of filth and abuse. He was so mad he couldn't see—not at Max any more, but at the whole situation—and his babbling was, I think, even more disturbing than had been his tri-umphant shriek at the first closure with enemy fighters.

Marrow was quieted at last by the queer shuddering of the ship as she let go her cargo, and by two words from Brindt, spoken not with Max's old aggressive exultation but in simple relief: "They're away."

Marrow took back the controls and stopped shouting.

2 /

All in all, Max had done a beautiful job, everything considered. Pictures taken on the raid showed that eleven of our Group's bombs fell within a thousand feet of the aiming point, and twenty-three within two thousand feet. This compared well with the —st Group, with a one and five record, and the —th Group, with zero and three. Two or three groups did better than we. As to the actual results in damage, our public-relations people put out a brave story that night about the raid's having given the German ball-bearing industry a nasty knock: ". . . severe damage . . . gutted . . . destroyed . . ." But a cooler appraisal, sent on by the British Ministry of Home Security the following week, after extensive reconnaissance, told a depressing story of futility and waste of men and machines, for we lost that day thirty-six bombers. In fact, the attacks on the ball-bearing plants at Schweinfurt caused relatively light damage. Two of the three main plants that produced bearings, Verenigte Kugellager Fabrik Werk II and Kugelfischer, were hit; the engineering firm of Fichtel and Sachs was slightly hurt; V.K.F. Werk I lost only an office building; and Deutsche Star Kugelhalter was untouched. The damage at V.K.F. and Kugelfischer was estimated to result in between one and four weeks' loss of output, which might amount to a loss of only about one week's supply of anti-friction bearings available in all of Germany. The sad fact was that the ball-bearing plants were ready for re-attack immediately after our raid, because the reduction in the rate of output was so very small.

Of course I learned all this much later, but when I did learn it, it seemed to put that whole day into a new, a much sadder perspective. We might better have stayed at home.

3 /

Marrow was flying again, and I had one hand lightly on the wheel in order to be able to press the talk button in case I needed to say something, and right over the target, not far beyond

the bombing line and just after we had taken the sharp left turn
that would carry us almost due north to the rally point, at 50°37'N–
10°34'E, nine minutes away, I suddenly felt as if I were getting an
electrical charge through the wheel. I looked across and saw that
Marrow had both hands off the wheel, above it, and his hands were
open, so he, too, must have experienced the same shock. He was
already looking at me, and I heard him say, "Jesus, the wiring's
shorted somewheres." That was what I thought, too. "Neg," Marrow began, "the wiring . . ."

Gingerly I approached my hand to my wheel and touched it.
It was dead; it was all right. I nodded to Marrow, and he took hold
again.

I said, "We must have been hit." The shock must have been a
factor of the blast on the elevators, reaching our hands through all
the gears and ratios of the cable system.

I hardly had the sentence out when Junior Sailen called and
in a tight, small voice said, "Number three's smoking."

One familiar word, "Braddock," flashed through my mind;
then something possessed me to answer as if I had been in command. "O.K., watch it closely," I said. "You watch it, Junior."

Maybe I took that liberty because the number-three engine
was on my side, or maybe I did it because of something about the
way Marrow was behaving. I don't know; I had acted on an impulse.

We reached the rally point at twenty-five past three, and Marrow buckled us around on a tight turn of less than ninety degrees,
and our high and low groups, having cut away from the target on
intercepting courses, hitched on to form our combat box. The second box joined up and came in trail with us.

"Still smoking," Junior said.

I was watching the manifold pressure on the number three,
and I saw it begin to drop, and then it began really to skid, and I
was aware that the prop might run away any minute, and, cool now
perhaps because of that day of rehearsal on putting out fires that
Marrow had given us, I proceeded, without checking with him, to
move the mixture control of number three to the off position, and
I cut the booster and pressed the feathering button for that engine and closed its cowl flaps. The propeller wouldn't feather for
the longest time but staggered along and wouldn't stop and

wouldn't quite feather, and again I was afraid that the r.p.m. might wind up tight like a windmill. But finally the blades feathered all the way, so they were slicing the wind, and with two or three twitching jumps the propeller stopped.

Marrow, far from complaining about my having stopped the engine without asking his permission, merely said, "Give me some coal. I got to get this speed up." We were supposed to cruise at one hundred fifty-five after the target, and we were running slow on account of the dead engine.

I jacked up the r.p.m.'s in the other three engines.

Then I said, "Kill the fuel to number three." I hadn't meant to put it that way, but it had come out as an order.

Marrow did what I had asked him to do. Didn't say, "Yes, sir," but obeyed.

I asked Junior how that engine looked, and he said he couldn't see any more smoke.

Prien came in on interphone from the tail, saying, "I'm sick. I feel as if I'm going to be sick. I didn't ever puke before on a raid. Oh. Don't let me pass out. I feel sick."

Of course it was Handown who said, "Take your mask off or you'll drown yourself. Use a helmet shell if you got one. Then get back in that mask in a hurry. Don't worry, Prien, we'll put in for a Purple Heart for you, boy."

Now Marrow, suddenly the old Marrow from nowhere, said to Prien in his familiar, self-assured voice, not angry but hard, "Listen, son, you're a God-damn yellow-belly. You pull yourself together."

This momentary restoration of the old rough Marrow worked magic for Prien. He must have gotten his mask off all right, but he didn't unplug his throat mike, and we could hear him gag. A few seconds later I asked, "You O.K., Prien?"

He answered that he was, and he ran an oxygen check.

Handown said, "Lieutenant Boman, you suppose we ought to shift the gas around in the tanks, empty that number three?"

Handown had by-passed Marrow and put that question straight to me.

I said, "I guess we better had."

4 /

Once Neg and I got started shifting gas, we really went to town. We saw some of the holes the flak had driven through the right wing—Neg said from the upper turret that he could see the ground through one of them—and we were worried about losing gas, because we couldn't afford to lose a cigarette-lighter full of fuel riding on three engines that far from home. So, with Handown on the valves in the bomb bay and me on the gauges up forward, we started transferring fuel back and forth, trying to outguess the holes, and what with half a dozen tanks to deal with, we worked that way for the better part of half an hour, and we were just about satisfied, when Max, from the nose, called in a flight of twin-engined fighters coming up from two o'clock, very low.

Handown scrambled back up into his turret, and I said, "All right, everybody, sharp eyes."

We had scarcely noticed the respite we had had from fighters for the past hour and ten minutes, so much had been happening. This was a deeper penetration than we'd ever made, and the Germans presumably hadn't been set up to cope with us so far inland.

We were near Hackenburg, about twenty miles southeast of the Ruhr. It was seven minutes past four.

There seemed to be about twenty-five fighters in the attack that was coming up. Their first passes were at the combat box in back of us, but soon they began mixing it up with us, too. Our experience up to that time had been that the pilots of German twin-engined fighters had been relatively inexperienced and cautious, and that they had often used to lob rockets or time-fused twenty-millimeter shells at us from outside the range of our fifties. But this bunch apparently hadn't heard about the timidity of the twin-engine boys, for they came in with a determination, persistence, and savagery such as we had seldom seen.

Not long after the attacks began, Clint Haverstraw called up and said, "Would you come down here a minute, Bo?"

I said, "What's the problem?"

"This next course change," Clint said. "Help me check it."

That was a peculiar request, coming from Haverstraw, because on all the missions we had flown he had never asked for help. Max had, more than once, but never Clint. I tapped Buzz on the shoulder and pointed below, and he nodded. I undid everything and crawled down into the nose and found Clint sitting at his desk, shaking like a man with d.t.'s. I plugged into the oxygen line on the left side of the compartment and bent over the desk, and Clint shoved some figures at me, and while I was trying to make them out, I saw him check his oxygen gauge on the right side, and it was low, and he pulled his plug out of the permanent system and put it in a walk-around bottle, and I said, "That's no good, you use my system over here, I'm going back to fly in a minute."

"Don't bother," he said. "I'm O.K. for a while."

Luckily, I bothered. It was the best thing I ever did in my whole life. It meant that I couldn't stay below for long—and that I was to leave the greenhouse just in time.

Again I tried to understand what problem was worrying Clint. It turned out that he wasn't worried about the course at all. He took off his right glove and wrote in large letters on a paper he had on a clipboard: "DID I KISS PLANE THIS MORNING?"

Poor Clint! That was what he wanted of me! He was shaking for fear he had forgotten to go through his ritual of tapping the sides of the hatch opening with his swagger stick and kissing the skin of the ship upon entering *The Body* that morning. He must have been afraid that we were flying without benefit of his incantations. So convincing was he, looking up at me with frightened eyes through his goggles, that for an instant I was taken in by his mad anxiety; I could not remember whether I had seen him perform the ceremony that morning. The morning seemed dizzyingly far back in time, and I could scarcely remember it at all. I suffered a sharp stab of fear, then I realized that all Clint needed was reassurance, and I took off my glove and picked up Clint's pencil and wrote: "YES."

He seemed better at once and gathered all his papers together in a neat pile. I pointed to his gun in the window on the right, and he readily jumped to it.

As I started to return to the co-pilot's seat I looked out the left-hand window, and far, far behind us, somewhat to the south, nearly ninety miles back, I saw smoke rising in a heavy, black tower thousands of feet high. I glanced downward and ahead, and through a beautiful afternoon, with traces of woolly clouds near

the ground, I saw the tiny Rhine, between Bonn and Koblenz,
with barely visible bugs on its silver stripe—the urgent barges of
German war traffic, I supposed. It was a nice day.

I crawled aft toward the passageway to the cockpit on one
hand and my knees, with my walk-around bottle in my other hand,
and I climbed up through the trapdoor and had just reached a
crouching position between Marrow's seat and mine, and was
about to rise to my feet, with my free hand reaching upward and
suspended, as it were, between heaven and earth, when I looked
forward and saw them coming in—four single-engined fighters,
meaning that a second attack had come up to join the first—from
twelve o'clock, away above us, at the very beginning of their run.
We were the lead ship; they wanted us; I knew that.

For a moment I behaved irrationally. My flak suit was near me,
stowed under my seat, and (possibly my eye had brushed across it,
making me aware of it) I suddenly wanted to remain huddled
there, to shrink smaller and smaller, to cover myself with the light
chest-protecting armor of the flak suit, which, because of its cum-
bersomeness, I had seldom worn since early missions. I reached for
it, but it would not come loose, so I braced my feet against the side
of the ship and tugged, but it was stuck, and for a few crazy seconds
I thought my life depended on getting it out, and all I seemed able
to do was use main force, for I had not the wit to stop and find out
why it was caught.

I gave up and started again to rise and was half up and half
down, and—*bingo!* and we had had it with the most terrific noise
I had ever heard.

I mean, for sheer noise, this was . . .

Almost simultaneously with the noise there was a blast of icy
air coming up the passageway from the nose.

The whole ship went over on one wingtip and into the beginning of a spiral, and I just had time to throw myself, belly
downward, across my seat and grab ahold for dear life. We seemed
to be falling.

CHAPTER TEN

THE TOUR

July 30 to August 16

1/

An announcement of a three-day stand-down, issuing from the Tannoy loudspeakers and rushing like a noisy flock of crows through the trees of the grove around the hutment, brought an end, at last, to the July Blitz.

With what strength remained to me, I pushed myself up from my bed, where I was lying fully clothed, and ran to the telephone booth in the officers' club and called Daphne's rooming house in Cambridge, and I found, for the first time in all my calls to her, that she was not at home. With a beer and a limp copy of *Punch* (Kid Lynch had smuggled it into the club!), I killed time and stayed awake, and I tried a second call, but she was still out. As I aimlessly wasted minutes until I could phone again I passed the officers' bulletin board and read an order that during the British bank holidays, from July thirtieth, which that day was, until August third, U.S. servicemen were not permitted to travel by rail. I was so tired that my mind was like a glass of warm milk, but somewhere at the edge of it was a dim recollection that on the day of Lynch's funeral Daphne had said something about the bank holidays. Had she said she had plans? I couldn't remember. I began to be afraid that she had gone off somewhere. Gone for five days! I was full of my separate peace with the enemy, my renunciation of all that was aggressive and hurtful in favor of self-

less love, which had come to me with the force of a vision in those
moments just before we touched down that afternoon, and I simply had to know that I could see Daphne soon and talk with her
about it. I called again; still out. This time Mrs. Coffin, Daphne's
landlady, who had no use for Americans, was distinctly short with
me. I was frantic. Excuse me, did Mrs. Coffin happen to know
whether Miss Poole had gone off on a trip for the holidays? . . .
Hers was a home, not a detective agency. . . . I simply had to talk
with Miss Poole. . . . Mrs. Coffin could not "materialoize" Miss
Poole out of thin air. . . .

In a folly of exhaustion and anxiety, I asked if Mrs. Coffin
would take down the number of the booth I was in and ask Miss
Poole to call me when she came in. Mrs. Coffin seemed to be taking down the number, but I could not be sure that she was.

Having rung off, I was flooded by new worries. What if
someone was in the booth when Daphne tried to reach me? What
if Mrs. Coffin didn't hear her come home? What if it turned out to
be late? What if she didn't come home at all?

I went to the bar and ordered a double Scotch, and I slugged
it down pretty fast. In my condition the drink rapped me on the
back of the skull—and the next thing I knew, it was nearly eleven
o'clock, and I was aware of having been asleep in a leather chair,
and my neck was stiff, and one whole arm didn't want to wake up.
I wobbled to the bar, feeling woozy and unsteady, and asked
Dunk Farmer if there had been any calls on the phone in the
booth, and Farmer, to whom, in his endless fantasy of transferring
from bar to combat duty, co-pilots were useless, said in his loud
cracker twang, "You cain't expect me to wait on six dozen alco-
holic maniacs and tend the telefoam, too. I ain' got but two
hands."

He grunted and was no help to me, so I called again, and
this time the telephone on the Cambridge end rang and rang and
rang, and I knew that Mrs. Coffin must have gone to bed, but I
held on, with my teeth grinding, and finally she answered, and at
first she refused to call upstairs for Miss Poole, but at last she did,
and this time Daphne was there.

What with having flown six raids in seven days, and having
seen the Kid so very dead, and having had my vision of selfless
love, and having taken that big slug of whiskey, and now hearing

Daphne's voice again, I felt drunk, and I didn't know, by the time I had hung up, exactly what I had said or what my Daphne had answered, either.

I had a vague recollection of her saying that she'd made some plans to go down to Devon with a girl friend, Judith Something-or-Other, and I *thought* she'd said she would call that off and meet me in London the next day but one ("I need sleep, oh, God, darling, I need sleep sleep sleep!"—that I knew I had said), August first, at ten in the morning, at the usual place, the Leicester Square tube station. I was pretty sure that was what she had said.

As I was falling into bed, I wondered whether I'd invented the part about somebody named Judith, or whether Daphne had. I'd never heard her mention a close friend named Judith.

Then I slept for twenty hours.

2 /

When I got up I squandered the little that was left of the day, July thirty-first, scrounging some transportation to London for early the following morning. I finally found a major who'd lined himself up a staff car, and he agreed to stomach my company.

I arrived at our trysting place a few minutes late, at about ten past ten. Daphne had always been ahead of me at our meetings, even when I'd been punctual, but this morning I was ahead of her. The city seemed ominously hushed, vacant, and purposeless, like a rundown clock which seems not to have any pulsating time in it. Stores were closed. It was a Sunday, and the bank-holiday weekend to boot. The air was mist-laden, and pigeons wheeled black against the sky. The newspaper kiosk beside which we always met was shut. Now and then an empty red bus ghosted along.

After half an hour, I began to wonder what Daphne had actually said during that phone conversation on the thirtieth. I telephoned Cambridge, but there was no answer from Mrs. Coffin. I went back to my post.

After an hour and a quarter I was convinced that there was no such person as the girl friend, Judith.

After two hours I remembered that Junior Sailen had said he had a ride up to London in a weapons carrier that morning, and I walked through deserted streets to the enlisted men's Red Cross Club that our crew frequented when on pass, and the place was obviously empty, but I asked a tired old Red Cross bag at the hall desk if a Sergeant Sailen had checked in, and she said mine was the first face she'd seen that morning.

"That's a poor start for a dull day," I said.

"I don't know," she said. "Your face isn't so bad, but all you young officers look alike to me. That's why I work in an enlisted men's club, because their faces, sergeants and all, each one's different, they have character. Know what I mean?"

I didn't see why I had to stand there and be abused by a sack of prunes just because I was lonely, so I told her to say ta-ta to Junior Sailen if he came in, from his co-pilot. I told her my boy Sailen had character, but it was only half life-size. Then I scrammed.

I meandered through echoing streets, and I tried whistling to buck up my courage, but the dead, damp walls threw my song, *Oh, Lady Be Good,* right back in my teeth, so I quit. I walked to the White Tower, in Soho, because once Daph and I had eaten there together, but it was closed, so I went and had a depressing lunch in a Lyons Corner House that looked like a cross between the Alhambra and Madison Square Garden, and in its huge cavern the clattering of my fork on my thick plate vied with those of only two other customers. Out of curiosity I took something that was called Bubble and Squeak on the menu and wished I hadn't.

I walked and walked.

In Hyde Park I saw a dirty duck in a pond and a pack of dogs, like a squad of noisy G.I.'s, chasing a bitch in heat and squabbling with each other; wild life seemed to have taken over the city.

I strolled along the Embankment trying to think realistically about my determination somehow to quit the work of killing and be free to live for and by selfless love, but I needed Daphne's help with all that.

I saw a tall bobby, and I asked him where the Tate Gallery was, and he told me, and I asked him if that was the museum that had the burning sunsets by Turner in it, and he said, "If you

please, sir, there's a handful of jolly fine Turners in the Tate. I
bring to mind two vivid sunsets."

So I walked to the Tate. I had no sooner entered the museum than my feet began to hurt, and I was just wondering why it
was that paintings in a museum always went in my eyes and
straight down to my feet when I saw one of the Turners. The sinking sun, reflected on water as I had often seen, from a plane, a
fiery orange light reflected on haze in an evening sky, just before
deep gloaming, burned my eyes, with a sensation of watering in
them, and I was so lonely for Daphne that I had to go outdoors
for some air.

It seemed that I needed to keep moving, but my shoes had all
those paintings stored in them, and I had to sit down, so I took a
ride in the Tube, to Charing Cross. Then I got up, took the magnificent escalator upward, then went right down again, and rode
the Tube to Richmond, where, in the park, Daphne had seemed
to be Rima one day. I stayed below and rode to Leicester Square,
but I couldn't face our habitual rendezvous, so I rode to Piccadilly
Circus.

3 /

By my watch it was six o'clock, and I went back to the
enlisted men's Red Cross Club, and this time Junior Sailen was
there, drunk, trying to sober up by playing ping-pong with a thin
corporal who was over six feet six inches tall; Junior looked like a
chipmunk tossing acorns to an Afghan hound. When Junior saw
me he ran to me and asked with extraordinary urgency if I'd go
out and have a drink with him.

We went to a pub called the India Sea, and Junior began to
cry and tell me about his wife. How could we have risked our lives
together so often without my knowing that little Junior Sailen
was married? It turned out, what's more, that his wife was not a
head taller than he, as one might have expected, though from
what he said she sounded strong for her size.

"I want out," he said, weeping. "Let me out of this rat trap!

I want to get back where people speak to you. I want my mother and my brother. They're not like officers, they're good to me. I owe them a big debt, and I love them, and I feel like they love me, and why can't I be with my wife? Who made a law that a man can't be with his wife? I'm no use overseas, she tells me what's right and wrong, she helps me decide. I'd like to have seven children, and I haven't got a one. I'm getting old in the service. I'm not a murderer, this worries me, I'm worried day and night in the Air Force. What good's back pay? It won't buy her any children out of me, will it? They're all mean bastards, except Major Marrow, he's a white man, he's like my brother, but I need my wife. She holds me when the mean bastards in this Air Force hurt my feelings. Why can't I be with her? I want her when you guys are mean to me."

Junior's line of chatter only served to mix me up even further about my own yearnings, about my separate peace, so I managed to get lost in the middle of a dart game.

4 /

I walked some more, in dark streets, and I thought that my torture came from the fact that my loathing of ugliness, of pain, of giving pain, was in direct conflict with my powerful pride, my sense of duty and responsibility, my always having wanted to give my best, work hard, win approval. Daphne had stirred up, at the expense of the striving side of my nature, my more magnanimous side. I needed to talk with her. Where was she? Where was she? Had I driven her away from me? Walking did not produce her.

Late at night, hanging around the front door of the enlisted men's Red Cross Club, I got wind of a weapons carrier that was going to take off for Pike Rilling at two in the morning, and I talked the driver into taking me, and I sat on a hard bench with unhappy men for what was, in that ungainly vehicle, a two-hour ride out to the base.

5 /

Next day I slept late. At the base post office on the way to lunch, I found a short note from Daphne, saying only that unless she heard from me to the contrary, she would come to our Bartleck room on Wednesday, August fourth, to stay, arriving at about seven in the evening. The letter was post-marked August first, but there was no reference to our phone call, and no mention of her plans for the bank holiday.

I went back to my room after eating and lay on my back and stared at the ceiling.

It seemed to me that my idea of a separate peace must have been somewhat the product of exhaustion. Not that I wanted to abandon it . . . I wanted to think some more. . . . Selfless love was all very well, but with Daphne dodging around . . . Daphne, Daphne . . .

I napped until supper.

The evening was one of the clearest and most mellow of the year, and after supper we all went outdoors to play softball or horseshoes or just lie around gassing. Marrow, in a ball game, was the loudest partisan on the landscape. You could hear his complaints against the umpire above all the laughter, and the low talking, and the pounding of feet, and the outcry of startled sparrows.

6 /

On Tuesday Sully got us up for a late raid, and Murika briefed us for Villacoublay airfield at nine o'clock, but the weather closed in, and the show was scrubbed. In the afternoon there was a severe electrical storm, and I sat in my room with the sky splitting and wondered why, after all my high-minded thoughts about what I was going to do, I had gone along with that morning's preparations for a raid, the same as ever. I felt as if I had no will of my own.

7 /

In the morning on Wednesday they briefed us for a Group practice mission but scrubbed it at the last minute. While we were waiting, Handown spoke to Marrow, in my hearing, about Prien. It seemed that lately he'd been vomiting his morning meal and sometimes one other meal a day. Between times he was constantly ravenous, but as soon as he sat down to eat in the mess hall and took two bites he felt as if he had food up to his neck. Sometimes he had the dry heaves. He would lie in bed all day whenever he could. Handown said Prien spoke enthusiastically about the crew—best anywhere. He was dying to finish his tour with us.

"Only thing is," Marrow said, "he wants to finish his tour without flying any missions."

Handown said he was a good kid and really wished he could get rid of his sickness.

Marrow said, with great vehemence, "He's a sissy, and he's going to get us all in trouble if we don't watch out."

I thought, standing by: We all say we're sick of it. Prien acts out what we only say.

8 /

The day dragged, but finally evening came, and I got dressed to the nines, and I went to our room, and Daphne was there, and it suddenly seemed as if nothing had changed, there had been no bank-holiday nightmare at all. She was, it seemed, as devoted to me as ever, and she wanted to hear, with her everlasting sympathy, all about the last part of the Blitz. When I asked her what had happened on Sunday, she told me, in such a way as to make it seem we had never talked on the phone at all, that there had been a serious mix-up with her former boss, for whom she had undertaken to do some part-time work the week before. The mix-up was about the deadline. She had stayed in Cambridge for the whole of the holiday, getting the promised work done.

There was no mention of Devonshire, or of a girl friend named Judith. With a sweet and innocent candor Daphne said that I had often spoken of her intuition, and that she felt she had it to a high degree, but sometimes she made serious mistakes in judging people's actions and manner, and she always realized after every such mistake that she had known in advance she was going to make it, but something had got in the way of her intuition. In short, she realized now that her former boss was in love with her. Perhaps her quitting had been a mistake. All this she put to me, as I say, with such open and disarming frankness that I thought nothing of it—at the time. I said not a word about my separate peace; the mood didn't seem to be right.

9 /

During a four-hour Group practice mission the following morning, which was intended to give the newer crews experience in formation flying, I made my compromise with myself. I believe that what brought it into being was my feeling that the crew of *The Body* needed me, and this had come to me strongly as a consequence of something that happened on the hardstand before stations time.

Prien had persuaded Doc Randall to excuse him from the flight because of his stomach, and the other sergeants were discussing our tail gunner.

Handown suggested that Prien's trouble was that he was afraid of being wounded.

Bragnani went pale at that, and said he hated the idea of being injured himself. "I used to imagine, when I was a kid, like a bruise was going to be blood-poisoning, or a stomach ache was cancer or something."

This sign of weakness and of honesty in Bragnani triggered his friend Farr, who turned on him with a torrent of scorn. I think perhaps it was the honesty that bothered Farr more than anything else. Bragnani, Farr told his crewmates, went wild in the presence of flak. He would get so crazy with fear that he would shoot his

machine gun at bursts of anti-aircraft fire, and sometimes, during a
bad predicted barrage, Farr said, Brag would cringe down against
the wall of the plane and sit huddled up with his arms wrapped
around his knees. Farr told all this as high comedy.

At the end of it, the would-be tough guy, Bragnani, blushed
and hung his head, and when Farr had finished he said, "My pal,"
and gave out an embarrassed laugh.

The other men turned away; it was too disgusting.

It struck me that there was something badly wanting in our
two loud-mouthed roughnecks, Farr and Bragnani. They just
hadn't ever been wired for moral fiber. I made a sharp distinction
in my mind between the immaturity, even the signs of apparent
weakness, in some of my other crewmates, such as Prien and
Junior Sailen, on the one hand, and the moral vacuum in which
Farr and Bragnani seemed to live, on the other. Not only did they
have no feeling at all for the crew or force or nation to which they
belonged, they could not even piece together, the two of them,
the slightest tattered rag of loyalty to each other. Their society had
failed them, and they were failing it. American life had meant to
them, somehow, nothing more than, "I've got mine, f— you."
There must have been terrible deficiencies in their education, and
in their homes; the Air Force had, in its wooden, cursory way, gone
through certain motions toward these two men that were known
as "indoctrination," but none of it was on the simple human level
that would cause them to want, at a minimum, to make sacrifices
for each other and for their shipmates.

I had seen plenty of cases among our crews of this shortage of
moral strength being bolstered, and fairly well compensated for,
by firm and valorous leadership, but our Marrow was too busy
being a hero to bother his head about deficiencies of character in
his crew. All Marrow could do was to jump poor Prien, who,
though exhausted by our trials, and perhaps weak and dependent
in some ways, had more decency and responsibility in him than a
dozen Farrs and Bragnanis.

These reflections gave me an inchoate sense of importance—
a sense, at any rate, that I might have a definite role to play in keeping our crew in one piece for the remainder of its tour. After all,
most of the men in *The Body* had only three more missions to fly.
My finding means to ground myself at this point might be very

serious for them. I honestly believe that I arrived at this conviction
without conceit or self-righteousness, for I was, after all, deeply
aware of my own fears, my many sorts of selfishness, my tendency
to rationalize, my own confused search for a way out. More than
anything else a sense of my worth, which Daphne had wordlessly
given me, provided me with the gall to think what I thought.

And what about the killing, then? What about all the frightful
and revolting hostile activities of which our life in the heavy-bombardment group was made up? How could I square my conscience
with them?

I decided, flying above the rugged coast of Cornwall, that I
would make this compromise: I would go along on the missions, to
do all I could to help my companions get through their common
tour alive, but I would try to do nothing in the plane that contributed to the death of anyone.

10 /

I was still most anxious to talk all this, and much more,
out with Daphne, but when I thought of meeting her I was filled
with a vague dread about what was happening to our relationship.

And so even with her, at first, I evaded. I took her that evening to a Red Cross show on the base, entitled *Step Lively*, and to
an impromptu party in the club afterward. Marrow sat with us
awhile, and he was charming. It was too late to talk when I took
Daphne home in a jeep from the motor pool, with a driver.

The next evening, however, we cooked supper on a hot plate
in our room in Bartleck, and I plunged into the many things that
had been on my mind. Daphne was in a curious mood, and my
talking seemed to drive her deeper into it. She grew increasingly
blue and quiet. In such depressed spirits Daphne actually developed a kind of blueness under her eyes, where the delicate,
waxy skin seemed to go translucent, showing, beneath, a pale dark
color appropriate to her sadness and stillness. She did not seem to
like what I was saying, but I could not get her to comment on it at

all. This had the effect of throwing me back on myself. She acted very strangely, as if she were having some sort of premonition. I soon gave up trying to get from her the support I had so long wanted for my thoughts and feelings, and she sat brooding, absorbed in herself.

At the end of the evening she announced to me that she was going to have to return to Cambridge to do another stint of work for her former boss; she'd try to be back in Bartleck with me in about a week.

I said, with a feeling of dead weight in my hands, "You're susceptible, aren't you, darling?"

"To him? Bosh! How little you understand."

At that, quite unexpectedly, she threw her arms around me and began, with a vehemence I can only think of as desperate, to kiss me.

I could not guess what I had done to fail her.

We made love, and the extraordinary thing was that the flow of feeling between us had never been more quick, strong, and deep. Daphne's intensity and her absolute dedication to me in those minutes were overwhelming.

11 /

Daphne left for Cambridge the next morning, while we were off on another Group practice mission in fine summer weather. Old Whole Wheat was dinning the close formations into us. The flying all around was excellent, and our crew, with Prien back, and apparently happy to be back, in his old slot, seemed to be on its toes, and I myself had a lift all day from Daphne's incandescent passion of the night before. Only Marrow behaved oddly with me: stiff, formal, somehow watchful. In five hours we covered most of England on a briefed flight plan, and when we landed I felt a pleasant tiredness, to which fear had contributed no part.

12 /

The ninth of August was cloudy and cold for that time of year. We had had no mission for ten days, and our crews spoke of their eagerness to go on and complete their tours. That afternoon Max Brindt and I went out for a walk along the perimeter track, and while we spoke of that ardor, which we all felt to some degree, he was, as well, deeply concerned about what we would find at home. A friend of his, a bombardier and a Happy Warrior, transferred back to training duties at Deming, New Mexico, had written Max that war heroes were a dime a dozen in the States, that people said, deeply impressed, "Oh, you were a *bomber* pilot," and then switched the subject to food. Worse than that, Max's friend had written, the Air Force didn't want his experience. The brass at Deming said to him, "Don't bother us, we know what we're doing, and we've got a nice cushy job over here in this section where you'll be out of the way of our actual training." Max was sore.

As Max rambled on I was flooded with what the end—if I made it, cross fingers—would also mean for me. Where would I be then with Daphne?

I hardly noticed, following that train of thought, that Max was leading me into the bomb dump. He sat, legs astraddle, on a five-hundred-pounder. He had a morose expression, and spoke of the bombs as s——. I think he wanted to drop them all; he had a deep mean streak in him.

That night I had, vividly, my dream of bombing and being bombed. It was worse then ever. It seemed, to put it mildly, that my compromise had not eased my mind.

13 /

At three o'clock in the morning of August tenth they briefed us for Schweinfurt—a calamity Marrow and I had been expecting ever since Curly Jonas had tipped Buzz off about the pre-

liminary plans for the raid and the viewing of the tiny city made
of sand. That briefing on the tenth was when Steve Murika spoke
of the "honor" we were to have of making such a deep penetration of Germany. We went, heavy-hearted, out to our planes, and
shortly after eight o'clock the order to scrub came riding round in
the cocky jeep with FOLLO ME printed on its tailboard, and we
cheered. Yet, powerful as was my own sense of relief at the cancellation, I began, soon after the scrubbing, to wish that we had
gone ahead, gotten that horror over with, because once the strike
had been set up and briefed I knew we'd get it sooner or later, and
we were so far along in our tour that I wanted as much as possible
behind me. As the days passed I developed a superstitious fear
of anything to do with Schweinfurt, and when I heard Farr say,
one day, by chance, in an unimportant context, "In a pig's satchel
I do," I thought of Curly Jonas' translation of the word Schweinfurt, and I snapped at Farr, "Don't *say* that," and he turned to
Bragnani and said, "Whatta you know? Teacher don't like us children to use naughty words. Gonta wash us mouths out with soap
and water."

I was all coked up, jumpy and restless, that day after the
scrubbing, having been keyed up so tight, and then unstrung, after
our long layoff, and I began fretting about Daphne, and I
couldn't sit still. I walked to our room in Bartleck and lay down
on our brass-framed bed, but after about five minutes of that I began really to be scared, and I hurried back to Marrow's and my
room on the station, and I tried, without much success, to focus
my eyes on a book, but that was bad, because I began to see words
that weren't there, such as "pig" for "big," and "fire" for "wire,"
and (how can a man's own eyes go subversive on him?) "death"
for "breath." I tried to write my mother, but my handwriting
looked like an old man's, and I tore up what I'd started. So, like
many of my colleagues, I went to the club, which was packed before lunch. In the Air Force shaking a dice cup was a respectable
way of having a tremor, and I had lost six bucks to Benny Chong
when a tech named Miglow from sick quarters came poking
around and said Doc Randall wanted to see me. It was on the tip
of my tongue to say that I wanted to see him, too, but I didn't.

What time did he want to see me?

Two o'clock, Miglow said, if convenient.

It was. It sure was. I was eager.

Doc sat me down and said that in relationships between men in the combat situation he believed in just as much honesty as the wingloading would carry, and he was going to start out with a pretty heavy weight of it. "Your pilot," he said, "the bluster boy, was in here yesterday. He said he was worried about your combat efficiency—afraid you might boot the whole plane one of these days."

I guess the worst sign about me was that I didn't, right then and there, call Marrow a son of a bitch. I didn't even say I was worried about *his* combat efficiency.

Instead I started in giving myself a hard time. "Well, Doc," I said, "it's true I don't sleep very well, and I feel awful jumpy to-day. I don't know just what it is. I must admit I'm scared I'll get the heebie-jeebies in the plane sometime and screw things up. But I know one thing, Doc. I really know this. I can't quit now and leave our bunch when we've only got so few to go. I couldn't do that. You wouldn't ask me to do that. But I do worry, I get the shakes. I'm not the only one who has troubles, but I don't want to endanger my crew. That's the last thing. . . ."

In this way, mouthing the clichés of combat fatigue, I managed to hide from Doc all that had been on my mind: killing, selfless love, Daphne, Lynch, Marrow, this rotten world.

And Doc, I suppose as a kind of opening wedge, came back at me with a cliché of his own. "Do you notice," he said, "that you're not afraid of the enemy but of yourself?"

I was just thinking that, much as I liked old Doc, this crap wasn't going to get us to first base, when the phone rang, and Doc, with a tic-like push to one side of his fine mustache, answered and said, "Oh, have you got that call through? Hold on a second." And he put his hand over the mouthpiece and asked me to step outside into the outer office for a few minutes; he had a call about a case. . . .

So I went out and sat in a straight chair, and then Marrow's perfidious, cowardly tattling hit me like a knee in the groin.

14 /

Doc Randall had never got used to the telephone. He seemed to think that telephone wires were tiny tubes; the longer the distance of a phone call, the louder one had to talk. At the outer edge of my slow take on Marrow I heard him now behind his closed door, talking in a medium shout in his office; I could hear the tone but not the words. Miglow and Train, the techs in Doc's anteroom, had the habit of taking bets on the terminal points of Doc's calls, basing their wagers on the volume of his voice.

"That's not so far," Train said.

"He got that frog out of his voice," Miglow said. "How far would you say?"

"Not quite to Portneath."

"Heck, no, that's no Portneath call."

"But it's farther than the Hall."

"You name it, bud."

"I'll say the evac hospital at Hocker Downs. The new one up there we sent those eight to last week."

"Not that far," Miglow said.

"I just happen to think it is that far," Train said.

"No, that's Cambridge," Miglow said.

"'Arf a crown?"

"What the heck, it's not money, sure."

So they checked with Doc's secretary, Mary Peadon, a WAC, not anything great, a blonde, brisk and saucy, much too careery for me, but a female, endowed with that thankful difference, and sufficient bait to lure in to see the old skull cleaner certain men who loudly proclaimed *they* didn't have any problems. The euphemism for going to pour one's heart out to Doc Randall was, "I'm going over to diddle Peadon." Train asked her where the Doc was calling.

"You two!" she said.

"Oh come on, Sergeant Peadon," Miglow said, mincing his words like a fag, "don't be so mean to us chaps."

"Cambridge," she said.

"Why, that son of a bitch," Train said, bringing the flat of

his hand down on his desk. "He's got ears like a God-damn switchboard."

"Who would he be calling in Cambridge?" Miglow asked.
"The garbage-disposal squad?" I supposed he meant the grave-
diggers at the American cemetery, and anger, like a napping animal, sighed and turned over in me and went back to sleep.

Then I came to.

"What number?" I asked Peadon.

Peadon looked at me in a peculiar way, as if to say, Train and
Miglow were bad enough, but these creeps with combat fatigue!

"I'm not authorized . . . ," she began.

"You heard the Lieutenant," Miglow said. "Give him the
number."

"He was talking to some flier's girl. I don't think it would be
right for me to give out the number."

"Number, please?" Miglow asked, a brutal note in his voice.

I was on the edge of my chair.

"You promise not to call her?" she said to Miglow.

"Oh, s——, Peadon!" Miglow said.

Peadon picked a slip of paper up from her desk. "Cambridge
one four seven six."

It was the number of Mrs. Coffin's rooming house. One
thought flashed through my mind: Was Daphne doing the work
for her boss in her room at home, and what kind of work would
that be, for a boss who was in love with her?

I spoke up right away, and sharply, to Peadon. "Did that call
come in from outside, or did Doc make it?"

Peadon looked at me and hesitated, but I guess maybe my
eyes scared her, because she said like a good girl, "Major Randall
placed the call."

I was really burned, and I'd no sooner been readmitted to
Doc's office than I said, "Doc, I think that was the dirtiest invasion of privacy I ever saw."

Doc didn't even ask me how I knew with whom he'd been
talking. He leveled those deep, sad brown eyes of his at me and
said, "Boman, there's one thing you'll have to understand. We—
meaning we the United States—have put something like twenty
thousand bucks into you, training you to do a particular piece of
work. Now, I don't know what you expect of me, but I'm not here

to be your mother"—and at that an involuntary bark of laughter, like a bursting sphere of bubble gum, erupted from my mouth—"but purely and simply to maintain you as an efficient fighting man. Your happiness matters to me as a man, but as a major all I care about is what kind of combat specimen you are. So it was my duty to check up on the information your pilot gave me, and one of the ways to do that was to call the person who knows you best."

How did he know about Daphne?

Doc said he kept pretty close tabs on people; he'd known about my girl for a long time. "What's more," he said, "you'll excuse my saying so, but I was pretty well acquainted with Pitt before he was shot down. I know about that girl. I'd say you've been lucky. I'd say I could wish the Pentagon would issue us medics a therapy for general use like the one you've had."

How did he get her number?

From Marrow.

Who'd got it, no doubt, from Haverstraw. The sly bastard! And what, if it wasn't privileged material, had my girl said?

"To my surprise," Doc said, "she wept quite a lot. I hadn't thought she was very much the crying kind. She said something very interesting. I took the liberty of asking her if she really loves you. She said she loves you more than any man she's ever known, but apparently, she said, you don't love her."

I didn't say anything. What does an aviator say to a military doctor who tells him stuff like that?

There was lots more. How Miss Poole had said she'd seldom been badly wrong in her estimate of a man, and she had considered me exceptionally capable of love as she understood the word. "It's a tricky word, all right," Doc said. And how she made allowances for the war. And how . . . But I was in a daze, and the next thing I knew Doc was staring at one thing after another and had begun to talk about eating in the mornings, calories, stamina, and then he came out with that crazy fable about the crow.

I don't know why, but I felt new when I left. I tried to call Daph, but she was out.

15 /

They were beginning to pack the morale to us in the Air Force, and that night we had a U.S.O. show called *Fun Marches On*, and I swear, I thought I'd have a hernia from laughing. What a crazy life!—the agony of stomach cramps waiting to go to Schweinfurt in the morning, and stomach muscles in another kind of pain—from mirth—in the evening; and queer thoughts of death and love all day. Was I sane? Were any of us then?

I tried to call Daph again before I went to bed, but all I got was an icy blast from Mrs. Coffin. Still out.

Not by so much as a flicker of an eyebrow did I betray to Marrow, either that day or the next, that I knew he'd ratted on me to Doc Randall. I was hurt and amazed, but I saw no point in confronting him.

In the morning, however, I was given one sort of vengeful satisfaction. A batch of mail came, and Marrow got a letter from an uncle, the first he had had from this uncle in more than three months. After reading it, Buzz was in a rage. "Your people at home," he said, "they're just like the Army, they try to do the right thing, but they tee you off."

I bided my time till he was cool, then I asked him what his uncle had done that made him so sore.

"He sold my car."

"What car was that?"

"The Olds. The convertible."

"Wasn't that the one you left at Floyd Bennett with the key in it? Only cost two hundred and thirty bucks? That you could have lost in a crap game and not missed it?"

"Oh, s——!" Marrow said, so taken up with his anger that he didn't seem to realize what a house of cards was falling down. "I cabled my uncle about that right after we got over here, so he picked it up. Uncle Ben. He's in the East all the time. So he drove the car home, the car was out home. He had no right to sell it without orders from me."

16 /

What happened on the mission of August twelfth showed the condition we were all in.

One of the troubles, to begin with, was the earliness of the starting hour. Sully wakened us at one, and the briefing, for a benzol plant we'd never heard of, at Gelsenkirchen, was at one thirty.

Out at the dispersal area, in black night, waiting for the take-off, which was scheduled for the first seepage of dawn at four o'clock, everyone was grumpy, but Marrow and Farr were particularly sour.

The effect on Marrow of his uncle's letter was amazing; his hurt and peevishness had not worn off, and at breakfast he had looked all squeezed, with a pinched face and rounded shoulders. He complained of having thrown a nightmare during our short sleep.

Farr was either hung over or still drunk from the night before —if it could be called that. Nobody counted drinks at Pike Rilling; aviators were presumed, usually with justification, to know what was good for them. A strict rule of our lives was that the moment we had an alert, all drinking stopped. No one had to ram that one into us; it figured. Thumbing your nose at that rule was considered as foolish as cocking your snook at the law of gravity. But this time Farr, who in recent weeks had been drinking rather heavily, had apparently set out to prove that he was bigger than common sense, and he was snarling and bitter. Said he was God-damned if he was going to fly a night bleeding mission—that was for the Royal Bleeding Air Force.

Marrow finally told him to hang up.

At that Farr said, "Not you or anybody else is going to force Ronald J. Farr to fly in a airplane in the middle of the night."

Bragnani and others did their best to straighten out his feathers, and we managed to push him into the plane at the last minute. "All right! All right!" he shouted. "I'll show you mother f——ers."

He did.

Our base altitude that morning was unusually high, above thirty thousand, and nine old planes out of our twenty-one had to

turn back because they couldn't get that far up. Farr greeted such
aborts as he saw alternately with scandalous abuse and with sarcastic congratulations. At altitude contrails were heavy.

Farr began to babble; I decided he was getting into the
brandy he always carried along.

About half an hour before the target we began to get vicious
attacks from enemy fighters, who came at us straight from the
morning sun in waves abreast of as many as twelve.

I worked at keeping myself cheered with the thought that
Daphne was coming back to Bartleck that afternoon, and, with the
self-delusion of a man in danger, I managed to restore to our relationship many of its earlier perfections.

After the third wave Farr called in and said his oxygen was out
of order.

Marrow blew. "I've had enought out of you lily-livered sergeants," he screamed, and he went on to dig that vein deep.

But Farr insisted, and Bragnani seconded him—said the ball
wasn't bouncing in Farr's gauge.

"Get on a walk-around," Handown—old mister practical—
growled.

"I tried it," Farr said. "It's my mask. Get me out of here! For
sweet Christ's sake, help me!" And he began to sound like a wall
climber.

Then he went silent.

Bragnani burbled, way up high, like a high-school girl; you
could piece it out that Farr had fainted.

Handown was on interphone again before the rest of us.
"Drag him in the radio room," he said. The reason for this suggestion was that we'd been briefed that morning for a temperature,
at altitude, of minus thirty-eight degrees (actually, we learned later, it hit minus forty-four), and in the waist compartment, with
the two open windows, a man without oxygen had only seconds
before he started turning blue. Not that the radio room was
warm; but you at least didn't have a direct blast of wind there.

As soon as Farr had passed out I had begun unbuckling, but
by the time I got back to the radio room quite a lot had happened,
which I pieced together later:

Bragnani had dragged Farr through the ball-turret compartment into Lamb's room, and Butcher Lamb, seeing that Farr's

mask had frosted up, had got the madly unselfish notion of putting his own mask on Farr. In order to do this he had taken his
gloves off, and he had in fact managed to remove Farr's dead mask
and get his own off and crudely applied to Farr's head when he had
begun to feel woozy. Bragnani had interfered then, trying to get
the mask fitted to Farr, and Lamb, in a preliminary phase of
anoxia, had gone delirious and had undertaken to knock Bragnani's block off.

As I entered the radio compartment, Farr was limp on the
floor and Bragnani and Lamb were wrestling beside him. Lamb
passed out. Bragnani went to work on Farr's mask. I put my own
gloves on Lamb, then found his and put them on my own hands.
I plugged in my interphone jack and excitedly said to Marrow:
"For Christ's sake, dive the plane. We've got to get down. You got
men dying back here."

A spare mask was stowed on the forward bulkhead of the ball-
turret compartment, and while we screamed down through a perfect sky with two fighters riding our tail, and Handown and
Prien steadily firing, I climbed uphill on my hands and knees
on the deck, got the mask, slid down, put it on Lamb, and plugged
it into a bottle.

I remembered the dive on our first high-level practice mission
—it seemed ten years before—when Prien had had his bellyache,
and how Marrow had laughed all the way down.

This time Buzz went right down to the deck and headed for
home. The Jerries dropped us. Lamb had come to at about nine
thousand, Farr at six. By some miracle there were no frostbitten
extremities.

I went back to my seat.

We were headed for home. I wish I could describe the elation
I felt. Far stronger than relief, it was a positive joy, such as I had
not felt since swinging out of the front door of Donken Elemen-
tary, back home, on the last day of school, in my eleventh year. I
remember the slap of the door, the rattle of the brass door bars,
and the whoop forcing itself up out of my neck.

Soon I noticed that everyone in the plane was in the same
mood. Marrow, who had started the morning so surly, began to
be chipper, and he joshed Lamb, and then I heard him do something he'd never done before—praise a crewman. Grudgingly, to

be sure. "For a sergeant," he said, "you got guts, kid, giving your mask away." We had a deal of narrative conversation on the interphone, and Handown, who sang like a sick dog, tried a snatch from *It's Delovely*.

We'd never flown at zero altitude over Europe before, and in Holland Marrow began a sightseeing-bus routine, on your left, ladies and gents, a windmill; on your right, a nice fat Dutch blonde in wooden shoes.

But over the Channel, where the sea was brown and the rollers broke with a hungry snapping of dirty wet white jaws, our wild mood cooled. We had to face it: This was an abortion. You could feel the shame oozing into the plane.

By the time we landed, our feeling of disgrace had turned to anger; we were all furious at Jug Farr.

Red Black was sitting on his tool box by the hardstand. He could scarcely believe his eyes when he saw *The Body* roll in. His face showed us the full horror of what we had done.

Farr was defiant. "I told you bastards. You wouldn't listen to a guy."

We had to face an interrogation. Haverstraw said to me, on the side, "I've had it. I want a desk job. I had a terrible time coming back today at low altitude. It works on me, always wondering where we are, whether I'm on or off in my navigation. I'm going to get grounded, I tell you, I thought I'd go off my rocker over the water. Down there in the front its different from where you are. Did you see the *color* it was?"

I reminded Clint that he only had three more to go, but that was a poor line of argument for that moment, because we weren't going to get sortie credit for this one. All our work and fear had gone to no account.

Haverstraw put a better face on things later in the day, but my own mood worsened. I found that I was scheduled for duty that evening. When the mission got in I tried to find someone to swap with, but no one would take it. Everyone was vindictive about our abortion—seemed viciously pleased that this discredit had fallen to the loud-mouthed Marrow, who got back some of the obloquy he had so nastily thrown at fliers who had aborted on other days. And some of this vengeful unpleasantness spilled over on me. At any rate, no one would take my duty. I had no way of calling

Daph, for there was no phone at all in our rooming house, so I
sent her a lame British telegram.

At about eight, as I was heading for work at the Admin block,
Marrow went bouncing down the corridor of our hutment, rather
sportively, it seemed to me, for a man who'd gotten a putrid razz
all day, and he said he was just going to have one lousy beer at the
club and then turn in, and I believed him. But he didn't get in
till two. It wasn't till two days later that I began to suspect he had
been with Daphne, my Daphne, once my only own.

17 /

On Saturday I went to Daphne, and it was in the first
moments of seeing her, as I stood in the doorway of the room and
she ran to me, with her head on one side, and said I was beautiful
—it was then that I began to sense the difference. That was the
afternoon when we went to the exhibition cricket match at Lishton. Marrow was there, and he avoided us most of the afternoon,
but once he came over and said he liked cricket, except it was slow,
but you could change some of the rules and put some pezazz into
it. There was something about the way Daphne happened not to
look him in the eye. . . . Later, when we walked in the village,
Daphne tenderly took my arm, but there was a difference, there
surely was a difference, and I began to suspect what it was.

And that was the night when, returning to our quarters, I
shook Marrow's shoulder and accused him of having been with
Daphne, and he denied it, but I felt that he was lying.

They sent us, late in the afternoon on Sunday, the fifteenth,
to bomb a German fighter field at Poix, in France, and everything
about the preparatory phases of the mission seemed to go, as Handown put it, "according to somebody else's plan." At ten in the
morning a priority message came down from Pike Rilling Hall
ordering each aircraft loaded with sixteen three-hundred-pound
fragmentation bombs. The ordnance crews had these bombs par-
tially installed when another priority message said there'd been an
error, the bombs should be general-purpose. The original target

message was supplemented at one fifteen by some corrections which appeared to be inaccurate, and after deducing the straight dope Group Ops and Intelligence called Wing, at two, and confirmed their guesses, only to receive still a fourth teletyped order with further conflicting data and numerous garbled co-ordinates. Not until two forty-five was the briefing information solid. Take-off had been set for four thirty. When we arrived at *The Body* she was still being loaded with big yellow bombs. Marrow was all on edge on account of the day's snafu, which Curly Jonas had described to him. Our departure was postponed till five fifteen.

The mission turned out to be a milk run, and the bombing was superb—even from my point of view, because it was directed at a runway and at fighter planes, not at human lives.

I hated Marrow. I sat there knowing that I hated him, whether or not he had gone to Daphne, and that knowledge made me miserable, for if a self-forgetting love was to be the guiding force of my life, then it should encompass everyone I knew; certainly it should be big enough to include a man to whom I had entrusted my life so often, whom I knew so well, and who was, in so many ways, vigorous, alive, magnificent. I hated him. I would never get over hating him.

We got back in the half-light of England's long day-fading time, and Marrow rode in at once, leaving everything in a mess in the plane for the rest of us to straighten out. Negrocus and I agreed that the number-three engine had been running extremely roughly on the way home, and we told Red Black about it.

In the interrogation the crew of *Miss Take* said they'd received fifty-caliber fire from the direction of *The Body*'s right waist window. It was awfully hard for gunners intently tracking enemy planes in the heat of battle to make absolutely sure that their line of fire did not swing into the paths of friends, but this accusation, being so explicit, had a nasty ring, and Marrow hotly defended Farr. He went to bed furious.

And he arose furious. The fliers were awakened, but he and I were not, by Sully at one forty-five. The noises of the men getting up roused me, and I got up and dressed and went to Operations and learned that *The Body* had been grounded for engine overhaul: a tiny fragment of flak had found a way into her number three. Being up, I went to the briefing, to pass the time, and learned that the Group was going to the Abbeville-Drucat airfield, and I was dismayed, for this would surely be another milk run. As the briefing was being time-ticked, at about three fifteen, Marrow came in, raising the roof about being left in bed. It was interesting to me to see how quickly, and how far, he subsided when he learned that I had told Red Black to check the number-three engine, and that Red had found a fragment in it.

Late in the morning, just before the mission was due back, I went to see Daphne. She was reading in bed when I got to the room, with her hair turned up in curlers and her face covered with grease, and she was chagrined to be seen, as it were, half fabricated, and she sent me walking in the streets for fifteen minutes while she completed the product. She was dressed, and her bed was made, and her face looked morning-proof, when I returned. I had braced myself to work into the Marrow business gradually, in an off-hand way, perhaps in mid-afternoon, but in fact I had not been there for five minutes when, sitting on the clanking bed with Daph opposite me in her straight-backed chair, demure and placid, I asked her if she had received Marrow in this our room.

She gave me a deep valedictory look and nodded, and as her head went down she said, "But wait!"

Wait? I stood up, and my chest like a bellows drove out one long-held word, "Why?"

Daphne did not answer then, but went to her closet, pushed aside the cloth that hung in the doorway, and disappeared. Soon she came out with a dented percolator and a can of American coffee I had brought her, and trying to hush the clatter of metal on metal as if any undue noise might awaken the reality that was sleeping somewhere in the room, she measured out the grounds and poured in water and set the pot to heat on an electric coil. She sat in the chair again and did not speak. I felt that something had come loose in my heart. Daphne lit a cigarette.

"Can we wait till the coffee's ready?" she said.

I went to the window and saw the back of a row of houses. The one directly opposite was made of brick with rough stone quoins down the corners; one of its chimney pots was askew. The bubbling began at last. I turned toward Daphne. She had such a pale and tired look!

"Sugar? . . . Oh darling, I'm sorry. I know you take three lumps."

Into that word, *darling*, to which in our weeks we had brought such renovation, she put, I felt, her whole heart, and that heart, if I knew it, was beating exactly as fast as mine was.

We were seated, and I scalded my lips on the first sip, and Daphne said, "Now, Bo, do you want to hear about your pilot?"

"Yes, I do," I said.

CHAPTER ELEVEN

THE RAID

1604–1656 hours

1 /

Marrow had one miraculous reflex left which pulled us out of that incipient spin, but I, still bellied down over my seat with my feet in the opening of the trapdoor, was so busy trying to put together in my mind what was happening that I think I lagged by several seconds in my realization that we were not, after all, falling. I was aware of a powerful, buffeting column of frozen air shooting up past my feet like a twister of prop wash forced through a funnel, and it seemed to me that we must have developed exactly that: a funnel, with the nose of the ship opened out as the outer cone, and the narrow passageway coming up between Marrow's seat and mine, the constriction of the trapdoor, serving as the spout; and out of the neck came this little directed hurricane at thirty-four degrees below zero. When my ears recovered from the crack of the first explosion, which like nearby thunder had been at a much higher pitch than one associated with its cause, I began to react to another unpleasant noise—a distinct sound of an engine running rough, if not altogether away. There seemed also to be sprinkles of air coming from my left, and I assumed there must be some holes in the instrument panel, but I was keeping my head down and holding on, and I had no desire to look. I was experiencing, within, a rush of feelings as swift and cold as the wind at my feet. I had been fearful before, when I had seen the Messerschmidts begin their dive at us, for it had seemed as if I *knew* that this pass, of all the enemy waves we had shouldered during the day, was the one that would cause us trouble, and I had been gripped by the paralyzing, numbing fear that had made my tussle with my flak suit so absurdly futile. The explosion had in an instant converted my terror to rage. It was not a noble anger at the Hun, but rather a fury of incredulity that this shame —yes, my first thought was of infamy—could be mine. I did not admit into my mind the possibility of being killed, but lying on my belly I had a picture of the boys in the hutment talking about the dope, Boman, getting himself shot down and having to spend the rest of the war in a prison camp, and I hammered with blind fury at the thought that this was happening to me. All this, of course, flickered through me in an instant, and was mixed together with my sensory reactions to our plight. It was only then that I realized, through a long habit of feeling with my body the relation of forces in flight, that we were more or less level; we were flying, not plummeting.

I pulled myself up in my seat, and before plugging myself in, I took one look at Marrow and saw that aside from a tiny cut in his right cheek he seemed not to have been wounded. Then, with a wonderful selective speed that was the fruit of experience, I turned my eyes to the manifold-pressure gauges, and I saw that the arrow for the number-two engine was jumping around like the needle of an oscilloscope, and, not wanting this time to cut an engine without Marrow's knowing, because on only two we would lose a lot of air speed and drop out of the formation, yet wanting to hurry because the unit was shaking enough to tear itself out of the wing, I tapped Marrow's shoulder, pointed at the number-two engine, beyond him, with a whole mitt, and then turned the glove in a flipping motion that simulated turning off a key. Marrow shrugged. How eloquent, in its indifference, that lift of the huge shoulders was! I killed the engine, and this time, in spite of all the vibration, the prop feathered in an orderly way. Our indicated air speed dropped at once to about a hundred and thirty, which was twenty-five miles per hour slower than the formation.

I looked out and saw that we were directly beneath our own squadron, perhaps three hundred feet down, and I had a vivid feeling of thankfulness that we had a good deal of formation, two whole task forces, in fact, to drift back through before we would be alone, straggling.

Vivid, I say. My senses, reactions, thoughts, and emotions had developed that remarkable post-critical fleetness and intensity which I had experienced once before, on the Kiel raid, the day the plane caught fire.

We were washing around, and Marrow, holding with bulldog jaws till the last moment to the one skill that was the essence of his narrow genius, his marvelous reactive skill as the manipulator of an aircraft, was fiddling with trim-tab wheels and throttles, to steady our line of flight. Our yawing, and the wind through the trapdoor, and the holes in the instrument panel, and Marrow's having shrugged, and the fact that some of our instruments had gone dead—everything I could observe made me think it was inevitable that we would bail out. I refrained from buckling on my chute just out of a rather morbid curiosity, mixed with admiration, I admit, for Marrow's smooth, automatic response to what was happening. I believe that Marrow had already broken down in every way but the one that mattered. Like a frog's leg that will kick, or a lizard's tail that will lash, after amputation, the essential force in Marrow—the flying touch—was holding onto *its* vitality, when all the rest was gone, and was keeping us aloft. I assumed, though, that we would bail out soon, and I was planning the steps —hand Marrow his chute from under his seat, pass one back to Negrocus, strap my own to my chest and click it on, right and left, and then move—when something happened that made me realize we couldn't do that. We couldn't leave.

I looked down through the trapdoor, and I knew the front end was blown out, and I knew I had just come back up from the front end, and my relief, my personal, self-interested relief at getting out of the greenhouse was so strong that I really had forgotten those other two up there, from the moment of the shock, and now I saw a hand. A left hand. It groped out, and then I saw the head, Max's, and he was dragging himself; the reaching hand and arm pulled him along, and the other arm was limp. I saw, as he moved rearward through my frame of vision, that his right leg was blown off right up to mid-thigh, pruned clean off, it appeared, though he was trailing tatters of flying clothes and was bleeding, and the furious wind made everything seem confused. He crawled

into the lower level under the trapdoor. I knew we couldn't push
Max out for a jump in his condition, and we couldn't leave him, so
we couldn't bail out.

Right behind him came Clint, on his hands and knees, dragging his parachute, and he looked to be in one piece, and he
crawled back, and slowly but methodically he took off his gloves
and jettisoned the escape hatch, and he kneeled at the edge of the
hole, perhaps praying, and he put his parachute on and then put
his gloves back on and remained there, kneeling, looking down
through the opening into the clear afternoon, with his hand on his
rip cord.

Just when he was about to go out, as I supposed, I had a
sudden idea, an impulse, "Well, now, I shouldn't let him do that."
Since the lower compartment was confined and shallow, I could
reach down and touch him easily from my seat, to dissuade him
from what he planned, but then I thought, "The lucky bum, getting out of this thing before it goes to pieces," so I didn't reach
out, for a moment. It seemed he would be blown out by the wind,
or slide out, because of the fluid of poor Max that was spreading
and freezing. And quickly I did reach down and touch him. That
was all it took. Clint gave up the idea. He didn't even look up at
me.

But I, as I leaned down, saw Max, lying on his back, writhing,
and he was still conscious, that was the worst of it, and I saw that
whatever had blown his leg off had also blown his oxygen mask
off, and his goggles, and his helmet; his face wasn't the least bit
scratched. Max was rational, and I saw him raise his left hand and,
with a pathetic begging expression, point to his mouth, so there
wasn't but one thing to do, the idea of which terrified me more
than anything I'd ever known, and that was, recognizing that Max
was going to die of anoxia and cold before he could get down to a
hospital bed with white sheets—I had lost that wonderful clarity of
thought—I hadn't listened to all those lectures you're supposed to
listen to in training—I was going to have to go down there in the
wind and give him my mask. Butcher Lamb, mild Butcher Lamb,
the radio bug, who liked to read Westerns on missions, had pointed
my way on that the day Jug Farr passed out.

As I started down Clint peeled *his* mask off, and I don't know
whether Clint had any thought that he himself might not be con-

scious much longer without a mask at that altitude, and I doubt whether he had any feeling that he was performing an act of truly selfless love, which he was, even when, having slipped the mask over Max's face, he got his reward from Max—a deeply moving look of contentment, for Max, using his good hand to hold the rubber against his face, settled back like a baby with a bottle; you could see him ease down and relax.

The only trouble was, the tube of the mask wasn't plugged into anything. I reached a walk-around bottle down to Clint, and he hooked Max into it. Clint ripped a big piece of flying suit from what was left of Max's pants and wrapped it and tied it, bloody as it was, around Max's head for warmth.

I thought of the spare mask back on the bulkhead of the lower turret compartment, and I decided to tell Butcher Lamb to bring it forward for Clint. I realized then that I wasn't connected with the interphone system, and I pushed my headset wire into the jackbox and heard a man screaming.

It was Junior Sailen, in the ball turret, screaming, really screaming, and a man screaming makes a horrifying sound. He was trapped in his ball turret. Knowing that we had two engines out, for he could see them from his post, and not having a parachute with him, and not being able to get out even if he had it, unless he were exploded out, which he may have expected to be, Junior had reached a pitch of helplessness that a dependent man could not bear. At times distinct messages came through his screaming, "I'm trapped. . . . Come help me. . . . Get me out," with some of the words drawn out into held notes. Everybody who was on interphone was forced to hear him, as he had turned his jackbox to CALL, which cut through all other talk. A piece of shell had come through the plexiglass of his turret and had knocked out the electric motor that made the turret gyrate and revolve, but also another piece, or perhaps the same one, had sheared off the handle which would have enabled him to turn himself up and get out. Fortunately our ball turrets were supplied with a second, external crank for elevation, so that a man outside the turret could move it.

Urged by the need for the mask for Clint and by Junior's cries I skinned back, as fast as I could, through the empty bomb bay and the radio compartment, where Lamb was at his gun, to the lower turret compartment, and I found that Negrocus Handown had been way ahead of me; he had already cranked the turret into line, and he opened the hatch, and Junior almost squirted out, and the two men embraced like brothers in a myth who had been separated as children and were seeing each other again as men.

I ran forward with the spare mask and two walk-around bottles and handed them down to Clint, who was already looking blue around the lips.

2 /

When I was plugged in again, I asked Marrow if he was getting on all right. He didn't answer. I thought perhaps the interphone was knocked out, so I called Prien and he did respond, though his voice sounded farther away than the tail of *The Body*. Then I ran a check all around, and I got a sassy answer from Farr; an echo of it from Bragnani; an absent-minded response from Lamb, who sounded as if he weren't on this trip but were sashaying down to Florida by Eastern Air Lines; no word from Junior Sailen, who had been removed to the radio room; the usual stout and reassuring boom from Handown, who was back up in his turret; no answer, again, from Marrow; and of course I didn't even try Clint and Max.

For a second I wondered whether Marrow had lost the power of speech. I couldn't get anything out of him. He just flew along, and his control was still subtle and smooth, but otherwise he was a huge, leather-clad robot. I supposed that his jackbox might have been ruptured.

Some of our guns were firing.

A brief glance outside the plane showed me that we had fallen back underneath part of the lead group, but we still had an umbrella. The air battle was continuing. I saw two new German *Staffeln* coming up, and (no credit to myself; just the astonishing persistence of the human mind in its habitual patterns of association and rambling, even during a cataclysm) I began ruminating about the efficiency of the Germans, and the obvious co-ordination of their attacks. One could suppose that they must have assembled, to meet both the Regensburg strike and ours, fighter squadrons all the way down from Jever and Oldenburg—we knew those units from our battles with them over Wilhelmshaven, Hamburg, and Kiel—and up from airports we knew in France, such as Laon, Florennes, and Eyreux, and since the planes had limited range they must have set them down for refueling along the way to us, somewhere near our expected line of flight but far ahead of us, and then got them up not only in time to meet us but also just in time to replace other squadrons who were having to retire. Such ingenuity put to the service of killing!

These thoughts, in their dreamlike detachment from our real situation, and in their vividness that was also dreamlike, took only an instant or two.

Then it occurred to me that we would do well to climb, to hug as closely as we could the remainder of our group, so that *The Body* could take maximum advantage of the formation's firepower and not be singled out, yet, as a potential straggler, and I suggested this to Marrow on interphone. I shouted, thinking his headset might not be giving him but a shred of sound.

No answer.

Then I tapped his shoulder, to convey by gestures what his ears apparently could not hear, and he turned his face, and my heart froze at what I saw. Behind his goggles, which intensified the horror of the sight, I saw eyes that seemed to aim at me but that were unimaginably far away. It was like being looked at through the wrong end of binoculars, or no—because that's a game all children have played—it was like being viewed through two infinitely distant telescopes. I hovered off Saturn; I was somewhere out in the black eternity of the universe.

I went through with the gestures I had planned. The telescopes simply swiveled away.

I saw then that one of the instruments on the panel in front of us that had not been shot away was the rate-of-climb indicator. It showed that we were descending, almost imperceptibly, at the rate of fifty feet per minute. With my right hand lightly on the wheel, I could feel that Marrow was trying, with all his deep-driven skill, to hold altitude. Our loss of it was not serious yet, but climbing to attain shelter from the formation was out of the question.

3 /

I heard a faint call on the interphone, and it was for me. "Bo! Listen to me, Bo!" It was Junior Sailen's voice. It did not even occur to me at that moment that for a sergeant gunner, and of all sergeant gunners formal Junior Sailen, to address his co-pilot by his nickname and not by his rank and surname was an act of unusual effrontery; I believe I may have felt faint relief and gratitude that Sailen had torn away a barrier between us. It was immediately evident why he had done so. Even though the interphone was fading, I could hear the pleading tone of his voice. "Can I get out? I want to jump. I have no gun, Bo. I'm no good any more."

I guess he was going batty sitting on a passenger seat in the radio room, doing nothing. Another guess about Junior: He had felt safe at his familiar post, locked into the ball turret, and he found rattling around in the radio room frightening.

A thought entered my mind which caused a leap of selfish joy in my chest: Junior Sailen had called me, not Marrow; he had asked *my* permission to bolt.

I looked at Marrow. He sat leaning forward, communing with the flight column.

Just at that moment, as it happened, Prien called in, with a hoarse shout, announcing an attack from the tail, and Marrow, though he had not responded to direct calls on the interphone in recent moments, automatically began to corkscrew *The Body* with the superb sinuous motions he had devised for self-defense at the height of his skill in the middle of our tour. He must have heard Prien.

I said on interphone, "Sailen! The answer is no. Repeat: No!" Because what if the others, Bragnani, for instance, heard an able-bodied man get permission to jump?

Junior could not (he did not want to) hear me. Far, far away I heard Junior shouting, "What? What, Lieutenant? What?" Yet perhaps he had understood me, after all, because now he called me Lieutenant, and, in any case, he stayed aboard, for whatever reason.

I called Butcher Lamb and tried to tell him the interphone was fading.

Butch heard me, I realized (some time later) when the interphone came in loud and clear; he must have left his gun and
gone down into the radio room and—I can visualize him—begun
checking out possible causes of trouble in the systematic, step-by-
step way of the born radio ham, concentrating on his work so as
to shut out all the rest of the world.

4 /

Right after calling Lamb—I suppose not more than four or
five minutes, at most, had passed since our nose had been opened
—I began to worry about Max Brindt. I leaned over and saw
through the trapdoor that Haverstraw was not doing anything
about Max. Clint was sitting by the big opening of the main hatchway, looking downward in a brooding way, and Max was still
conscious, and for a moment the stump was exposed to sight there
in that wind, the blood still spurting and coagulating and freezing
on him and all over the deck, and I could see that I was going to
have to do the most distasteful piece of work I had ever done in
my life. I got up and unclipped the first-aid kit from the wiring-
diagram box on the back of my seat and started down.

Going down through that small trapdoor was easier thought
than done. We were making about a hundred and thirty miles an
hour through the air, with the front end splayed out and wide
open, funneling the air as if through a Venturi tube so that the
blast in the trapdoor was tremendously powerful and concentrated,
besides being thirty-four degrees below zero. It took all the strength
I had, on top of all the courage I had, to force myself down
through it. I had to ease myself past the revolting form of Max. The
escape hatch on the left was open and looked very void and vacant,
and a lot of the wind was being driven out through it, so the hatch
opening was like the mouth of a vacuum-cleaner tube; once in a
while something would pull loose and fly out through it, and you
felt you might, too. The front end of the ship was pretty much as
I had imagined it, with all the plexiglass gone and some of the
metal bent outward, and Max's seat and Clint's desk and chair in

a tangle, and wires flapping, and equipment all mashed and confused. And suddenly, like a blow in the chest, the thought hit me
that I had no parachute.

Worst of all, there was Max, his eyes open, begging me to do
something.

I tried to remember all those lectures on first aid, in large,
warm auditoriums, often with a quite satisfactory and unhurt WAC
modeling the slings or handing the bandage rolls to the fat, bald
major who was demonstrating, on a stage, what one should do for
every sort of imaginary injury. I had a moment's flash of anger at
the image of one steak eater of a medical major, because I remembered his saying that the best thing you could do for a wounded
man in a plane was to leave him alone. "Cold conditions, flying
clothing, harness, and limited fuselage space render the giving of
effective first aid to such a man during flight a matter of extreme
difficulty, and the less he is disturbed, generally, until the skilled
assistance of a trained physician is available, the better." What did
that fat slob know about kneeling in a murderous gale of cutting,
boreal wind on a sheet of ice made of your crewmate's blood and
seeing his eyes, looking out at you from a bundle of bloody trouser
material, saying, "We've been through very much together, Bo, we
took a walk together just the other day, so please, for the love of
the God I didn't know till a minute ago I believed in, please,
please, Bo, please, please, please." Suddenly there was a marked
degree of love in the eyes, and though I had always, until this
moment, considered that I despised Max and assumed that he
despised me, here I was, struck to the very seat of my soul with
horror and receiving messages of brotherly love from him. I believe this tender begging look increased my sense of terror by many
fold, because I hated Max, I really did hate his deep aggressive
drives, the love of dropping bombs that made him jump on his
seat, after bombs-away, like a baby on a kiddy-car. I think he was
one of them, one of the men with the taint Marrow had, a war
lover—not so poisoned, maybe, as Marrow, but one of them. And
his eyes were saying, "My dear Bo, my dear fellow man, my
brother, sharer with me of life, do you understand what I am trying
to say with my eyes?"

I began to attempt to order my thoughts. First aid. I took off
one glove and crammed the glove between my knees and lifted

the lid of the kit; my skin stuck to the metal, it was so cold. A small blue bandage box flew from the kit and out through the escape-hatch opening without even touching the floor. I turned with my back more to the wind and hunched way over and opened the lid again. I saw a morphine ampule. Morphine, pain, Max. Brother in life. I took the ampule out and crammed the first-aid box into a safe vee between an oxygen bottle and the wall of the plane, and I banged Haverstraw on the arm, to bring him out of a trance he seemed to be in, and he, without taking his gloves off, bared some of the leg above the stump, and I held the ampule in front of Max's eyes, and then he looked into mine with more love than ever, and I stuck him, and Max winced at that pin prick—goodness knows how Max felt it through the torment of his leg—and I be-lieve the pricking sensation itself gave Max relief, because he closed his eyes (which gave *me* immeasurable relief) and looked contented; in spite of the fact that I had not succeeded in getting much, if any, of the morphine into him, because it had seemed thickened by the cold, or, at any rate, had oozed out on his skin and had not gone in him. I put my mitt back on.

Tourniquet. My thoughts, like the pain-relieving fluid, were thickened and sluggish, on account of the very, very cold atmos-phere of man's madness with which that cavern in the war plane was invested, but at last two thoughts—bleeding, tourniquet— came slowly together, and I reached for the box, and took out ma-terials marked for a tourniquet and saw that a loop had to be formed of the cord that was provided.

Kid Lynch came into my mind, and I guess that, at that, I had had enough of war, really enough, because I simply had to leave.

I carefully stowed the first-aid kit by the oxygen bottle and handed the tourniquet cord to Clint and made a circle with my hands to show how big it should be, and I started to go up to the flight deck. Unfortunately as I was going across above Max he dreamily opened his eyes and a look of such gentle surprise came into them, mixed still with that other look, of trusting family love, that I did something I had least expected to do. I straightened up my head, shoulders, and arms through the trapdoor, turned my head to glimpse at Marrow, who was driving woodenly along as if mushing down Broadway with nothing but a few taxis to worry about, and then I reached for my parachute, which was under my seat and on top of my flak suit, and was not stuck, and I backed down again, pulling my chute pack after me.

Max's affectionate eyes took one look at the parachute and rolled to the left and saw Clint's chute on his chest, and the love fled from them, as he must have concluded that the whole crew was about to bail out. He began to flutter and roll from side to side. I've never seen a human being who affected me more with abject fright than Max reacting to the idea that we were going to leave him, in his condition, alone in a ship gliding down the sky on automatic pilot.

I pulled my mask loose and leaned over and yanked the bloody pants material aside and shouted in Max's ear, "Don't worry, chum, we're not going to leave you."

That worked better even than the prick of the ampule needle. It seemed to me that tears of joy came into Max's eyes.

Chum? Since when was Max Brindt my "chum"? The word was one of many commonplaces used around the base, expressive of a rough, sometimes sarcastic affection: chum, pal, friend, son, doc, bud, buddy, old man, brother. But not as between Boman and Brindt! I despised him with his "*Banzai!*" at the dropping of bombs. I really did not like him.

Clint had the loop made and handed it to me, and now came the job of getting it over the leg, and it was then, and only then— I'd been so shocked and braked by the whole deal, especially by the brotherly love in that man's eyes, that I hadn't realized it until then: that there was a shoe, with a foot in it, beating, or kicking, Max in the face, and it was his own right foot, and it was still attached to him.

I had a flash memory of Mrs. Krille, in something like seventh grade, telling us about Achilles, brave and generous warrior, slayer of Hector, who died when Paris struck with an arrow the Peleid's one vulnerable spot, the tendon above the heel, vulnerable because his mother, dipping him in the Styx as a baby to make him wound-proof, had held him by the heel, and Mrs. Krille (I could remember of her face only the sweet mouth, the warm eyes behind shell-rimmed glass, the astonishingly long black hairs in her nostrils) saying that this tendon had an extraordinary strength. "In animals," she said, "it is called the hamstring."

The bone was gone, flesh and pants were mostly gone, the

flying boot had been blown off the shod foot, yet a ragged, tenacious length of tendon and muscle and back-of-the-knee sinews and more muscle, a living rope, in places an inch thick, had held firm, and in the terrible wind the foot had blown back and now was banging against Max.

I hadn't noticed it, and indeed I hoped it had just started blowing that way, and my idea was to try to keep him from realizing that his leg was cut mostly off and that his foot was striking him, so I grabbed the shoe and pulled it forward, and I forgot the knife in my boot with which I might have severed the tendon, and finally, being very heavy-handed, very slow, my fingers stiff, my heart and mind sick, I laboriously worked the tourniquet cord over the foot, and threaded it up the tendon.

While I was doing that, I noticed that Marrow was executing some exceedingly rough and even crude maneuvers. They seemed not like his.

I concentrated as best I could on getting the loop of the tourniquet in position, but we seemed to be bouncing as if in a front.

I felt a rage at Marrow. All this, Max's anguish, the insane work I was doing, *all* this was somehow Marrow's fault. He was the one whose natural climate was war.

Clint—having something to do was nourishing him wonderfully, and he was growing more and more alert—handed me the turning stick, and I inserted it and turned it, and the flow of blood stopped. I tucked the stick into the loop.

Then (I think because I saw a bundle of spare interphone wire stowed next to the oxygen bottles, back underneath the upper deck, beyond Max's head, and also because we were bouncing around in such a peculiar way) I got the brainy idea of trying to make Max more secure, so Clint and I dragged him back farther and we made the intercom wire fast to the back of Max's harness and lashed that to the foot of one of the top-turret stanchions. We had to stop and put our gloves on and whiff our oxygen every few seconds. We finally finished that absurd work. We gave Max another shot of morphine, and he seemed to be resting all right, and I was about to go back to my seat when he spoke again with his eyes—a piercing, questioning stare into mine.

I loosened my mask again and leaned down and shouted into the rags around his head, "Don't you worry, Maxie boy, we're

going to get you back to England. England's in sight right now."
How I wished that were true!

And the eyes, in the watery, bluish light of that recessed place,
were flooded then with love, more and more of it, love of his
friends, I guess, and of England, of home, of an uncertain, abstract,
marvelous everything. Above the mask the eyes were so full of love
that the emotion seemed intolerable, overwhelming, and then all
that feeling drained out very quickly and the pupils rolled upward.

5 /

As I started, empty and numbed, up to my seat, I beck-
oned to Clint to follow me above to the flight deck, where he could
be out of the worst of the wind and could be plugged into the
permanent oxygen system. He climbed up after me and went back
to the radio room.

Marrow was flying very badly. He was like a beginner, over-
correcting, and jolting the controls.

I sat down and hooked myself up and looked at my watch. It
was four thirty-nine. We must be past Eupen. We were supposed to
get P-47s at Eupen.

The Body was now definitely a straggler. The last of the formation was three quarters of a mile ahead of us and six or seven
hundred feet above us, in a sea-blue sky, and there were German
fighters plunging into the squadrons of Forts, but for the moment
they were leaving us alone. We were having some of what Marrow
would have branded in the early days as *his* luck. They could have
sent up a Fiesler Storch, a tiny single-engined scout plane like a
Piper Cub, and armed it with a twelve-gauge shotgun, or maybe a
slingshot, and they could have potted us with it.

I saw no P-47s, but I thought we might as well put up a straggler's signal just in case they were somewhere around but out of
my sight, and besides, this would be something for Junior or Clint
to do, and since there was a spare jackbox in the radio compartment, I called on interphone, "Haverstraw? You on there?"

The answer came back clear as a bell. Lamb must have shot

the trouble, whatever it had been. Clint was on and asked what I wanted.

I told him there was a flare canister at the forward end of the ball-turret compartment; he should get out a green-green flare and fire it. There should be a pistol in a clip-rack next to the canister. He could fire it out of Butcher's slot.

"Roger," he said, and there was that old ironical lilt in his voice; doubtless he was delighted to have something to do.

"Wait a sec," I said. "Do you remember what time we were supposed to get fighter support?"

"Sixteen sixteen hours," Clint said, "same time as course change at fifty degrees thirty-eight minutes north dash oh six degrees oh three minutes east." That number-dogged mind of his was clicking; he could have told me the number of Jenny in Minneapolis or of Peggylou in Biloxi, if I had asked, I'm sure.

Then Prien came on and said, "What's green-green, Lieutenant?"

I said, "It means, 'My ass is dragging, friendly fighters take note.' "

Next it was Bragnani; brave, bully-boy Bragnani. "We going to make it, sir?"

There is a mimic that lives in all of us, whose job is to hide our true selves from the world by pushing masks out onto our faces and sneaking others' gestures into our hands, and I was on the point of saying, "Listen, son, you fire your gun," but I paused a second, over the thought that the boys in the back didn't know what was going on, not a thing, and I said, instead, "The nose is opened up. Two and three are feathered. We're losing altitude, about seventy-five a minute now, but we're holding one-thirty i.a.s. . . . They got Lieutenant Brindt." I thought I might as well tell them that.

Then, clear and strong, almost like a vivid memory, we all heard Marrow's voice, "Lamb? You awake? Give me a fix, kid."

"Yes, sir," Butcher said.

There was a silence, a long one, and then Marrow, "Come on, come on, come on."

Lamb must have been trying to get cross bearings on the radio compass.

A floodgate of abuse broke open. That monotonous, whining

voice which made you cringe. In the middle of it, on CALL, there
was an unintelligible phrase in Farr's voice. More of Marrow's
cursing. Then Farr, "Aw, f—— this, I'm through with this crap."
Farr clicked out and Marrow was still going. Lamb tried to cut in
with the fix, but Buzz didn't want it any more. Marrow was flying
now with really dangerous want of co-ordination—washing all over
the sky, careening, flirting with death and shouting at it. That is
surely what some deep part of him was doing. Not only with his
own but with ours.

Farr pushed his button and rasped, "For Christ's sake, do
something, even if it's wrong. . . . Ah, s——! I can fly till I'm sixty.
I'll do five hundred missions. They can't hit me no more than . . .
I'm telling you, you son of a bitch, I'm no rookie. I'll outlast every
mother f——er of you. You can't knock me off. They tried! The
bastards plugged the s—— out of me, but they . . . This is so
dumb. I could've told those God-damn toidy-seat generals. . . .
How dumb can you get? . . . Don't you put a finger on me, you
bastards. . . ."

I saw Marrow, across the way, unbuckle his seat belt.

I said, as sharply as I could, on CALL myself, "Farr!"

He paused, and I said, "Bragnani, get that brandy away from
him."

Marrow reached under his seat, pulled his parachute out (I
remembered with a start that I had left mine below), and half
stood up. As he did so the plane slowly climbed till it was on the
edge of a stall. I pushed the column forward, and *The Body* fell
off to one side and after a long, swooping plunge picked up buoy-
ancy again.

Marrow settled back in his seat. He seemed puzzled, un-
decided, old.

I said, "I'll fly her awhile, Buzz."

Marrow grabbed the wheel and tensely held it.

"Give her to me," I said. "Let me fly some."

No answer. Marrow was leaning forward toward the column.

Prien said, "Four fighters coming in, six o'clock level."

I stood up in the aisle, just in back of the trapdoor, and I
tapped Marrow on the shoulder, and when he turned his head I
jerked my right thumb toward my seat. For what seemed to me a
long time nothing happened, then slowly Marrow unplugged his

suit-heater cord and his headset jack, and he put his hands on the sides of his seat, pushed himself up, slid out from under his wheel, straightened up in the aisle, and then in the over-cautious way of a senile man sat down in my place. I moved into the pilot's seat, and that was all there was to it.

CHAPTER TWELVE

THE TOUR

August 16

1/

"He came in here," she said, "uninvited, with a bottle of whiskey in one hand and a medal in a box in the other." Daphne looked at me with her head on one side, as if to ask me if I really wanted her to go on. "He's huge, isn't he?" she said. She told me that he had paced around the tiny room with his powerful shoulders bent forward, and he swayed and glanced resentfully, like a cooped animal, at the low slanting ceiling and the confining walls. At first he brimmed with vitality; his voice was loud and resonant.

"Bear in mind," Daphne said, "I hadn't seen Marrow more than five or six times altogether in these months. But I knew him. It was amazing how well I knew him—through your eyes . . . and because he's so like my Dugger. . . . I'm sorry, dear Bo: I have to try to be honest with you."

She told me Marrow had poured whiskey in teacups and acted the part of a hero.

"Max Brindt," he said, at one point, "is the only *soldier* on my crew."

Daphne, out of her full intuitive knowledge of what Marrow was like, said, "What about that gunner Bo has told me about— is it Farr?"

"Nah, he's a blowhard sergeant. Max is an officer, a gent, and Max likes his work; he likes to bomb 'em. I guess the reason he's

so good is he's a Hun, he's a Wisconsin Heinie. Those Germans
know how to fight better than anyone."

They're murderers." Her father.

Daphne said that Marrow looked at her pityingly, as if she
were unutterably small and weak, and he said, "Listen, kid, what
do you think soldiering's all about?" Marrow spoke with such benign good humor, she told me, and was so tolerant of her woman-
ish ignorance of the world of men, that he seemed radiant and irresistible. He spoke of what a good sport the German fighter was;
the old wheels-down, respect-for-chutes routine.

"Now you take your boy friend, Bo. He's a nice guy, I'm not
going to run him down, don't worry, but the point is, he's just not
made for fighting. Not real gutsy, sojery fighting. He's too educated
or something."

"Wait a minute, Daph," I said. "How did you say he referred
to me?"

She said, surprised at my question, that he'd used my nickname; her tone said, ". . . of course."

"Are you sure?"

"Positive. He never called you anything else all evening. Bo
Bo Bo."

"All I can say is, that's mighty odd." I told her that he had
never, that I could remember, used my nickname to my face.

Daphne said Marrow had gone on, cheerfully and bluntly, to
belittle me. He wasn't going to run me down—much. "Why do
you suppose he's a co-pilot?" And he said, "Him and his pal Lynch!
The only thing Lynch ever said that I like was once he was talking
about our engines, and he said we had more horses in one B-17
than all the horses Julius Caesar brought along in his invasion of
Britain. Now, that's *power*."

He was drinking his whiskey in gulps, Daphne said, in a way,
she added, that any girl with experience would have recognized as
preparatory.

He began to tell her—and he seemed to her to be getting
larger and larger; his chest looked as if it would burst, and he had
discarded his tunic and his upper arms bulged through his thin
shirt—about how he had always loved to fight. "Once when I was
just a kid, me and my best pal . . ." A friendly argument about
cars—the Overland versus the Chevrolet; in the right angle of a

wooden fence, a corner of an empty lot, covered with sour dock and pepperweed; Chuck, subject to temper and hay fever, both bad. "I darn near killed him." Marrow laughed at the picture of Chuckie with just enough life left in him to sneeze.

And when he got to high school, Marrow said, he asked to be taught how to fight. "We had this coach"—Daph said she'd forgotten his name—"he called it 'The Manly Art of Self-Defense,' but . . . defense! It was how to get *rid* of the other guy. How, if it was going bad, the knee in the b——s . . ." He was beginning, Daphne said, to use language that was, like his drinking, part of what he apparently considered the ritual of preparation; as if filth were an aphrodisiac.

I broke in then, I guess because her talk of Marrow's belittling had reached the self-blaming part of me. "You know," I said, "I think Buzz may have been right about me as a fighter. You remember I told you once about my boxing. I'm a congenital runner-up, a co-pilot. The thing I remember best about my whole boxing career is the nightmare of *not* remembering, being amnesic, once, about what had happened in the last round of a match. Guess it was nice to forget."

It came back vividly: lying on the rubbing table, the gray nowhereness gradually giving way at the center, and then a flickering of images, as when a movie film flaps free of the sprockets in a projector, and finally unblurred sight and a clear orientation to everything in the rubdown room: Moose Moohan, the trainer, with his hairy arms and his great expanse of belly under a sorely stretched T-shirt, and the smell of eucalyptus ointment and of the armpits of the mighty, and the glass cylinder containing Moose's sparkling bandage scissors with the duckbill at the end of the blade to slide under gauze—everything clear and familiar in the rubdown room, yes, but what was beyond the door? That room was my world. I could remember not one single thing in the whole world outside that room. There was no otherwhere. My whole life would be spent on that table in that room. . . .

The memory of non-memory, at that moment, in the context of Daph's account of the blustering boasts of my pilot, was important to me, because I had often thought of that knockout as my first death, and I knew now that I was not afraid of the process of dying or of what lay beyond it, but only of cessation—of the pos-

sibility of forgetting the marvels of the big world of life; and besides, Daphne now said, replying to my words, "But, Bo, you're
strong, you're truly strong."

She shook her head, then, and said, "He kept shouting, 'I love
to fight . . . *fight!*' "

He got onto speed, too. (Daph said she couldn't remember
the order of things exactly, but she was trying to tell me all she
could recall.) "Once I drove all the way across Louisiana in a Lincoln Zephyr with a cop on my tail. S——, he couldn't catch me. A
cop'll very seldom go over eighty on a motorcycle—you know?—
and after all, I'm a flier, I'm used to speed. I drove across the country once in a friend's car in seventy-seven hours' time, with a stopover at home. I dropped the guy who owned the car in Omaha, so
he could get some sleep—we spelled each other at the wheel—and
I called this chick in Holand, and told her to wait up for me, and
she did, and I screwed her, and the next morning I picked the guy
up and we went on and *still* made it in seventy-seven hours flat,
stopover included."

He began talking about his various cars, and he had the gall to
tell Daph, for the second time, his yarn about leaving his car at
Bennett Field with the key in it. This was the very day after Marrow got the letter from his uncle about the car having been sold.

He showed her the medal—said he'd brought it along to show
her the misprint of his name. "A sergeant, they'd have spelt *his*
name right."

When he said he liked to fight for fighting's sake, she said, one
of the implications was that he had nothing else for which to fight.
Certainly, not on account of his identification with a group. She
remembered that he spoke once of our crew as "Boman's little
men's club."

"*The Body*," he said, "is my body. And when I fly I'm just
pushing along with *The Body* sticking out in front of me. It's part
of me."

He told Daphne about various missions, and of course I had
told her all about every one of them. "And I remember them, Bo,
I've always felt as if I'd been with you on all of them. And Bo, he
changed everything around. You never took credit for anything,
but I know you, and I know what happened. About the Hamburg

raid, when you went around the second time, he told me how he thought everything out and decided . . ."

All this time he was expansive, cheerful, and magnificently healthy-looking.

He reached in the watch-fob pocket of his trousers and pulled out two fifty-dollar bills and threw them on the bed. "My mad money. I'm mad for you, kid. Want 'em? I don't give a s—— for money."

"I could use a hundred U.S. dollars," Daphne told me, "but I was not pleased about the prospect of becoming a 'hundred-buck hoor,' as I think your friend would put it."

"Prospect?" I said. "You knew it was coming?"

"I've tried to tell you, he was making that kind of man's preparations all along."

"But I mean, you knew you were going to submit?" I was trembling.

"Wait, Bo," she said. "We'll come to that."

"Better come to it now," I said.

"I've tried to tell you, Bo. You're the only one."

"Who're you trying to kid?"

"I have a side, too. There are two sides to this."

Anyway, she began to tell me the story of it. Marrow was talking about his contempt for his commanders, and he paid a special tribute of scorn to Wheatley Bins, calling him yellow and "not a man." Then he said, "To hell with leadership! I get my bang out of flying."

"Bang?"

"Bang's the word. Listen, baby, I get a . . ." Then, Daphne said, he broke off, and his eyes gave her a signal. He was ready. She thought the word "man" might have triggered him. Marrow made no attempt to court, to charm, except that he said, "You sure must have something, you sure put roses in Boman's cheeks." He laughed. He stood up, and Daphne told me she had the impression his head was bumping the ceiling, and his arms were tensed and huge, and he said, "O.K., baby, take your clothes off."

Daphne did, and he undressed.

She was trying to tell it quickly, get it over with, but I began to beat my fist on the metal bedstead.

"Nothing came of it, Bo," she said. "Please listen. Nothing came of it. Not that he couldn't. He was able. He wasn't as much of a man as he imagined—I mean, not as big as a Flying Fortress, as he seemed to think. He was able, though, and quite eager on the surface, but as soon as he touched me, I knew he was exactly like Dugger, disgusting, wanting to use me to make love to himself. I drew back, got off the bed and put my slip on, and he said, 'Because of Bo?' and I said, 'No, because you don't want me. You don't want anyone but yourself. You want to be the manliest man this side of Casanova, but you only want *that* in your own head.'

"He was furious, and he began to argue with me, as if he could seduce me by talking me down, but by this time I knew all about him, he was so much like Dugger, and I could see the hint of relief under his bullying talk.

"Then something happened that was almost funny. Bo! I hope you can see that it was funny. There was a knock on the door, and I wish you could have seen the big hero's face! He must have thought you'd found some way to get off duty and had come to me, and that you were right outside the door, and, darling, he grabbed up his clothes and jumped behind the curtain of my closet door. I whispered, 'Major Marrow, you left a sock at the foot of the bed,' and he pranced out in his underdrawers and did a double bend for his sock and tip-toed back again. Then I opened the door. It was the telegram from you."

2 /

"When he came out of the closet there was a definite change in his mood. He was *smaller*. The boastful ring was gone out of his voice. But he was more dangerous; I was warier than I had been before. I got fully dressed, first thing, and I said I thought he'd better, too, but he lay on the bed in his drawers. He asked me who that had been at the door, and I told him it had been the girl from the post office who delivers telegrams—hadn't he heard her voice? But he was suspicious. 'You can't kid me. Come clean,

baby.' I'd put the telegram down on my dressing table, and now
I picked it up and I waved it, to show him. He wanted to know
who had sent it, and when I said it was from you, Bo, he narrowed
his eyes and said, 'You're a clever little bitch,' and he got up and
came over and reached out a hand for me to give it to him. I handed
it over, because it wouldn't have taken much of his strength to get
it away from me, and he read it and crumpled it up and threw it
on the floor. He began to praise you. 'Son of a bitch Bo. Time and
again we wouldn't have gotten back, wasn't for him.' He poured
himself another teacupful of whiskey and got back on the bed, and
thoughtfully he said, 'You know, Bo would have made a p——
cutter of a squadron commander, group commander—and they
didn't even let him be a first pilot. He's got guts *and* brains, that
boy.' He had a canny look; I didn't trust him. Those remarks were
to show that he was better than you—*he* was a first pilot. I said he
was talking in a very odd way, considering the fact that he had
gone to Major Randall to try to get you grounded. He said, 'You
know everything, don't you, you smart little hoor?' Then he
laughed. 'That was a hot one! Bo was in good shape, as good as
me.' But his laughter was brittle, and he asked me how I knew
about his having gone to Doc. I said Major Randall had telephoned me. Marrow blushed. Really! Red as a beet. But I saw, all
too well, that he was angry. He didn't stir on the bed. He said, 'You
and Boman and that horse doctor been discussing me all along?'
And I thought, Oh, yes, Marrow, you *are* like Dugger—because
one of the things Dugger couldn't stand was the idea of exposure,
of having people know anything about him except that he was the
best flier in the R.A.F. I said you hadn't ever said a word about him
that wasn't nice, and he got up from the bed, and he said, 'That's
a lot of bull s——.' Then he began to be quite nasty about you, Bo.
I was becoming more and more apprehensive, because I felt that
he was smoldering. He paced back and forth now like something
trapped. 'I suppose you talked with that son of a bitch Bins about
me, too?' he said. You see, it was getting unreal. He said, 'They
rigged that whole thing up, for Bins to get it instead of me. That
God-damn Doc was in on it.' Then he looked at me, and he said,
'You better skin those clothes off again, baby. If you think you can
refuse *me* a f——, you got another think coming.' I sat there not

moving. I just tried to be as still as I could. Sure enough he tacked again—went off in a completely new direction. 'I clobbered the bastards at Hamburg. Just like flies. They'll never take that away from me.' If you hadn't looked at him closely, you'd have thought he was smiling; his lips were pulled back in a set way, almost prim. He was marching up and down like a sentinel. He began all over again at the very beginning: Who was that at the door? Then: Boman hadn't made first pilot; Boman and Doc and I had been whispering about him; he knew all about the plot to install Bins in command while he, Marrow, was away at a rest home; he was going to get me back in that bed, no woman could . . . It went around and around. But it got worse and worse, too. You've told me, Bo, about his tirades on sergeants. He got filthier and meaner and louder. Finally he stopped in front of me and said, 'You want to know something, baby?' He had a vile look in his eyes, and his teeth were clenched. He was very dangerous, creeping down into the slimy place in himself where things begin—snakes, toads, spiders, mud. I thought, He's Dugger. . . . He's going to say he used to bomb beetles, on the cart tracks on the farms, dung beetles, to see them squash. Or, he had a canary, he . . . I kept saying to myself, 'He's just like Dugger, I know what to do.'

"And then he gave me my chance. When he reached the point on his circle that concerned Doc Randall, he said, 'Want to know why I went to Doc? Because . . .' He went to my dressing table, where the medal was lying in its box; he picked it up. 'You know something?' His voice broke into a kind of petulant scream, and he shook the box and said, 'That p——, Boman. This is *his!* He won it. It's his, his, his.' His voice rose higher with each word, and he turned and threw the box at the wall with his great powerful arm. A very violent thrust. The box was crushed and fell open, and the little bronze propeller shot across the floor, dragging its red, white, and blue ribbon after it. 'Oh, I hate the pint-sized son of a bitch.'

"I stood up. I kept the bed between him and me, and I asked him, 'Is the reason you hate him that you can't bully him?'

"And he said, 'He's strong, all right, the little p——.' "

I was simply astounded at what Daphne was saying, and I saw that many of my thoughts during the tour, the stands I believed I had taken, were based on cockeyed premises, and I was amazed at how little I really knew about my pilot after these months of inti-

macy. How much less I must have known about myself! Well, I
was twenty-two; I was a blind kid—old enough, though, to be
asked to lay down my youthful life in a war. It was crazy, crazy.

"Marrow," Daphne said, "turned on me then—I still had the
bed between us—and he said, 'If you tell that little s—— I've been
here tonight, I'll . . . I'll bomb the bejeezus out of you. . . .
I'll . . .'

"I was absolutely still.

"Then he said, 'Don't you make the mistake he did. Don't you
get it in your head that the reason I didn't want to go around the
second time was because I was chicken s——. Oh no, baby. The
only reason was, I didn't care where the f—— we dropped those
bombs, as long as it was on a city. You can't win a war being
squeamish. Chicken s—— doesn't win wars. You have to kill *somebody*. . . .'

"Suddenly I grasped, thank heavens, how to manage him. I
understood, then. It was from Dugger that I understood. I said, 'I
know all about you.'

" 'What do you mean?' He halted, like a soldier challenged
by a guard at night.

"I said, 'That feeling when the plane shudders because the
bombs are falling out.'

"Yes! It was going to work. I saw already a subtle change on
his face. It was as if he was fighting back one of those grins that
aren't about anything funny.

"So I went on. 'The feeling you have—you have that stirring
down there, don't you, Major?—when you start the bombing run.'

"Now he looked astonished. And you could see creeping into
his face the first sign of caving in, the first realization that the world
knew all about him. Six billion pairs of eyes staring at him. He was
trembling.

"Those lines about his feelings had come from things Dugger
had told me; now I remembered, Bo, your having told me about
the shout when you first meet fighters each time, and I said, 'And
when the Hun takes his first pass at you, and you can feel the trembling of the ship when your own guns begin to shoot . . .'

"He sat down. All the flame was out. He hung his head and
squeezed his hands between his knees.

" 'You little bitch,' he said. Then he put his hands over his face and began to shake out dry sobs. He's much farther gone than Dugger ever was. In a minute I asked him if he didn't think he'd better put his clothes on, and he did; he was docile and quiet.''

3 /

"There it was, Bo. What I'd come, through agony, to know about Dugger, and what I'd thought all along about your pilot. The stuffing came right out of him." Daphne stood up, and she was angry in a way I'd never seen her. "Why do you men have a conspiracy of silence about this part of war, about the pleasure of it?" She was unusually disturbed. She said men pretended that battle was all tragedy—separation, terrible living conditions, fear of death, diarrhea, lost friends, wounds bravely borne, sacrifice, patriotism. "Why do you keep silent about the reason for war? At least, what *I* think is the reason for war: that some men enjoy it, some men enjoy it too much." She said she didn't mean just the life of campaigns, getting away from everything humdrum, from responsibilities, from having to take care of others. "More than that," she said, "I mean, the pleasure your pilot gets." She said something about the gratification that wells up out of "the dark slimy place of toads and snakes and hairy men"—from deep, deep down. At one point she said, "I think we ought to worry less about the future life, in peacetime, of the ones who break down in battle, and more about what's going to come of those who enjoy it too much. They're going to inflict their curse on the rest of us in peacetime. . . . Knives, billies; all that . . . They're going to pass it on to their children. We'll have other wars. Oh, Bo, I don't know what we can do about these men, how you can educate this thing out of them, or stamp it out, or heal it out—or whether you can get rid of it at all." She just had a feeling, a woman's feeling, that this was where all the trouble came from. We couldn't have a real peace while these men still had that drive in them. "Diplomacy won't make peace; diplomacy's just a mask." And she said, "Economic systems, ideologies—excuses."

But I wasn't ready, yet, to think about all this that Daphne was so vehemently pouring out. I was feeling bruised and sullen, and I said, "If he's so horrible, why did you undress for him?"

Daphne blushed; a hot red glow of shame burned her face. At least I thought at first it was shame. Partly it was, I still believe. But partly it was anger.

"Because I have a life to live," she said. "Life goes on. You men in a war think the war's all there is, you mistake risking your lives for taking responsibility, and you think that having taken that responsibility—which incidentally you never do by deliberate choice; you claim someone has forced it on you—you think then you can abandon all others: to your families, to your conscience, to women. Women aren't made to sleep around."

"Then why do you do it?"

A funny little smile curled Daphne's lips. "I want to be fought over," she said. "I want to cause a war."

Her sudden elusiveness made me sarcastic, for my first and only time with Daphne. "The face that launched a thousand Flying Fortresses?"

In a small voice Daphne said, "Bo, your tour's almost over."

"So you were willing to get in bed with Marrow because my tour was almost over? His tour's almost over, too, you know. I don't get it."

"Do you remember that Sunday of the bank holiday, when I didn't come up to London? That was the same thing, Bo. I was looking around; don't you see that I have to look around, now that your tour's almost over?"

"You can look. You don't have to get into bed with a guy's pilot, do you?"

"I got into bed with you, Bo, the first night I went out with you. I didn't hear you criticize me for that."

That line slowed me down.

"You see, my Bo, I was forced to realize, you forced me to realize, as your tour went along, that you didn't really want me very much more than Marrow does—though there was a big difference, darling, darling; you gave me a lot. But you see, you didn't want me, a woman; you just wanted a camp follower, a stopgap till your tour was over and you could go home to your other life. You just wanted a war girl. Isn't that right?"

I didn't feel like facing quite so much quite so fast, and I lashed out again. "How come you loved this Dugger character if he was so repulsive, like Marrow?"

"I was a child, Bo. It was during the Blitz. It's so chancy, the kind of people you meet."

"Yeah," I said, "but how could you think you loved a guy like that?"

"You had your Janet. You've told me all about her, Bo. We shouldn't have to account to each other for our educations, should we?"

Touché, but I didn't say so.

"And besides, darling, I broke off with Dugger as soon as I realized that he didn't love me, he only loved war."

"And you've been breaking off with me because . . ." I thought of Doc Randall's report of Daphne—how she had cried on the phone with him and had said that she loved me more than any man she had ever known, but that I didn't love her.

"You're not a war lover, darling. I know that."

". . . because I never brought up the subject of marriage?"

Daphne reacted to that word with another blush, and again there was anger in her warmth. "All your talk about selfless love," she said, "what was that except a kind of vague yearning for . . . for justification? I mean justification for the use you've been making of me. Selfless love! And even your not wanting to kill—"

"Now wait a minute," I said.

"I don't deny that part of it may have been genuine. What you have to do *is* revolting. But your compromise, darling. 'I'll go in a bomber but I won't kill,' can't you see that there's a lot wrong with that idea? And that what's wrong is that you can't go all the way, you certainly can't give all humanity a complete love when you can't even give it to one human being?"

There was too much to think about, and I guess I was too young to think about all of it clearly. I was a kid. It isn't fair, for the older people to make young kids fight their wars for them. I went back to the subject of Marrow, as if *he* were simpler to think about than myself.

4 /   "He sat down on the edge of the bed with his elbows on
his knees and his head in his hands. I think he was rather drunk. I
watched him closely. He began trying to get me to mother him. I
tell you, Bo, one whole class of heroes is nothing but babies! It
was surprising how far he let down the bars. 'I'm not as good as
they say I am.' And, 'Why was I passed over?' He kept saying he
was a failure, always had been. Sent down from his college. Made a
poor show of his work for—what was it, a grain merchant? A flying
bum, he called himself. Failure, failure, failure. Said he'd always
wanted a lot of money, the mad money was a pretense, he was a
skinflint. Said he was easily discouraged. Once, he said, when he
was about twelve, he got a job at a small apartment house that was
built in Holand, really a kind of tenement block, he was supposed
to sweep down the stairs and empty the garbage for five dollars a
week, but there was a dog, a Doberman pinscher, he was afraid of
the dog, and he took to skipping days, and the owner came to the
house one evening and sacked him, in front of his parents, and his
father bellowed at him, but when his mother tucked him in that
night, she said he didn't need to bring money into the family because he brought luck into the house."

Marrow's luck!

" 'The fellows never wanted me. We had a Y in Holand, it
was a rickety gym and a library and a room with a piano, and one
night, I was maybe thirteen, fourteen, there was this whole bunch
wanted to beat me up, or something like that, after a basketball
game, I wasn't even on the team, the game got them excited, and
they stood out in the yard and chanted my name, and Mr.
Buckhout, he was the Secretary, he kept me in his office till it blew
over.'

"He said he was puny and pigeon-chested, he bought some
springs from Sears, Roebuck to build his shoulders and arms. He
said he never got good marks in school. 'Something made everybody hate me.' "

Daphne said Marrow admitted that all his aggressiveness was
"bluster and bluff." " 'Why do you suppose Haverstraw is my favorite guy on the crew? Because he's an officer and a weakling. It's

easy for a guy to feel like a big shot when he associates with children.'"

And that reminded him: Once, he said, he'd been playing with his friend Chuckie, and a blast of dynamite had gone off on some construction job, on the edge of town, and he thought it was thunder in a clear sky, and he was terrified that it was some sort of *message* or *warning*, and he ran home to his mother. And next day Chuckie called him a coward. "Ever since then," he said, "I've been scared of being scared."

Daphne was positive that it was right after telling this anecdote that he volunteered to her that all his stories of his great swordsmanship were imaginary. "The only thrill I get, it's flying."

I tried to pin Daphne down. "What is he, then? What is it about him that makes you call him what you do?"

"I'm not an expert. This is just a woman's theory."

"I fly with this guy, don't forget that."

Daphne thought a few seconds and then said, "One who loves fighting better than the things he's fighting for."

I tried to think what Marrow might be fighting for. No ideas, no hopes or dreams, certainly. I pictured a white frame house, vintage about nineteen twenty-five, in Holand, Nebraska. Some evergreens that had been put in as "landscaping" have grown far too high for their purpose, and the living room and dining room are dark in the daytime. There is a collie sleeping on the porch. A man in black trousers and a white shirt, with suspenders hanging down and his detachable collar detached, and an unlit half-smoked cigar in his mouth, walks slowly back and forth behind an underpowered motor lawn mower which is spewing out clouds of thick blue exhaust. A woman, nearly white-haired, with a look under her eyes as if a pair of grasping hands had ahold of her cheeks and jaws and were pulling the slack flesh to the sides and downward, comes out onto the porch; the screen door slams, and the collie, who is very old, painfully rises. . . .

"He's a superb flier," I said, "and if he loves war so much, why *was* he passed over?"

Daphne was frowning. "A war lover—my Dugger—your pilot: he's a hero, as I see him, in every respect except that he gets a tiny bit too much satisfaction, 'bang,' Marrow called it, out of some deep-down instinct for . . . perhaps hunting." Daphne was

having a hard time with this. "I'm trying to tell you. . . . It's silly
for me to try to analyze it, Bo; I'm a woman. It's just something I
feel. . . . It has to do with death. That's close to it. I guess when
you say the things a man's fighting for, you mean: life. And Marrow doesn't want that, he wants death. Not just for himself, but
for everyone."

I remembered Marrow's flashing eyes, that day the three of us
lunched in Motford Sage, and the sound of the ladle jangling in
the soup tureen when he pounded his fist on the table and said, "I
want to kill death." Even death. Death was a bastard, a sergeant. I
had a picture of the man in the black pants with the suspenders
hanging down: he was skulking in the obscure corners of the dark
house, laying an ambush for the boy, ready to roar, ready to jump
the boy. Death the Father Almighty.

"So the heroes," I said, "are Marrow, Brindt, Jug Farr? Is that
it?"

"No, no, no," Daphne said, "there can be the other kind, who
fights fiercely, Bo, when he has to, much as he hates it, because he
loves what he's fighting for more than himself—life, I guess. Dunkirk. You only have to say a word like that. London when they
blitzed us."

"That stuff you told me about Marrow, here . . ." I shook
my head.

"He can't make love, because love has to do with birth, life.
When he gets in bed, he makes hate—attacks, rapes, milks his
gland; and thinks that makes him a man. . . . You're stronger
than he is, Bo—how could you not have known that? He said the
medal's yours. It's still on the floor. You can have it if you want it."

I got up and went across the room and there, under the dressing table, was the Distinguished Flying Cross. I picked it up and
held it in the palm of my hand: my medal.

"But the tough thing," I said, "is when you have this character
on your side, in your own airplane. What are you supposed to do
about that?"

"That's very hard," Daphne said. "These people can make
you think you love them. I guess the first thing is to know who they
are and what they want. . . . But be *careful*, darling."

I was so full of rushing thoughts and feelings that I hardly
knew what I was saying or what I was hearing. I was utterly be-

wildered; nevertheless, I felt stronger than I had for weeks; yet I felt somehow desperate, too. I heard myself saying to Daphne, "Do you think we could make a life together?"

"I don't know," she said. "I don't know, now. I've never loved anyone as much as I did you, yet . . ."

"Did?"

"Darling, you're so American. You get what is and what you want all mixed up together in your head."

CHAPTER THIRTEEN

THE RAID

1656–1739 hours

1/

And so it was Marrow who had broken down and not I.
He simply sat in the co-pilot's seat and stared, and this was the
most terrifying thing Marrow, the flier, could do—suddenly to go
passive.

The four planes Prien had called in raked through from the
rear before I had got set in Marrow's spot, without touching us,
and they flew on to hit the main force. They, or others, would
surely attack us again, for a plane couldn't straggle and be as lucky
as ours had been for long.

I called Clint and asked him if he'd fired the flares, and he
said he had, and I asked him how far he thought it was to the coast.
Thought! He knew exactly. It was three minutes to five; our task
force would be between Brussels and Ghent; we were now about
twelve minutes astern of our former position in the force, so we
would be perhaps ten miles short of Brussels; if we were holding a
hundred and thirty, we would be at the coast in approximately
thirty-five minutes.

Clint followed these steps out loud on the interphone, but the
calculations that were embedded in them he must either have
made beforehand or else have worked out like lightning as he
spoke; in either case, he was being astonishingly efficient, with
none of his equipment at hand. It was all straight in his head.

Where was the foggy Haverstraw whom Marrow had so often caught daydreaming? . . . My own mind (my heart was low; I felt irretrievably sad) was still enjoying the remarkable clarity that followed, like a stalker, after trouble. I began piecing together the duties of all the crewmen.

I ordered Lamb to put out a distress call on MF/DF and to open the pulse of our IFF to "very wide" and turn it on, even though this was early for it. I visualized the whole process far ahead: how some listener in England would pick up our MF/DF call and would relay the message to the Main Locater Station, and it would get in touch with the control station to which Pike Rilling was attached; that control station from then on would give priority facilities to *The Body*. And a little later the scanners of the homing apparatus, seeing our pulsation on the special "very wide" band, would follow our track all the way in and would report our progress to the Main Locater Station, which would, in turn, pass on every detail to our Wing Headquarters in Pike Rilling Hall and, in case we might be forced to ditch, to the Sea Rescue Organization. This was the first time my mind had dared to leap ahead to England—and to the possibility of survival.

I checked the rate-of-climb indicator and saw that if it was still functioning properly we were dropping much faster than before, for it said we were now losing about two hundred feet a minute. The altimeter indicated that we were at just over thirteen thousand feet. I was about to tell the crew that we could knock off oxygen in a few minutes when something went wrong with the controls.

The wheel wrenched itself forward, the nose went down, we began to dive.

I thought a cable must have parted.

I grabbed the wheel and pulled with all my strength and managed to get the column back a little, but we still were out of control.

Then I looked across the way and saw that Marrow had slumped forward onto the co-pilot's column. I was fighting his weight; and I thought: Even in unconsciousness, he's trying to kill us all, his innermost center really does want death for everyone.

I called Handown to come down and help me with something—fast. When he showed up I was tugging on the pilot's wheel with my left hand and trying to pull Marrow back with my right. Marrow was half conscious. He'd rouse up and sort of flap his arms and his head would roll around on a loose neck, and I'd be able to gain a little on the column, and then he'd crumple forward again, and I'd lose what I'd gained. Handown pulled his shoulders back, and at once I was able to ease back and level us off.

We had lost four thousand feet.

Marrow, who was hovering on the edge of consciousness, wouldn't stay put. And with the nose guns and ball turret out, and Lamb away from his gun on the radio at least part of the time, we couldn't afford to have Handown in the cockpit being Buzz's nursemaid. I indicated with my head that Neg should try to drag him out of the seat and get him aft. But that was not easy to do. The trapdoor between the seats was open, and in his gear Marrow weighed two hundred pounds, and he had just enough fight in him, besides, to make his weight squirm. Negrocus got Marrow half out of his seat and saw that that wasn't going to work, so he propped him back up in it, and, holding Buzz with one hand, Neg worked out of his own parachute harness with the other, and he used his harness to strap Marrow's chest and shoulders and arms to the back of the co-pilot's seat.

Then Handown went up in his turret, and the first thing he did was to come on interphone and say, "Listen, you jerks, Lieutenant Boman is now first pilot of this ship. Do you understand what I'm saying?"

"What happened to the Major?" It was Farr, sounding sober.

"He resigned," Handown said.

"You a pretty good flier, Lieutenant?" Farr again, sounding drunk.

I said, "Everybody off oxygen. But check in first."

Prien didn't show up with an answer, so I sent Junior Sailen back to see what the matter was, and Junior, having plugged into the jackbox in the tail position, reported that Prien was gone. The little escape hatch back there had been kicked out. That dip and dive must have made Prien think he'd taken complete leave of his digestive equipment, and he'd bolted. I asked Junior if he could work Prien's guns, and he said he'd try.

I think it was Prien's having cleared out that made me say, "Listen, you guys, what do you want to do? If you want to bail out, we're over Belgium. Or do you want to try to get home?"

There was a very long silence.

Clint said, "We've got about fifty minutes to go beyond the Belgian coast to hit an airdrome."

Farr said, "I'm game," but he didn't say for what.

Junior said, "Kind of windy back here." The hatch was open and doubtless tempting.

I said, "Neg, how about you?"

He said, "I don't think I ought to say, sir. If the fellows want to jump . . ."

Only then did I remember that Handown's parachute harness was holding Marrow back in the seat across the way. Buzz's head was flopping around. Handown didn't think he ought to say!

"Let's give it a try," I said. "We can always ditch this thing if we have to. O.K., everybody?"

The only answer was from Farr. "Teacher, I'll go along if you fly real nice."

I remembered that my parachute was down below, alongside Max's dead body.

We were all quiet for some time. I felt horribly depressed. I got Haverstraw to come forward and take the oxygen mask off Marrow's face.

Neg Handown announced fighters coming down from overhead. "The whole bloody Luftwaffe," he said. "This is going to be interesting."

For the next six or seven minutes we were treated to the vicious acrobatics of some twenty Messerschmidts, most of which, fortunately, kept coming in from abeam; they never caught on that we were defenseless from head-on attacks.

Since we were not under pressure to stay in formation, we did have far more than usual leeway for evasive maneuvers, and I guess I did everything except turn *The Body* over on her back. I motioned to Clint Haverstraw, who was still forward, to plug himself into the co-pilot's jackbox, and he stood behind Marrow calling out attacks in the front sectors. When planes did come in from ahead, I turned the ship to one side or the other to uncover our waist guns.

I began to get calls of encouragement from the boys.

"Attaboy, Lieutenant, swing her over. More! More!"

"Rack it to 'em, Teacher."

Junior Sailen shouted, "I got one! I think I got one! Oh, Jesus God, I think I really got one!" In all our missions Junior had never made a claim.

We took a hit in our left wing, and the number-one engine began to backfire in an alarming way, but after a few coughs it seemed to catch on again—though its pressure fell and our speed dropped off to about one twenty-five.

In the midst of the worst of all this, I suffered an attack of yawning. Not once, but three or four times, my face stretched, my neck muscles drew tight, my mouth gaped, my eyes squinted. I could not help myself. I thought with amazement that I might drop off to sleep at the height of the worst danger and greatest responsibility I'd ever known. But when the yawns passed I was wide awake.

Suddenly the Germans were all gone, and a Spit-5 came in close, after lifting its wing at a distance, and it throttled down and flew right alongside, and I got on the VHF band, and I heard, very plainly, one of those warm, genteel voices of the R.A.F. "Hello, Big Friend," the voice said, in parlor tones. "Is everything tickety-boo?"

"I got an engine and a half," I said. "Sure, I'm putt-putting along." Daphne had given me the sort of ear that made me go all understated when I talked with an Englishman, even when I was so scared I may have had a load in my pants. "But I sure am glad to see *you*. Any more like you at home?"

"We'll circle you."

"Thank you, Little Friend, that's very good news."

I switched over to CALL, and I shouted to the crew in quite a different tone of voice, "Listen! We got Spits! They're going to stay with us."

There were cheers on the interphone, but I can't say that I was happy. Marrow's head was lolling back on the seat, his mouth was open, his face was white except for the red oval crease where his oxygen mask had pressed the flesh.

The altimeter said we were at eight thousand seven hundred feet.

"How much longer to the coast, Clint?"

"Shouldn't be more than ten minutes now. You ought to see it pretty soon."

"And how long did you say from there?"

"Fifty minutes, maybe a little more, the way number one's rattling."

I studied the gasoline gauges, and I did some figuring, and I said, "I guess we're going to have to ditch this old *Body* in the sea."

2 /

Soon I saw the coast, which looked at first like a long edge of cloud shadow, and I began to doubt the wisdom of my decision to go as far as we could and land on the water. With her front end opened up, *The Body* would not breast the waves but would scoop and dig. I had no idea how much sea was running, how high the heads of the waves would be, with their madwomen's hair of foam. I recalled some earlier ditchings in our Group: three lost; all hands lost; all rescued; six lost . . . I tried to remember our drills on ditching procedure on the land—our jokes about the sea of mud on which we seemed to have set sail; and our boredom, for who could have thought it would ever happen to us?

I became unsure of myself, thinking I should not be bull-headed just because I had announced my decision to the crew; perhaps I should wheel around and order everyone to jump, with *The Body* gliding toward the sea.

But somehow I wanted to get to the west, as far as we could go, and I kept plodding along on one and a half engines, unsure, and about that time Junior Sailen called up. He said he'd been hit in the arm by a piece of the shell that had jammed his turret, and he asked if he could bail out, and being in the midst of my doubt about ditching I said, "Go ahead, if you want to." I was sorry he'd been hit; he'd certainly been quiet about it. We were thirty miles from the Channel, and he said, "I can't swim so good, is it all right with you if I get out?" Junior had been wanting to jump for a long time, he must have been eying that empty hatch opening back there in the tail and envying Prien, and of course he

could simply have skipped, the way Prien had, and no one the
wiser, but Junior had to square everything with the people who
took care of him, so he made it clear: he was hurt, he couldn't
swim, he wanted permission. I didn't mind. I was depressed and
fearful of my judgment. I wasn't going to force Junior to drown
with the rest of us, if that was what was in store for us. I told them,
I said, "What I'm going to do is stick with this thing as long as
possible and give this ditching a try. It's been done before, let's
give it a try." Then I said, "Anyone that wants to hop off here is
welcome to." Junior said in his politest manner, "If you don't
mind, Lieutenant, I think I'll go," and I had Marrow's clipboard
with a map on it in my lap, and I said, "We're just past a town
called Saint Nicholas, I guess it's farm country, don't rip too soon,"
because I remembered Kozy's body flapping like a ribbon when
he went out of the tail of Braddock's ship, and Junior said,
"Thanks, sir," he wasn't calling me by my nickname any more.
That was the last we heard of him. He bailed out, and he was
killed by some civilians, I heard later, some black Belgians, or whatever they called them.

3 /

I saw three separate flights of Germans diving down from
the upper sky; I supposed our friendly fighters were driving them
off from the task forces. They ignored us.

My behind was sore. The right cheek had a stabbing pain
in it.

The coastline was vivid now, the meeting place of green and
blue. Under a clear sky the sea was thankfully blue; I don't think
I could have ditched in that grayish-brown liquid we had so often
flown across. To the southwest the glare of the lowering sun was
spread wide on the water.

Marrow was stirring, and when I looked across at my seat,
where he lolled, his mouth open, I felt as if my chest were banded,
like a barrel, with iron straps of sorrow. I could hardly bear to look
at him. I had loathed him for three days, yet now I could only

think of the magnificent aviator he had once been, hunched forward over the column, arrogant, steady, holding between his finger tips, like a flounce of satin, all the power of *The Body*. I tried to think what had broken him. That babbling of Farr's had driven him over the edge; the great war lover couldn't stand the sound of a man's fear. But he had obviously been lost long before that final collapse into passivity. We had often talked in the hutment, and in the club over comfortable drinks, about fear, and fliers had frequently said that everyone had fear in flight and in danger. Fear was the constant; what varied was each man's capacity for holding it at arm's length. That was courage. Fear was the common lot; courage was given to some. That was what everyone seemed to believe—except Marrow, who said that was a pile of s——, *he* wasn't afraid in an airplane. The others and I called him a liar. But now, with Daphne's help, I believed him. Not only had he been free of fear in combat; he had enjoyed our missions, he had enjoyed them too much, and it may be that he had come at the end to fear not the clashes and killing but his enjoyment of them. For to enjoy, even to enjoy horror, was to live, and much as he had shouted about his zest for life, I believe Buzz had found life, at the innermost heart of it, unbearable. Death gave me terror; for Marrow death was home. And I think Max's having reached this longed-for home before him was more than Buzz could stand. He'd been passed over again. Besides, *The Body*, his body as he imagined, had been opened up to let death in. He was maimed. His power and manliness were not untouchable at all; they were being taken away from him. Because of the inner drive for death he did not know he had, he passively welcomed his emasculation and disarmament. Now he was hurrying home. As Prien had acted out the sickness many of us had felt, Marrow had begun to mimic, with heartbreaking authority, a final approach to the death he unknowingly wanted.

It was terrible to watch him. I remembered his galloping across a field with a bucket of coals from the ash heap behind the enlisted men's mess, whooping at Braddock; his cheek-splitting grin as he stepped back to the ranks after getting his medal, while the fliers cheered and the nurses waved their pretty caps; his eyes popping as he told a story of getting some lucky girl to put her face down on his eight-dollar pillow. I had been completely taken in by his seeming vitality—and so, I'm afraid, had he. But now he looked like a very old person who had reached the stage of bidding death to come right in at the mouth, the nostrils, the eyes. There was the faintest look of surprise on his face.

I had hated him, but I felt only despair, looking at him. It did not make me proud or happy to be sitting in his seat under these circumstances.

Now that I think of it, I had almost no fear. We were over the coast, about to leave the enemy shoreline, and we kept losing altitude, gliding lower and lower, with the four Spits circling around us in a radius of a couple of miles, in a crippled ship that couldn't make England. Why was I so much less afraid than I had often been in much less danger? I think because of my feeling about the men who were left with me: Handown, Haverstraw, Lamb, Farr, Bragnani; and Brindt's body; and Marrow's living shell. Maybe courage is love. I had disliked Max; hated him, I believe. But I must have cared about him, too, for I had fought to keep him alive. (There had certainly been courage, alias love, in Max's eyes at the very end of his life; too late.) I had no use for Farr; I had thought I loathed Marrow. But I guess they mattered to me. Love, like fear and anger, floods and ebbs in us, and I suppose I had just enough in me that afternoon to keep me functioning, though I felt rotten, rotten, rotten.

4 /

We left the coast north of Ostend, with the blue inlet of the Wester Schelde off to the right, at twenty-nine minutes past five. We were at six thousand one hundred feet, and we were dropping now at nearly three hundred feet a minute.

I said, "Clint, you busy?"

"I'm on the tail gun." He must have gone back there of his own accord after Junior had jumped.

I said, "Look, we've got to get ready."

"Ah'm ready, massa boss," Clint said.

"Listen, everybody," I said, "we've got to get all the weight out of this thing that we can. Leave your guns till last, and leave a

few rounds leading into the guns. Then you can dump the rest of
the ammunition. Lamb, hold onto your MF/DF, your IFF, and
your liaison, but you can dump all the other equipment. Everybody start with the loose stuff—flak suits and all like that."

The men began tearing things apart, dumping thousands of
dollars' worth of apparatus into the sea.

Handown was keeping a lookout, revolving his turret slowly
round and round. When we were at about fifty-five hundred feet,
he called in some twin-engine fighters diving down on us, and
everyone went to his gun, and the Germans came through on us in
spite of our Spitfires, and we fired the tag ends of our ammunition,
just to give them an impressive show. But one of them made a
pretty good pass, and I think he hit the number one, because it began to wind up, though in truth it had been misbehaving for some
time. They only took the one pass and then went off looking for
other stragglers.

During this run by the Germans, Butcher Lamb, for the first
time in his career as a gunner, was suddenly animated. He shouted
on the interphone, swearing at the Germans, and calling on me to
roll it, shake them off our tail. What had got into him?

We were just riding, at that point, I didn't dare pull any evasive maneuvers, because we were staggering along not too far above
critical air speed. I had thought that the lower we got, the denser
the air would be, and I would hold up better with the same power
settings, but by this time I had every bit of emergency war power
poured to those two engines, and the temperatures were up as high
as they could go, the pressures were way too high, and number
one began missing a beat here and there, and winding up. So naturally there was a tendency for the number four to pull us off
course to the left, and when Lamb shouted to me that he had made
contact with the control station on liaison, I flipped my jackbox
switch over, and there was one of those polite English voices,
sounding as if it were on a phone in an adjoining room, asking me,
"Are you veering from your intended course?" I looked at the
compass and I was way to the south of our course, flying about
two fifty degrees. I felt suddenly as if someone in England was
watching over me, and "Oops," I said, "beg your pardon," on liaison, and got back on course. They must have plotted me several
times and found me drifting off to the south and they must have

thought, "Oh-oh, that joker's getting way off his course, he's maybe going to miss England altogether," so they worried about me, and now they had told me to get back on course again—only, having that built-in politeness of Englishmen, they hadn't told me, they'd asked me. Talk about love. I loved that voice.

5 /

I loved England. I wanted England. Dimly in the distance to the left I could see the tall bluffs of the east coast, the stretch from Dover to Margate, where the glare path of the sun ended in shadow. I was straining every nerve and muscle to get as far as I could, mushing the plane, with the nose up high, just a hair faster than stalling, it seemed, yet moving enough so as not to lose any more altitude than I could help. I wanted a miracle to buoy me to England. I wanted to make it and knew I couldn't. I wanted to fly just once more over the amazing multiplicity of greens, the aimless lanes and hedges, the hamlets in evening peace, Ely on its hilltop, the Dutch drainage canals, a wide loop over the ancient courts of Cambridge, where, I knew from Daphne, great minds of an individualistic people had taken nourishment—Bacon, Ben Jonson, Cromwell, Milton, Dryden, Newton, Pitt the Younger, Byron, Darwin, Thackeray.

I wanted Daphne. I wanted, just once more, to be with my Daph, to lie on my back in a meadow by a sluggish stream, with my head in her lap, talking about us. Couldn't I see her once more, to tell her I'd meant to handle things differently? I wanted another chance at life. Couldn't a man try again, and get it right this time?

I was so weary! I yearned for my sack at Pike Rilling. I'd sleep for four days and four nights.

My left hand was at my throat. I'd taken off my mitts, and my hand was bare, and it was fingering something soft . . . a piece of silk—my scarf, cut from Kid Lynch's parachute. Then, with a flood of anger and fear, I realized I wanted more than I was going to get. I wanted Lynch back, and Braddock, and Kozy, and Colonel Whelan, and Silg, and Stedman, and Curly Jonas, and all the

cemetery-full at Cambridge where the backhoe and loader and
dozer had worked so hard for so many months. I wanted it all un-
done; to be back in Donkentown, where the wag of a collie's tail
was all there was to notice, in a moment, like this, of summertime,
except for the hum of a bluebottle, and in the distance the clanking of the bascule bridge being raised for a coal barge to pass.

I very much wanted Marrow back, the way he was supposed
to be—impossible to live with; I wanted Prien back, and Junior.
And Max.

Oh, my God!

"Clint, would you come up here a minute?" This was something I didn't want to broadcast on the interphone.

In a few seconds he was at my shoulder. I screamed at him
over the whistling of the wind through the holes in the instrument
panel, "Look, Clint, I've got to ask you to do something tough." I
couldn't look at his face. "Would you crawl down below and un-
tie . . . the . . . the whatyoumaycallit . . . and put it out the
hatch?"

"You mean Max?"

"Yeah. You know, so he won't be trapped in there." I
couldn't bring myself to say, So Max would have a decent burial
at sea.

Clint got the idea right away. "Sure. Sure, Bo," he said, and
he ducked down and fought his way through the gale in the trapdoor.

It should have been wrapped in a parachute, with something
to weigh it down—a machine gun, or a couple of the radio transmitters we had dumped. But there wasn't time; there was never
time. I poked my head over, after a while, and saw that Clint had
slid Max over to the hatch opening. Clint seemed to be hesitating.
I said out loud—but no one could hear me, "We commit this
body. . . ." That's all I could think to say.

Clint came back up in a few seconds. I shouted to him, "Listen, could you get Neg and come up here and the two of you drag
him"—jerking my head toward Marrow—"back to the radio room?
We're going to have to help him get out."

So Neg and Clint went to work, and I'm sure it wasn't easy
work, physically or mentally.

After a bit I got on interphone and said, "All right, let's dump those guns. And listen, Lamb! Have you got us tuned in on the control station?"

"Yes, sir. They been telling us we're doing jolly well." Lamb was livelier than I'd ever heard him. Mimicry now. There was, in all of the crew, come to think of it, and in my own heart, a crazy kind of willingness, eagerness, merriment in those last few minutes of that long dreamlike flight.

I flipped the jackbox switch over and told the control people I was down to about twelve hundred feet and that I was going in in three to five minutes.

And the kindly voice in the next room said, "Righto. We've been talking with the Sea Rescue chaps. They'll be onto you in a jiffy. . . . Good landing, old man."

Then I told Lamb to screw down his distress-call key and have his afternoon snacks. All the secret call letters and frequencies were on rice paper which the radio operator was supposed to eat before a ditching.

In a minute he called up and said, "M-m-m. So nourishing, so *good*."

Then the ship began shaking, and I realized a gun was shooting, and I said, "For Christ's sake, whose gun is that?"

It was Handown's. I guess he loved his guns too much to have heaved them into the sea. I remembered his cuddling them in the truck going in from the plane that time, with his cheek laid tenderly against the barrel. Neg said a Heinie had jumped us. Some Marrow with a German name, I thought.

I told Neg to come down in the co-pilot's seat, because I was going to need him when we went in, and I ordered everybody to get Mae Wests on and get into the radio room. And put a Mae West on Marrow, somebody.

We still had five hundred feet, but the water seemed very close. The waves were not bad; the wind was not making the feathery streaks that it made when it was fresh. I swung slowly in a more northerly direction, to be heading into the breeze. The German had left us.

"Everyone got a Mae West?"

There were no answers, and they knew enough to keep a couple of fellows on interphone back there, so I supposed everyone was set.

I decided a little formality couldn't hurt. "Stand by for water landing," I said.

I fastened my safety belt; Neg already had his tight. I opened my window; Neg's was open.

Then I remembered a pilot named Cheeney, who'd been rescued from a ditching, sitting in one of those fat leather chairs in the officers' club, taking a sip from a drink and putting it down on a table and pointing at his glass and saying, "You think it's soft when you swallow it, but when you land in it"—he struck a fist into an open hand—"landing in it is like hitting a stone wall in a car that's doing sixty."

But then there was lots to do, and I forgot Cheeney.

Handown knew every step—he lowered the wing flaps, cut the engines, feathered the props, cut all the fuel and ignition switches. We were screaming back and forth to each other all the time.

Suddenly we were in silence, but for the whistling of the wind. The waves—the rows of stone walls—seemed to be passing us very fast underneath.

I was really feeling our way on the wheel, holding the wheel in my finger tips, and in my throat I was conscious of the shape, if not the sound, of, "Daph, Daph, Daph."

I was gliding in, a normal slow landing, with full flaps, and I gave the last gentle pull, to level us, and we skimmed and skimmed and skimmed, in a three-point attitude, with the tail maybe a tiny bit lower than usual.

We hit. My eyes were shut. The shock was astonishing. I had my forearms up to protect my face. I opened my eyes. We were completely under water, water was pouring in the trapdoor between the seats, and in my window, and there was a score of tiny fountains coming through the instrument panel. I felt that my weight was forward. I was leaning on the wheel with my arms. I reached with my right hand for the catch of my safety belt.

Then daylight broke through the windshield!

We settled back in a level position, and the water stopped pouring in from all directions. I dimly realized that the nose had buried at first and then the ship had quickly settled back in a normal attitude.

Next thing I knew I was out the window, and in the water,

and I jerked my Mae West tabs, and I saw Lamb standing on the wing trying to release a life raft from the bomb-bay fairing. The rafts wouldn't release themselves the way they were supposed to do, and Lamb was energetically tugging and cursing. Very soon the wing was awash, and I climbed up on it and saw Bragnani and Clint beyond it. Lamb had the raft free. It would only inflate part way, but we four got into it.

I shouted, "Jesus Christ, she broke in two!"

Clint said, "All we had to do was walk out."

Apparently the water, like a maul hitting a bung, had knocked the ball turret up through the ship, and the fuselage had split apart there. The tail section was taking a dive. The forward part was still level. There was a sound of a long sigh, as the air seeped out of the wet wings.

"Oh, jiminy, I forgot something," Clint said, and he jumped out of the raft, but I grabbed his collar and hung on. The lunatic wanted to go back for his lucky swagger stick. I convinced him it was down in the opened-up front, already far under water, and he climbed back in with us. I guess he had gone out of his mind for a few seconds.

We paddled through between the two halves of *The Body*, both of which were settling fast, and beyond we saw Neg Handown in a raft with Farr hanging onto the side of it by one arm, looking as if he couldn't get in.

I glanced around, and I saw Marrow; he was bobbing against the fuselage, just back of the right wing. I jumped in and swam to him.

His face had fallen forward into the water. His Mae West wasn't inflated; the air in his jacket must have been holding him up.

I wrestled with his bulk, and suddenly his head came up, and his hands thrashed, and he was saying something, but I couldn't make out what. Maybe it was, "Leave me alone," or, "Don't touch me." There was a kind of ferocity on his face; the lips were pulled back, the strong teeth bared. His eyelashes glistened with sea water. He pushed me away, and he paddled forward along the fuselage and out over the right wing. The ship was going under fast now. Marrow pulled his way along what little of the number-three engine was still awash, and he reached one of the blades of the propeller, and he threw his arms around it and hung on, yes, for dear death. The blade took him down.

I swam horrified back to Handown's raft and got in. It was shot full of holes like the other one, and Neg already had the hand pump going.

As the last shoulder of the plane disappeared, "Poor guy," Lamb quietly said.

The Body was gone, and we six were alone on a big sea.

I saw that Farr couldn't climb into the raft. His left shoulder was covered with blood. Neg and I dragged him aboard.

I asked him when he'd been hit, and he said it had been over the target. So the brandy had been medicinal after all. He had been brave, surely above and beyond the call of duty. I thought of Junior Sailen's long silence about his wound, and I thought: My God, what human beings will bear for each other's sakes.

A Spitfire dipped down out of the evening sky, and we waved and cheered, and it circled us, and half an hour later, more or less, a launch came into sight. There was a man in a yellow slicker out on deck holding a handrail on the wheelhouse roof, and he began waving from a distance. Neg and I pounded each other on the back.

When the launch drew near, the crewman, who was wearing a heavy blue turtleneck sweater under the slicker, called out, "Anybody hurt?"

"Just my feelings," Handown shouted. "Those bad old Germans."

I got it across that Farr was hurt. "Righto," the crewman called. "Just hold on half a mo'. We'll have you fixed up splendid." The launch eased close to us. "All right, maties, lend a hand, give a shove, that's it!" And we had Farr aboard. What did they give him to fix him up splendid? Brandy.

We were all on the rescue boat soon, and with a roar it lifted its head and raced toward England. I looked back. There was a broad wake of churning spindrift, almost like a contrail in the sky. Except for that path the sea was barren. There was not a trace of Marrow, who had loved war, or of his ship, which he had named *The Body*.

A Note about the Author

John Hersey was born in Tientsin, China, in 1914 and lived there until 1924, when his family returned to the United States. He attended Hotchkiss School, was graduated from Yale in 1936, and then went to England to study at Clare College, Cambridge, for one year. Upon his return to this country, he was private secretary to Sinclair Lewis for a summer. Hersey has been a writer, editor, and war correspondent for *Time* and *Life*, a writer for *The New Yorker* and other magazines, and an editor of '47. Since 1947 he has been devoting his time to fiction.